The
UNINVITED

Dorothy Macardle

With an introduction by Luke Gibbons

TRAMPPRESS

First published by Peter Davies, January 1942

The Uninvited © copyright The Beneficiaries of the
Literary Estate of Dorothy Macardle, 1942, 2015

This edition published 2015 by Tramp Press
www.tramppress.com

Introduction © copyright Luke Gibbons 2015

A CIP record for this title is
available from The British Library.

3 5 7 9 10 8 6 4 2

ISBN 978-0-9928170-7-7

Thank you for supporting independent publishing.

Set in 10.5 pt on 14 pt Minion by Marsha Swan
Printed by GraphyCems in Spain

The Uninvited: An Introduction

Luke Gibbons

Did the key to the whole thing really lie in our hands?...

IN THE SUMMER of 1944, Eamon de Valera visited the Savoy cinema, Dublin, to catch a screening of *The Uninvited* (directed by Lewis Allen), based on a novel by his close friend, Dorothy Macardle. The film, lauded in William Everson's *Classics of the Horror Film* as 'quite possibly the movies' best ghost story,' did not impress the Taoiseach: 'Typical Dorothy,' was his cryptic response. The *Irish Times* was more positive in its review: 'I doubt if even Hitchcock could have made a better job of it.'

Lewis Allen's film was an adaptation of Dorothy Macardle's first novel, *Uneasy Freehold*, published by Peter Davies in January, 1942, and bearing its more well-known title, *The Uninvited*, in the United States edition. The novel won critical acclaim and was an immediate commercial success, its inclusion in the Literary Guild of America's books of 1942 greatly helping its sales. Following the success of the film, *The Uninvited* went into a Bantam mass market paperback edition and as late as the 1960s, was still in print in a Corgi Books 'selection of fine reading' that listed *Catch 22*, *The Ginger Man*, and *Lolita* among its other attractions. Then, for all practical purposes, the novel disappeared from view, a development that is somewhat surprising as subsequent decades witnessed the rise of the women's movement, the outbreak of the Troubles in Northern Ireland and, not least in the literary domain, a re-evaluation of the gothic genre in fiction. Perhaps the reason for the novel's neglect was Macardle's own defiance of conventional categories: a feminist activist who was also a radical republican; a universalist civil liberties humanitarian who was also a nationalist; a defender of Irish neutrality during World War Two who moved to London to participate in the fight against the Nazis; a brilliant lecturer who held no teaching position; a journalist and historian who was a critic and novelist of distinction; a psychological rationalist who also put in a good word for ghosts and extrasensory experiences.

Born in Dundalk in 1889 to the wealthy Macardle brewing family, Dorothy Macardle was educated at Alexandra College and University College, Dublin, where she graduated with a B.A. degree in 1912. Steeped in a love of literature from the outset, she moved to Stratford-on-Avon to pursue her Shakespearean interests, before returning to teach English at Alexandra College. This period in her life provided the milieu for several of her publications, including an edition of *Sir Philip Sidney's Defence of Poesy* (1919), *Selections from Sir Thomas Malory's Le Morte d'Arthur* (1922), and the posthumous *Shakespeare: Man and Boy* (1961). As in the case of the 1916 leader Thomas MacDonagh, this love of things English did not prevent her, however, from gravitating towards Republicanism in the Anglo-Irish war, and taking the anti-Treaty side in the bitter Civil War. Dismissed from her teaching post at Alexandra College, she was imprisoned in Mountjoy and Kilmainham jails, and participated in a mass hunger-strike protesting against conditions in the prisons. On her release, she published 'Kilmainham Tortures', an exposé of the ill-treatment she received with other female prisoners, which was followed by her first exercise in investigative journalism, a chilling account of atrocities in Co. Kerry during the Civil War, *Tragedies of Kerry* (1924).

Throughout this period, Macardle's creative energies were devoted mainly to theatre, writing eleven plays, many of which are lost or survive only in manuscript form. Three of her plays were produced at the Abbey Theatre – *Atonement* (1918), *Ann Kavanagh* (1922–1932) and *The Old Man* (1925) – while one, *Dark Waters*, was produced at the Gate Theatre in 1932. This interest in drama led to her appointment as theatre (and sometimes film) critic for the new *Irish Press*, launched in tandem with Fianna Fáil's accession to power in 1931/1932. Her work as a journalist also extended to social issues, not least the lip service paid to ideals of the family in Ireland while mothers and children, living in abject slums and in conditions of chronic unemployment, were reduced to poverty and criminality. In a series of powerful crusading articles in the *Irish Press*, ranging from 'Some Irish Mothers and Their Children' to 'Children and the Law: A Test of Civilisation,' Macardle insisted that pieties about family life mattered little when working class mothers and children were deprived of the basic material conditions of life. 'Irishmen are said to be sentimental about their mothers and no wonder. No wonder at all in a man who grew up in a small, struggling home and who, looking back, must realise what a miracle of patience and courage was the mother who kept the Grace of God about her children in such a pitiless world.' These issues surface again in her fiction, relating early damage to affective ties to subsequent emotional paralysis and the incapacity to love, but by no means limiting the nurturing of these ties to the family, as conventionally defined.

In 1924, Macardle published *Earth-Bound*, a collection of short stories written mainly in prison, and which contained the classic 'The Portrait of Roisin Dhu.' This story, a feminist reversal of Oscar Wilde's *A Picture of Dorian Gray*, features a painter, Hugo, who sets out to depict Ireland as the mythic 'Dark Rosaleen,' only to discover that the image on canvas drains life, vampire fashion, out of his real-life model, Nuala: ''Tis not good to be put in a picture: it takes from you.' This can be seen as a dress rehearsal for one of the key themes of *The Uninvited* – that the idealisation of the female, particularly the symbolic figure of the 'Mother,' is often achieved at the expense of the actual experience of women in an unequal, patriarchal society. *The Uninvited* charts the tragic fate of two women, both artist's models, whose deaths lead to the abandonment of an imposing house, Cliff End, on the North Devon coast: the 'virtuous' Mary Meredith, once married to the bohemian painter Llewellyn Meredith, and the artist's Spanish mistress and model, the 'wild' Carmel. Cliff End is purchased fifteen years after their passing from Commodore Brooke, Mary Meredith's still grieving father, by an aspiring Anglo-Irish playwright, Roderick ('Roddy') Fitzgerald, and his sister, Pamela, both hoping to start anew away from the pressures of life in London. The story (narrated by Roddy) revolves around the Fitzgerald's attempts to make a success of their dream home, but the experience turns out to be closer to a nightmare. The Commodore is the over-protective guardian of a granddaughter in her late teens, Stella, who lived in Cliff End as a child but was orphaned when her mother fell to her death over the cliff behind the house. Roderick's and Pamela's dreams of a quiet life begin to unravel when local gossip, aided by their matter of fact but superstitious Irish housekeeper, Lizzie Flynn, hints at disturbances at Cliff End, and these take effect when the melancholic Stella begins to visit her former home.

Though the story has its share of supernatural contrivances, what is most noticeable is the air of psychological realism, as if uncanny or spectral occurrences are themselves ways of dealing with gaps in the psyche, or profound psychological wounds. So far from psychology explaining away the extrasensory, Macardle notes in her Irish novel *The Unforeseen* (1946) – a follow-up to *The Uninvited* – that even a rationalist such as Sigmund Freud 'after stiff resistance to the idea of telepathy, has accepted it.' The extrasensory happenings at Cliff End in *The Uninvited* concern the violation of primordial attachments, the yearning of a daughter for her missing mother, but also with the obsessive desire of a mother, cut off in her prime, to be reunited with her own lost daughter. Drawing on Henri Bergson's idea in *Matter and Memory* (1896) that perception of the world is not a function of the present but is also, in Bergson's apt metaphor, 'impregnated with memory-images which complete it as they interpret it,' objects and places at Cliff End are imbued with residues from the past: 'I suppose it's fifteen years or more alone since that tragedy happened, but stories like that linger in a lonely place.' Or as another character surmises: 'Isn't there a theory that violent emotion can impregnate matter, saturate floors and walls, and then, with a sensitive person in a receptive mood, it is reproduced?' The young Stella Meredith is that 'sensitive' person, and as Roddy, Pamela and Lizzie are absorbed into her re-awakened world, they also succumb to the ghost. Questions of haunting, in this sense, have less to do with truth and illusion than with pain and loss, coming to terms with memories lodged in the physical – 'hysterical' – body, already incorporated into the material world. Stella's earliest memories relate to feelings of warmth and light, and being suffused by love and the smell of mimosa, and it is this scent that first hints at disturbances in Cliff End, followed by sounds of weeping and a mysterious light under the door at night.

It is striking that that 'the sainted' Mary Meredith, whose memory is cherished by the young Stella and Commodore Brooke, is also revered by her austere friend, Miss Holloway, who took Stella into her care at the 'Centre of Healing through Harmony' following the death of her mother. As in the case of Miss Holloway's cold comfort, Mary's virtue and piety leave a chill in their wake, not unlike the portrait of 'Roisin Dhu' in Macardle's earlier story. Perfection in this case, rather than redeeming reality, shows up its faults and is used to moralise on its transgressions. In this, it is difficult not to see traces of maternal ideals of the Virgin Mary cultivated by the confessional Free State in Ireland in the interwar years, and given institutional expression in the 'veneration' of the mother, and the sanctity of the home, in de Valera's 1937 constitution. Mary Meredith is indeed compared to the Madonna, and Stella's room is described by Pamela as a 'shrine' to her: 'Pale blue walls – her mother's favourite colour; marguerite's on the hangings – her mother's favourite flower; Mary's pictures – Florentine madonnas … even a statuette of her mother – a white plaster thing. It's a *culte*. Oh, the piety, the austerity, the pure virginal charm! Any sensitive girl would come under the spell – and I doubt if a man is born who could break it.' Nor would any man want to break it, a factor which leads Mary into a doomed relationship with the artist, Llewellyn Meredith: 'Mary's faith in her father would lead her to idealise men. Very probably she had romantic illusions about Meredith.' The representation of the longing mother again proves her undoing: on being confronted with Llewellyn's strange portrait, Stella's mother rushes out in a storm to hurl herself over the cliff.

Pamela and Roddy set themselves the task of lifting this spell, and it is perhaps this demythologising of sainted figures that lies behind de Valera's remark, 'Typical Dorothy,' in his response to the film *The Uninvited*. Macardle's own disillusionment is evident here as, for over a decade from the mid 1920s to the mid 1930s, she had worked on her monumental history, *The Irish Republic*, telling the story of the Republican contribution to the fight for Irish Independence, and the defeat of the Republican cause in the Civil War. The publication of the 1000-page book by Victor Gollancz's Left Book Club in 1937 coincided, however, with the introduction of the new Irish Constitution, awarding special recognition to the Catholic church, and restricting women's presence in the public sphere and the workplace through 'protection' (as de Valera called it) of her place in the home: when Stella attempts to break out of the confines of her home to visit Cliff End in *The Uninvited*, the Commodore asserts his control: 'You'll do no such thing.' Though Macardle was reluctant at first to criticise de Valera – *The Irish Republic* was, after all, dedicated to him – she joined with other leading feminists and Republicans including Maud Gonne, Hannah Sheehy Skeffington and Dr Kathleen Lynn in opposing what were perceived as betrayals of the commitment to equal citizenship in the 1916 Proclamation. Writing to de Valera, she expressed her dismay: 'As the Constitution stands, I do not see how anyone holding advanced views on the rights of women can support it, and that is a tragic dilemma for those who have been loyal and ardent workers in the national cause.'

It was at this point that Macardle set her sights further afield, towards Europe and, in a deteriorating international situation, towards opposition to fascism. Having observed the League of Nations at close quarters in Geneva while covering its proceedings for the *Irish Press*, her growing internationalism led her to London at the outbreak of World War Two, where she applied herself particularly to working with the Czechoslovakian government in exile. In keeping with her life-long concern with the breakdown of familial attachments, Macardle focused on the plight of dispossessed children in Europe following the catastrophe of the war, publishing in 1949 an early landmark in Holocaust studies, *Children of Europe; a Study of the Children of Liberated Countries: their War-time Experiences, their Reactions, and their Needs, with a Note on Germany*. Working with psychoanalysts such as Anna Freud who stressed the importance of attachment and emotional bonding in childhood, this comparative exercise in applied psychology reiterates the themes of *The Uninvited*. For most damaged children, memory was repetition, reproducing the original hurt rather than offering an escape: 'Many children who had been deported could hardly be persuaded to step on to a 'bus or a train.' Macardle concludes that there may be no cure for profound loss, and that certain kinds of surface calm belied deeper scars underneath: 'Adults who rejoiced to see children apparently ridding themselves of neurotic troubles learnt, nevertheless, to be cautious about relying on the completeness of the cure. It was too much to hope that children could sustain experiences and separations of the sort that these had undergone without deep-rooted injury: impossible to say how much of the psychic trauma remained latent when immediate symptoms had disappeared for a time.' Even at that, the deepest scars had to do with the absence of affection: 'Dr [Anna] Freud often finds a certain retardation in these children. In particular, they are all sometimes slow in learning to speak. Most serious loss of all, however, is the lack in their lives of individual cherishing love.' In recent decades as the sustained abuses of incarceral regimes in Ireland have come to light, it is precisely the violation of affective ties, the bond between care-giver and child, that throws the longest shadow.

It is clear from this why Macardle takes issue with placing motherhood on a pedestal, as in the norms implicit in the 1937 Constitution. Stella's problem in *The Uninvited* is that the perfect mother is motivated by virtue rather than love, the chill call of duty and discipline: 'I thought mother loved me a little bit just because she was good and did her duty, but it isn't that: it is really loving [that is required], as if she – as if she delighted in me and wants my love, too.' Return to home in this sense has more to do with the capacity for love in the present, notwithstanding dislocation and loss. This underlies Macardle's 'realist' novel, *The Seed was Kind* (1944), which opens at the League of Nations as a young girl, Diony, joins her Irish grandmother and French grandfather to attend school in Geneva. Diony's grandfather, Louis de Chauvigny, an eminent French thinker, is completing a book, *After Guernica*, warning about the imminent death of the League and the sleeping sickness overtaking France in its hour of danger. We are told that 'neither his long residence in Geneva nor the internationalism of his creed had weakened his attachment to France,' and it is this desire to reconcile national attachments with displacement and internationalism that presides over the novel – and, indeed, much of Macardle's writing.

Considered in this light, the 'exile' of the Fitzgeralds in England and their summoning up remembrances of things past in *The Uninvited* may be viewed as a commentary on Macardle's own divided loyalties. Though the action is set in Devon and features quintessential aspects of English life, it can also be seen, in Elizabeth Bowen's description of Sheridan Le Fanu's gothic classic *Uncle Silas* [1864], as 'an Irish story transposed to an English setting.' As if with Macardle in mind, a letter to Pamela in *The Uninvited* from a cousin reminds her that 'you might find Dublin your spiritual home,' to which Roddy adds: 'Well, that's always a refuge if all this becomes too much for you.' Irish allusions and references abound in the novel, and no more so than in the name of its protagonists. 'Pamela Fitzgerald!' Stella exclaims, when she learns the name of Roddy's sister, on their first meeting with the Commodore. 'The Commodore hasn't heard of my famous ancestress,' Pamela responds, before going on to explain:

> 'She is said to have been a daughter of the Duc d'Orleans,' she told him, 'and an exquisite girl. She married Lord Edward Fitzgerald, who led the Irish rising of 'ninety eight. She was not really an ancestress of mine, I am afraid, but I am charmed to have been named after her. I don't know any story more full of heroism and romance.'

'I am afraid, 'the Commodore answered stiffly, 'that I am not well acquainted with Irish rebel history.'

The invocation of the memory of the dead might have ended there, but the subsequent gloss on the relation between haunting and home prefigures much of what is to follow later in the novel. Roddy seeks to change the subject, as Pamela continues:

> While I tried to divert our host with journalistic small talk, she was telling Stella how Pamela had actually been seen at Frascati, her old home near Dublin, in broad daylight, at a garden party a short time before.
> Stella was enthralled.
> 'I am not really surprised,' Pamela went on. 'You see, she had been happy at Frascati. I am sure that, if spirits walk, it is in spaces that they have loved. That is why it seems foolish to be afraid of them.'

Having no homes to go to, ghosts are led back inexorably to worlds they have lost. It is for this reason that the unrequited ghost remains hidden at Cliff End, and only returns to her one place of happiness through the 'medium' of the present day Pamela Fitzgerald. Pamela makes a habit of re-appearing and when she moves to Ireland in Macardle's subsequent novel, *The Unforeseen*, she announces a house-warming party for her new home in Donnybrook: 'Her husband, giving her a quizzical grin, said she would have no uninvited guests.'

Writing of uprooted young Jews unable to live with loss, Macardle wrote in *Children of Europe*: 'Disillusionment and nostalgia threw them back onto tragic memories. They were some in whom melancholy brooding had spread deep roots and the habit of sorrow was ineradicable.' *The Uninvited*, however, raises the possibility that *disillusionment* itself may be liberating, if by that is meant dispelling romantic illusions and hopes of 'spiritual' salvation. The 'disillusionment' of Republicans following the shattering experience of the Civil War is often commented on, but Macardle may be suggesting that the best way of revisiting Frascati is to return to the present, free from the enchantment of Romantic Ireland or, indeed, of the island of saints and scholars. In a mood reminiscent of Beckett's *Murphy* (1938), Roddy muses at one point in *The Uninvited* when Stella seems to be losing her mind: 'This situation was atrocious; it could not go on. It had been bad enough already. The cult of the sainted mother, this fixation on dead virtue, dead standards, dead taste. What ordinary mortal could hope to interest Stella while she worshipped that pattern of perfection?' This kind of ghost, like the idealised portrait, reduces the living person to a still life, frozen in time and space. By contrast, the paranormal in *The Uninvited* works to unsettle the normal, and the extrasensory to bring people back to their senses.

Dorothy Macardle: Published Fiction

Earth-Bound: Nine Stories of Ireland (Worcester, MA: Harrigan Press, 1924/ Dublin: Emton Press, 1924).

Uneasy Freehold (London: Peter Davies, 1942)/ *The Uninvited* (New York: Doubleday, 1942).

The Seed was Kind (London: Peter Davies, 1944).

Fantastic Summer (London: Peter Davies, 1946)/ *The Unforeseen* (New York: Doubleday, 1946).

Dark Enchantment (London: Peter Davies, 1953)/ (New York: Doubleday, 1953).

Dear Garry,

Here is your book. It was you who insisted on my writing it.

I understand your pertinacity. The extraordinary events of that summer will never be credited – we shall even doubt our own memories, unless the facts are recorded without more delay.

I know you understand my reluctance. The occurrences which you regard as of 'evidential and scientific significance' were inextricably bound up with matters of a personal character. Every effort that I made to separate them from this intimate story failed. I have been able to do as you wish only by forcing myself to forget that what I was writing would ever be read.

I have not spared either you or myself – your legalistic scepticism or my own ill-considered acts and slow-witted refusals to face the truth.

I wonder whether, when you have read this circumstantial narrative through, you will feel as acutely as I do that

Our indiscretions sometimes serve us well,
When our deep plots do pall.

What strange interweaving of destinies began with the reckless mood of that April morning when Pamela and I first saw Cliff End!

Yours,
Roderick

Contents

The
UNINVITED

Chapter I

CLIFF END

THE CAR SEEMED to share the buoyancy of the morning, humming along over the moorland roads and taking the twisting hills in top.

I was glad we had taken down the hood. There was a heady exuberance in the air. The sky was a high, light haze; the trees and hedges were sprayed with young colour; birds were busy and lambs ran lolloping and bleating about the hills. Pamela pulled her hat off, otherwise the breeze would have sent it flying. It was her doing that we were on the road before nine in the morning and heading for the sea.

That in itself was reckless, for we were two hundred miles from London already and I had to be at my desk by twelve the next day. Even on a paper as smoothly run as *Tomorrow* and with a chief as easy-going as Marriott, you cannot stretch a weekend farther than from four o'clock on Friday to Tuesday at noon. But I was not going back to town without saluting the Atlantic from those famous North Devon cliffs, and Pamela had insisted on seeing this house.

She was a little delirious with enjoyment of the spring morning, and talkative. 'It's going to be warm. Roddy, look at that blackthorn;

3

it's dazzling! I feel lucky this morning – do you? Isn't "Marathon" a gorgeous name?'

'And that,' I replied, 'is your reason for wanting to see it! You ought to have discovered by this time how much innkeepers' recommendations are worth! If it was any good it would be on the agents' lists.'

'Agents' lists!' Her tone washed them out. It was true they had not proved much use. 'This must be the village. Turn to the right.'

I turned off the tarmac on to a steep by-road; the Hillman topped the rise easily, and we came in sight at the same moment of the house and the sea. I drew up because 'Marathon' was written on the gate-posts, but I did not stir from the wheel: the house was a drab barrack with its face to the northeast and a blind back to that superb view.

Pamela's first 'Oh!' was a cry of elation, her second a groan of disgust. She sat glowering. '"And Marathon looks on the sea"!' she quoted wrathfully: 'Exactly what it doesn't do! The man who built a house like that in a place like this should be condemned to haunt it for all eternity.'

I drove on to where the road dwindled and a track led across the down to the edge of the cliff. There lay the ocean – or is it still the Bristol Channel here? No matter. I strode over the turf; Pamela sprinted ahead of me and pulled up – she is temperamentally incapable of keeping away from edges; I followed and grabbed her elbow, digging my heels in, tensed against the blare of the wind.

The bay seemed to laugh at us, delighting in our surprise. The water glittered and danced in the windy light; to right and left the coast swept in broken arcs, its rocks hewn into caves, arches and islets, the cliffs topped with yellow gorse; there were green headlands near, silvery and hazy headlands beyond, and Lundy lay far out, like a giant's barge. Every hour of every day the scene would be changing, taking new colours and forms. I felt that I had been hungry since childhood for that view and would hunger for it for the rest of my life.

Pamela said bitterly, 'If only there had been no house in this place!'

We turned away and walked back to the car, drove down to the main road, studied the map and set a course for the shortest route to London, the golden mood of the morning dead.

We were sunk in silence, our thoughts pursuing the same path to the same dismal conclusion: our hopes had been preposterous; we were fools.

At length I spoke: 'We have just got to make up our minds that what we want doesn't exist.'

Pamela did not reply for a while, then in a subdued voice she said, 'We could make something of the farm at Ghyll Bridge.'

'My dear girl, you would spend your entire day filling lamps and bath-tubs, and I would be hewing wood and drawing water instead of getting on with the book! Where would be the sense in that? No,' I persisted ruthlessly: 'a mouldering old mill in Sleepy Hollow or a bright "Linga-Longa" or "Cotta-Bunga" slightly detached, we could have for our money, but a plain, honest house, with space, light, air, services, and privacy, England no longer offers to the likes of you and me.'

'We could have Littlewood for three years.'

'And paint and carpenter, plant and dig, every spare minute, for somebody else! I have told you: lease a place I will not.'

Pamela fell silent and I was dismayed. She had caught her lower lip between her teeth – a sure sign, in childhood, that she was going to cry. To my relief, she laughed. She said, 'We'll have to advertise for a haunted house.'

It was too bad. I had been thankful to see Pamela set her heart on anything and now this scheme, which had promised escape, solution, and fresh adventure to both of us, seemed doomed to fail.

SIX YEARS of nursing our father had changed Pamela a great deal. When he died I had persuaded her to come and live with me in Bloomsbury, thinking she might find new interests and regain her spirits in my lively bachelor flat. The plan had appeared sound enough but it had not worked so well. Actually, most of the people who crowded around were not altogether congenial either to her or me. Then there was my affair with Lorette. It was obvious, apparently, to everyone but myself, that Lorette would prefer the spotlight with Johnny Mayhew to anything I could offer her, in the end. Pamela worried lest she would marry me and lest she would not and went all hypersensitive and self-effacing just when her school-girl form, her rampageous imagination and capacity for ridiculing sentiment, might have helped. She started a course in library work but realised that this would only lead her from one cloistered life to another and gave it up. Finally she told me that she wanted country life and was thinking of buying a cottage and growing raspberries, sharing with Gillian Long.

I at once realised several things – that London had let us down; that the sooner I snapped out of Lorette's orbit the better; that I would miss Pamela; that my book on the British censorship, designed to cause that animal's death by exposure, was not progressing, and that I could now earn as much by freelance writing as on the staff of *Tomorrow*. I said, 'Why not share one with me?'

Her delight was flattering; enthusiasm seized us; the plan expanded. A complete break with town, a life with air, space, and growth in it was what we needed. We knew it, and the search began. This weekend was our fifth defeat.

NOW THE SEA was out of sight; the road ran down between pines and up over moorland; the surface improved. At crossroads, a sign reading 'Biddlecombe' indicated one of those villages that run head-long to the sea in cleeves of the Devon hills. This one started with a good-looking inn; I would have liked to try its cider, but recollected that the day was too young.

Pamela began to chatter. 'How depressing it is to turn one's back on the West! Why did the ancient races all drive one another west-ward? And the fairy isles are all in the western seas. And western people have more magic, haven't they? And music – Oh, Roddy, what an alluring lane! Do just run up it! There must be a grand view from the top!'

'It will be the same view,' I grumbled. 'However, if it will get the West out of your system!'

To please her, I backed and turned up a gorse-lined smugglers' path. It coiled up among rocks and larches; forked, sending a rutted

6

farm-road off to the right, changed to a straggling drive among budding rhododendrons and came out on a small windy plateau high on the cliffs. The view was the same but there was more of it, for here a little headland ended and the sea lay out to the south as well as the west.

Pamela was first out of the car; she rounded a clump of trees to the left but, instead of walking forward, stood, staring, her back to the view. I joined her and saw an empty house.

Stone-built, plain-faced, two-storeyed, so beautifully proportioned that one would have halted to gaze at it anywhere, it stood confronting the bay. A wooded rise sheltered it on the east and on the north was the wind-break of trees.

'Roddy,' Pamela said. 'It's a house!'

'So it seems.'

I walked round it. It was a solid structure – Georgian, I thought, with large windows on either side of the door and three windows above. There was a flat-topped, pillared porch with a fanlight over it, and the ground-floor windows were set in shallow arches which repeated the fanlight's curve. The house faced south. The shape was odd, for its sides were much longer than its frontage, the ground floor projecting at the back with a flat roof. The man who built the house had evidently intended to add rooms upstairs. There was a yard with out-houses, and a stable opened on to the drive. The place had been neglected for years; the storm-shutters which protected the ground-floor windows were denuded of paint and one of them hung askew, and a small greenhouse, built out on the west side, had lost most of its glass. The walls, however, looked sound. The garden beds, which had been made here and there where the out-cropping rock allowed, were matted with weeds and the leafage of pinks; rough lawns, sloping down on two sides to the cliff's edge, merged with the heather, unkempt; there were clumps of short, fleshy daffodils in the grass, and a forsythia laid sparse yellow bells over a windowsill. I walked to the edge. Not a building was in sight except a lighthouse and a coast-guard station away on the left. I listened, and heard only the rumble of the sea, a gull's cry, and the distant bleating of sheep.

The cliff fell steeply to the sea; on the west side, the edge was not a hundred yards from the house; there was a little creek here, and at its inner point stood a dead, twisted tree. Standing there, I looked down and saw, beyond juts and shelving rocks, the amber gleam of a minute beach. I was seized by covetousness. One could run down by some zig-zag track in the rocks and swim. There were men who could own places like this …

'Roddy, Roddy,' Pamela was calling. 'It's for sale!'

She was in the drive, near the stable. She had found a faded placard, half-hidden by shrubs.

'It's worth twice our money, derelict as it is: forget it!' I said,

'Commander Brooke, Wilmcote, The Avenue, Biddlecombe,' Pamela read. 'Roddy, come on!'

WE NOW HAD good reason to call at The Golden Hind. I thirsted for cider, but it was early, and we were in England; its coffee was vile. The motherly body who served us showed the liveliest interest when we asked the way to Wilmcote and stood watching us from her door-step when we left. Pamela laughed, 'She sees a prospective customer in you.'

The wooded estate which included The Avenue could be seen on the slope of the hill to the north on the opposite side of the village from Cliff End. One could walk through the village and climb a steep path to the right, or drive along the main road and take a winding course round the hill.

The village allured us; one could see down the steep, straggling street to the small wharf at the end where fishermen were busy with boats and nets; the whole place had a fine, sea-weedy smell; but we were torn with impatience and drove off.

Very trim, very ship-shape, Wilmcote appeared, with its clipped hedge, edgings of box, looped muslin curtains, and knocker of polished brass.

When I had rung the bell I suddenly felt embarrassed, realising that it was scarcely ten o'clock. The door was opened quickly but not, as one would have expected, by a neat maid. The girl who looked at us with dismayed dark eyes had her hair enveloped in a turban of pink towelling, and her cheeks were pink from the heat of a fire; the effect was charming and I smiled; this made her flush more deeply and she asked us quickly to come in. We murmured apologies for coming so early, and she accepted them with a grave mandarin nod.

'I thought it was our daily maid; you must please excuse me,' she said.

She looked a child, but her manner would have been appropriate in a hostess of thirty.

'Quite by chance,' Pamela told her, 'we have seen the house called "Cliff End." We would like to look over it if we may have the key.'

'My grandfather is out; I am sorry,' the girl answered politely. And then her face came to life with a look of almost incredulous excitement.

'Oh,' she breathed, looking from me to Pamela and back again, 'you are going over the house?'

'If we may,' Pamela replied.

'I have no idea where the key is!' She spoke despairingly then reflected and added, 'But I will find it. Forgive me if it takes a little time. Won't you wait in here?'

She left us in a small, formal dining-room but came back very soon with a key. It was large and rusty.

'I think this must be it. I expect you may have it. Or could you possibly wait?'

She looked a little worried. I explained that we had a day's driving before us and were anxious to lose no time. As though the decision were a serious one, she handed me the key.

'Take it. I will explain.'

She heaved a sigh of frustration. 'I can't possibly come with you because I have just washed my hair. What a misfortune!'

'Don't let us keep you in a draught!' Pamela said anxiously. Again came that smile, a little surprised, and a glance, frank, yet shy, into Pamela's eyes. I felt, when the door was closed behind us, that she sent longing thoughts after us and that it *was* rather a misfortune that she had just washed her hair.

THE KEY would not turn in the lock of the front door. Walking along the east side of the house, under the hillside that rose close to its windows, we found a small door and this, with much creaking and sticking, let us in. We passed through a scullery to a big flagged kitchen. It was dim, for the windows were overshadowed by the rising ground and were caked with dust. Every corner, the sink, the taps, and the piping were festooned and canopied with cobwebs cradling dust. But the room was wired for electricity, had a generous sink and boiler, and, Pamela thought, a tolerable range.

'Not labour-saving,' she pronounced, 'spacious, however: room for Lizzie and her cat.'

This was quite a point. Lizzie Flynn had cooked for us from the time when I was seventeen and Pamela eleven until we gave up the Wimbledon house. She had comforted Pamela when our mother died, trained her to take the mistress's place, and stood between her and father's tantrums. I had found them mingling their tears in the kitchen when some ambitious concoction had been sent untasted away. Lizzie had sworn, when we parted, that she would come back to Pamela at any time, to any part of the world, provided her ginger cat might come too. And Lizzie required space.

'These would appeal to her!' Pamela was looking into larders and pantries, a dairy, a wash-house, and two or three store-rooms which opened off a passage behind the kitchen, taking up the space under the flat roof.

We cast hasty glances into these and the servant's bedroom and hurried to the front of the house. A wide corridor led us straight to the front door. Standing with our backs to the door, we looked at the hall and stairs with delight. It was a fine entrance, broad, balanced, ample – remarkably so for such a small house. The stairs were shallow and had a mahogany banister which curved gracefully on the upstairs landing, doubling back along the corridor to the left.

At the foot of the stairs, on our right, was a door with good, simple lines, and one exactly similar faced it across the width of the hall.

'Elegant!' Pamela exclaimed, opening the door on the right.

This would be the dining-room. It was almost dark, the shutters only letting in thin blades of light, but one could see that it was a long room, high-ceilinged, with a beautiful marble mantelpiece. The south window would look over the bay, and the window in the east wall had been set forward to escape the shadow of the knoll. What a room to breakfast in!

'Heavy silk curtains,' Pamela was murmuring; 'ivory paint; a Wedgwood frieze; an old refectory table; the Waterford glass.'

I crossed the wide hall to the door opposite, opened it, and stood silent. I had seen no lovelier room. It was in a submarine dimness, but I could see the perfect shape of the room, the beauty of the cornices and of the mantelpiece; I could imagine it with its windows open, all the lucent charm of sea and moorland flowing in.

Pamela, standing beside me, drew a deep breath. 'The divine proportion, surely?' she murmured.

The room was a pool of peace; our footsteps, loud on the parquet, violated its ancient quiet. Here, nothing that would disturb or frustrate the mind's creative impulse would intrude. I felt that I could beggar myself to live here, but I did not tell Pamela that.

Mute with excitement, Pamela ran upstairs and I followed. She stood at the landing window looking over the radiant bay. I opened a door on my right. Here, over the drawing-room, were two rooms with a communicating door. Unexpectedly, the front room was the smaller; the other was almost square; from its windows I looked westward over that magnificent broken coast and the open sea. In the foreground the dead tree, all its boughs grown inward, made a black, fantastic figure against the blue sheen of the water. I said aloud, without turning: 'I want this view.'

'You may have it,' Pamela called back, exultant. 'I want this room!'

I found her in the room opposite which, like the dining-room, had windows east and south. Sunlight and sea-light danced on ceiling and walls.

'"Farewell, thou art too dear for my possessing!"' she sighed.

I looked into the room behind it, which opened near the head of the stairs, and called to her: 'Don't despair: here's the snag!'

The east window had been blocked up, and a very large window in the north wall looked over the flat roof to the yard. The brick fireplace was much too small; the built-in closets too narrow and deep. And the room struck cold. It was dim, graceless, wholly without charm.

'Somebody's studio,' Pamela said. 'I would hate to be a painter and live out of the sun. The spiders like it, don't they? It would have to be the guest-room, just.'

I jeered at her notion of hospitality.

'It's you and me and Lizzie who matter,' she contended, 'and you must have a study. Lizzie will have to sleep downstairs.'

The bedroom accommodation ended here; other doors on the landing revealed a large bathroom, linen-presses, and a sort of lumber-room with a ladder to the attic, and that was all.

'It is really a small house, isn't it?' Pamela said wistfully. Her face was taut, as if with hunger; she wanted it; so did I.

'An architect's plan,' I said, summing up; 'electricity; plumbing; in very fair condition; no tennis-lawn and no room for one; telephone would have to be brought from goodness knows where; too isolated for most tastes: there's a bare possibility – an almost totally naked one – that it might be within our price.'

She stood immobile for a moment as though she were listening.

'I believe it is,' she said; 'I believe we are going to live here – Come and see!'

Chapter II

THE COMMANDER

THE COMMANDER was at home. The maid who took my card in returned at once and showed us into an office-like room at the back. He stood waiting for us, a man not far from seventy, with white hair and beard, his head erect and blue eyes alight. He had the air of a man going into battle. He said, 'Good morning, Mr Fitzgerald,' bowed to Pamela, motioned us into leather armchairs, and, sitting in his swivel desk-chair, waited for me to begin.

He listened to my questions studiously and replied with precision. Yes: except for a brief period, the house had been untenanted for some time – for fifteen years, in fact. Yes, no doubt, the roof and out-buildings would need repair. It was a well-built house, however; the man who designed it had been an architect and had built it for himself.

'Five generations of my family,' Commander Brooke said, almost defiantly, 'lived there in health and comfort. Considerable sums were spent on improvements about twenty-four years ago.'

It was for sale, freehold; the rates were negligible; the property included the knoll on the east side and part of the larch-grove, also the sandy beach from which bathing was safe at low tide.

'And the price?'

'In its present condition, fourteen hundred.'

I shook my head. I saw Pamela's face change and the old man glance at her keenly from under his jutting brows. He seemed to be studying her.

'Perhaps the Commander would consider an offer?' she said.

I offered a thousand, pointing out that repairs would certainly cost a good deal. He sat absorbed in thought and did not reply for a moment, then he looked up, saying, 'I beg your pardon?' I repeated my offer, and he said, impatiently, 'Yes, yes, that would do … '

His tone was so inconclusive that I wondered what there was that would not do – Pamela or myself, perhaps?

'You would sell for a thousand?' I asked, not certain that he had understood me. He sat motionless for a moment, his face stony, and then, like a man forcing himself to some ordeal, said, 'Yes.'

Pamela opened incredulous eyes and relaxed with an immense sigh. I had as much as I could do to keep a business-like rigidity and remember to say that I would like to examine the place thoroughly with an architect and have his report. Still abstracted in his manner, the Commander told me that there was a good man at Barnstaple, he believed, and, telephoning to a bank there, secured the address. His telephone was at my disposal, if I would like to make arrangements at once. 'A report will commit us to nothing,' he added, as though thinking aloud.

I reflected that it would commit me to the architect's fee, but agreed. The reluctance in the old man's manner made me nervously anxious to secure the house before he should change his mind. One could not fail to see that the whole transaction was distasteful to him and that our enquiries affected him as an intrusion. I wondered whether he disliked the house or disliked letting it go.

I telephoned. Good! Mr Richards could run over from Barnstaple; he could be at Cliff End at three o'clock. No, he was, sorry; he could not make it earlier than that. I asked Pamela how she would feel about driving most of the night; she said that she would enjoy it, and the appointment was made.

As I hung up the receiver I caught the Commander's eyes fixed on me searchingly. I felt diminished under that luminous blue gaze. His face, narrow and aquiline, stamped with experience and authority, had a look which, I imagined, it wore rarely – a look of doubt. Was there some defect in the house which he feared the architect might expose? No, the man had rectitude in every line of him; it was not that. Was he uneasy about the sort of people with whom he had to deal? I returned, his stare with a frank regard, perhaps a little amused, and, as though reassured, he turned to Pamela and said, with a courteous gesture, 'May I invite you to drink a glass of sherry?'

He rang, ordered the sherry, and, after a moment's reflection, told the maid to ask Miss Meredith to come in. The girl goggled at us inquisitively as she left the room: evidently, morning callers were rare at Wilmcote.

While we waited the Commander talked about motoring, which, he said, he had never learnt to enjoy, and about the vehicles of his early days. Pamela responded gaily, and I had time to look around the room. It was not interesting; there were filing cabinets and shelves full of old books; no fire; no flowers; no photographs except of ships; no new books; no papers except some nautical journals and *The Times*. There was only one work of art in the room, a large portrait in oils over the fireplace, and that was not very good.

Yet, on second thoughts, that picture had quality; one would remember it. It was the portrait of a girl. The artist had scamped labour on the hands and hair and white muslin dress, but he had painted a living face.

The girl was beautiful – fair-skinned, fair-haired, with large, ice-blue eyes. Her hair was piled high above a noble forehead; her mouth was set in sweet, stern lines; she held her hands like a nun's, crossed on her breast. I could imagine her pictured so in a stained-glass window with a halo about her head.

The Commander, catching the direction of my gaze, became silent. I hesitated to speak of the picture and there was an awkward pause. It was a relief when the girl of the turban came in, with decanter and glasses on a tray. The old man introduced us.

'This is my granddaughter, Miss Meredith: Miss Pamela Fitzgerald; Mr Roderick Fitzgerald. They are considering purchasing Cliff End. The house,' he explained to us, 'actually belongs to her.'

A flash of excitement lit the girl's composed little face, but she bowed formally, setting down the tray. Her hand shook slightly as she gave us our glasses. She looked seriously at Pamela and then at me.

'I hope you will be lucky in it,' she said.

What an odd, well-behaved child! No, not a child! Now, wearing a brown dress with cream collar and cuffs, her brown hair parted and held as smooth by combs as springy curls would allow, she looked quite seventeen. Her manner would still have served for thirty or more, but not all the time. Again she rested that frank, searching gaze on Pamela's face, transferred it to mine, and smiled.

'I believe you will!' she exclaimed, and very slightly saluted with her glass before she drank.

We told her how charmed we were by the house, the sunny rooms, and the view. She listened greedily.

'It must be fabulous,' she sighed.

The Commander turned to her. 'How's the commissariat, Stella? Can we give ourselves the pleasure of inviting our new acquaintances to lunch?'

'Yes! Yes!' she responded eagerly. 'That would give us great pleasure,' she amended, under her guardian's repressive glance. 'If you will excuse a very simple meal.'

We accepted, and Pamela was conducted to Stella's room.

The Commander offered me a cigarette. There was something about which he wanted to speak to me alone; that was evident. He began awkwardly.

'Miss Fitzgerald looks a little delicate. The air here should do her good.'

That, I conceded, was one of our reasons for leaving London.

'Yes,' he went on reflectively; 'a delicate, hypersensitive type.'

'Scarcely hypersensitive,' I protested.

'I beg your pardon.' He was sincerely apologetic; the last man willingly to commit an impertinence, I felt sure.

'The air at Cliff End,' I suggested, 'must be superb.'

He was abstracted and did not reply directly. 'Does wind affect her?' he asked.

'Not too much; we both rather enjoy a storm.'

'It makes melancholy sounds,' he murmured, 'blowing over the moors.'

'That won't worry us.'

'It is, of course, a lonely spot ... '

'A writer has to be able to be alone, and Pamela makes friends ... '

I broke off. What was the old man driving at? I thought I had better let him come out with it, and waited. He was tapping his blotter with an ivory paper-knife, as if giving some imperative signal. At last, he spoke abruptly:

'A clear duty is imposed on me,' he said.

'Yes?'

'I told you that six years ago the house was occupied for some months. I must inform you that the people did not stay very long. They experienced disturbances there.'

'Experienced!' I smiled at his word; most men in his place would have said 'fancied,' or 'imagined,' if they had thought it necessary to mention the matter at all.

'As long as the cause was not rats,' I replied lightly.

'It was not rats.'

I waited. Was he going to tell me any more? Obviously not. His mouth set in a firm line; he was looking out at a cat on the garden wall.

'I felt obliged to mention it,' he said.

So, I was to take it or leave it at that.

'A story like that will be quite an attraction to my sister,' I told him.

'Indeed?'

He turned to his desk and wrote down for me the address of the solicitor in London who had charge of all business concerning the house. I could see that he wanted to be rid of everything connected with it, and I admired, the more, the integrity which had forced him to warn me about 'disturbances' and the delicate consideration which had made him, rather than mention these before Pamela, reluctantly invite us to lunch. A complex personality – hard on himself. Was his hand heavy, I wondered, on the girl?

Conversation with him was difficult in this mood, and I rose with too much alacrity when Stella returned, summoning us to lunch.

We had a delicious meal: chicken with asparagus and potato croquettes was followed by a trifle on which the custard was still warm, with ratafia biscuits lavishly scattered on it. The Commander poured an excellent hock. At table he exerted himself to be affable and entertained us with stories of the ways and characters of Devonshire men; under his dry, sometimes caustic, humour, his strong regard for these men could be felt. Pamela, who was in tremendous spirits, questioned him with lively interest.

'Is there a Celtic strain in North Devon?' she asked. 'You would expect it, wouldn't you, here, between Cornwall and Wales?'

'None!' he replied rather sharply. 'The Welsh are an entirely different race.'

And an inferior one, his tone conveyed.

Stella, who was seated at my right, looked at her plate and visibly turned her mind on some other track. Was she very reserved or very transparent? I could not guess. Her face, firmly moulded on delicate bones, with a wide smooth forehead and hollowed temples, had a reticent look; yet little shadows and contractions, continually in play, betrayed what lips and eyes might conceal. In our honour, she had replaced the comb in her hair with a velvet ribbon and hung round her neck a locket on a thin gold chain. Our visit was an exciting interlude and the sale of her house a climactic event. She would have asked a thousand questions had good manners allowed. Now, as though trying to grasp some elusive memory, she half-closed her eyes. She opened them suddenly, exclaiming, 'Pamela Fitzgerald!'

'Stella!'

The tone expressed horror; the girl paled under the Commander's freezing stare; tears brimmed her eyes and her throat worked; she was unable to speak. Pamela smiled.

'The Commander hasn't heard of my famous ancestress,' she said, and turned her attention on him.

'She is said to have been a daughter of the Duc d'Orléans,' she told him, 'and an exquisite girl. She married Lord Edward Fitzgerald, who led the Irish rising of 'ninety-eight. She was not really an ancestress of mine, I am afraid, but I am charmed to have been named after her. I don't know any story more full of heroism and romance.'

'I am afraid,' the Commander answered stiffly, 'that I am not well acquainted with Irish rebel history.'

Pamela, once she gets her Irish up, is not easily crushed. While I tried to divert our host with journalistic small talk she was telling Stella how Pamela had actually been seen at Frascati, her old home near Dublin, in broad daylight, at a garden-party, a short time before.

Stella was enthralled.

'I am not really surprised,' Pamela went on. 'You see, she had been happy at Frascati. I am sure that, if spirits walk, it is in places that they have loved. That is why it seems foolish to be afraid of them.'

She had said it lightly but the effect was startling. Stella stopped eating and turned to her a face irradiated with wonder and something like relief.

'You truly think that?' she breathed, 'You do really believe … '

Her grandfather cut in with a glance of such displeasure at Pamela that I grew hot with indignation. 'You cannot possibly,' he said, his voice edged with contempt, 'you cannot possibly hold those views! With what flippancy, with what reckless levity, people speak of these things!'

Pamela gazed at him; was she going to be sarcastic? She can. No; she spoke slowly and thoughtfully: 'You are perfectly right: they do.'

There was a pause. Really, I felt, Pamela had not been fortunate in her choice of topics; Welshmen, ghosts, and rebels did not appear to be among the old man's favourite themes. Stella was nervously crumpling her handkerchief; a strong, flowery perfume came from it; the Commander noticed it and frowned with his nostrils pinched. Dismayed, Stella hurriedly put it away. She spoke gently: 'I am sorry, grandfather; I forgot how much you dislike my scent.'

'I supposed that you had forgotten,' he replied.

She stood up and with a little bow to Pamela said, 'Excuse me,' and left the room.

Nobody came to the rescue, and the silence continued until Stella returned. We tried to engage her in talk about the neighbourhood and its entertainments, asking whether there were dances sometimes or amateur acting; where could one hear music? There was a tennis club, she told us, and a cinema – 'rather a comical one' – no music; no plays.

'My granddaughter,' the Commander informed us, 'has recently returned from a school in Brussels. It is an exceptional school; the pupils attend concerts and visit galleries. I hardly think that the local choral society would interest her, after that.'

The girl took up her cue and talked appropriately about the amenities of life in Brussels. Coffee was served at the table and then it was time for us to return to Cliff End. Stella had such a look of eagerness held in leash while we prepared to leave that I contrived to ask her privately whether she could not come. She smiled sadly and shook her head.

'You ask,' she whispered.

I signalled to Pamela, but she had already had the same notion and was saying, lightly, to the old man, 'Would you come with us? Both of you, perhaps?'

'Thank you,' he replied, 'but I dislike motoring, and the walk takes an hour.'

'The proprietress, then?'

Surely he could feel the child's eyes, eloquent with pleading, though he did not glance her way?

'I am sorry: I cannot spare Stella this afternoon.'

He produced a great bunch of old-fashioned keys. He and his granddaughter would be occupied, we gathered, when we called to return them. They bade us a polite goodbye.

Stella had shown no sign of disappointment, but her face was set in resigned, sad lines; it was the expression of the face in the painting, and I resented it; for a long time, in spite of the excitements of our enterprise, I could not get it out of my mind.

In the car Pamela dangled the bunch of keys joyously and read out the labels – 'stable,' 'studio,' 'potting-shed,' and so on. 'They make me feel like a land-owner,' she said.

'We have been a bit precipitate,' I warned her: 'didn't stamp on the floors or examine cupboards or look at the woodwork; it's probably full of dry rot.'

'Dry rot!' she exclaimed, as though it were a term of abuse. 'That's what's the matter with the old man!'

'You did put your foot in it up to the elbow,' I said. 'Curmudgeon!'

'Queer. Does he want us to buy the house or doesn't he?'

'He has to sell it and hates being made to.'

'Probably.'

'Do him good!'

'You were a monkey, turning his own table on him like that!'

'Well, I should think nobody has stood up to him for five generations. And I couldn't stand it – snubbing that enchanting child!'

'Child!' I mocked. 'What's the difference between you? Five years?'

'Just about. She is eighteen.'

'She doesn't look it.'

'She is not permitted to grow up.'

'Did she say so?'

'Heavens, no! She hasn't realised it yet. Something will happen when she does.'

'She seems all thrilled about the house.'

'Yes. She left it before she was three and has never been in it since.'

'That's odd – I wonder why.'

'Her mother died there.'

'That's not a reason.'

'I know … She was the girl in the picture and as good as she was beautiful, it appears. Stella's father painted it – Llewellyn Meredith. Do you know his name?'

'I do not. Ha, a Welshman!'

'An entirely different race,' Pamela mimicked wickedly.

'Now don't get up one of your prejudices!' I begged.

We were in the drive.

'Roddy, think of those rhododendrons in blossom!'

'You couldn't make much of a garden here, you know; there's hardly any soil.'

'I'll guarantee to make one of some sort.'

'Curious, the way the house hides itself.'

I pulled up outside the stable and we walked round the trees. The house was splendid, standing there in its austerity and steadfastness among the wildness and freedom of moors and sea.

'Are you sure you will be satisfied,' I asked Pamela, 'living up here on the edge of the world?'

'Satisfied?' She laughed, inarticulate with love at first sight.

'Come practical, now!' I adjured her as we went in.

'Cupboards!' she responded, making for the alcove under the stairs. 'Cheers, Roddy! Big enough to telephone in!'

Behind the alcove, I found a small cloakroom. The maid's room was opposite, and I looked into that again. Shrubs darkened the window; I would have to cut them down, then it would have the westward view. Beside it was the old bathroom with a hideous rusty bath on iron feet.

'Glory, have we missed a room!'

Pamela was at a door between the drawing-room and the bathroom, trying keys in the lock. She opened it with one which had no label. We looked straight through a bay filled with sunshine to the twisted tree.

It was a charming, odd little room. The bay had been built out of it, and, standing there, Pamela was in a flood of light. On the right was an alcove large enough to take a couch, and opposite it was a fireplace with yellow tiles. The sun-bleached wallpaper showed a faint pattern of small yellow garlands still.

'It's a gift!' Pamela said, enchanted. 'What do you suppose it was used for?'

'Smoking-room; sewing-room; still-room; powder-closet,' I suggested, but Pamela was not listening; she was examining the door to the garden, of which the upper half was of glass. She pulled, and the glazed panels opened inwards, leaving a half-door locked.

'It's bolted outside!' she exclaimed. 'The steps are covered with a board. It's a gangway! Oh, it's a gangway for a pram! It's the nursery – Stella's room!'

I felt sure she was right. Outside, too, there was a screen of strong wire trellis which had probably been kept locked, but the hasp of the latch had rusted and fallen out, and a growth of weeds held the screen open wide. Yes, this was Stella's room.

'It's the prettiest room in the house! How she will enjoy spending a night here!' Pamela said.

'Hi, there! You're exceeding the speed limit!'

The bolt was stuck. I swung over the half-door and went across the lawn and stood again by the tree, looking down at the bright crescent of sand. To own that would be to own the ocean. My skin prickled with a longing to plunge in here and now. I would be happy in the sea if I were to be hanged in an hour. I laughed, suddenly visualising Lorette in this setting. She would be bored to frenzy in a week. Even the memory of her would be blown away by these breezes. Well, that was what I wanted!

'Roddy,' Pamela was saying, 'think of it! To own soil and rocks and trees and a beach!'

'I *am* thinking of it. Come and see about the garage,' I replied.

The stable would make a garage for two cars. There were endless possibilities in the small rooms, some with windows, others without, opening on the yard. Stone and labour had been cheap when Cliff End was built and planned for an increasing family. Of that family, Stella was the last, I supposed.

We returned to the nursery.

'We can't make this journey again,' I told Pamela. 'Better take measurements in case ... Have you the notebook?'

'This room must be all yellow,' she said. 'Painted furniture; daffodils in a jug; perhaps a green mat by the bed ... '

I was working with my beautiful steel measuring tape which coils up or stands on end like the Indian's trick rope. Conversation was erratic.

'Alcove, six foot six. Are you taking it down?'

'I am. Liberty's have curtain stuff, woven, yellow and green ...'

'Window, six ten … Come into the drawing-room; that's more important.'

The drawing-room floor was too large for my carpet, I could see at a glance, and the parquet needed none.

'Windows,' I dictated, 'nine foot four and a half – the old velvet curtains might do. That architect's late … Llewellyn Meredith – I believe I *have* heard his name. Max will know about him if he was any good.'

'An R.A.,' Pamela answered. 'Flat pelmets, arched, don't you think? Stella has the misfortune to have her father's colourings and that's an abiding grief to the old man. He thinks she inherits an irresponsible strain … '

'Where on earth,' I exclaimed, 'did you dig out all this?'

'Psychological deduction! … Stair-carpets will cost a lot.'

'Then we won't carpet the stairs.'

'Scrubbing's a bother.'

'We won't have linoleum!'

'Ugh, no! On those stairs!'

'Anything we buy,' I pronounced, 'must be what we mean to live with. We can't afford makeshifts.'

'I agree!' Pamela said.

'Of course, we haven't bought it yet!'

'Of course not!' She was smiling … 'He thinks that stern discipline will keep her in the strait and narrow path. But he's fond of her and good to her in his way.'

'Twenty-two steps.'

'Only sometimes her father breaks out in her and then he pounces like a hawk – I wish I knew where she found that mimosa scent! He doesn't know it, but he is stunting her, spoiling her spontaneity.'

'Blast that architect! We've two hundred miles to drive.'

'Blast him! … He's breaking her nerve. He'll create a complex if he doesn't look out.'

'Lord, woman!' I straightened up and stared at Pamela. I hadn't heard her rattle away in this fashion for years.

'How did she find time,' I asked, 'to tell you all this?'

'Tell me!' she chuckled. 'That reserved young person? Roddy, have sense!'

'Oh, you're just spinning a yarn?'

'I'll have a bet with you it's true!'

'You're a public menace!'

There was wine in the air of Cliff End; I blessed it; Pamela was herself again.

Chapter III

THE VILLAGE

EXTRICATING ONESELF from London is a desperate business; you are fighting an octopus; as soon as you have loosened one tentacle, you are clutched by another. First there was Marriott: he had always been so decent; I could not let him down. He was ordered abroad for spa treatment, and I had to take his place all May. Then Clement Forster, who was to succeed me as literary editor, insisted that he must have a long holiday first. I needed masses of notes for my book from the British Museum and had only the evenings in which to work there, and so it went on.

On the nineteenth of April Cliff End became ours, equally and jointly, free of rent forever – 'from the centre to the sky,' Pamela added. About the sky, in these days of aeroplanes, I was not so sure.

It was infuriating, but I saw no hope of escaping finally until July. Pamela simply 'threw London overboard,' as she expressed it, and went. She put up at The Golden Hind; I snatched a few days with her there, engaged workmen, and left her in charge. Her reports were a bit elevated, but, even deducting a percentage for temperament, I was satisfied that the job went well. I ran down for three weekends and found that she was managing capitally and enjoying it all no end. I was savage at having to miss the fun. No help or interest seemed to be forthcoming from Wilmcote, but that neither surprised nor troubled me; the old man, I thought, was difficult and better left to himself, and I had no doubt whatever that Pamela would make friends with his granddaughter sooner or later.

Strange child; she made me think of a narcissus just breaking out of its sheath.

When Forster went off I moved into his flat and despatched our furniture; a week later I saw Lizzie off at Paddington with her collection of hampers and her cat.

'That's my Whisky,' she chuckled as the porter handed in the basket. 'I have to have my Whisky wherever I go, night and day.' She was not tired of that joke yet. This porter was her equal. 'That's right, ma'am,' he replied with a twinkle. 'Don't lose your spirits, whatever happens.'

How Lizzie laughed! And when Lizzie laughs she shakes in all her ample being; her eyes run, her cheeks grow crimson, and everyone within hearing is forced to smile. She would be talking about this porter for weeks.

'Whisky and gossip are your only vices,' I told her as the train pulled out. Still convulsed with laughter, she contrived to call back: 'Goodbye, Mr Roderick! Take care of yourself!'

From my twenty-first birthday on, Lizzie had taught herself, carefully, to say 'Mister Fitzgerald'; it took a parting to make her forget. It would be nice to be looked after by Lizzie again. Meanwhile, how I was going to loathe these weeks, neither travelling nor at home! And Max was out of town.

But July was perversely pleasant, with shade in the parks and sun and breeze in the streets. London, abandoned to honest workers like myself, began to seem my proper home; I was not sure that I wanted to give it up. And I was going to miss the paper – the office politics, the hasty lunches in pubs with our odd, amusing drift of contributors, and the weekly rush. Marriott was a grand fellow in spite of the dictatorial ways which so often enraged me, and the office staff were such an uncommonly decent bunch. Tomlin seemed genuinely upset at my leaving – 'Who'll keep His Knobs in his place now?' he fretted; and Knoblock declared that, lacking the Buffer, Tomlin would get him down. I had rather resented being known as the Buffer, but it had been a friendly tribute, after all. When should I hear it again?

Marriott called me in for a cup of tea and a farewell chat. He said my decision was a blow to him, quite a blow. 'Your name means a lot to our readers, RDF – quite a lot. You must send us plenty of stuff; don't let us down. If you care, any time, to suggest a series, I'd be glad, very glad. Not too highbrow. Er – what about "Country Life"? "A Pen Man in Devonshire" – something like that?'

I pointed out that I was not yet a qualified countryman. This snack-bar writing was just the sort of thing, though I hope I concealed the fact, from which I wanted to get away.

'What about "Some First Nights Recalled"?' was his next suggestion. A retired septuagenarian's theme, but I agreed. I was going to miss the theatre more than everything else put together. Oh, Jiminy, had I made a mistake?

Lorette provided the answer to that question. I thanked the stars she was out of town, but she rang up from Sussex, and while she complained and mourned in her crooning voice, I could see that drowsy kitten face, feel her soft little clinging hands. Johnny wasn't being kind; she didn't think she could bear it much longer; what *was* she to do? She *must* have a lovely long talk with me and she was coming to town. When I told her, perhaps in too light-hearted a tone, that I would be gone, she changed to abuse and rang off.

Well, that was salutary! I wanted wind, sea, the Devonshire cliffs! I wanted people who kept their bargains and knew their own minds.

The name of the Great West Road is tonic. I had few regrets as I drove out of the city at the dusty end of a sweltering day, left the wilting suburbs behind, and accelerated into the spacious dusk. I had none at all when I woke in the morning to the cheeping of birds and the gurgle of running water, in an inn on the edge of the Marlborough downs.

I had slept heavily and was late away. The morning was hot and glaring, but on the uplands a breeze blew and by mid afternoon

I could feel in it the vigour of the sea. I felt thirsty from head to foot. The road kept cheating me of a sight of the water, dodging down into wooded valleys and winding behind high banks, but at last the bay lay before me; I was seized with a crazy elation and speeded wildly until I drew up at Cliff End.

For a minute the whole scene quivered, then I saw it clear, in the pure, strong colours of childhood, as if a gap had been torn here in some veil that dulls the world to older eyes. The house was alive; new paint shone; polished windows glittered; upstairs white curtains waved; from inside I heard Lizzie's welcoming shout.

Pamela came flying out of the house, a rich colour in her sunburnt cheeks, grey eyes alight. She wore slacks and a white jumper and looked eighteen.

'The girl's rejuvenated!' I exclaimed.

She studied me, laughing and disapproving. Lizzie, too, while crushing my hands in the warmth of her welcome, shook a commiserating head.

'God help us, you're looking badly,' she exclaimed with relish.

'Poor, town-blighted son of a hangman's ghost,' Pamela said; 'we've got you just in time! Quick, Lizzie – tea! We're having meals in the kitchen still, Roddy. I know you want to bathe first, but you can't; the tide's too high.'

'All right, tea first! Gosh, Pamela, you look fine!'

'Everything's fine!'

She made me begin my inspection of the rooms at the top, chattering all the time.

'It doesn't *look* as if much had been done, I am afraid, and there's mountains waiting for the master's hand. No carpets down or hangings up. But the lights light and the boiler boils and the cooker cooks and your sacred telephone is working at last.'

To my surprise, the rooms looked larger than when they were empty. Most of them had been washed in light green, the hall and passages in ivory; I liked the effect. And the grand-parental furniture, which had looked elephantine in London, seemed in place here. In her bedroom Pamela had the half-tester bed, the sofa, the bow-fronted chest-of-drawers, and the wardrobe, broader than it was tall, as a wardrobe ought to be. The room had a rich and permanent air and looked rather dramatic, one end dim and the space by the windows brilliantly lit. I found the tall-boy in my bedroom, between the windows. I would not have believed that a room could be at once so peaceful and so exhilarating. I decided to change the position of the bed: I wanted to wake facing that view. In the room opening off it was my flat-topped desk. Sunlight poured over it; a jar of pinks spiced the air; my parcels of papers, each with a label corresponding to its drawer, were set out on top. Ten minutes' work would make this my home.

'You have done pretty well,' I said.

'The studio isn't papered yet,' Pamela told me. 'The plaster's too bad to take paint. And we'll just, for the present, have to shut the dining-room up. It's an arrogant room and won't tolerate makeshifts. It will have to wait till we're rich.'

The lovely drawing-room had accepted its role as general living-room with a good grace. The colourless birch of the dresser, dining-table, and chairs, and the faded rose of the arm-chairs and chesterfield, and my book-cases, painted green, settled pleasantly together. The window-seat was piled with cushions; at the opposite end of the room, by the fireplace, my book-reviewing corner was complete, with deep chair, low table, and bridge-lamp, and the radio within reach. Pamela's lamp and sewing-table were on the other side – not that Pamela ever sewed, except in occasional day-long orgies. Nothing had been bought for this room, and seeing our old things in it made me dizzy for a minute, as if the past and future had collided here; then the future settled – became today. On the mantelpiece cabbage roses flopped heavy heads and in the broken-down greenhouse one superb red azalea glowed, proclaiming how flowery, how delicately coloured, silkily draped, and graciously furnished this room ought to be.

'What spending there'll be on it,' Pamela said, 'when your book is sold!'

I did not tell her that a book like mine never brings its author a fortune or that the room teased me with its suggestion of potentialities unfulfilled.

'Any callers yet?' I asked.

'No, thank goodness! We are safe, Lizzie says, until the curtains are up.'

'Nothing from the Commander?'

'No.'

'No "disturbances"?'

She hesitated: 'I wouldn't have any difficulty about imagining things.'

'As far as I know, you've never had much difficulty about that,' I responded as Lizzie came to bid us to tea.

A lavish tea was spread on the check cloth. Lizzie jammed our splits for us, more generously than in schoolroom days, and piled them thick with clotted cream. Sterile years dropped away.

'Tomorrow,' Pamela said, 'we will hang the drawing-room curtains and settle the books and put up the chandelier. Charlie Jessup is coming to help in the afternoon. He's a useful neighbour. There's nothing he won't undertake to do. "I be a bit of a tomato grower," he'll tell you one day, and "I be a sort of a blacksmith" the next. The trouble is, when he is half through one job a passion seizes him to begin another. He and his aunt were supposed to care-take the house, I believe, and to clean, it up for us, but it was left in rather a mess.'

This surprised me; I should have thought that Commander Brooke would be scrupulous in a matter like that.

'Anyhow,' Pamela went on, 'he loves hanging round and doesn't seem to care whether he's paid for his work or not. I think it's in love with Lizzie he is.'

'In love with my Irish stew,' Lizzie chuckled.

'I wouldn't blame him,' I said, remembering that dish – hot, meaty, redolent of good flavours; but not for July.

I asked Pamela whether the Commander had offered her no help at all.

'Very little,' she answered. 'Just that formal note, asking me to let him know whether everything was in order, then a list of local addresses for which I asked him; not another word.'

'Nothing from his granddaughter?'

31

'Not a sign of life.'

'I thought she would be running up on every pretext.'

'It is not that she wouldn't love to, I'm certain of that. It's the Curmudgeon.'

I felt a little flat. I had counted on Stella's companionship for Pamela. And, I began to realise, I had looked forward to taking her for drives and picnics, or to swim – in short, to giving the child a good time.

'Yes,' Pamela said, with her disconcerting habit of reading my thoughts aloud. 'A spot of knight-errantry is wanted there.'

'Rot!' I replied.

Lizzie came round with her vast brown teapot, filled up my cup, and put in cream and sugar, two large lumps.

'Idiot!' Pamela responded, automatically, and passed me the gingerbread.

Lizzie said: 'Language, language!' in admonishing tones.

I felt my solar plexus beginning to quiver. How old was I? Seventeen?

Pamela was not amused. She was thinking her thoughts. Pamela can look grim, her brows very dark and level, her eyes very grey, the line of her jaw firm, and her shoulders square.

'I am not going to stand it,' she said.

'You are not proposing to fight the Commander?' I asked. 'I wouldn't, my girl! That's a formidable old man.'

'I am going to make friends with Stella.'

Her tone was one of unshakable resolution.

'Lizzie,' she added, 'is learning to make Devonshire cream.'

This was not one of Pamela's irrelevancies; it was part of a planned campaign. My laughter exploded; I choked on a piece of cake; with expert violence Lizzie pounded my back; Pamela's laughter and Lizzie's rang out together, fiddle and big bassoon. Recovered, I dashed out to the car for the bag which contained my bathing suit and a vast new bath-robe. I was upstairs and into them in two minutes, but remembered the rocks and cursed because I had forgotten to buy sandals. In the sitting-room Pamela had put a record on the gramophone – an old thing full of reckless gaiety – 'Sous les Toits de Paris.'

'Come and swim,' I shouted.

'There are espadrilles in your cupboard,' she called, running to her room.

They were the right thing for the jagged, zig-zagging track that ran down to the beach from behind the knoll. The sand was not yet uncovered; small waves rippled lazily over a smooth, flat rock which served as our platform. We are both strong swimmers. Pamela made off round the cliff while I headed out into the bay. When I tired of the crawl I turned over and paddled on my back, looking up at the cliff and the sky. Cool, clear, and buoyant, the water bore me up. I was in the place where I wanted to be.

It seemed no time before I heard Pamela hallooing and saw her waving imperiously from the rock; I swam in and followed her up the path; there was work to be done.

Presently, in the stone-floored dairy, the unpacking of books began.

SOON AFTER SUPPER Pamela, although still garrulous, was incoherent and yawning. Like many people who have active imaginations and dream a good deal she is a morning sluggard and likes to breakfast in her room. This suited me very well, because my best notions come to me in my bath and I prefer to breakfast in the company of a writing pad. This morning, it transpired, she and Lizzie had been up at seven, 'to put a face on the house for the master.' I sent them off to bed.

I was sleepy, too, but I sat up to do some budgeting. I had been gripped by a suspicion that we were doing a madly extravagant thing. I could scarcely believe, in spite of all my meticulous calculations, that it was possible for us to live like this, so I pulled out account books and, sitting at the kitchen table, went over the figures once more.

The quiet was absolute – almost frightening, after the rumble of Bloomsbury. One did not hear even the sea. As though feeling the stillness, Whisky rose in his basket, stretched himself, stepped towards me doubtfully, then sprang on my lap and lay purring, heavy and warm. He was a nice cat, with just enough Persian mixed with his ginger blood to give him a lithe body and long, fine fur. He approved of his new home.

So do I, Whisky; but are we ruining ourselves?

Pamela had been clever about renovations and done them economically. These were a charge on me, while she provided movable furnishings, it being more probable that I would some day want to buy her share of the house than that she would want mine. As to housekeeping, she earned her half. Living expenses would be much the same as in London – less, Lizzie swore, when she had a few hens. We saved garage and, this summer, at any rate, would not want to travel. As to entertaining, house-guests could stand against cocktail parties. Yes – incredible as it seemed, the thing could be done; there was no need to worry; we could carry on, and on our usual scale; we could even carpet the stairs. Only, until my work was bringing in more, the drawing-room must remain shabby, the greenhouse and garden must be neglected, and the dining-room locked up.

That would not be for long: I was convinced of it. That germinating excitement which invades a writer out of space and silence was surging through me already. What a massacre the London traffic makes, daily and nightly, of half-born thoughts! Here, ideas would grow and grope their way to daylight, fantasies put out their antennae and suffer no obstacle, no shock. Here was the freedom of peace. The cat was asleep; I heard the clock ticking and the embers settling in the grate, and no other sound.

I put Whisky in his basket without waking him and went round my house, bolting doors. A burglar would have small difficulty in getting in by the nursery or by the greenhouse, which opened into the sitting-room by a warped door, half of glass; but there was nothing in Cliff End to interest burglars. I turned the keys in the locks of the inside doors, put the chain on the front door, and went upstairs to bed, filled with satisfaction,

shut up in infinite content

I woke to the crying of gulls, breathed the air from the sea that was blowing in through my windows, and rose, lord of a new heaven and a new earth.

I ran out in bathing kit, startling a rabbit who was nibbling his dew-bit on the lawn and sending him scuttling back into the heather. The sun was drawing rich fragrance out of gorse and larches and fern. The water was cold. I swam until I was hungry, and even Lizzie was satisfied by the breakfast that I demolished when I came in. I was arranging the papers in my study when Pamela emerged from her room.

She put her head in. 'Well? Feeling less Bloomsburied? You look a bit more human already.'

'I'd rather look inhuman than like the picture on the cover of *The Jolly-Holiday Magazine*. That's what you're turning into! Do you want things from the village? I'm going for walk.'

'Men are so unselfish! *I* am going to hang curtains. And Biddlecombe, please note, does not consider itself a village: it is a market town.'

She made me a list and added, in charity, that everything could wait to be sent except half a dozen eggs which were wanted for lunch. I was to get those, and the butter and cream, from Mrs Jessup at the farm.

Jessup's farm, I learned, not only supplied us with milk, butter, cream, eggs, and Charlie, but gave Cliff End a right of way. Where the lane forked one might turn left, walk over the dips and hillocks of Jessup's pasture, pass the village school, and go down a steep, winding by-road to the quay. I said that I would go by the lane, the high-road, and The Golden Hind, and return through the farm. This involved delivering to Mrs Robbins of the inn a guide-book which Pamela had promised to lend her; it naturally involved, also, a chat.

Mrs Robbins heaved a sigh of relief when she saw me and invited me to take a glass of cider with her; it appeared that she had felt anxious about Pamela, 'up there alone with nobody but the woman, out of sight and call. A fearful courageous lady she must be; I hope she met with no trouble?' she said.

'Why, what trouble should she meet with?' I asked, amused. 'It is the most peaceful spot I have ever been in.'

'I'm glad indeed that it be peaceful,' she said resentfully. 'Such a gay, kind young lady, too.'

I wondered whether the danger was supposed to be from ghosts or gypsies but thought it more discreet not to enquire, so thanked her for my cider and hurried on.

The post office yielded the envelopes, spices, and vinegar from Pamela's list. Chicory I failed to find. At the tobacconist's was a tray of picture postcards – local views, badly photographed and reproduced. One of them showed a roof and chimneys which I thought must be those of Cliff End; it would be useful for sending 'change of address' to friends.

'That's Cliff End, isn't it?' I asked the rheumatic old fellow who kept the shop.

'That be it; a fine house, too,' he replied, laboriously wrapping up my cigarettes. 'I'm thankful to hear there be folk in it again.'

'Have you a dozen of these?'

'Likely I have.'

He opened drawers, pulled down boxes, and at length collected ten, talking meanwhile.

'Maybe you are the new owner? Well, well! I hope you and the lady will bring it back to itself. They last lot weren't no good. Went away owing eight pounds very near in the village. Wrong 'uns, they were. And making excuses to get out of their bargain by starting ugly stories about the place.'

'So that's what started the stories? Hard on Commander Brooke,' I said.

'That's what I do say. There's others says different. But that's what I do say.'

He sounded combative. The smack of a paper on the counter behind me made me look round.

'Don't 'eed 'ee, mister,' said the irate old man who stood there, in ancient leggings and earth-stained corduroys, wrath in his rock-brown face. 'Don't 'eed 'ee: 'ee ain't got no right to talk that way, and so I be telling 'ee this longful time. You should take shame, Will Hardy, to be talking slanderous of they that's not here to speak for theyselves.'

'Be it slander,' retorted Hardy, 'to say as they left Biddlecombe owing money to every trade in the place?'

'They owed but a little,' the Parkinsons' champion retorted.

The two had squared up to each other: it was as well the counter was between them.

'And could you blame them, mister,' he appealed to me, 'if they was stone broke after paying twelve months' rent for house as warn't fit for Christians to bide in?'

'You believed their stories,' sneered Hardy, 'because they paid you well to believe them and to scatter them around.'

''Tis a lie.' A grimy hand was banged on the counter. 'For gardening and for fencing they did pay me and paid me proper, and good victuals with it at midday, and e'er a penny of their money outside the rightful ever crossed my hand.'

'Ah, they got sick of the place! The gentry didn't fancy them and they got lonesome, perched up there like puffins, and made up their excuses to quit. That's all there was in it,' declared Hardy, maddeningly assured and calm.

The old gardener was dancing with temper.

'And if they did mean to quit would they have planned out the garden like a paradise? A show place her had in mind to make it, with blossom shrubs. Cruel fond of the place her was. And the Commander – didn't 'ee give 'em back half what they paid? Doesn't that show and prove that 'ee were in the wrong?'

'It proves 'ee's an honest man, and they were rogues that took it from him.'

'"Not fit for Christians to bide in!" That's what the cook says to me. Be you listening, mister? Swooned away the cook did, with seeing a white face on the stairs; and no wonder after Mrs Meredith dying in it, so pitiful.'

'Do you want *Amatoor Gardening*, or do you not?' Hardy demanded, with the grin still on his face.

'I do want it – not that an amatoor paper be useful to me,' the gardener thought it necessary to explain to me, 'but my new summer lady, she do read it in secret like, and she come out and talk wise to me out of it, but her baint a garden person at all. The start of her life I did give her last week – "that's what *Amatoor Gardening* says, ma'am," I says, "but I do say different," says I. "Oh," says she, her face going red, and back with her into the house. Give it 'ere to me, and there's tuppence and good-day to 'ee. Don't 'eed 'ee, mister.' And the old fellow stumped out of the shop.

'What chance has the Commander with that sort, I ask you?' Hardy demanded of me.

'Such stories could do a house no good,' I responded ruefully enough, but my point of view did not interest the man.

'The poor Commander,' he went on. 'Things are changed with him indeed. He and his daughter, they used to live there in pride; everything of the best. I did have to import his tobacco from London; now he takes it ordinary.'

At the thought of that downfall the man looked ready to weep.

'Well,' I said, 'you are probably right about the Parkinsons and their stories; we'll hope so, at any rate.'

I left my order for newspapers and strolled down to the quay.

The Parkinsons' cook and her fainting fit had impressed me no more than Mrs Robbins' solicitude, and pleased me no more either. Some day we should want to let Cliff End for the summer and go to Ireland or abroad; such legends as these would pull down the rent. On the other hand, they had, no doubt, pulled down the price; perhaps we ought to be thankful to the gossip-mongers after all – as long as Lizzie did not take fright or Pamela start seeing faces … It was odd that she had not mentioned these stories. And what was this about Mrs Meredith's death? Gosh, if the poor old Commander believed any of it, one could understand his discomfort about selling the place!

Some tourists were chattering in and out of a café. In the small, cobbled marketplace an artist had set up his easel and was making a conventional sketch of the crooked houses, the jetty, and the boats.

This was a busy little place, full of strong, briny smells and cheerful noise. Some very old houses crowded together at the lower end. The marketplace was separated with chains and stanchions from the wharf and jetty, where small boats of all sorts were drawn up. Some fishermen were spreading their nets to dry in the mid-day heat, and women came out of the houses and settled to mending them. There was a babble of jocular talk in strong, deep voices. I caught curious glances which were quickly followed by nods of greeting as I passed. I wondered whether Max Hilliard would feel that he could paint in this place. It would be grand to get Max down. Well, one could loiter hours away on the quayside, but it was too hot for hurrying and I had a steep road to go.

A stiff climb it certainly was on the cobbles; I was glad to come out on the moorland where there was a breeze and to accept an invitation to 'step inside to the cool and take a sup of buttermilk' when I arrived at the farm.

Mrs Jessup, small and alert, with wrinkles enough for a centenarian but the agility of a young woman, studied me with keen brown eyes as she moved about between her living-room and dairy, putting up the things for which I had asked. It was an event in the life of the farm, the opening of Cliff End – the beginning of a new era – and the old woman wanted to talk.

"Tis a real comfort to have neighbours again,' she said warmly, 'and such a kind, considerate lady as Miss Fitzgerald. Pays me every Saturday, regular, and mentioned the extra pint that I forgot. Not like they Parkinsons that did let their great dogs chase the sheep and paid ne'er a penny for three that were scared over the cliff. Unchristian it may be, but I blessed whatever it was chased they out of Cliff End. I do pray, though, that you and Miss Fitzgerald will have peace.'

'Thank you, I'm sure we will.'

'And so you should. For why would anyone wish to frighten a kind lady like your sister? Certainly not the gentle soul that's gone.'

'The Commander's daughter?'

'Ay; his only child. She wouldn't hurt her worst enemy, would Mary Meredith. Threw her life away, striving to save that wildcat, Carmel – that's what most believe.'

This was the first I had heard about Carmel. It was really extraordinary that neither Pamela nor Lizzie had mentioned this local legend. Well – I had evidently come to a fertile source of information; Mrs Jessup wanted nothing so much as to pour the story into my ears.

'Who was Carmel?' I asked.

'Who was she? God only knows. An artist's model folks did say. They brought her back with them from foreign parts. Supposed to be a sort of lady's maid to Mrs Meredith, she was, but a queer sort of a maid, if you ask me; wild as a gypsy in her ways. She'd dress up in her shawls and ribbons and dance on the lawn, then she'd break out in passions and weep and give out curses in her foreign lingo and threaten she'd throw herself over the cliff.'

'Is that what happened?'

Mrs Jessup gave me a doubtful glance, eager to say more, yet undecided how much to tell. She went to her dairy and came back with butter on a plate. Standing at the table and shaping up her butter with wooden pats, she answered at last.

'No living soul knows what happened, Mr Fitzgerald, or ever will know. Unless,' she added, her eyes on her work and her voice lowered, 'the nurse knew more than she'd say.'

I had to play up to my cues if I wanted the story.

'What did the nurse say?'

'She said she saw them there at the edge of the cliff. Carmel was running and Mrs Meredith after her. It was dark night and a gale from the south-west. It was as if the wind took Carmel and flung her into the tree: she could see her, in her black dress, clinging to it, Miss Holloway said. Mrs Meredith couldn't stop herself on the slope; 'tis steep there; she flung herself sideways, making a grasp at the tree, but fell back and went down. That's what the nurse said, but by the way she said it, I thought she could have told more.'

'Was Mrs Meredith killed?'

'You didn't know that?' The brown eyes were startled; she shook her head. 'Broke her back, poor lady; not a scar on her lovely face, but a bruise, they did say, on the side of her head.'

'What a terrible tragedy!'

'It broke her father's heart.'

'And the girl she was trying to save – Carmel? She was all right?'

'Ay, but not for long: dead in a week she was; died in her bed up at Cliff End. Ran off, that night, in the storm, no one knew where. My own uncle Jacob it was that found her, two days later, sick and raving, up in Hartley's barn. Old Mrs Hartley was afraid to take her in, so they put her in a farm cart and brought her home. She died in Miss Holloway's arms.'

'And Meredith – what happened to him?'

'Him?' The way Mrs Jessup slapped up her butter was more eloquent than words. 'That man had no heart to break! Finished his picture and took himself off abroad. We saw nor heard no more of him for maybe three years, when the news came he'd been drownded somewhere at sea. There were no tears spilt in Biddlecombe for him.'

She packed the things firmly into a basket and then, having kept me all this time waiting for them, said that Charlie was coming to us after his dinner and would bring them along.

'I'll take six of the eggs, please; they are needed for lunch,' I said.

'Well, I suppose it's fifteen years or more since that tragedy happened, but stories like that linger a long time in a lonely place.'

'Ay, they linger,' she said. There was something depressing and ominous in her tone. She extracted the eggs and put them in a paper bag.

'Well,' she concluded with a sigh, 'Mrs Flynn says there's not a stir in the place. She's a kindly body. 'Tis nice for me and Charlie having her in and out. Goodbye, sir, and I hope all will be well.'

She stood watching me from her door. I could feel her goodwill and her foreboding following me as I walked over the rutted field, perplexed and amused.

Here was a fine mesh of gossip weaving between Cliff End, the village, and the farm. I wondered how much of it Commander Brooke took seriously. How much had Stella heard? And why on earth had Pamela – the communicative, dramatising Pamela – kept all this to herself? Lizzie could not possibly have failed to collect and relay every word of it long ago.

I struck across the heath where a beaten track meandered in the direction of the house. This was a grand place to walk in, with the sea crashing against its crags below on the right, the gable of Cliff End ahead, and springy heather and ling underfoot. I came to neither hedge nor fence and wondered where the Jessups' land ended and ours began. Pamela had surveyed it with the map; I must take her tramping the boundaries with me.

The track led me through a gap in our rhododendrons and into the drive, just opposite the yard door. Pamela called to me from the nursery, took the eggs, and delivered them to Lizzie and joined me on the lawn.

'It's fun shopping in the village, isn't it?' she said. 'Did you get everything?'

'I did, and a fine parcel of gossip into the bargain.'

She nodded. 'I thought you would.'

'The whole place is bubbling with it,' I told her: 'attempted suicide, suspected murder, haunting, and the dear knows what! We seem to be at the centre of a legend. It explains the Commander's manner. It explains a lot. In the name of goodness, why did you send me out in naked ignorance among the natives to learn it from them?'

She took my arm, and our steps led us to the twisted tree. It was a larch, long dead, bent inland, its roots clinging precariously to the cliff's edge, half-exposed where turf had fallen away.

'This is where she fell,' Pamela said.

'And was caught on that ledge, I suppose?'

'So Charlie says; and lay there, dying … '

'Queer kid you are, never mentioning it!'

'Roddy, it is such a dreadful story – really tragic, not just romantically so. At first I couldn't get it out of my head; it seems, somehow, so close.'

'But, look here, you told me Stella left the place when she was a baby; it must have happened about fifteen years ago. That's not exactly close!'

'I know. It was silly of me. I've got over it now. I didn't want to spoil your first day by blurting it out, and I told Lizzie she mustn't.'

'Good heavens, you don't suppose I'm going to mourn for a woman I never knew? What's Hecuba to me?'

She sighed and laughed. 'Oh, Roddy, you good old buffer; I'm glad you've come!'

'I do believe you've been lonely!'

'I wasn't, really – at least, I don't think so.'

'Those "disturbances," by the way,' I told her, 'were apparently invented by "they Parkinsons" as an excuse to get out of their contract; they went off without paying their debts.'

'That's an agreeable theory; I must tell Lizzie that.'

'How does she react to all this?'

'Enjoys being at the centre of it and would love to have a story to tell; but she couldn't stand a real haunting; Catholics abominate that sort of thing.'

We strolled up to the nursery bay. The broken hasp still hung down and I made a mental note to mend it. Leaning over the half-door, I saw Whisky asleep on the camp bed which, with garden chairs, was the only furniture in the room.

'Whisky loves this room,' Pamela observed.

'Cats have a flair for comfort that is positively psychic. Do you remember Minnehaha and her winter quarters in mother's fur coat?'

'Yes.' Pamela smiled, but her face looked a bit pinched; she was brooding over the Meredith story still.

'It is hateful,' she said, 'to think of the child – losing such a mother; left to grow up with a heart-broken old man. I wonder whether she knows what happiness is?'

So that accounted for Pamela's obsession! Her own girlhood had been so spoilt and shadowed by an old man's bitter moods, she had suffered so much nervous and emotional strain that she rebelled against the thought of Stella suffering in the same way.

'Well,' I suggested, 'perhaps something can be done about that.'

She replied, drily, 'There appear to be obstacles.'

I grinned, remembering gymkhanas in County Wicklow.

'You always did win the obstacle race.'

'"Nursery" sounds silly,' she said. 'We'll have to call this the "yellow room".'

'We can try!'

I was ready to bet that 'nursery' it would remain.

Lizzie came along the corridor carrying a steaming dish. I sniffed and recognised a smell out of pampered holidays long ago. 'Cheese souffle!' I exclaimed.

'It is,' Lizzie called back, delighted, 'and let you come and eat it before it collapses on me!'

Lunch was in the sitting-room; the curtains were up. Lizzie beamed as we seated ourselves at the sun-flooded table. She uncovered the dish with a flourish. 'And now,' she said, 'Mr and Miss Fitzgerald are at home.'

Chapter IV

STELLA

TO A WRITER, every occupation that is not his own brain-grating task seems a delightful idleness; I took a holiday, made the greenhouse my workshop, and laboured like a navvy with saw, plane, and hammer, glass-cutter, brushes, and paints, stopping only to eat, sleep, and bathe. Pamela's sewing-machine hummed in the nursery. In alcoves and corners, shelves and cupboards went up. We had never enjoyed ourselves more. On the tenth day after my arrival, suddenly, Cliff End was a home. The transition stage ended when the last stair-rod went down. In order to enjoy the full effect of the prospect we walked out of the house and in again at the front door. No entry could be more enticing. The carpet was blue, and spikes of delphinium glowed sapphire, mauve, and azure against the ivory paint of the landing and hall. Sunshine, streaming through the fanlight, twinkled on the face of the grandfather clock, on the copper bowls and hereditary warming-pan.

'How *could* this house be all those years empty?' Pamela asked of the air.

'Jessups,' I replied. 'They and their kind,' I added, 'will make it impossible to sell or let the place if we ever want to give it up.'

She touched wood. 'Roddy, don't speak of such a thing!'

'Lost your heart?' I asked.

'Hopelessly; it would shriek like a mandrake if you tried to uproot it now.'

The evening turned cool enough to justify our first sitting-room fire. It was a fire of logs from our own timber and they filled the room with a fine country smell. With the books in their places, our ancient curtains of pale gold velvet drawn, and the lamps lit, we settled to an evening of leisurely work. As usual, Pamela's sewing-table proved to be crammed with cuttings from newspapers and periodicals to be pasted up for her files. This was a hobby which I encouraged as useful in the sister of a journalist. I had de la Mare's stories to review. All we lacked was a cat, but we had discovered that nothing would induce Whisky to leave the kitchen at night; even when Lizzie went 'Jessuping' – Pamela's word for her frequent visits to the farm – her familiar spirit remained in her citadel.

After half an hour or so, when I paused to re-light my pipe, Pamela said absently, 'The weekend after next, don't you think?'

'For what?'

'I told you! The house-warming.'

'Did you tell me? All right. But who's going to be the party?'

Pamela smiled. She had been thinking all this out.

'Wendy, for one.'

'Wendy Flower! Where is she?'

'Playing at Bristol.'

'And Carey?'

'Of course!'

'The Argosy Company, I suppose?'

'Yes; I had a card. Wendy says they're collecting pubs and want to try a weekend at The Golden Hind; they are free on Monday nights, and would we invite them to a meal. It would be rather fun having them here.'

'Would it? Perhaps … '

The idea was intriguing – those two at Cliff End! I had never quite learnt to think of them as ordinary mortals; they were Pierrot and Pierrette, as they were when I saw them first. That was in a revival of *Prunella* at the Matinée Club. Those two exceedingly young people had startled me. They had poetry in their work, and a kind of wildness, and played to one another in a way that made the piece one lyric. I said as much in my notice and it brought them luck – an engagement together in Hassan. They wrote me a joint letter all rapture and gratitude, and a sporadic sort of friendship sprang up. They came a good deal to the flat. Pamela imagined that they did not have enough to eat and sometimes invited them to supper. I thought them quite light-weight people, in spite of their talent, but both surprised me – Wendy, by reacting with great sweetness when I gave her a severe notice, and Peter, by repaying money that I had lent him at a time when it must have taken some doing. And now he had given up dancing for stage-design: a precarious adventure.

'And who else?' I enquired. Her answer startled me, as she had meant it to do.

'Max and Judith,' she said.

'Lord, how you do fly at things!'

'You'd like it, wouldn't you?'

'You bet I would! But where are they? We can't ask them to come hundreds of miles.'

'Still at Chipping, I think; and Max is always ready to do things; they'd come.'

'I believe they would, too! But aren't you rushing it? The studio isn't fixed.'

'There's only the papering to do, and Charlie can help. If we don't finish up in a rush it will wait for months.'

'Well, it's your funeral!'

'Good! You write to Max. Ask them to come on Saturday week and stay a few days.'

'Well, that ought to warm the house right enough! Bright child! – What about the local gentry? Are you inviting any of them?'

'Dr Scott,' she replied. 'I think he's rather a newcomer here. He keeps asking me to play tennis at the club but I've wangled out of it; I just *can't* dress up and go out to tennis clubs and get let in for callers yet. He was kind when Lizzie scalded her hand, and so careful not to seem curious about the house that I promised to invite him some time.'

'Very good … And?'

'And Stella, of course.'

Stella, of course. So the house-warming was to be the first engagement in Pamela's campaign! Funny Stella! How those cheeks would flush and dark eyes light up when the invitation arrived! And then what would happen? 'I fear I cannot spare you that evening'?

'I'm afraid there's no "of course" about Stella's accepting,' I said.

'I know; I shall have to write very carefully, but I think I see how it can be done.'

'I wouldn't put it past you!'

I wrote the letter to Max and went out to post it. The letterbox was near Jessup's but there was no finding the short cut in the dark, so I went round by the drive and the farm road, a good twenty minutes' walk. A fine rain was falling and the air was soft; the sea made a low drowsy sound.

I hoped Max would come. He would like this place. It would be grand to show him the house and walk, and talk, and swim. I was anxious to know, too, how this marriage was turning out. His first marriage had taken a lot out of Max. His work had lost a good deal of the attack and audacity which had been so exciting in it. How he had ever come to marry that chit, Mitzi, was an insoluble problem to his friends. It was just before the break that I met him first, at Lorette's. She and Mitzi belonged to the same set. They behaved like two scratch-cats that night; Mitzi ignored Max pointedly, and Lorette was sarcastic in public to me; Johnny guffawed; I could have throttled the bounder. I don't know what impulse it was that made Max show extraordinary friendliness to an obscure and much younger man. We saw a good deal of each other after that. A man who talked little, as a rule, and rarely offered advice, he said a few things to me about his problems which threw a flood-light on my own. I pulled up just in time. When I told him of my decision to leave London he had said with strong feeling that he was very glad, and did not say why. It would be good to see Max.

When I returned, Pamela had gone to bed. I sat up late, working, and wrote the warmest appreciation of a book that I had sent in since my 'prentice days, and perhaps my best. The hour suited the book. The rain ceased; the last smouldering log crumbled and died into white ash. The curious, living stillness, with a tremor of the invisible vibrating in it, that de la Mare creates in his stories, possessed the place; the sound from the sea was no more than the breathing of nature in her sleep; my lighted room floated alone in space. I shivered, then laughed: I had made myself nervous, reading those queer tales. I went to bed.

TWO DAYS LATER, in the middle of the morning, a telegram came from Max: 'Both delighted.' The message was characteristic in its promptness, brevity, and warmth. Suddenly we felt rather excited. Pamela and I are gregarious creatures, and I suppose a lurking fear of feeling isolated had bothered her as it had me. It was splendid to be able to collect friends like this. I telephoned the theatre in Bristol while she wrote notes to Stella and Dr Scott.

Mr Carey was rehearsing, a charming girl's voice told me. Would Mrs Carey do?

This was startling.

'Hold on a minute, would you?' I called Pamela, covered the mouthpiece, and said: 'Did you know Peter was married?'

'He can't be! He hasn't a cent!'

'He is, so! Do we assume it is Wendy, or what?'

'It *can* only be Wendy. Ask.'

It seemed the only way.

'Hullo, are you there? I say, who is Mrs Carey? Who was she, I mean, please? Oh, of course! Yes, do please ask her to come to the phone.'

Wendy's light voice was full of laughter.

'Yes, darling, we've done it! We were dying to for months. Didn't you know? But you see, there was a simply ghastly dilemma and we couldn't see a way out … Goodness, no! Peter and I don't care a hang about cash. No, but our names, don't you see? Our atrocious, disastrous names! And they were both beginning to be known a wee little bit, so he wouldn't change his and I wouldn't change mine; but to go through life as Peter and Wendy just wouldn't be bearable, would it? So in the end I promised on my honour never to call him Peter; so we were married; and we'd simply adore to come. And we've been dying to stop at The Golden Hind.'

I relayed all this to Pamela to the best of my ability. She was pleased with the news, as was I. Those two made a gay and a decorative combination; if only they could secure engagements regularly all should go well, but they had no resources except their own talents and rather exotic looks.

'Good luck to them,' Pamela said. 'They really are Siamese souls, you know – almost too twin. Come and vet my letter!'

Very good, I considered. She had struck a nice balance between the prerogatives of a grandparent and the emancipation proper to eighteen. 'Some rather young friends' were coming from Bristol and we were inviting Dr Scott. Would Miss Meredith come? We should be so happy if Commander Brooke would entrust her to us for the evening and she should be escorted home in a car at whatever hour was decreed, though we hoped it would not be before twelve. Our enjoyment of the tranquillity of Cliff End was expressed and we sent the Commander our kind regards.

The letter, approved, was addressed and stamped and I put it in my pocket to post it after tea.

Work on the studio had begun. Charlie had fixed up a trestle-table and was pasting paper with vast flourishes of his brush, his snub, scrubbed face pink with importance. The paper was a good buff. With the reddish carpet and my favourite old curtains, patterned with tropical birds on a buff ground, the, new twin beds and woven covers, the room should warm up.

'It can be made a nice room to go to bed in, anyhow,' Pamela remarked when we returned to the job.

'It is too large for a plain paper,' I objected.

Pamela agreed, but said that amateurs were apt to go wrong with patterns and stripes. Our expert looked round. He grinned and saved his dignity neatly.

'You didn't know you were going to find the like of Charlie Jessup in this place, did you, miss?'

'What we would have done without you, Charlie, I can't imagine,' she replied, mounting the steps and carefully laying her pasted strip on the wall.

Honour was not satisfied. Charlie came forward and neatly peeled it off. 'They edges is overlapping,' he said reproachfully. 'Now, now, this baint proper at all.'

Heavens, how slow the fellow was! How rapidly I had covered my share of the wall! Were we doomed to spend the whole gorgeous day in this lugubrious room? I wanted a swim. Pamela showed no intention of quitting, however, so I worked doggedly on.

'You can hardly believe, in here,' I grumbled, 'that there's bright July weather outside. Some day I'll have that east window knocked out again.'

'The hill-side's so close,' Pamela replied, 'that it wouldn't do much good. Nothing will make this room attractive in daytime.'

'This be the room,' Charlie announced, 'that they Parkinsons locked up.'

I saw Pamela pause in her work, startled, but only for an instant. She spoke lightly:

'Yes, and left the closets full of junk! Simply shut them and papered over them, lazy sluts!'

Charlie said nothing.

'Or perhaps,' she teased him, 'it was you who did that, when you got the place ready for them?'

'Locked the room up and never set foot in it after,' was his reply.

More gossip! Between the recurrence of this rubbish, my boredom with the job, and irritation at Charlie's slow pace, I was ready to snap on the least provocation.

'I suppose they had their own reasons for not wanting to use it,' I said.

Charlie was not crushed. He replied darkly, 'There be no doubt whatsomever but they had.'

I was not going to encourage any more of this. I said: 'I think you were using rather too much paste.'

He was offended and maintained a palpable silence until we told him to go down to Lizzie for his dinner, when he departed with a hop, a skip, and a grin.

'Queer cuss,' I remarked, working at the table. 'How old would you say he is? He could be anything from twenty to fifty with that leprechaun face.'

Pamela did not answer. She was standing by the window, quite idle, watching me; there was a look of trouble on her face. After a moment she asked, rather seriously, 'Are you sleeping well here?'

'Like a dormouse,' I answered. 'Aren't you?'

She did not reply to that directly; she said: 'I haven't wanted to worry you. I thought, perhaps, it wouldn't come back, but it does. Roddy, there *is* something – at night.'

I turned and faced her; her brows were drawn and her eyes rested distressfully on mine.

'What is there? What do you mean?' My voice sounded rough.

'Haven't you heard anything, Roddy?'

'Of course not!'

'Not last night, or the night before last, when you came up so late? The night we had a fire?'

'I heard the sea – nothing else. There wasn't the ghost of a sound in the house.'

'There *was* a sound, Roddy; I heard it just before I heard you come up,'

'What kind of a sound?'

'A sigh – no, a sharp, shaky breath, a sort of gasping sob, as if someone had had a shock.'

'That's the wind, Pamela; it would make queer noises between the hill and the house.'

'There was no wind those nights.'

'That's true … Have you heard it before?'

52

'Yes.'

'Always at night?'

'Yes. But the last two nights it has been much more – sort of *actual*. Roddy, it is a heart-breaking sound.'

Pamela's voice shook. I stood there and said nothing, stiff with dismay. Whether it was fact or fantasy, this was going to smash up Pamela's peace of mind. Those damned superstitious gossip-mongers! What could I say or do? Pamela was such a rational person: one could not simply dismiss her idea.

'You realise, don't you,' I said slowly, 'that suggestion could account for all this? After all those stories. And they have been very much on your mind.'

'Yes: that's what I said to myself at first, but it isn't that.'

'Where do you think the sounds come from?'

'I can't make out.'

'From this room, do you suppose?'

'Perhaps.'

'Why didn't you come and call me?'

'I made up my mind to, Roddy; I would have; last night I tried; I tried to make myself get out of bed, but I – couldn't make myself move.'

'You were dreaming,' I declared. 'It's a common dream sensation, that paralysed fright. I am quite sure you would never have felt it, awake.'

She shook her head. 'It wasn't a dream. I wish you had heard it too.'

'In the name of all that's rational, Pamela, why? So that you could think there *is* something wrong?'

'No, Roddy; so that I would know that I wasn't alone with it.'

I paused; she was in dead earnest about this; then I asked, 'Does it go on for long?'

'Only a few minutes.'

'It's something in the house, Pamela – birds in the chimney, Or mice, or a bat.'

'Perhaps it is.'

Relieved by her acquiescence, I spoke lightly:

'We'll get Whisky along! Shut him up here. He'll chase your *revenants*.'

'Whisky won't stay in this room.'

'Wise cat; I wish I needn't.'

Pamela seized on this. 'Charlie's fairly good at the job, Roddy – shall we leave him to finish it and take tea down to the beach?'

Now it was my turn to set an example.

'You say he doesn't finish things; better see it through,' I replied. But I was not sorry, a few minutes later, to hear Lizzie's bell ringing for lunch.

When Pamela throws off a fit of depression she does it thoroughly, becoming buoyant and voluble all at once. Over lunch, she began making plans for the party with so much zest that I felt reassured: whatever it was that made strange sounds night must be harmless, I told myself, since its effect on her could so quickly be shaken off.

'The Liberty curtains have come,' she said; 'they're lovely. The nursery will be the ladies' cloak-room; I'll fix up a dressing-table with petticoats. Lend it your long mirror, won't you? I'll have to lend Judith my beautiful triple one: she uses a good deal of make-up and uses it exquisitely. She looks about thirty, doesn't she, Roddy? And she's at least six years older than Max.'

'That shouldn't matter,' I replied. 'Max is rather old for his age and he has had too much of the company of volatile youth. I thought Judith quite beautiful when I saw her, and that was at the Queen's Hall where most women look frumps. I wonder how she and Wendy will hit it off?'

It was amusing to realise what varied types we were inviting to meet one another, and to speculate how they would mix. Max would like Stella, I thought. It would be disappointing if Stella did not come.

Charlie returned from his dinner in high good-humour. Pamela and I meekly accepted our proper places as his assistants and the work went better, but, as each half-hour dragged on, I more angrily regretted not having given in to Pamela's proposal and gone down to the beach. I grudged every minute spent in this room and I felt a headache coming on. When, just as four o'clock struck, Lizzie appeared, Pamela and I shouted, as one man, 'Tea!'

'Whisht!' Lizzie signed to us. She was out of breath and spoke in a thrilled whisper: 'Miss Meredith has called.'

'Devonshire cream!' Pamela ordered, and whipped off her overall.

When I joined them ten minutes later I found Pamela on the window-seat and Stella on the high-backed tapestry chair; between them was a table laden with splits, jams, and cream, while the tea-trolley stood near. Stella gave me her hand, saying, 'How do you do?' with no intonation of interest but with a joyous smile. She wore a soft brown silk thing on her head, half jockey cap and half bonnet, with a curve to the brim which made the effect much more *chic* than she knew. Her tussore frock was a school-girl's, but she had pinned on a rose of just the colour that pleasure had brought into her cheeks. She spread a modest smear of cream on her scone.

'Try a mountain of it, like mine,' Pamela urged. 'It was for this,' she said gravely, 'that we came to Devon. Perhaps you don't like it, though? One never knows with natives.'

Stella laughed and piled on a spoonful.

'I love it. Grandfather always sent me some for my birthday when I was at school.'

'Did you enjoy your school in Brussels?' I asked her.

'It is a very good school, but I suppose no school is precisely enjoyable,' she replied.

She searched her mind for some appropriate topic which she had, doubtless, prepared. Her brow cleared.

'Do you think you will like living in the country?' she asked.

'We are quite sure we shall love it,' Pamela answered warmly. 'And we hope you don't feel too sorry not to be the owner any more of this lovely house?'

When Pamela thought that ice needed breaking she usually just walked on it. This time it worked. The girl was brimming with eagerness to talk about Cliff End.

'I thought I would be if anyone ever bought it; but now I'm glad.'

There was a compliment to us in her shy smile.

'But it is very curious for me,' she went on meditatively, 'because I didn't think of it really as a house, as a live house, I mean, that people would eat in; I thought it was only a memory; a memory, and stone walls.'

'Is this actually your first visit since you lived in it?' I asked. She nodded.

'Grandfather … ' She hesitated. 'You see – it was very natural – he didn't understand my wanting to come.'

'I see.'

Stella had finished her scone and, omitting to wait or ask permission, began walking around the room. She gazed at the view from the window and then stepped into the greenhouse. She turned, suddenly, came back and sat down.

'I do beg your pardon!' she said.

'Never mind; but won't you have some more tea? Tell me,' Pamela asked, pouring a second cup, 'do any memories come back?'

'Nothing fresh,' Stella answered, concentrating, her hands in her lap. 'There is just one memory I have always had, because it comes again and again in my dreams. You see, I was not quite three when – when I went to live with my grandfather.'

'I would like to hear that memory if it isn't a depressing one,' I said.

'Only parts of it are depressing. I am in a room alone in the dark. There is a black thing outside, clutching at me – perhaps it was that tree. I am frightened in the dark and I cry. I cry for a long time and then somebody comes in. She leans over me and whispers some pretty words – I never know what they are, and then she lights a light. It is lovely and I am happy, but someone else comes and puts it out.'

'And you cry again?' Pamela asked.

'Then I am too frightened to cry.'

'Please remember next time you dream that,' Pamela said firmly, 'that I am coming to light it again.'

Stella gazed at her very seriously. 'Thank you,' she said.

We talked about dreams and I found myself propounding, with more explicitness than I had achieved before, the theory that dreams are an abstraction of a repressed conflict, disguised in symbols borrowed from the happenings of the day. Stella followed with an intense absorption, less like the average girl's attentiveness, which is often mere personal flattery, than like a small boy's when he is being shown how the clock-work works. When I spoke of the common flying dream she exclaimed, 'Why, I am always dreaming that!'

'Do you have an admiring audience in the dream, as I have?' Pamela asked.

'No,' Stella chuckled, 'and I am glad I don't, because I go just a little way and then come down plop.'

'I used to flop down once,' Pamela laughed. 'Some day you'll fly.'

We told Stella about the party and said how much we hoped that she would come.

'The whole house will be ready then, except the dining-room, and I'll show you all over it,' I promised.

'Oh,' she sighed longingly, 'if only I possibly could!'

'I'll desert the party if necessary and drive you home in good time.'

'Please, what time will it be?'

'We shall begin at eight,' Pamela said.

She shook her head. 'I couldn't possibly manage it.'

'That's very disappointing. Come some afternoon, early, won't you,' Pamela asked her, 'and we'll take a picnic tea to one of the places you told me about. We haven't even been to Clovelly yet.' She turned to me: 'Did you ever hear such alluring names, Roddy: "Deadman's Rock" and "Rapparee Cave" and "Gallantry Bower"?'

'You know this coast well, I expect?' I said to Stella.

'I used to explore in my holidays,' she answered eagerly, 'when I could save up enough for the buses and the funny little trains. But grandfather says I am too old now to run about the country like that. It seems strange to have less freedom because you are growing up.'

She checked herself. She regretted having appeared to criticise her grandfather, I thought. She looked from Pamela to me, hesitating. There was something a little difficult which she felt she ought to say.

'Please, Miss Fitzgerald – Mr Fitzgerald, please will you not feel hurt with my grandfather because he doesn't pay you a call?' She looked anxious.

'We don't expect it,' Pamela said quickly. 'You see, we know about the terrible accident. The thought of this house must be very painful to him.'

As though not satisfied, Stella went on: 'My mother … she was his only child, you see, and she was so beautiful and good. You saw the portrait, didn't you, so you know?'

'An angelic face,' I responded.

'And she died before he could come.'

She paused and then asked impulsively, as if pent thoughts were escaping against her will, 'Am I undutiful to want to come here? Is it unnatural and morbid of me?'

What a clouded face! She was obviously quoting the old man. Pamela deliberated.

'On the contrary,' she said, 'I would think it morbid of you not to come. It is different for old people. Young people have to make themselves get over things.'

'I see,' Stella responded eagerly. Then she said, 'Thank you,' and stood up. 'And now I am afraid I really must go.'

I told her that I had letters to post and would come with her as far as the farm.

'That would be nice,' she said.

I took a scone for the seagulls; I could never tire of their planing and swooping.

Stella said goodbye to Pamela on the doorstep and turned to give her a little bow as we rounded the corner of the house. They had taught her deportment at that school, and, I imagined, she had habitually spoken French. The young English-woman of today did not use these gestures and phrases.

As we walked to the edge of the cliff, Stella's eyes rested sorrowfully on the dead tree.

'I will cut that down some day,' I said.

Yet on second thoughts, one would miss it in the foreground, that, grotesque shape which, in a wind, would become, in turn, every character in *Macbeth*.

A gull caught a morsel in mid-air; another and another dived. Stella tossed scraps to them, laughing at their greed.

'I saw sea-gulls once from the boat at sunrise. They rose up against the light and they looked as black as crows, then they swept down on the other side and they changed to pure gold. It was magical.'

'Who painted that portrait?' I asked her, as we walked over the heather.

'My father. He was Llewellyn Meredith. Have you seen any of his pictures? Do you know his work?'

She would have loved me to say 'yes.'

'No,' I had to tell her; 'but that is because our parents' generation is always the one we are most shamefully ignorant about. Do you study painting?'

'At school I did, and I hope to again some day.'

We had come to the farm road. She paused, embarrassed, and then looked up at me.

'Please, if you don't mind: I am sorry: I would like you to come with me but I would rather not.'

'I have letters to post.'

'May I take them and post them for you?'

'I wanted the walk.'

'As you wish.'

This was awful! I had been teasing her, treating her as a child; now I had been reminded that I was forcing my company on a lady who did not desire it. I stood still and spoke, half-seriously: 'You would like me to come and you would rather I did not. I don't understand!'

'It is of no importance.'

I had been a clumsy oaf! Of course! The way down would pass Mrs Jessup's door; this visit was clandestine – not to be reported abroad.

'I beg your pardon, Miss Meredith,' I said sincerely; 'I will turn back now.'

She flushed, distressed at having seemed stiff and unfriendly and wondering what she could say or do, and I was wretched at having spoilt her pleasure in the visit like this. We looked at one another, both understanding the situation, realising one another's difficulty and equally at a loss. Suddenly I had a notion, and smiled.

'If you will be so kind, put these in the letterbox for me. The top one is important, as you can see.'

I handed her the letters and, involuntarily, she glanced at them.

Frowning in a puzzled way, she looked up, then her brow cleared and her laugh rippled out; in a moment her face was demure again.

'Certainly, Mr Fitzgerald.'

'Then we shall see you before long?'

A shadow descended. She glanced doubtfully at the letter. Was she afraid that it would cause a direct prohibition, perhaps? She did not express her thought. She said gently, 'It would be a pleasure. Goodbye.'

She hurried along the road, not glancing back, and was soon lost to sight round a heathery hummock. It made me smile as I walked home to think what a child of the place she was, with her gaiety that flashed and vanished, her candour and her reserve. There was something, too, or I was greatly mistaken, like rock. She was drawn by some deep fascination to the house and yet not one hint had come from her about the local gossip, not a sign of inquisitiveness.

We should see Stella again: her grandfather might try to keep her from visiting us, but he would not succeed. She and Pamela had taken to one another, and Pamela was tenacious in friendship. The old man would have to give way.

Chapter V

THE STUDIO

I HAD MADE myself an impressive timetable of work. Jobs in the house and garden were henceforth to be counted as recreation and confined to the hours between lunch and tea. The late afternoon and evening were reserved for articles and reviews, while every morning from ten until one o'clock was stringently allocated to the book.

Very promising, and yet *The History of the British Censorship* did not progress. What ailed me? My study was comfortable, sunny, and quiet; files were in their places, books in their shelves; my last lot of plays from the Drama League Library lay spread on the window-seat and all was set for good steady work; yet my chapter-heading, 'The Ibsen Hysteria,' stared from a mangled page. I had once rushed at this task in the spirit of a crusader, mockery for my sword, but now anything and everything interested me more than those idiocies of long ago. I prowled, idled, and groaned.

Pamela's prescription was simple: give the summer mornings to Cliff End, then, in September, go full blast at the book. Specious, but I knew too well that the longer the respite the more painful would be the labour of a fresh start. I began to fear that I might never be able to take up this book again. I was afraid that I might be undergoing one of those periods of transition on which Clement Forster used to dilate. Your entire outlook on life changes, he declared; you grow a new mind, and you have as little use for your former style and ideas as for your out-grown clothes. You've got to discover a new writing personality in yourself. I had actually watched something of the sort taking place in him, and it did him good: he got rid of a lot of sentimentality; developed realism, humour, and poise. All very fine in journalism, but it would be awkward if that sort of thing were to happen in the middle of a book.

There was no accounting for it; some indefinable ferment was going on. Struggling against it resulted in a crammed waste-paper basket and a temper in flitters. I decided on a compromise: I would abandon the book for a couple of weeks and see what happened. Pamela approved.

'There's still plenty of occupation for you,' she said.

There was.

One long-ago Christmas my godmother gave me a toy theatre from Spain. It had sets of scenery and cardboard figures, the complete stuff of some half-dozen gorgeous plays. I had not supposed that life would ever again bring me such a sense of riches and mastership. But that thrill was almost equalled in the days that followed, while I surveyed our boundaries and planned the use of the outhouses. I would have a photographic darkroom at last, and a carpenter's shop. Why not a pottery – set up a potter's wheel and a furnace and experiment with the local clay? Who could I get to help me to build a boat?

There were electric fittings to be seen to, also, in the house. Just as soon as I could afford it, I was going to have a new circuit put in. I wanted more points for desk-lamps, two-way switches for the hall and landing, wall-lights for the stairs. Meanwhile, I did what I could with adaptors and yards of flex, while Pamela made pink shades for the party.

'It is a scientific fact that people talk better in rose-coloured light,' she declared.

Stella was coming. In a stately little letter she informed Pamela that her grandfather appreciated our kindness in inviting her and that she gave herself the pleasure to accept. Dr Scott had been good enough to promise to bring her and drive her home.

'It was Dr Scott who did it,' a postscript said.

Max wired 'Regret postpone Sunday weather,' which meant that he was at work on one of his cloud studies and must take conditions while they served. In my opinion, there was no one painting in these islands whose skies could compare with his, at his best. The change meant that our entertaining would start with dinner for our four old friends on Sunday. The housewarming proper was to begin on Monday at nine.

On Saturday, while Pamela and Lizzie did things with prawns and duck and mushrooms, I completed my lighting scheme. Now, the drawing-room had the lovely little chandelier and floor-lamps; every bed had its reading-lamp and each dressing-table a flattering strip-light. After dark we switched everything on and surveyed the effect. Pamela had been to Honeysett's nursery garden and filled the house with flowers – roses and stocks in the rooms and gladioli on the landing and in the hall. The whole place glowed softly. I envied no man his house. Even the studio would look inviting when there was a fire in the red-brick hearth.

'We must have one tonight and all day tomorrow, to air the room,' Pamela decreed, but it was easier said than done. She and Lizzie and I spent twenty minutes wielding bellows, holding up newspapers, throwing on oil, and even, scandalously, sugar, trying to persuade the fire to light. When at last the coals caught, Lizzie rose, disgruntled, and stood looking round the room.

''Tis pretty enough,' she admitted, 'but what I don't understand is how you have the conscience to ask anybody to sleep in it. I'd sooner lie on the rocks.'

'Why, Lizzie,' Pamela exclaimed, startled, but I broke in:

'She has been listening to Charlie, who knows nothing whatever except that the Parkinsons shut it up. They were fools and they fooled him. For goodness' sake, Lizzie, don't let Charlie fool you.'

'I'd not mind that scatter-brain,' Lizzie went on doggedly, 'but 'tis what Mrs Jessup says.'

'That Mrs Meredith's ghost walks, I suppose?'

'Yes, Mr Roderick. God rest her soul!'

'To be sure they say that, Lizzie! Why wouldn't they? A lonely house, a beautiful lady, and a violent death! Would anyone in his senses lose the chance of making a story out of that?' Pamela supported me.

'We haven't seen anything, have we, Lizzie? I don't think we need worry,' she said.

'Well, 'twill be on your souls, not mine, if harm comes – if that fire goes out again I'll put furniture-polish on it, so I will,' Lizzie concluded, and took herself off.

Pamela said slowly after a moment, 'I could give them my room – the bed's big enough – and sleep here myself.'

'Giving in to Lizzie and Charlie?' I said drily. 'I hope you're not going to start that.'

'No, of course not!'

'This is a perfectly good room.'

'Yes, it's really not bad.'

I asked casually: 'Been sleeping all right?'

'Perfectly, thanks.'

'No more midnight sighing?'

'Not a sound.'

'Splendid!'

'Yes, it is.'

I myself, although I was not going to tell Pamela this, had once imagined just such moaning sounds as she had described. It was on the night after Stella's visit. I had a queer uneasy dream about her. I had taken her to the Zoo; there was a great cage full of birds; Stella was somehow inside the cage, crying and frightened, unable to get out. I was trying vainly to get to her when I woke, and it seemed as if the crying went on. It ceased in a moment, however; it had evidently been an hallucination caused by the dream. Pamela's experience had been something of the same kind, no doubt. I was glad she was free of it at last.

I DROVE to Bideford station to meet Max and Judith on Sunday afternoon.

Bronzed, lithe, and untidy, Max had the air of a man filled with health and content. I looked at Judith, praising her inwardly. Serene and composed, with her smooth dark head, controlled movement, and quiet voice, she was a woman out of a different world from Mitzi's, yet not Max's world, either, one would have thought.

These tranquil women defeat me a little; when a pool is so still, how is one to know whether it is shallow or deep? When no emotion is permitted to trouble the surface, can there be any sharing of life's fiercer experiences? I wondered whether some of Max's rock-like quality was not wasted on a person so admirably poised.

'Max fell in love with a bank of cumulus,' she explained apologetically. 'I had no influence. When these things happen I cease to exist for him. Fortunately, the affairs are necessarily brief.'

'Has he immortalised his beloved?' I asked.

She replied in a low voice, 'He is doing a lovely thing.'

Max smiled: 'Judith has her prejudices.'

Good, I thought: she cares for his work.

'You have no rivals today, at least,' I remarked.

The late afternoon was as calm as Judith's eyes.

Max had been silent as we drove, gazing about him.

'Could I get out and walk?' he asked. 'Is it far? Should I get to the house in time?'

I dropped him at Biddlecombe crossroads, describing the short-cut to Cliff End, and stopped to pick up the Careys at the inn.

'He's a new man,' I said to Judith when we were alone; 'all appeased and relaxed. He looks younger than when I knew him first.'

Her lips parted in a peaceful smile.

'It is charming of you to say that, Roderick – We'll say "Roderick" and "Judith," shall we? – I have wanted to ask you: isn't the secret of making Max happy simple? Isn't it necessary only to be happy oneself?'

I reflected: it was probably true. Mitzi had never been without some tragic obsession about her health or her relationships or her prospects on the stage; if one thing failed her by turning out well, another would serve her appetite for melodrama by going wrong. Was that what had worn Max down?

I said, 'I feel sure you are right.'

The Careys appeared, like visitants from some far star, Wendy's head aflame above a skimpy sea-green garment, Peter in white silk shirt and scarlet cummerbund. They were rapt, and his ecstasy filled Peter with melancholy. He looked more than ever like a beautiful dying Pierrot.

'We've hiked twenty miles,' he told me in sad, musical tones as we drove on, and Wendy said with her Ariel lilt, 'It's the scrag-end of our honeymoon.'

Judith smiled and Peter raised arched enquiring eyebrows.

'It's the poetry of your aspect and the realism of your phrasing,' I explained.

'Carey, my chuck,' sighed Wendy, 'I have begged you not to say "hike."'

'We have roved, we have rambled, we have wandered, O my Soul's Illumination!' he responded to that.

'There's your sister!' Judith exclaimed, as we drew up at the garage. Pamela ran eagerly to welcome her guests. She and Judith, who had not met more than three or four times, greeted one another with warm pleasure, and Pamela gave Wendy the kiss due to a bride. When I had put the car away and followed them into the house I found Peter floating about, studying every corner from every angle, while Wendy just breathed, 'Oh, Roddy, it's swell, it's swell!'

'Marvellous potentialities,' Peter concluded. 'I'd do it in silver and geranium, with purples and just a streak of jade.'

'I like it just as it is,' Judith said, 'refusing to bow down to Mammon, yet full of harmony and ease.'

Pamela was pleased.

'The perfect tribute, Judith. It makes me wish I had given you my own room.'

IT WAS WELL that the ducklings were fat; our friends were hungry. It was a picturesque group that we had assembled, I thought. Pamela, who had refurbished her wine-coloured taffeta, cut on the Nell Gwyn model, looked a stately chatelaine, and Max, with his soft brown beard, was patriarchical and comfortable in a brown velvet coat. Judith wore filmy black with a raised pattern in gold and long filigree ear-rings hung from her delicate ears; svelte and sophisticated, she made an entertaining contrast to Wendy, whom she regarded with amused, kind eyes.

Max was a little preoccupied. When I asked him eagerly whether he thought he could paint in these regions, he frowned: 'I have got to think about it.'

Judith sighed: 'My poor Max! Don't say it is picturesque!'

'*Touché!*' he confessed, smiling. 'That's the trouble: huddled houses, all colours, stained with age and storm; church spire bosomed in foliage; quay-side, fisher-folk, small boats, and what have you?'

Judith nodded: 'It's just too bad.'

'Now what can we do about that?' I wondered, and Pamela said that we could take him to see the Ghouls – her private name for curious rock formations on the southward coast.

'If there's time,' he agreed, 'but I have to get back on Tuesday afternoon.'

'Having left your clouds in mid-air?' I conjectured.

'Just so!'

Max cast off his cares then and engaged Peter in theatre talk.

The youngsters were in rampageous spirits. The god of chance, under whose aegis they had married, had rewarded them: Wendy had just been cast for her first professional lead. It was Salome. Carey had to design the dresses and sets. He called us all into session on the question of the colours which Wendy ought to wear to make her look utterly decadent and set off what he called her orange hair and the pale green tints of her skin. Max bent serious thought to the question, and between us, after dinner, a scheme of seven veils was devised which ought, we thought, to conjure Oscar Wilde out of his grave.

'We'll sketch it, tomorrow,' Max suggested. 'Carey's got hold of something original there.'

We cleared the floor then and called upon Wendy to rehearse the dance for us, but she was too fey to produce anything but a hilarious caricature with a toby jug for the prophet's head. The fun might have gone on until morning, but Max broke it up, saying that Pamela must have rest. Judith, in her cool, soft voice, said that she, too, felt a little tired. She smiled very sweetly at Wendy, whose ebullient youth had charmed her. Judith looked thirty and was twelve years or more older; she had beauty, dignity, sweetness, but no longer that vibrant joy.

The night was warm and scented; the bay lay entranced under a high half-moon. Max and I walked with the Careys to where the road forked, then strolled home across the heather and along the edge of the cliff, talking, as we often did, about the backward currents that were setting in all over Europe and their effect on art and literature.

'They subordinate the whole to the part,' he said bitterly. 'It is no longer life they are celebrating, nor nature, but some crude, fanatical party creed. I am afraid that doing things for their own sake will soon be a luxury for children and, perhaps,' he smiled, 'for freaks like you and me.'

Max was generous; he was an artist of considerable achievement – I, a journalist barely beginning to be known. He read my thought.

'Don't be surprised,' he said, 'if this place changes you and your work. It may push you towards something creative. It's exciting. Glad, aren't you, that you faced the break?'

'Thoroughly glad.'

'Those two,' he said gravely, 'are making a mess, and I am afraid neither of them will ever make anything else.'

'Mayhew's a cur.'

'He is.'

Neither of us added an opinion of Lorette, but I dare say the same term occurred to us both.

Standing on the edge of the cliff, I chucked a stone over. I heard it fall with a plop – I knew that for me, forever, Lorette had sunk out of sight.

Max was standing beside the dead tree. 'That's interesting!' he said.

'Interesting in more ways than one,' I replied, and told him something about the story of the place. He had half a memory of Meredith's name.

'It will come back to me; there was some rather discreditable picture, I believe.'

'He seems to have been an ugly character, according to local legend, and the odd thing is that the girl he married is regarded as almost a saint.'

We were walking up to the house.

'Marriages can be surprising.' Max paused. He took his pipe from his mouth and knocked it out against the porch, then glanced at me with his deep smile.

'You worried a bit about me at one time, Roderick. I want to tell you: Judith is perfect. Life can be grand.'

'She looks happy,' I said.

'She *is* happy.'

Alone in the sitting-room, over whiskies and soda, we talked for another half-hour. Suddenly Max remembered Meredith's name. 'Lyn Meredith! That's he: Llewellyn, and called Lyn. By Jove, that man painted a picture – He made himself famous with it for a season; notorious rather; but not through its merits. It was one of those "story pictures" that become a popular rage. I wish I could remember the subject, but it's clean gone. I have the volumes of Royal Academy photographs somewhere; I'll look it up. The odd thing is, I remember his tricks of style: crude brush-work; impatient, even violent treatment of background, but a devilish clever knack with the face.'

'His daughter idealises him, I'm afraid.'

'Ah,' Max replied sympathetically. 'Orphans who have lost their parents in infancy tend to do that. It's natural, isn't it? She need probably never hear that he wasn't first-rate. What's the girl like?'

'You'll meet her tomorrow.'

It was time for bed. We took off our shoes and carried them, there was so deep a quiet in the house, and tip-toed upstairs. I liked my carpet's muffling pile. Before reaching the top we paused simultaneously, halted by a sound – a gasping, long-drawn sob. It came from the studio. In an instant Max had pulled the door open. He exclaimed, 'Judith,' in amazed distress and went in, shutting the door.

Yes; it was Judith's voice, weeping, babbling, hysterical. What on earth had happened? This was appalling. What could one do? Judith must have hurt herself or be ill. I hurried to Pamela's door, but before I reached it she opened it and stood there, her white dressing-gown clutched around her, fear on her face.

'Now do you hear it, Roddy?' she whispered, shuddering.

'Hear it! Good lord, of course I do! It's Judith!'

Astounded, she listened. The sobbing was rhythmic and desolate now.

'It *is* Judith! Oh, Roddy, thank heaven it isn't … But Judith – she was all right; she was in my room! I must go to her.'

'Don't! Max is there.'

Max came round the well of the stairs.

'For God's sake, Pamela, take Judith to your room,' he implored. He was pale and stupefied.

'There's nothing wrong,' he told me when Pamela had gone; 'nothing whatever. It's pure hysterics. I've never seen her cry before.'

The poor fellow paced up and down the corridor. He knew hysterics and he was in hell.

'I only make her worse,' he said despairingly, and drew back with me into my room as they passed – Judith weeping helplessly and Pamela angrily telling her to be quiet, that she wouldn't have Lizzie disturbed with such rot. She drew her into her own room and shut the door. Presently there was silence, and after a little Pamela came to us.

'Go in to her, Max, and beat her!' she said. Max went to her room.

I gave Pamela a cigarette. She was shaking.

'You sounded pretty ruthless,' I said.

'If I had taken her seriously, she would have gone off her head.'

'Has she seen a ghost?'

'No.'

'Heard something?'

'No, nothing at all ... Steady a minute: I've got to think out whether I can tell you; it's very much a woman's trouble.'

She sat smoking, and gradually her colour came back.

'You'll think it's something serious unless I do,' she reflected aloud.

'I certainly shall.'

'When she sat down to cream her face in front of the mirror she thought she looked old. It gave her a hideous shock.'

'But, good heavens, that's not enough to throw a woman like Judith into such a frantic state!'

'She says it was ghastly: "stark old age – death's-head old age." Roddy, it *would* be a shock.'

'But it's grotesque! Judith couldn't look like that.'

'I know; even distraught, like this, she has a lovely, lovely face. I made her look in my hand-glass; that did reassure her a little.'

'The thing's incredible; there must be more in it than this; I can't understand.'

'Nor can I, Roddy. But you've seen people suffering from shock, haven't you? That's her condition. She can't go back to that room tonight. I'll give them mine and go in there.'

'You'll get into my bed, Pamela. Push the sofa into my study and I'll sleep there.'

Max came out to us; his face was dull with misery. He had heard what I said.

'No, Roderick; she'll have to come back and look in that mirror again; she has got to be convinced that it was her own imagination and, perhaps, the light.'

'It's not the light,' I replied.

'And the mirror is a good one,' Pamela added. 'Max,' she went on, 'Judith is really ill. Don't put any strain on her tonight. Please stay in my room. I'll have Roddy's.'

'I'm not ill: it isn't that.' Judith was standing in the doorway, tears streaming down her face. She was blanched to the lips. She leaned her head against the door-jamb and wept.

'You'll never be able to forget this. Oh, poor Max! Poor Max!'

She and Max looked like broken creatures. It was true that none of us would be able to forget. Desperation made me say the first thing that came into my head, and I said it in a tone of conviction that astonished myself.

'Judith: it's not you. There is something wrong with that room. Pamela and I were sick with depression while we were working in it. The last tenants kept it shut up. We've both heard things. We ought never to have put you in there.'

Max stared at me, hoping that what I had said was true. Judith's tears ceased to flow; she turned pleadingly to Max.

'Oh, it is, it is something outside me! I never felt like that, and I *couldn't* look like that, could I, Max?'

'The sighing,' Pamela said tremulously, 'it must have been from that room. You never told me that you had heard it too! Oh, Roddy, it *is* haunted! The house is full of some misery that can't die! What shall we do?'

Now Pamela was breaking down; this was too much.

'We'll shut up that room and forget it,' I said. 'We were crazy to put them in it; Lizzie was right. Judith has had a horrible shock, and instead of shouting for us she tried to fight through it alone. The proper thing to do when you see a ghost,' I said to Judith, 'is to yell. You plucky women are the dickens to deal with!'

Between light, diminishing sobs, Judith smiled.

'Oh, you are nice, Roddy! Max, isn't he nice?'

Pamela had run downstairs for brandy; Judith took a minute sip. We hauled the sofa into the study and said good night. For the present, there was no more to say. Pamela left a note for Lizzie, telling her not to call us but to start breakfast when she rang, as we had been up very late. As soon as she was settled in my room and all the doors were shut, I went into the studio. I intended to spend the night there and see for myself.

I saw nothing. And there was nothing wrong with the light. The mirror gave out a pleasantly softened reflection; my face, with its long upper lip and untidy eyebrows, looked less rough-hewn than usual.

I got into bed and put the light out and the whole wretched episode sank to the back of my mind; yet I could not sleep.

A phrase Max had used bothered me. I was not to be surprised if my work underwent a change. I might find it becoming more creative. What the hell had Max meant by that? What was wrong with my work as it was? Fiddling journalism; nothing sustained about it; conventional, facile, all on the sound old traditional lines? No doubt that was how he saw it: did he suppose I had not seen that too? Why else had I undertaken the book? And what was the book, anyway, but a compilation, a re-hash of old newspaper articles better forgotten – no more 'creative' than Pamela's scrap-books. And even that I hadn't the capacity to finish. It would never be finished. I saw that now. It would not be finished because I had nothing to say. What I had mistaken for talent had been no more than the afflatus which makes every second swelled-headed adolescent suppose he has a vocation to write. It was a folly which had made me turn my back on the chance of a solid profession, got me as far as a sub-editor's desk on a London weekly, and led me to walk out from that into the blue. I had imagined that I had something to say, and behold, without the drive of a play to report on, a book to review, or a controversy to join in, I was empty: I dredged into my own mind and found nothing there. My youthful energy was already exhausted. I was finished: finished at thirty. And Max had seen that.

I heard the clock in the hall chime three, four, and five. It was nine when I woke – too late for a swim.

Pamela came down to breakfast somewhere about ten, refreshed; then Max and Judith arrived, declaring that they had slept beautifully and looking only a shade subdued.

'It is Roddy,' Pamela said, 'who looks as if he had seen a ghost.'

'Where did you sleep?' Max asked quickly.

I began to realise what it was that had happened.

'In the studio,' I told them, 'and I had an experience very like Judith's.'

Neither Max nor Judith concealed their relief: any explanation was preferable to the thought that Judith had behaved like a hysterical egoist. As I elaborated the picture of myself which had appeared to me in the small hours her soft laughter rang out; a delighted guffaw from Max started me on a vein of comedy, and gales of laughter swept away the cobwebs left by the night.

'But it is not funny if your beautiful house is haunted,' Judith said, and Pamela nodded: 'It's not.'

'Look here,' I appealed to the three of them, 'we could discuss all this and nothing else the whole day; the subject of hallucination is bottomless. And what would happen to our party? I propose that we cut it out, at least until we've all had one good night's sleep.'

They agreed.

'And I suggest,' said Pamela, 'that we do a little camouflage in the bedrooms, or Lizzie will smell a rat.'

'Ha, ha,' I quoted, 'I smell a rat, I see it floating in the air, but believe me, I will nip it in the bud.'

We were barely in time. Pamela waylaid Lizzie in the hall and lured her back to the kitchen while the rest of us, feeling like guilty children, made readjustments upstairs. Our dispositions were just finished when Pamela ran up to inspect. She declared us first-class conspirators, then beckoned me downstairs, whispering: 'Come and see what I've found in the nursery.'

It was a parcel labelled, 'For Roderick and Pamela for the party,' in Peter's ornate hand. A box of fireworks! Grand! I have a pyromaniac's passion for fireworks. When had Peter discovered that? This would be splendid at midnight on the edge of the cliff.

We arranged them on trays which we secreted in the greenhouse, then, leaving Pamela to her sandwich-making, I took Max and Judith down to the rocks.

It was a hot, lazy August day, and the sea held a stronger blue than the sky, with fans of violet here and there. The beach was covered. Max chose a ledge and took headers into deep water again and again, revelling in the vigour he found in himself. Judith was quiet and tired and content to be so. She swam a little, then lay on the smooth rock watching Max. There was the shadow of a smile on her face all the time which deepened when their eyes met. She was a different Judith from yesterday, more securely happy, released from some kind of strain. It must take courage, I thought, for a woman to marry a man younger than herself: the other way round, a difference is all to the good.

'Tired?' Max called to her, standing over her on a rock. She smiled up at him.

'Beautifully tired.'

'Beautifully!'

'I suppose I ought to go and give Pamela a hand,' I murmured. Nobody heard me; I was as much alone as that flying gull who had the sky to himself.

I clambered back alone up the rocky path.

Chapter VI

HOUSE-WARMING

THE PARTY sailed away on a high tide; I had no work to do except to try to get acquainted with Dr Scott. He came rather late, and Stella, in her dark hooded cloak, hurried away with Pamela, leaving me to thaw him out. He had come from examining a patient and was quite obviously revolving his diagnosis; he felt out of place in this irresponsible atmosphere and did not in the least mind showing it. A lanky, loose-jointed man, clean-shaven and tanned by the summer, he looked about my own age and was anxious to appear a good deal more. When Wendy floated past in her rainbow chiffon he stared as if he could not believe his eyes. I introduced Peter: they gazed at one another like creatures of alien species and drew apart with stupid smiles. I was thankful when Max pulled alongside. In a few minutes he had Scott talking with absorption on the subject of dogs. Judith and Wendy insisted on putting on a foxtrot which made Peter look faint with pain. Marriage was wearing him out, he complained, as he helped me to clear the floor. It seemed that he and his wife, in face of the deadly danger of merging into one soul, which would drift through eternity as Peter-and-Wendy, felt it important that each should keep studiously doing things which it knew the other disliked. 'One is forced to cultivate differences, and it is so fatiguing,' he moaned.

'And, you see,' Wendy cried above the music, 'the one who begins to forget first will be lost!'

Judith, fascinated by this philosophy of marriage, asked questions which produced a babel of exposition, but it died down; all the chatter in the room quieted, leaving the music crooning to its end. Pamela had come in with Stella, and Stella was beautiful.

The talk and laughter bubbled up again instantly, but that pause had been actual; it had been a tribute to this dark-eyed girl who moved shyly in her straight, rather stiff, ivory frock by Pamela's side. She came to me at once.

'How did Dr Scott do it?' I asked.

'I imagine,' she replied seriously, 'that he made my grandfather think it would be unfair not to let me come, and grandfather is never unfair.'

She waited for introductions and, as Pamela and I made them, gazed with candid wonder into each face, as though longing to know everything about everyone all at once. While the rest danced a foxtrot I stood with her in the door of the greenhouse, telling her the stories of my friends. And, in the telling, what vital, gifted, dramatic individuals they became! And so they were; so were Pamela and I, myself: we were free, clever, friendly, and fortunate people, living changeful, progressive lives; it took this imaginative child to see it, looking out from between her prison bars.

'May I have this dance, Miss Meredith?'

She shook her head.

'I am so very sorry, I can only waltz. Oh, how beautiful they are! Oh, look!'

She was right: Judith's dancing was perfection, and Peter had torn himself from the ballet only out of his passion for design.

Scott steered Pamela along conscientiously, his head bent in earnest talk the while. Stella chuckled as Wendy went by with Max,

Max moving, as so many large men do, with buoyant ease, both too much lost in the music to talk.

'She is like the girl in the fairy-tale who kissed the good brown bear and then he became a prince.'

'You have got Max in one,' I said, delighted. 'Now tell me about the others. Carey and Judith, who are they?'

She pondered for a minute, then said, 'Endymion, I think, but not Diana. Your sister is Diana, isn't she?'

'Right!'

'Or, perhaps … Yes, if this were a fancy-dress party … ' She paused.

'Go on!' I demanded.

'Are you sure I'm not being rude?'

'You are paying charming compliments.'

'Well, then, Jeanne d'Arc.'

'The only saint Pamela tolerates! Well done!'

'I love Jeanne! … And Mrs Hilliard, a queen, of course: Marie Antoinette.'

'Perfect! Our next party must be a fancy-dress dance, that's certain! And who will you be?'

I had a fleeting vision of Stella floating down the stairs in the snowy billows of the Pavlova swan dress, but waited to see what she would say. I would have staked a lot on this opening with most girls, but Stella evaded it.

'I shouldn't think anybody could choose for themselves, because you can't, can you, look at yourself in that imagining way? No, I really prefer a party like this, where people are themselves.'

'A waltz now: may I have the pleasure?'

'I promised Dr Scott.'

'But I believe you're a débutante?'

She laughed: 'I believe I am.'

'Your coming-out party! And a débutante should dance first with her host.'

'So this dance will be a *faux pas!*' she laughed, delighted with her little pun as she danced off, on air, to be brought to earth very soon by the sober paces of Scott.

'Roderick,' Judith asked as we waltzed together, 'why does that child look so joyous? It isn't just a "party" look. She is really starry-eyed.'

'Would you call her beautiful, Judith?'

'But, yes! She startled me.'

'She is in love with this house.'

'It *is* lovable.'

'It has been a dream-house to her for years, and now she is here.'

'Where has she lived?'

'A prim school in Brussels and a neat little villa in Biddlecombe – the fashionable side.'

'Ah, now I understand! – Roderick, don't let them put her back in a cage!'

Pamela put on another foxtrot and danced with Max while Judith went round sedately with the doctor and Peter taught Stella the step. Telling Wendy about the bear and the fairy, I begged her to sit out with me and save me from being compared to a waggon hitched to a star.

She wanted to talk to me, she declared. She wanted me to use my influence with Peter, who, in a sudden access of marital responsibility, was swearing that he would give up the theatre and open a shop.

'It would kill him, darling; don't you know it would kill him?' she grieved.

'He won't do it,' I assured her, 'but he'll always talk about doing it, just to hear you say he mustn't. You keep it up.'

'He does hardly earn any money, but some day somebody will recognise his genius; don't you think so?'

I told her, truthfully, that I thought Peter had more originality than most of the big noises in stage design and, less truthfully, that recognition was bound to come soon.

I never liked thinking about the future of these two – they issued such a reckless challenge to life.

When that dance was over I took control of the gramophone and put on 'Invitation to the Waltz.'

Stella did not talk while she danced. Her movements were light and precise and her enjoyment was evident, but she was a little anxious and rigid. That would change, I thought, and then she would dance beautifully. I recognised the scent she was wearing: it was the mimosa that her grandfather so intensely disliked.

Judith was resting in a corner; she smiled at Stella when our dance ended, and Stella went and sat with her on the couch. There was eager chatter among the others, and Pamela called, delighted: 'Roddy, they're going to do the Pierrot dance.'

'We'd love to; it's our mascot dance, isn't it?' Wendy responded.

'That's so; but it's a bit acrobatic,' Peter remarked. 'We may wreck the room. Have you got the apology?'

We went through my records and found the music. Peter had given it to me long ago as a peace-offering after having been extremely rude about a criticism I had written of Wendy in a modern part.

I put out the floor-lamps, leaving a pool of light in the middle of the room.

It was a lovely performance. Certainly, when these two danced together they had only one soul.

'I am exhausted with enjoyment,' Judith sighed when they finished. 'Who could have foreseen such a treat?'

'That was perfection,' Max said.

Scott looked dumfounded; he muttered, 'Incredible, incredible!' And Stella, who was sitting beside him, laughed.

'You are wishing you could see their skeletons, aren't you?' she teased him. 'They haven't got any, I believe.'

'Oh dear, that was our secret,' Wendy cried distressfully, sinking down on the fender-stool. Stella looked at her gratefully.

'You have given us a pleasure that we shall remember always,' she said.

Judith smiled at the gracious little phrase, spoken so spontane-ously, and came to me, murmuring, 'What an engaging child she is!'

'She is nearly nineteen; hardly a child,' I heard myself say brusquely, and felt Judith's surprise. How absurd, and how rude!

'Forgive me, Judith!'

'I forgive you, Roderick,' she smiled.

It was time for supper. A bar and buffet had been set up in the hall, and here Lizzie presided in supreme satisfaction with her decanters and carafes, ladles and tea-pots and urns. Mrs Jessup was in the kitchen, and Charlie, his face crimson with heat and excitement, acted as runner between the two. The door was open on to the moonlit night; glasses and plates were carried to the porch. Scott waited assiduously on Pamela; he had become talkative at last; I heard her telling him that she would like very much to have one at Cliff End. What would she like to have here? I wondered. Oh, a dog!

I heard Judith's laughter; Peter was spinning her one of his sad, fantastic yarns, sitting with her on the stairs. Max was in the porch with Stella, talking about painting. She listened, radiant because he knew her father's name. He came along presently, offering to relieve me at the bar.

'I wish Miss Meredith could study,' he said thoughtfully; 'she seems to have a painter's instinct. I would not have expected Meredith's daughter to have such integrity of mind.'

I signed to Stella from the stairs and she joined me.

'I haven't forgotten my promise,' I told her: 'this is our chance. Do you want to see the kitchen first?'

'No, no, they are too busy; it wouldn't be fair. Just – just my mother's room, if nobody minds.'

'I have full consent,' I told her. 'You'd like to see the studio too, wouldn't you? This is it.'

She stood still in the middle of the room.

'Mr Hilliard has seen my father's paintings,' she said happily. 'I wish I knew more about him; grandfather has never talked about him, nor has Miss Holloway. They disliked him, I'm afraid.' Miss Holloway had been her nurse and then her governess, she explained.

'Were you fond of her?' I asked.

Stella looked a little perplexed.

'She is a very fine person and was my mother's devoted friend; I ought to be fond of her. But you could never become exactly attached to a governess, could you? Because it's her business to make you different from what you are.'

'Is it? I find some of your theories a little austere.'

'Theories?' She was puzzled.

'Some young people love their governesses and enjoy their schools.'

'But then life would be just a dream!'

'Whereas it is "real and earnest"? Never mind – Your tenants,' I told her, to give her a cue, 'kept this room shut up.' She nodded.

'I heard about it. Our servant told me. Grandfather was very angry with her.'

'Some of the local people maintain that the Parkinsons made the whole story up.'

'I do hope that is true.' She paused with her head bent, then lifted it and looked at me frankly.

'It made us both very happy to know that you find the house peaceful,' she said. 'We were truly afraid of your being disturbed. I know that my grandfather warned you.'

Nothing would have induced me to tell her that all was not well.

'We appreciated his candour,' I replied.

'I felt sure myself that it would be all right, because Miss Fitzgerald is not afraid of ghosts.'

'How do you know that?'

'She said so, don't you remember, at lunch?'

'And you think they won't come if one isn't afraid?'

She deliberated and answered: 'It's more that I think they might come if one were.'

'I see.'

'Troublesome spirits, I mean. Gentle ones would do no harm.'

'So you worried about us?'

'Just a little.'

'Well, don't worry any more. Come and see the other rooms.' I showed her the linen-press in which Pamela took such delight, my own room, and my study. Stella paused beside the bookcases, smiling.

'What a nice workman-like room,' she said. 'Do you work very hard? Do you write everything over and over again? If I thought that the words I wrote were going to be read by thousands of people I could never stop altering them.'

I tried to analyse for her the training of a writer's technical sense, expounding how judgment at length becomes instinct and the personality develops its essential style. She listened so intently that I felt sure she would not forget one word of what I was saying. I hoped I would remember it myself: it was too good to waste.

I asked whether she would like to borrow a book, and she asked for the stories by Walter de la Mare.

I found the book under a pile of journals, wondering how she had known that I possessed it. One would hardly expect to find *To-morrow* in the Commander's house.

'It was intriguing, what you said about it,' she murmured, glancing at the wood-cuts: 'that "he brings us into the world of the unseen, not by enshrouding our senses in veils of fantasy, but by lifting veils away."'

When had I been so charmingly flattered? Stella had my very syllables, and they sounded musical, spoken with such slow pleasure.

'How, please,' I asked her, 'did you recognise RDF?'

'You mentioned the paper to grandfather and then I guessed.'

I could have enjoyed more of this but I had my duties to our other guests. I took Stella across the landing to Pamela's room.

'This was probably your mother's room.'

She stood with downbent head, as if waiting for some quickening of memory or listening for the echo of a voice, then looked up at me with a little sigh. There was a gentle grace, which was not childish, in the movements of her head.

'What a pity that one forgets!' she said.

'No,' I replied tersely, 'it is one of nature's best dispensations. You should be living in the future, not in the past.'

'But, you see,' she explained, 'those years in this house with my mother were beautiful. I *know* that. "She made a heaven around her," Miss Holloway said. But the future ... '

She broke off. Was she afraid of the future? Had she nobody except the old man?

'The whole house is lovelier than my dreams,' she said as we went downstairs, 'but the little room where we left our cloaks is the one I love best. Miss Fitzgerald thinks it must have been the nursery.'

A crowd had collected in the hall around Wendy, who was telling fortunes, Pamela's green witch-ball between her hands. Max was teasing her, trying to distract and tempt her with every sweet from the table in turn. 'If you don't eat you'll go up like a bubble,' I heard him say warningly, to which she replied: 'Salome should.'

She looked up at me, laughing: 'Come and breathe on it, Roddy.'

I obeyed, and she gazed into the patch of dissolving mist with a tense and solemn expression.

'Oh, there's a brilliant future for you!' she cried. This raised a friendly cheer.

'I see a great building,' she went on, 'and paper is falling on it like snow. Manuscripts! You're pouring them out of a horn; and I see a comet with a flaming tail – that's a star, of course – an actress – she's starring in every one of your plays. The tail is her orange hair … '

A shout of laughter put an end to this prophecy, and Max, standing on the stairs with a glass in his hand, called out that he was going to propose a toast. Judith, with an amused glance at Peter, whispered a warning to Max. He laughed.

'To Wendy Flower! May her shadow never grow more! May her Salome cause the critics to lose their heads.' That was followed by a toast to Peter Carey: 'Success to all his designs, for his life, for his wife, and for the theatre.'

Peter, called to his feet, spoke in wistful, musical tones about the tragic hardships of the theatre-man's lot and the bitter contrast afforded by settled domesticity such as Pamela's and mine. His contrasted pictures of his old age with Wendy, and ours, were extremely funny and made us laugh a great deal, but he did it just a little too well.

When he had sunk down, as one overwhelmed by despair, I proposed a toast to our débutante. Stella's reply was a shy and flowing 'Thank you.' Scott, who had cheered up considerably, called upon her for a speech; Stella shook her head and said something in a low voice to Judith, who nodded and stood up to make a very gracious little speech, wishing good luck to Cliff End.

It was past eleven, and Stella had to leave at twelve, so I asked her which she would prefer to see, the fireworks or charades. Without hesitation, she chose the fireworks, and I hurried Peter to the green-house, where we collected my trays and a lantern.

'Seriously, Roderick,' Peter urged as we prepared our display at the farthest edge of the lawn, 'seriously, you ought to write a play. The company is famished for new stuff, and look how well our last big find went – *Undertow*! It was at the Duke of York's for more than a year. You boosted it no end yourself. Milroy would gobble up some-thing from you, and the Great Man goes by him.'

'Avaunt, Beelzebub!' I replied to all this. 'How many honest critics have been thus seduced? How many led up the garden path "that leads to the eternal bonfire"?'

The night was warm; our audience gathered on the steps of the porch. I could distinguish the silhouette of each against the glow in the open doorway. 'I like house-warmings,' I thought.

Our flowers and fountains and trees of fire soared into the blue night, saluting the moon, and broke, and showered flakes of flame into the sea. The last flung a flaring banner over our heads, which quivered, like the Aurora Borealis, and died away. For a minute the group in the doorway was still; then, with a babble and clapping, it broke up. Pamela called me: Scott and Stella were hurrying towards his car.

'Cinderella's time is up,' Judith said.

Stella said 'Goodbye' to everyone, with a special little smile for Max, and, for me, a shy 'Thank you.' I heard her say to Pamela, as she leaned from the car, 'I have never been so happy in all my life.'

'Don't forget: four o'clock on Monday!' Pamela called.

'Cinderella? No,' Judith reflected: 'the Sleeping Beauty, just waking, I think. I wonder what will happen next?'

A bonfire was blazing on the edge of the creek; Peter had robbed my wood-pile. He and Wendy were acting a wild scene about wreckers, peering over the cliff, pointing, crouching, dashing about from rock to rock, describing the approach of the victim ship with such vivid-ness that one almost saw it, and Wendy's shriek became the death shriek of the doomed crew. Her frenzy as she bashed clambering phantoms on their heads, and her dance of gloating and triumph, made Judith declare that Wendy must have been a wrecker in a previous incarnation.

'I was,' she declared, kneeling on the grass, erect and excited, 'and gods, what a life! Duping the fools, seducing beautiful ships! Flaring your beacon and watching them change course, watching them head for the rocks – so proud, so near home, so puffed up with their brave voyage! And then, the crash, the yells – and the loot!'

'Shut up, you little demon!'

Peter looked scared; the rest applauded. I said, 'I want to see your Salome, after that!'

Before they left, our promise had been given: Pamela and I would go to Bristol for a night and see the play.

They had to be back for rehearsal at three o'clock next day; reluctantly they said goodbye. I offered to drive them back to the inn, but they wanted the walk down the hill-path and through the sleeping village. Max went with them, and Pamela and Judith and I returned to the quiet house.

Lizzie had disappeared from the scene. The chaos was too complete to be tackled at night. Judith went upstairs, while Pamela and I ate blackened banana sandwiches and sipped lemonade. We emptied ash-trays out of the front door, bolted it, and latched the ground-floor windows, leaving the nursery open for Max to come in by.

'Why don't you sleep here, Roddy?' Pamela asked as she switched off the nursery lights. 'This isn't a bad little bed.' I told her I hated sleeping on the ground-floor and that the sofa did very well.

'All right,' she said absently, standing within the room, and added, 'How curious!'

'What's curious?'

'I noticed that she was wearing it, but it was faint, and now it is over-powering, isn't it?'

'What are you talking about?'

'Don't you notice it – Stella's mimosa scent?'

'I do not.'

'But, Roddy, you must!'

'Well, now, of course, you have made me imagine I do.'

86

Pamela looked at me incredulously. 'Well, "only Goodness knowses,"' she quoted, '"the noselessness of Man!"'

As we went upstairs Judith came out of her room.

'My dears,' she said, 'you have the loveliest house, you give the most delightful parties, and you have the most charming friends! I would like to say "thank you," please.' She gave Pamela a quick, warm kiss, smiled at me, and went in.

The sofa was comfortable; I liked lying in the study, among my books; the sea made a drowsy sound. I was sleepy; there was a soft warmth in the night, a flowery sweetness – a small, secret room … I heard Max come in and then fell asleep.

I thought it was a sound that had roused me. Pamela had not called: there was only the door between us; I listened; there was no stir in there. Could it be Judith in trouble again?

I was out on the landing in an instant, listening at their door, but no sound came from that room. There was not a sound from the studio either, or from anywhere: a heavy cloak of silence shrouded the house.

I did not turn on the light; I waited, leaning over the banister, looking down. No moon shone through the fanlight; there was neither sound nor light down there – or so I thought for a moment, but then I became aware that there shone, very faintly through the half-open door of the nursery, a pale, pulsating gleam. It was not moonlight: it moved.

A sense of deep uneasiness held me rigid. I was uneasy because I was eavesdropping there. It was an intrusion; this house was old; long before we were born it had its occupants, living and dying here. We were aliens and trespassers in their hereditary home. Now I knew that they were in possession of the house once more, their timeless-ness closing over our intrusion as water over a stone. Down there, in the nursery, things were as they had been; somebody moved and sighed there; somebody moaned.

I had been listening in a half-trance. I roused myself suddenly, and the shock of astonishment came. I had seen a light and heard a voice – a young voice, moaning. Now light and sound were gone.

They had not been natural: my own pounding pulses told me that. Someone out of the world of the dead was moving about the house.

My hand groped, trembling, for the light switch; I turned it on and ran bare-foot downstairs. Everything was as we had left it: a white cloth, thrown over the laden table, made it like a bier; the nursery was empty, the curtains closed; face-powder strewed the dressing-table; the scent of mimosa lingered, potent still.

I leaned against the wall, waiting for my heart to recover its natural beat, but a cold shivering had taken me and I longed for my own room. I turned the lights out and tried to go upstairs.

I could not do it; I trembled at the knees and shuddered convulsively, sick with the chill that seemed to shrink the flesh on my bones and wrinkle my skin. My breast was hollow and a breath blew over my heart. If I had not clung to the newel-post, fighting, I would have panicked; I would have shouted for Max or pulled the front door open and torn out of the house. I thought something was coming down the stairs.

I saw nothing; nothing came; my eyes lost power to focus and everything looked blurred. At last, step by step, hand over hand on the rail, I dragged myself up the stairs. By the time I was on the landing I was faint with the deathly weakness that comes when one has lost too much blood. I reached my room and huddled under the blankets, clammy with sweat. There was no interval for thought; no sooner had the thudding of my pulses stopped and warmth come back to me than I slept.

I CAN force myself to recall that experience now, but I was scarcely able to believe in it, in the morning, when I woke. I stood at my window, looking out at the radiant morning, telling myself what happened, unable to credit the tale. Today joined up with yesterday, and the night between them was no more than a night of dreams. My thoughts were full of our friends and the pleasures we were going to enjoy here and the work that I was going to do. We had made a good beginning at Cliff End. It had been a good party. A pity Stella could not have stayed till the end; she would have revelled in Wendy's acting. Wendy was a bit of a witch.

I was in my bath when an idea came to me which held me enthralled while the warm water grew cold. There was a play in that reincarnated wrecker of Wendy's – a play which I could write. Not a reincarnation story – Heaven forbid! But a tendency; an inherited strain; a restless, uncanalised craving to watch people heading for the rocks: a male passion in a weak, nervous girl. Not a Lorelei or siren affair, either – for once, sex would not be either the motive or the lure. It would be the game for the game's sake. A psychological crime play; a melodrama, rooted in character; a thriller, true to life … Bristol was waiting for it; London was waiting for it; Peter, for once, had talked sense. This was what Max had meant when he spoke of my doing something 'creative'. All my avid reading of plays, my dramatic criticism, my devotion, since childhood, to the theatre, pointed to this. The book could wait.

I went to the kitchen and demanded a large and immediate breakfast; Lizzie was in a good humour and fried potatoes, bacon, and sausages for me at once.

'That is what I call a party,' she said with satisfaction. 'Did you ever see the like of the mess that's in the sitting-room? I have been up since seven clearing the kitchen. Let you eat here, in decency, while I attack in there. I'll ready it, just, before they come down. You could maybe,' she added persuasively, 'get Miss Pamela's when you're done?'

'Maybe I could, but she'll come down, as there are visitors.'

She would have to come down, I realised, in order to conceal from Lizzie the changes we had made upstairs.

'Maybe she would,' Lizzie persisted, 'but she needs the rest.'

'Very good, ma'am: I'll do it. Go and put a face on the room!' Obediently, when I was finished, I boiled an egg for four minutes, made tea and toast, and carried a tray upstairs, accompanied by Whisky, who expressed his resentment eloquently with his tail. He had the habit of a morning call to cadge the top of Pamela's egg, but he thought the proper person to bring it up was Lizzie and did not approve of its going to my room.

Pamela was splashing in the bathroom; I set the tray on the table by the bed and went in to tidy my sofa. When she returned she called in a tone of dismay, 'Lizzie's been up!'

'It's all right: "Alone I did it"!' I informed her through the door.

'Come in and talk to me.'

She was back in bed, Whisky at her elbow, purring, and the tray on her knee.

'Want to smoke? The egg's perfect: bless you, avic. I had a marvellous sleep – did you?'

'Part of the night.' I sat on the window-seat, lit my pipe, and drew at it, meditating. No, I hadn't the right to keep this to myself. I said, 'I feel it my duty to inform you that I experienced disturbances.'

'Roddy!'

'I did: I heard moaning and I saw a light.'

Pamela turned a little pale but interest lit up her eyes.

'A light! Where?'

'In the nursery.'

She spoke slowly: 'Do you remember what Stella told us about her dream?'

'Yes. I went down. There was nothing.'

'How did you feel?'

'A bit – over-excited.'

She looked at me hard: 'You're keeping something back.'

'There was a sickening chill in the place,' I confessed.

'A chill? Was that all?'

'Absolutely all.'

'I am immensely relieved that you heard … '

'I can understand that.'

'It's rather dreadful to think … '

'Don't think! We'll get used to it: people do. Remember Mrs Comerford's house? It's a glorious morning: forget it! Low tide's about midday, and Max and Judith needn't leave till two; what about an early lunch on the beach?'

REGARDING a feast of remnants – salads, trifles, cakes, and sand-wiches, spread on the sand about us – Max sighed and wished loudly that he was about nine. He had been for a walk and had good news for us: he wanted to come back in the autumn and paint.

'Grand!' Pamela said. 'I do hope,' she added, 'that we shall have a peaceful room for you by then.'

But Max meant to put up at The Golden Hind. 'I am no good as a guest when I am working,' he declared.

'I shall not be satisfied,' Judith said quietly, 'until I have slept in the studio.'

There was a pause. It was sheltered and very hot here in the creek, between the beetling rocks and the sand. The sea glistened; the air quivered with heat. Max, in his white flannels, the vivid green of Judith's wrap, Pamela's sky-blue bathing-suit, and the plates and glasses scattered on the coloured cloth made a dazzling picture. I wanted to say something about what had happened in the small hours, but it all seemed incredible. Rather casually I told them what I had heard and seen – nothing of what I had felt. Judith and Max looked so concerned and distressed that I regretted having said anything. There was a shocked, troubled, silence, and then Max spoke perplexedly:

'I wonder what on earth can be done?'

'Shut up the studio; shut the whole thing out of our minds,' I replied.

Pamela shook her head:

'I can't shut it out.'

'You are getting used to it already; you are learning to sleep through it,' I reminded her.

'But it may come again, any night, Roddy, and it is such an incon-solable sound.'

'Well,' I asked her, 'what do you want to do?'

'I would like to understand what the *cause* is. Who is grieving and weeping, and why? What keeps the spirit lingering on?'

My mood was unsympathetic to all this; my mind was secretly revolving my play, and part of me was angry because Stella was not with us here. I replied thoughtlessly: 'Revenge is the classic motive.'

Max looked doubtful: 'The atmosphere in the studio doesn't suggest revenge.'

Pamela's brows were contracted; she was rubbing the sand from the whorls of a pink shell and murmuring, 'If we could only find out what would give it rest.'

Max asked, 'Have you any idea as to who it is likely to be?' Pamela's eyes met mine, but nobody answered. Probably we all had the same thought and felt the same reluctance to speak the name.

Judith had been silent; she spoke thoughtfully now.

'Do we need to suppose that there is any restless spirit at all? I think it may all belong to the past. Isn't there a theory that a violent emotion can impregnate matter, saturate floors and walls, and then, with a sensitive person in a receptive mood, it is reproduced? Mightn't something of that sort account for my experience and for Roderick's, too?'

It might, we all agreed.

'But how would you deal with these miseries out of the past?' I asked.

Judith smiled.

'Simply by living in the house as you are living in it.'

I said, 'Good!' and Max, 'I agree,' together, but Pamela looked doubtful.

'I am afraid it is not that,' she sighed. Then she laughed and produced one of her misquotations:

> The time has come, the walrus said,
>   To talk of many things,
> Of shoes and sand and bathing-wraps,
>   And trains and leave-takings,
> And why weekends should ever end,
>   And whether Max has wings.

We were all laughing as we packed up and climbed the rock-path, where a fresh breeze caught us and blew our towels about.

Judith was right, I thought. Life was active and rich and free at Cliff End; it would be strange, indeed, if the vigour and content of the living could not banish the lingering sorrows of the dead.

Chapter VII

FATHER ANSON

MY PLAY GALLOPED. In three days the three acts were mapped. My Barbara's dark passions swept the action along, and I, too, was carried away. Even the grim conviction that the house was haunted, which I could resist no longer, failed to distract me from my work.

I heard the sighing again, and I lay and listened; I assured myself that it came out of the past and no more told of immediate and present sorrow than would a gramophone disc. I do not think I believed that argument, but it served. I fell asleep again and, in a sort of half-dream, absorbed the tragic mood into my play. To my relief, Pamela told me she heard nothing on either the Tuesday or the Wednesday night.

I had a fine distraction for her on Thursday. By seven o'clock that evening I had made sure that the plot would hold water, contrived my ending, and determined to go on with the play. I came down and found her laying the table for dinner and told her what I was at. I told her the story, after forbidding her to let her invention loose on it – for in two minutes she would kidnap a story, ride off with it, and make it her own.

She was pleased out of all proportion to the cause.

'I just thought you were at something different,' she exclaimed. 'You looked so alive. That book was becoming a dead weight on you. This is the grandest idea! And think what success with a play might mean!'

I asked her what she would think of a night in Bristol. I had my central character and main lines of conflict fixed but the other characters were still more or less fluid. Since I had Wendy in mind for Barbara, I thought it would be well to see the company at work before planning the rest. There is no doubt about it: the personality of a player can give a dramatist no end of help in creating a character. They were doing *Death Takes a Holiday* this week – a play we both wanted to see.

'I'd love it! Let's go tomorrow,' she said.

'I've got to get two articles off tomorrow. What about Saturday?'

'Tennis with Dr Scott! The third time of asking, but I'll put him off.'

'It's on Monday, isn't it, that Stella is coming to tea?'

'Yes.'

'If we started really early I could see the show twice on Saturday. All right, let's do that – what about Lizzie, by the way? Will she mind sleeping here alone?'

Lizzie looked dubious when we put the proposition to her. She ranged the coffee-cups on the table with unusual precision, pursing her lips.

'You're going to supper at the farm on Sunday, aren't you?' Pamela asked her. 'Perhaps you could go and sleep there on Saturday night.'

'And have them thinking they had scared me with their bogles?'

The struggle in Lizzie's mind was visible. It would be a fine boast at the Jessups' table to say that she had slept in the house alone and it would be tremendous to have something to tell; but she was nervous.

'Well,' she concluded, 'if there were ghosts in it they would have shown up before this. All right, I'll stay! Go off and enjoy yourselves, though it's early days in a new place to start gadding out of it!'

'Business, Lizzie! Serious, sober business,' I protested.

'I wouldn't doubt it,' she replied drily. 'Yours is a cream of a trade.'
I sighed.

'The workers of the world will never recognise writers,' I complained when Lizzie had taken herself off. 'We'll all be put to scrubbing, some day.'

But Pamela looked worried.

'We're cheating her, Roddy. I think she really had better sleep at the farm.'

'I would leave it to herself; you bet she'll be all right,' I replied firmly – so complete was the obliviousness which screened from my waking and working mind the sense of what I, myself, had experienced that night on the stairs.

THE LONG DRIVE to Bristol was a delight: we went over Exmoor, planning to come back by the sea; we were certainly surrounded by magnificent country. There was a pleasant excitement in being again in a big, busy town. Bristol pleased us, with its steep streets, wide vistas over the valley opening suddenly, cranes rising behind old houses, and steamers thrusting in among trams. Pamela had no end of purchases to make for the house, and I needed books. I opened an account at George's shop. At a flower-shop, with the inauspicious name of Withers, we ordered crimson roses to be sent to Wendy on the first night of *Salome*, then lunched hastily and went to the theatre, where I was given seats and received a note from Milroy, pressing us to go round after the show.

It was a curious experience to watch the actors in this delicate, sophisticated piece and try to cast them in imagination for my robust play. Fortunately we thought Wendy good and liked Peter's sets immensely, so we were able to say nice things to everybody when we went round.

The welcome which a friendly critic receives behind the scenes in a theatre never fails to go to my head. Ought one to discount a good deal of it? Is this exuberant pleasure partly politic? I believe not: theatre people keep a youthful candour longer than most of us do. I was less open: I said not a word about my work to any of them, though Milroy backed Peter in begging vehemently for a play. Over tea at a café I lured Wendy and Peter into talking, widely and wittily, about the several members of the company, their best parts and weakest points.

It was a profitable afternoon; we both enjoyed the evening's performance, which had more pace and atmosphere than the matinee, and when we set out homeward on Sunday I had a packet of useful notes.

We could not resist the challenge of Porlock Hill. The car took it like a bird. Pamela's sigh of pleasure as she looked back at the moors unfolding below us made me turn my head unwarily and run the car up a bank, but no harm was done. What country!

The immense greenish reaches were brushed with distant showers and the moving purple shadows of clouds; a low hill rose like a wave. An exultant, irrational sense of possession filled me: I had chosen Devon and made it my own. The inflating consciousness of new riches was still with me when, late in the afternoon, we reached home.

As we walked to the door we saw Mrs Jessup and Charlie going home by the shortcut. Pamela laughed: 'Lizzie hasn't been too much alone.' She turned her key in the lock and went straight to the kitchen; after a moment I heard her calling me and went in. They were sitting at the table, both rather pale.

'Roddy,' Pamela said, 'Lizzie has seen a ghost.'

I sat down. This was more than gossip. Lizzie was changed; she sat with her forearms heavy on the table, sagging over, her face blotched and dull with trouble and shock. She looked at me in deep distress.

'Oh, Mr Roddy, and you after buying the place and fixing it up so comfortable! But you and Miss Pamela daren't go on living in it – you daren't, indeed!'

'Lizzie dear,' Pamela pleaded, 'do try to tell us; tell us quite clearly what you saw.'

'I ought to be able to tell it, Miss Pamela, for 'twill be cut and carved on my heart till my dying day. In the hall, I was, locking the door. That top bolt's a bit high for me; I had to get up on a chair. I had the hall-light, only, on; it was dark upstairs. 'Twas Whisky I noticed first: I heard a fierce snarl from him, and, Heaven shield us, there he was under the chest, flattened to the floor with terror, his two eyes glaring like lamps and his teeth savage. It was a lady, Miss Pamela. I screamed like mad, because it gave me such a fright to see anybody, thinking I was in the house alone, but I had no thought at first but that she was as real as you. Standing there, leaning over the banisters, she was, just as you might yourself, and staring down into the hall. All in white, she was, with long fair hair. But oh, pitiful saints, the awful look in her eyes!'

'What kind of a look was it?' Pamela asked.

Lizzie began to cry.

'Don't ask me, miss! I wisht I might ever forget it. Blue her eyes were, and terrible, as if she was looking down into hell. It went through me like a blast of ice. And then, in a wink, she was gone. I near fell; I near fainted; my heart was beating fit to break my side; I could hardly get to my room.'

'Poor Lizzie,' I said mechanically, 'you've had a shock.'

'I couldn't sleep a wink, believe me, Mr Roddy. I thought I'd lay-in in the morning, but I couldn't rest. I got up and went to early Mass and had a lovely talk with the priest after. He is a grand, wise man, is Father Anson – he says I'm not to stay alone in it again.'

'We wouldn't ask you to, Lizzie,' Pamela said.

So she had told the priest.

'And what did Mrs Jessup say?' I enquired.

'She says, another time, I'm to sleep at the farm, and she says there's no doubt the Parkinsons saw the same. She says, by the blue eyes, it is the lady who was killed on the cliff.'

We left poor Lizzie to quiet her nerves with her work and walked round the knoll. The heat was intense and the light from sea and sky glaring. The dismay with which I had listened to Lizzie's story passed off.

'I am not inclined to believe it,' I told Pamela. 'It is too like the conventional apparition – the white lady with long fair hair. And Lizzie *wanted* to see a ghost; it was up to her, living here; she'd lose prestige if she failed to see something, sleeping here alone.'

Pamela shook her head.

'But the condition she was in, Roddy! Imagination wouldn't do that.'

'Auto-suggestion can do anything.'

'Her description is very like the portrait.'

'Exactly! She has heard Mary Meredith described.'

'I wonder why you are so sceptical, Roddy; it doesn't help.'

'Will it help to let hysteria run amok? I am not entirely sceptical: I think there *is* something wrong – something psychic in the place. But don't you see, if there is, it depends on a receptive mind in order to manifest? The more you expect something, the more you get attuned to it and the more subject you become to obsession. We have got to shut it all out.'

'Roddy, Roddy, that can't be done!'

'What else is there to do?'

Pamela walked in silence for a while, then lit a cigarette and absent-mindedly dropped the match. The heather was as dry as tinder; I had to stamp out a flourishing little fire. I pointed the moral:

'You see what brooding on such things does for you!'

After that we turned back, hoping that Lizzie would have some tea for us.

'Listen, Roddy,' Pamela said gravely, 'I believe that Lizzie did see Mary, and I'm glad; because now we know one thing, the essential thing: we know who haunts the house. Now we have to find out why. I have the strongest feeling that if we could discover that we should be able to put everything right.'

I was impressed.

'I suppose that is a possibility.'

'Do let us tackle it from that end, Roddy. You've got just the right sort of mind to investigate a problem like this, because you can both imagine and analyse. My mind *invents* too much. Do let's make enquiries – discover everything we can about the Meredith household and try to work it out!'

'But where are we to begin?'

'I know – that's the difficulty: the Commander is the obvious person, of course.'

'Can you see yourself confiding in him?'

'No: he'd be a clam.'

'Mrs Jessup has told us all she knows, and more; I'm quite sure of that. I can't go round scavenging gossip about the Merediths, after all.'

'I know, Roddy; it's not easy, but do promise to try.'

'I'll think about it,' was all I would say.

But all day I scarcely gave it another thought. A fine handful of lively characters occupied my mind. I had a fascinating job on hand, the weather was glorious, and tomorrow Stella was coming to tea.

The pleasure which that thought gave me was disturbing, and I did not want to be disturbed. I had left London and come to this remote village for peace. I had found my work and I wanted to get on with it. This 'engaging child,' as Judith had called her, was a charming friend for Pamela ... Charming, yes ... but I must keep my balance.

So I told myself, but I was not so equable when, on Monday at lunch-time, a telegram came: 'I am desolated unable to come.'

'Why a telegram?' I demanded. 'Why not a telephone call?'

'There is something,' Pamela said slowly, 'that Stella didn't want to discuss.'

She sat at the table, crumpling the telegram in her hand. Her voice was depressed.

'Do you think that the Commander is going to cut her off from us again? Never allow her to come?'

I saw it in a flash.

'I do. The Commander has heard that his daughter's spirit is haunting this house.'

'Oh, Roddy!' Pamela's eyes filled with tears.

I went to the greenhouse and set up a shindy, sawing and hammering, mending the shelves. I wanted natural noise and action; I wanted something I could handle and master; I would not be baffled by the dead.

WE HAD a caller, however, that afternoon.

At about three o'clock Lizzie announced Father Anson. She had an air of mixed pride and sheepishness, as if this were her doing and she did not quite know how the priest would be received.

The old man came in a little diffidently, but was quickly at ease. He sat looking about the room and talked with lively appreciation about the pleasures of settling into such a home. He had himself just moved into a new – a very new house. 'It is convenient, but I prefer the charm of old, lived-in places,' he said.

He was taking our measure, sensing the atmosphere and approving what he found. We took an instant liking to him, both of us. He was half Irish, like ourselves.

'You are the luckier,' he said; 'you have the benefit of the name – a very noble name, in every sense.'

'Yes, I don't want to change it,' Pamela said.

He smiled kindly. 'And yet you will surely do so, my child.' He looked not far from seventy, though hardy. He was not a tall man; his air of authority came from his bearing and his strong, thoughtful voice. His weathered face was creased with lines of experience and humour; he had a slow, comprehending smile and a direct, steady, blue regard from deep-set eyes.

He said that he felt glad when young and ambitious people had the courage to leave London and that it needed courage, he believed. 'In the city so much of your life is lived for you by others; you are required to fill so small a space. But here, as it were, the spirit has play in a more spacious body, and that is better, if the spirit is rich and strong.' He smiled at me. 'Your criticism interests me: you are fastidious, yet liberal, and aware of the subtler currents of our time. But you will find criticism is not enough to satisfy you, among these horizons, I dare say.'

Just what Max had said! This was curious. I was tempted to tell him about my play, but refrained: the pot boils better with the lid on.

When Lizzie brought in the tea he smiled at her and asked whether she would come and teach his housekeeper to make soda-cake. 'But it needs the air of Ireland to raise it, I am afraid; it never takes the true flavour this side of the water,' he said.

'Let's see, now, what you think of this, Father,' she replied, delighted, 'and if you give the word, I'll come.'

He praised the soda-bread and ate a substantial tea. I wondered whether he would leave soon afterwards, for he was probably a hard-worked man.

'I have lived in Biddlecombe for twenty-five years,' he told us, and said no more. He would not open the subject of Lizzie's experience but was hoping that we would.

'Lizzie told you about the ghost, Father Anson?' Pamela said.

He nodded.

'I am very sorry, Miss Fitzgerald. It is grievous for you all.'

I told him that if he could spare the time we would like to consult him about it, and he looked up with a smile.

'I would feel grateful for your confidence.'

We told him everything – more than we had told each other. Pamela learned for the first time about the sickening sense of cold and fear which had come over me on the stairs, and I, for the first time, realised that, while she and Lizzie had been alone here, the sound of sighing had often roused her at night and kept her wandering about the house. We told him of the Commander's warning and spoke of the portrait of Mary Meredith and how closely Lizzie's description of the apparition resembled it.

The priest's scepticism, I realised with satisfaction, was of the same brand as my own: he cross-examined us closely about detail and discounted a good deal; finally, however, he shook his head slowly, and there was compassion in his tone.

'A residue remains; undoubtedly a residue of the inexplicable remains. I fear you may find that you cannot live in this house.'

I felt too dismayed to speak, and Pamela's voice trembled as she asked him: 'Father, can nothing be done?'

'My daughter, we can all pray.'

'But, mustn't we,' she persisted, 'try to understand – to do something?'

'Keep your own spirits calm.' He paused. 'In the last resort, there is exorcism.'

I felt a strong recoil. The idea was abhorrent to me, redolent of superstition, the devil, and sulphurous fumes.

'Don't you think, Father,' Pamela urged, 'that it might be possible to do something that would give the troubled spirit rest?'

He smiled. 'If there is, indeed, a troubled spirit – and if you have the faith and the courage,' he said.

'And the knowledge,' I put in. 'We know very little about the Merediths. The Commander seems to wish to have no intercourse with us or even to allow his granddaughter to visit us, and village gossip is not a reliable guide.'

'Ask me whatever you wish,' the priest answered. 'I may have to use a little discretion in answering, but you will understand that.'

Pamela's first question was very direct: 'Did Mary Meredith die by an accident?'

'As far as I know, her death was accidental,' Father Anson replied. 'As far as I know.'

'There was some doubt?' Pamela went on.

'I understood that there was a doubt in Miss Holloway's mind.'

'Do *you* think it possible that the girl – Carmel – struck her?'

'It is not likely, but, at such a moment of terror, not impossible, perhaps.'

I asked him whether he had known Carmel. He bent his head. 'She was one of my parishioners.'

A Catholic, then! That surprised me: I had thought of the girl as a gypsy, a pagan.

When I asked him whether Carmel had been very attractive Father Anson hesitated, then said, 'I believe some admire the type; she had bright eyes, a fresh colour, a pretty smile.'

'Is it true that she was Meredith's model?'

'Yes. She was a dancer, I understand, but posed for him a great deal in Spain.'

'That was before his marriage, of course? You know nothing of any – any other relationship?' I asked.

He answered the first part of my question. 'Just before. That was the time when he and Mary Meredith met. She was wintering for her health in Seville and studying art. After the marriage she insisted on returning to England. Mary was all in all to her father and she would not leave him alone. The Commander gave them this house.'

'And they brought the girl with them? That seems extraordinary!' I exclaimed.

'Yes, but it seems that Meredith insisted that he could not lose his model, and Mary' – the priest shook his head – 'well, great magnanimity is seldom accompanied by worldly wisdom, and Mary loved to do a generous thing.'

'I have wondered whether she was unhappy,' Pamela said.

'Meredith was not a man to keep his wife happy,' the priest replied.

'I see.'

Pamela sat thoughtful. I felt depressed. Was the house impregnated with the anguish of a woman who knew that she was betrayed? If this were so, what could anyone do?

Pamela asked, 'Was she – Carmel – here for long?'

'She came twice. Her first stay lasted, perhaps, six months; then, in the winter, they all went abroad. Mary was delicate and our winters are harsh. In the spring they returned – Meredith, that is, and Mary and their baby, who had been born in France.'

'Stella?'

'Little Stella. I was told that Meredith was devoted to her – his saving grace. They had no other child.'

'What had become of Carmel?' I asked.

'Mary had found a post for her in Paris – as a mannequin, I believe. I understood that the pay was excellent and the firm a respectable one. Mary would be scrupulous about that. Protestant employers,' he added generously, 'often have a sense of responsibility which some of our faith might well emulate. Carmel remained there for two years, or less; then she threw it up.'

'I expect she was bored,' Pamela said.

'It is probable,' Father Anson replied. 'But a hard time followed; she was poor, even, I fear, destitute. The poor child exercised commendable resistance to severe temptations, I thank God. She became ill. When she came back I was shocked: she was pitifully changed.'

'She returned, then?' I said.

'Yes: she came to this house almost, you might say, a beggar. Mary took her in. She nursed the girl, gave her clothes, tried her best to restore her to health of body and mind.'

'She had become unbalanced?' Pamela asked.

'Over-emotional. Sick people sometimes do.'

He was silent for a time, then said, 'I am afraid that is all that I can tell you. It ended as you know.'

'But, Father, we don't know how it ended,' Pamela protested, 'and it is surely on knowing that that any hope of a solution depends? What are we to believe? Was Mary murdered? Is it the old story of the spirit of a murdered victim "ranging for revenge"?'

The priest looked shocked.

'My daughter, Mary Meredith was not a heroine of melodrama. Mary was almost a saint. Revenge is unthinkable in connection with her.'

'Then is suicide a possibility?' I suggested. 'You teach, do you not, that suicides die in sin?'

'Mary was not a Catholic,' he answered gravely, 'but I am certain that she shared that belief. It was not suicide.'

Pamela looked troubled.

'It was either an accident, then, and that suggests no cause of haunting,' she said, 'or she was struck. And that doesn't guide us to a motive either, since you are sure revenge would not be one.'

Father Anson spoke very gravely:

'You must not ask me to believe that the spirit of Mary Meredith is not at rest.'

Pamela met his reproachful look firmly.

'I am afraid, Father Anson, that I feel almost certain of it. And I want to know *why* she is restless: why!'

'I trust you are not right, my child, but if it will give you ease of mind, I will try to think along this line.'

'You are very kind, Father; I feel that if – if we can know what was in her mind – know about the last scene with Carmel ...'

'Perhaps,' I broke in, 'you were with Carmel when she was dying?'

An expression of stern anger hardened the priest's face.

'Unhappily,' he said in a low, vibrant tone, 'unhappily, I was not with Carmel when she died.'

'But as her confessor,' Pamela said quickly, and stopped, flushing under the priest's quizzical look. 'You didn't mention it, Father: I just supposed it was so.'

'As her confessor,' he agreed, 'I ought to have been with her. I was not sent for. I saw her twice while she was delirious and I did not see her again.'

His anger about this was profound. I should not like, I thought, to incur that undying condemnation. I asked whether it was the doctor's fault.

'He was not with her, either, when she died.'

Pamela asked, 'Who nursed her? This Miss Holloway was it?'

'Carmel died of pneumonia. Nurse Holloway was in charge.'

'Miss Holloway!' Pamela exclaimed. 'She lived with them all. Do you think we could find her and talk to her?'

Father Anson hesitated, his lips compressed, then replied: 'She lives in Bristol now; she is not a very approachable woman, I fear, but if you should decide to approach her, I could obtain her address.'

I was remembering Mrs Jessup's story of Carmel, dying from exposure, sent home in a farm-cart. I said: 'There was a good deal of prejudice against Carmel in the village, it seems.'

'I suppose they thought her a sinful woman,' Pamela said.

The priest had risen.

'We are all poor sinful creatures, and the wiser we grow, the harder it is for us to avoid falling into sin. I sometimes envy the very simple.' He smiled at Pamela and pressed her hand. 'Try not to worry, my child! You may become accustomed to these little disturbances, or they may cease. I will pray for you. If you need my help, send for me: at any hour, day or night, I will come, and remember, the Church has had centuries of experience in quieting such troubles. And now I will talk to Lizzie, if you please.'

We thanked him, inadequately, it seemed to me, and I went up to my study to work. An hour later I saw him walking across the fields, his head bent against the rising wind.

Chapter VIII

MARKET-DAY

'YOU'LL SEE, now, the house will be quiet,' Lizzie said confidently after Father Anson's visit, and it was: night after night went by without trouble of any kind.

'I'm beginning to believe you were right, and Lizzie did have a hallucination,' Pamela said; 'or else Judith was right. Anyhow, I'd like to run up a flag.'

'Yes, I wish we could tell the world.'

I wished that we could tell the Commander, for the silence from Wilmcote was complete. A few days after the arrival of the telegram Pamela had written Stella a note, but it remained unanswered; he must have forbidden Stella to write – selfish, tyrannical old man!

I resented the situation vehemently; chiefly, I told myself, on Pamela's account, for I was working like a beaver and she was spending the days in the garden alone.

It was not possible, we had found, to neglect the garden. This soil, poor and sandy though it might be, was our own, and weeds were taking final possession of it under our eyes. One morning I came on

Lizzie standing in the middle of the small, brick-walled patch, like an Epstein figure of gloom. 'One year's seeding, seven years weeding,' she muttered, contemplating the groundsel and dandelions which were giving up the ghost in the wind and sending their winged progeny all abroad.

It had rained in the night; I stooped and drew out two handfuls of groundsel; sweetly the roots came up. I kneeled and cleaned a patch all round me, and so the return to the land began. I had released an atavistic passion; you cannot see clean earth, your own, and not fill it with visionary crops. Now, in her mind's eye, Lizzie saw bean-rows and salad-beds, winter stores of fat marrows, strings of onions and jars of scarlet fruit; Pamela gathered imagined flowers, while I ate luscious raspberries and infantile peas. 'Our fate was sealed during our holidays at Laragh Castle,' Pamela declared. 'I remember Aunt Kathleen saying: "Garden in childhood and you'll garden in age."' She wrote for expert advice to our cousin Nesta, who was running a nursery garden near Dublin with great success.

For me, gardening was truancy, and I stole only an hour for it now and then, but Pamela worked all day. She made herself red dungarees and was seldom out of them.

'For one thing,' she said, 'they scare the puffins.' This was her name for the local ladies who, avid for inside knowledge of the haunted house, were making afternoon calls. One of them, to her delight, misled by her cropped curly head, sunburnt arms, and work-manlike way with her spade, had taken her for the garden-boy. I gave her no help with these ladies: for me, tea on a tray in the study was the rule just now.

I was lost in *Barbara* – that served as the working title of my play. The pace at which it raced alarmed me: such slick, rapid writing could not be good. It was dangerous, too, to live so obliviously in an imagined world; almost anything might be happening in the actual world, or even in my own house, and I not know. All the time, absorbed though I was, part of my consciousness was intensely aware of some action waiting to be taken, a situation that must be brought to an end.

One breezy morning the spell snapped. I found myself sitting at my desk, my play a mere sheaf of paper under my hand. My mind was moving in the world of reality again and a fierce restlessness possessed me. I went out.

I had had an illusion that everything was waiting, changeless, for me to step into it again and find it just as I had left it a week or two ago. Now I found myself vaguely afraid. I went to Pamela where she was working in the alleged kitchen garden – now promising soon to deserve its name. 'Look here,' I demanded, 'all this peace and quiet is beginning to seem too good to be true: are you keeping things back?'

'Cross my heart,' she replied, 'I wouldn't keep anything from you of that sort, Roddy, because if there is haunting it has to be fought. I've not heard a sound since we came back from Bristol: eleven quiet nights.'

'Fine! Come for a walk to the village?' I suggested.

She shook her head. 'Don't want to leave this. Oh!' she added. 'It is Thursday – market-day; could you bring back some of Corney's cream cheese?'

I struck off by the short cut; the wind was strong here; this was the turn where Stella had refused to let me come any farther. I had treated her as a child that day, and how sweetly dignified she had been! This silence from her was intolerable; somehow it must be broken down. I would go through the village, I decided, and up on the other side. I would walk by The Avenue to the pine-wood and the bowling-green, where old gentlemen took their constitutionals. One might meet the Commander up there.

Biddlecombe market was quite an important affair, to judge by the carts, piled with produce, which thronged the tributary roads running down from the hills. The stalls had been set up in the cobbled square by the wharf, their awnings making patches of shade in the hot, lively scene. The place was populous: women chattered, poultry squawked, competing with the clamour of gulls, children dodged in and out, sucking sweetmeats on sticks, and fishermen strolled around, carrying strings of glittering mackerel and gossiping with their inland friends. The smell of shellfish pervaded the place. I found Corney's stall, secured the cream cheese, and paused at a flower-stall.

The face of the old man who was in charge looked familiar. He recognised me, too, took his clay pipe from his mouth, and leered up at me with twinkling eyes.

'Who was right, now, mister, eh? Who was lying, eh? It warn't the Parkinsons, was it, nor yet their cook? What be your cook thinking about it, mister, eh?'

I left him to his toothless cackling and dodged to the far side of the next stall, sheltered by a bank of daisies and phlox. I disliked carrying flowers, but the house demanded them, and I really owed Pamela some attention. These were drooping, however.

While I contemplated the phlox I heard a soft, excited voice say: 'Mr Fitzgerald,' and turned to see Stella looking up at me with flushed cheeks and troubled eyes.

'Tell me,' I asked, 'are these fresh? How long would they last?'

She examined the cut ends of the stalks.

'Yes, they'll revive in water,' she said. 'They might like an aspirin.'

She chuckled at my astonishment. I bought the flowers.

'And now have I got to go to the chemist's and buy aspirin for them? Is there anything else you feel they should have?'

'I am quite sure Miss Fitzgerald has aspirin.'

'Why would she? We don't have headaches.'

'I bet you she has aspirin,' Stella repeated, smiling.

'To be sure!' I had to confess. 'She gave some to Judith. Well, you women know one another's ways.'

Feebly I made conversation, intent on keeping Stella from vanishing again into the blue. She was not going to embark on apologies or explanations in the middle of the marketplace, I could see.

I had an idea.

'I'm hot and thirsty,' I said: 'aren't you? What would you think of an ice at the Lavender Cafe?'

She hesitated, then nodded.

'Yes, thank you; I would like it.'

We went into the dark little shop with its awkward steps and ostentatious oak beams. Stella deposited her parcels neatly and settled into a corner seat. I sat as silent as she while she pondered, her transparent face revealing all her doubts as to what she might and might not say.

'You disappointed us,' I said at length.

She nodded. 'Yes. And I was rude. And just after you had let me come and meet your old, best friends.'

'That part of it doesn't matter. But – is this the kind of ice you like? Have some wafers with it, won't you?'

'I would have written to explain, but I couldn't think what to say … Even after my horrible, horrible telegram – and Miss Fitzgerald wrote me the friendliest note … As a matter of fact, I did write an explanation, quite an elaborate one: I sometimes get chills, and I said that I had had one – but I – I just couldn't send it – not to your sister.'

'Don't bother about explanations, they don't matter; but when will you come?'

She flushed painfully.

'That is what makes me so unhappy: my grandfather doesn't wish me to come.'

'Do you mean – ever?'

She nodded and bent her head over her ice, trying to eat it; she was upset.

'I wonder why you can't tell me the reason: you know it, don't you?'

She whispered, 'Yes,' then looked at me very seriously and said: 'I give you my word of honour that it is not because grandfather feels – unfriendly or anything, to you or Miss Fitzgerald. It really has nothing to do with you at all.'

'No,' I replied, 'I am aware of that: it's the house.'

She looked immensely relieved but said nothing.

'You didn't want to tell us for fear we should feel worried about it?' I guessed.

'Yes.' She waited eagerly.

'Somebody has told the Commander that the house is haunted, and he believes it: isn't that so?'

'Exactly! Oh, I am so thankful that you understand! But, you see, I thought there might be no truth in it and that you would both begin to worry if you knew what was being said – I do hope,' she added quickly, 'that it isn't true.'

I fenced a little. 'Tell me what is being said and I may be able to tell you whether any of it is true.'

'I haven't heard very much,' she replied, 'because the minute Susie mentioned the rumour to grandfather he paid her and told her to go. She came back to the kitchen in a temper, saying he ought to have been grateful for the information: she said a white nun walked up and down the stairs, wringing her hands, and your maid saw her and fainted and you found her in a swoon on the floor.'

I grinned. This was not as bad as it might have been.

'I can assure you nobody has seen a white nun.'

'Oh, I am glad!'

'Did your grandfather speak of this to you?'

'Yes, because I said something to him. I said that I should think you wouldn't mind very terribly if the house were haunted, because Miss Fitzgerald was not afraid of ghosts. And I said that perhaps my great-grandmother's spirit visited Cliff End sometimes. Because, you see, the house was built for her and she loved it very much.'

'Your great-grandmother has not appeared, either. What did he say?'

'He was angry; he said the whole subject was morbid and abominable and he forbade me to mention it to him or to visit Cliff End any more, and' – her face tightened – 'he made me send that horrible telegram.'

'Please don't worry any more about the telegram, but listen – this really matters: I am going to tell you something that I want no one else in Biddlecombe to know: some strange things have happened at Cliff End and we believe that there is some kind of psychic atmosphere there, although, probably, there is no ghost.' She listened with profound attention while I talked about emanations and subjective phenomena, the impregnation of matter by emotion, and all the rest. I was not wholly candid; I said that Lizzie had had a vague hallucination but gave her no description of the figure which she thought she had seen; I did not mention the light in the nursery and talked mostly about the sighing sounds and the sense of depression in the studio.

Stella sat for a while in dejected thought.

'I'm dreadfully sorry,' she said then: 'it spoils a whole room in the house; it evidently isn't a happy spirit. Then,' she added, flushing a little, 'I am afraid that one of my great-uncles drank too much; he may have, sort of, left nightmares behind.'

I laughed. Posthumous delirium tremens would be about as nasty a haunting, I thought, as one could conceive.

'I'd certainly prefer your great-grandmother,' I chuckled; 'but, in any case, it seems to be all over now,' I told her, 'and I would like you to tell your grandfather that.'

She shook her head. 'I am so happy that it seems to be all over, but I am afraid that to tell grandfather would be no use at all.'

'That seems a pity.'

'Yes.'

She sat drooping, a sad little figure of defeated youth. I deliberated: the situation seemed absurd – outrageous – and I decided to persist.

'Tell me,' I asked her, 'would you be afraid to come?'

'Oh, no!'

I hesitated.

'But you feel obliged to respect his wishes, is that it?'

Stella flushed. 'Well, I am afraid I rather often do things that I know grandfather might not like, but once he has forbidden something, I don't disobey.'

'I see. And you don't feel that you can make an exception this time?'

'I … I have been trying to decide.'

'I hope you will decide in our favour.'

Her smooth brow became furrowed with troubled thought.

'It would be purely selfish of me, wouldn't it? And unkind. Because he is fair about it: he doesn't absolutely forbid it any more. He did at first, but the other day, when Miss Fitzgerald's letter came – imagine, after what I had done, writing to say that she hoped I would come when I could! – when that came I told him that I did, really, very, very much want to go, and he said nothing for a long time; he looked worried to death; then he said: "If you go, it will be against

112

my wishes and against my judgment." Then he told me that I must decide for myself. He said: "You are eighteen, and I have never been a tyrant, I think." So I said that I would think about it; and I have been thinking ever since.'

She was clearly longing for me to offer her some advice, but what could I say? It seemed atrocious that an old man's morbid fears should deprive Stella of friendship and pleasure, quite apart from my own desires; but dared I counsel a course which might destroy the relationship between the two?

'You see,' I explained, 'I mustn't advise you, because I am an interested party. We want to see a great deal of you, my sister and I.'

Her face lit up. 'Really and truly?' she asked.

'Really and truly! Does that seem so strange?'

'It does, a little. You see, your sister is so – she has so much *savoir faire*, and I haven't any, I'm afraid. They said at school that I was *farouche*.' She laughed. 'I didn't mind their calling me that because I thought it was a lovely word.'

'I think that school of yours sounds stuffy. Weren't you glad to leave it?'

'I was! Especially at first.'

'Then you began to feel that Biddlecombe is too far from the world?'

'Exactly! Is that silly? Because, where is the world? We were in the world at your party, weren't we? I expect you are in the world wherever you go.'

'Look here,' I asked her, 'how much do you want to come to Cliff End?'

She checked an impulsive reply and hesitated; my question had not been a fair one. Her reply was a little constrained: 'I want it very much.'

'You don't feel that you could come, and say nothing?'

She shook her head.

'That is what I was tempted to do, but, next thing, I would be telling grandfather lies. It is dreadful, but when I am nervous lies do sometimes just pop out of my mouth: quite cunning ones, too. I can't understand it, because my mother was absolutely truthful – as clear as crystal. She never told a lie in her life.'

'Any time,' I said, 'I'd prefer a fight to a lie.'

'I believe you think I ought to tell him I'm coming.'

'I believe I do.'

She looked into the distance, her eyes, with their long, dark lashes, large and sad, the sensitive profile set. I saw that Stella would be a beautiful woman even in old age. I saw, too, how easily that gentle expression might become one of resignation. But she lifted her head, saying, 'I believe I do, too.'

'Splendid!'

'I will decide tonight.'

'Fine! And if the decision is favourable, will you come to tea tomorrow?'

'But that would leave you and Miss Fitzgerald not sure whether I am coming or not.'

'If you don't mind finding Pamela in dungarees and gardening with her, that doesn't matter a bit.'

She smiled. 'Oh, I should like that … And now I will go home. Thank you for the ice and everything.'

'I'll explain to Pamela,' I promised.

I waited in the cafe until Stella had been gone some minutes, then took the steep road home.

When I recounted this interview to Pamela she blazed. 'What a rotten shame, distorting life for the child like that! It is tyranny, and a mean form of it, that's all!'

She tore out a deep-rooted plantain and flung it on the weed-pile, as if she were disposing of an enemy.

I felt called upon to protest. Perhaps I wanted to put the case against myself in order to hear it refuted.

'Look here, supposing he really believes that his daughter's spirit is haunting this house, isn't it natural that he should be nervous for Stella?'

'Parents ought to endure their nervousness and let young people live.'

I pointed out that if Stella should ever hear that her adored mother was supposed to have been seen here, it would be pretty disturbing for her.

Pamela snapped.

'Then why did you encourage her to come?'

'I took a chance,' I answered, 'and it was a bit unscrupulous.'

'No,' Pamela said firmly, 'it wasn't. We can't go through life avoiding the natural thing to do because there may be a ghost, and I think we have to chance it for Stella, too. If she gives in to the Commander about this, she'll give in about everything and she'll just wilt.'

'I don't know about that.'

Pamela's energy was doing me good: I was quite ready to be encouraged in inciting Stella to revolt.

'Roddy – can't you see her, in another ten years, with a sad, sweet face like her mother's, walking beside the old man's bath-chair, all her faith in happiness dead?'

I could, right enough, and the picture pinched my heart.

'All the same,' I said, 'I feel sorry for the old man. He appears to have doted on Mary, and now Stella's all he's got.'

'Yes; and he tries to re-model Stella in Mary's image, twisting her into something she can't become, in order to have Mary with him again in his old age! She's her father's child, too, an artist's, after all. It's like those mediaeval kings who had children made into dwarfs.'

'How you exaggerate, Pamela!'

She stood, holding her fork like a challenger's staff, her head erect. There was nothing conciliatory to be looked for from her. I began to feel angry.

'If only you were not so prejudiced!' I protested. 'Think how much you could do if you and the Commander were on good terms! Look here, Pamela – if you ever have the chance – if you meet him, do try to be nice! You can do it jolly well when you like.'

For a minute she retained her David-against-Goliath stance, then she relaxed, rested her eyes on my face seriously, and said, 'All right, Roddy: I'll do my best.'

Chapter IX

THE NURSERY

FRIDAY WAS a day of nervous fever such as I had not experienced since my early twenties. The play was racing to its close. I lunched in my study on coffee and a sandwich and, when I began to feel hungry again, rang my bell as a signal to Lizzie that I would have my tea upstairs.

It exhilarated me to be able to do this. Stella was coming: I was convinced that she would come, and I was a great deal too much aware of that simple fact. The workman in me felt challenged. Had it come to this? Because Stella was coming must I break off the most critical day's work I had ever attempted, lose way, waste an impulse that might not be capturable again? The thing was winding up in a fine flare of action and passion; I would not slack it down.

The battle which it cost me to make this decision and stick to it added tension to the scene. The passage between Barbara, trapped and frantic, and the cool, amused Frampton was written then. Once I wavered; I had heard the sound of Stella's laugh from the garden and caught a glimpse of a yellow frock. So she had come! I put down my pen and looked out of the window. They were building a weed-fire at the foot of the knoll. That barrow was much too heavy for Stella: I ought to go down …

I sat at my desk again. Jennifer's entrance came now. This was difficult: a spirited girl, clear-sighted, ambitious, whose life had been deliberately wrecked by Barbara. I had to make her forgive, and even fight for her tormenter, without seeming soft or a fool. The first draft was quite inadequate here; could the thing be made convincing? Yes: I knew that it could. There is often a well of reckless compassion in youth.

At last it was done; the play was finished; I wrote 'Curtain,' stretched like a cat, and went out. Gosh, it was nearly six o'clock! I came back to realities with a sense of remorse.

Pretty behaviour this! Why must I always be showing myself to Stella as a mannerless churl? I had persuaded her to face a hard ordeal in order to visit us, and absented myself when she came. How on earth could I make her feel that I had a valid excuse?

She was absorbed in her weeding, kneeling on a sack on the grass. When I greeted her she looked at me over her shoulder, smiling, and then stooped to her work again.

'So the battle's fought and won?' I enquired facetiously.

'There was no battle,' Stella replied.

Pamela pushed up the barrow full of weeds and tipped it over beside the fire, which was filling the air with a sharp autumnal reek; the smoke wavered, almost levelled by the strengthening breeze. She forked the weeds on to the heap.

'What have you to say for yourself?' she asked.

I said: 'That fire needs a bigger hole,' and began to wind a stick in its side. 'I suppose,' I went on defensively, 'that you are both like Lizzie – feel no end superior because you have been getting hot and grubby while I kept cool and clean at my "cream of a job"?'

Stella turned round and surveyed me, kneeling upright on her rug.

'"Hot and grubby" is quite right,' she said, smiling; 'but you don't look shamefully tidy yourself.'

Pamela remarked, 'I can always tell whether he has done an honest afternoon's work by his hair.'

'Well,' I grinned, standing up, 'does it give me an excuse?'

Stella studied my appearance carefully and nodded: 'I think so.'

'That's really nice of you,' I said. 'It was outrageous of me, and I was well punished up there. I'd rather make a weed-fire than anything; I felt quite sure you were guzzling cream for tea, and I had only a sandwich; I felt as cross as a boy kept in from cricket, but, well, you see, I was finishing a play.'

Stella sprang to her feet. I had worked for my effect and secured it. She opened her eyes wide. 'Do you mean you have really just finished a play?'

Pamela, too, swung round. 'Properly finished? The whole first draft, Roddy? Oh, good work!'

'Is it historical? Is it a poetic play?' Stella asked eagerly. 'What is it called?'

'It's modern and in prose, and for the present it's called *Barbara*. Honestly, it was bad luck on me, its winding up this afternoon. I didn't dare leave it, just.'

'Of course! Oh, but of course!'

Stella understood; I was forgiven.

'*Barbara* is a rather good title. What happens next?' Pamela asked.

'I'll read it to Milroy and see what he thinks of it. When could we go to Bristol? When does *Salome* come on?'

'It starts on Tuesday. They're doing two Coward one-acters with it – queer mixture. Would Friday do? I have just surrendered to siege and engaged Charlie to do gardening for a week, and I daren't leave him alone.'

'Fine: that gives me a week to trim it up.'

'When are you going to read it to me?'

'Whenever you like.'

'This evening?'

'H'm – I ought to start an article, but I haven't the energy. All right!'

Stella sighed; her face made me smile, there was such a war on between her greedy interest in the play and the demands of social behaviour; the latter won.

'I hope you will have an extravagant success with it, Mr Fitzgerald. And now it is time for me to go.'

'That is too bad,' I grumbled, 'just when I am free.'

Pamela stacked up the tools, and she and Stella took them to the shed while I followed with the barrow.

'Do you feel we are too old to be called "Roderick" and "Pamela"?' I heard Pamela ask.

'They are lovely names and I would like to say them,' Stella replied.

'By the way, Stella,' I said as we returned to the house, 'when are you coming to bathe from our beach? It's the grandest bathing I've ever known.'

'Yes, isn't it!' she exclaimed.

'You have bathed there often, I expect?'

She confessed with a little smile: 'Yes, but nobody except Mrs Jessup knew.'

'But why the secrecy? It was your own property.'

'I was afraid my grandfather would say it was dangerous.'

'You went all alone, then?'

'Yes.'

'That is a rather dangerous thing to do. I hope,' I told her, 'that you will bathe there often, but not by yourself.'

'Pamela has invited me to come next Tuesday.'

'Good! Can you dive?'

'No.'

'You must let me teach you.'

I thought Stella had not heard: she did not reply.

'We'll light a fire,' Pamela said in the hall, and asked me with her eyebrows whether we should invite Stella to stay on. I assented.

'Stella,' she said, 'would it make difficulties for you, or could you stay to dinner with us and hear the play?'

'Oh! Oh!'

Stella stopped dead and looked from one to the other of us, as if we had dangled the keys of Paradise before her eyes. 'How I should love it! And it *is* possible. Grandfather never comes in on Fridays until after half-past ten.'

Now what had we done? The same thought struck Pamela's mind and mine; I caught her worried glance. This was taking a chance indeed – to keep Stella so late.

Stella was explaining: 'He goes to supper on Friday with Captain Pascoe, who is an invalid, and they play chess, and as a rule our daily help comes back on Friday evening to keep me company and we do the silver, but we haven't one just now. The silver won't be done until tomorrow, that's all.'

'Do it good!' I said. 'I suggest dinner early, and I'll read immediately afterwards and drive you home before ten.'

'It's too late to have dinner early,' Pamela said, and hurried away with Stella to wash, while I lit the sitting-room fire.

I looked forward to the reading but made a mental note to leave out certain passages which would not be approved by the Brussels school.

Stella came down presently, all tidy and proper, and sat in Pamela's chair.

'I am glad there was no battle,' I said, standing by the mantelpiece. For a moment she did not reply. Her face was turned away; she was watching the clouds which, kindled by the evening light and teased by the wind, were stretching a golden fleece over the sky. She said at length, a little sorrowfully, 'All the same, it is as if something had gone.'

'No, no! He'll get adjusted to this.'

'He looked at me for such a long time, as if he did not think it could be me at all, and then he said, "So you have passed out of my control." For a minute I very nearly gave in. And at lunch he hardly talked. He did try to, and so did I. He doesn't mean to punish me but I think everything's changed.'

'I hope you don't regret holding out, Stella?'

She shook her head. 'No. Besides, it had to come some time: a person has to grow up.'

'Yes; that is important,' I replied.

Lizzie came in to set an extra place at the table. Stella smiled at her and said, 'Good evening.'

'You should be hungry after your afternoon's work, Miss Meredith, and I wish I had known you were staying,' Lizzie said. 'You're not one of them that refuse potatoes, I hope? What about a look at the kitchen? You were wishful to see it, Miss Pamela says.'

'Oh, thank you. I expect it's enormous, is it?'

They went off together and I went to the study to bind up my script. Pamela put her head in, and I told her that Lizzie and Stella were making friends.

'By the way, Roddy,' she said as we went downstairs, 'I'm sorry, but you are not to be permitted to bathe with us.'

'Not to bathe! Good heavens!' I exclaimed, disgusted. 'That damn puritanical school!'

'No,' she replied in a low voice: 'Miss Holloway! Miss Holloway told her that her mother did not like mixed bathing.'

'But that's preposterous!'

'Isn't it?'

'After all, things have moved! You've got to break that down, Pamela.'

She shook her head. 'I tried a little, Roddy; it's useless. Her mother's ways and ideas are sacred still.'

It was half-past seven when dinner began and after eight before Lizzie had cleared it away and, with coffee bubbling beside us on the low table, Pamela in her chair, and Stella on the fender-stool near her, the reading began.

While I read, the room darkened. I switched on my lamp. The wind was whining on a low note outside; the logs crackled, and with the accompaniment of those sounds only, I read on, more dramatically than I had intended to, to the end of the first act.

Pamela exclaimed, 'Roddy, it's masterly! And only three weeks' work. Man, you're a dramatist! Why have these things been hid? What a character! Where on earth did she come from?'

'Wendy and her charade, of course.'

'Do you think Wendy has the stuff in her to play it? That sort of consuming, unholy fire?'

'She's an actress, and intelligent. How's the exposition?'

'Slick!'

'And the curtain?'

'Terrific!'

'Anything you think should be changed?'

Pamela is a fairly acute critic. She made three or four points; I fought her on all of them, in order to thrash out the pros and cons, and gave way on two.

'There's one stage-direction,' she said: 'that moment when Barbara sees Jennifer and Frampton together: when the devilish idea first comes into her head. I am afraid she's got to have words or a gesture there, or it may not get across.'

We had both ignored Stella, sitting there, rapt.

'Oh,' she murmured slowly, 'I saw her standing stone-still: *really* like stone.'

'That will do it,' Pamela said.

'Right! Yes! She must suggest implacable coldness,' I declared. Stella repeated 'Implacable coldness,' with a sigh, and said, 'Oh, please go on.'

I went on, wishing that the play might ever, in the theatre, have such an audience as this.

The second act satisfied Pamela less. It was the most difficult. Barbara, launched on her career of wrecking, has, at the same time, to retain the adoration of a young girl and the devotion of an intelligent man.

'She gives herself away too completely,' Pamela protested. 'You think that they are fools to care for her and you lose sympathy with them.'

'What can I do?'

'Can't you make her almost deceive herself; bamboozle herself into thinking that her motives are pure?'

'That's not quite the theme ... '

A searching discussion followed. I became rather ill-tempered, thinking that Pamela was failing to see the difficulties of the devices which she proposed. The noise of the wind, shrilling through the broken greenhouse, was getting on my nerves; it was too like those ghostly moans.

'We must curtain that door,' I grumbled.

'Go ahead, Roddy; read on,' Pamela urged. 'The third act may suggest what you want for this.'

'Are you enjoying it?' I asked Stella. I had clean forgotten about leaving out passages on her account and wondered what she was making of some of the relationships.

'It is exciting me so much that I can hardly bear it,' she replied; 'but there are bits that I don't understand: I mean, Barbara does some things that seem quite natural and they are evidently part of her wickedness, but please go on.'

For the opening of the third act I wanted a song; it was to be sung off-stage in the half-dark, by the Welsh lad who was in love with Barbara's maid and has given up all hope of winning her heart. I explained what I wanted – something grave, tender, perhaps with a religious tinge – and asked Stella whether she happened to know such a song. She pondered deeply for a moment, then said: 'I think, perhaps, "All Through the Night."' I remembered it vaguely and asked her whether she could sing it or hum the tune.

'I did learn it once, and it doesn't matter, does it, how badly I sing?' Then, looking into the fire, oblivious of everything but the words and their feeling, she sang. I remembered the old song now, with its wistful, moving cadence; Stella's voice, a true and very sweet contralto, suited it so perfectly that you could have thought it was being sung for the first time.

I thanked her rather absently when she ended, and Pamela's murmured comments left silence after them. I did not want to break the silence; I did not want to go on reading my play; I wanted to rest there and look at Stella, sitting so still, not lifting her eyes from the fire, but flooded, as I was, by an overwhelming apprehension of the dangers and the sweetness of love. A pulse was throbbing at the side of her throat.

I rose and crossed the room to the window. The sky was quite overcast and twilight was merging into night. I drew the curtains, went back to my place, and took up the play again.

In reading the third act, I omitted one rather grim passage, giving an evasive summary of it, and then read to the end. I looked up and met Stella's eyes fixed on me, aghast.

'But she was worse than a murderer! There isn't any crime people can be hanged for worse than what Barbara did.'

She was shocked, as though the thing had happened in real life. I laughed: 'I'm glad you feel that way.'

Pamela held out her hand for the script. 'Show me that bit you cut, Roddy; what a maddening thing to do!'

She stood by the lamp reading it, absorbed, and I watched her face; I was anxious about this bit: it involved a sharp change of key and was on the edge of sensationalism. She shook her head: 'I don't like it; it is too violent; there's the wrong sort of shock.'

'Poetic justice! Barbara deserves her fate.'

'Barbara deserves anything, but I think illness is dangerous in a play; it has too many associations outside the theatre; once you suggest it, the whole human tragedy breaks in.'

'I'll just put my things on,' Stella said a little anxiously, and slipped from the room.

'Hurry!' I called after her, dismayed to see that it was past ten o'clock. Not for the world would I have made her late. I threw down the script, snatched my torch, and ran through the greenhouse to the garage. Pamela came with me to help with the warped old doors, which always set up a wrestling match when you tried to open them in a wind like this. I backed the car up near the greenhouse and we put up the hood. There was rain in the west wind.

'Better get a coat,' Pamela said as we came in again. She called Stella from the door but turned back to say to me: 'Roddy, I'm thrilled to the marrow of my bones. I don't know when I've seen or read such a play. It's tremendous!'

'You think it will go?'

'Bound to! It's got everything: original characters, nice, dry, ironic humour, juicy dialogue, and plot.'

I was really delighted. The world was mine oyster which I was going to open with this play. And then …

Pamela had run upstairs, and a sharp cry sent me racing after her. Stella was lying on the landing unconscious.

I carried her down and laid her on the couch; her face was as pale as wax, her breathing so faint that, for one agonised moment, I thought she was not breathing at all. Her hands were cold; she looked like a dead child. My heart was constricted with fear while we worked to restore her, and Pamela's breath came in choking gasps, but there was no trace of terror on Stella's face.

I asked Pamela whether she had seen or felt anything wrong on the landing and she shook her head. She ran up to her own room for *sal volatile*, smelling salts, and a shawl and told me that everything was as usual up there.

It was a profound faint; for a long time there was no sign of recovery, then, just as I was panicking, thinking that we must wake Lizzie, call Dr Scott, her breathing deepened and colour began to appear in her lips. She opened her eyes. I felt as though my own spirit had fled to the edge of death and come home.

'What is it?' she whispered. 'What is wrong?'

'Nothing, darling,' Pamela answered. 'You fainted on the stairs; lie still for a little.' Tears were streaming down Pamela's cheeks. She poured out brandy, but Stella was shaken by tremors and could not drink; she tried patiently and swallowed a little at last. For a moment she shut her eyes, then opened them and looked at us, and a smile deepened the shadows in her cheeks.

'Don't be worried: I didn't see anything,' she said faintly.

My relief was immeasurable, and Pamela drew a long breath. She busied herself, settling cushions under Stella's head, stoking up the fire, and lighting the lamp under the coffee-pot.

'I wonder why you fainted?' I said to Stella, and added, 'But never mind.'

'I don't know at all,' she answered, and asked me what time it was.

It was only twenty to eleven: that seemed incredible. She asked me to telephone to her grandfather: 'Please just tell him I have one of my silly chills.'   •

'Is she fit to go home?' I asked Pamela. 'What shall I say?'

'I don't think she should go out,' Pamela replied anxiously. 'She might faint again. I would like to put you straight to bed here, Stella,' she said.

'Yes,' Stella pleaded: 'do please let me sleep here.'

She was very pale still, and the trembling went on. It would certainly be better for her to keep warm and go to sleep as soon as possible, but was this house fit for her? Was it safe? I stood looking down at her, tormented by indecision.

Her dark eyes met mine, troubled and shy. 'Please, please, don't look so worried,' she said.

'Are you sure you would prefer to sleep here?' I asked her.

'Oh, yes!'

'You are quite sure you didn't see anything that frightened you?'

'Quite sure.'

Her voice was weak and shaky. Yes, she had better stay.

Commander Brooke answered the telephone. There was no anxiety in his voice. He probably supposed that Stella was in her own room. When I mentioned my name he repeated it, his surprise and displeasure undisguised. I could only ignore his tone.

'Miss Meredith dined with us,' I told him, trying to sound as if that was something of which he would naturally approve, 'and I am sorry to say she is not feeling well. It seems to be a chill. She is over the little attack and is resting. My sister would like to put her to bed at once, if you agree.'

There was silence, then, in a constrained voice, he asked, 'Can Stella come to the telephone?'

'We were anxious to keep her warm and it is in the hall.'

He spoke slowly: 'Stella is subject to chills; they are said to be a nervous affection. Has she – has she had a shock?'

'No.'

'Are you sure of that?' He was in acute anxiety.

'She assures us that there was nothing of the sort, and we have no reason to think there was.'

'No reason?'

There was bitter, almost contemptuous, scepticism in his tone I answered firmly:

'No, Commander Brooke! And I am glad to have the opportunity to tell you this. Our servant spread a rumour which, no doubt, you have heard; we have no reason to believe that it is true.'

'Can you assure me of that?'

'I have already assured you.'

'Have you had no such experience?'

'There have been faint, unaccountable sounds; a glimmer of light; certain moods of depression – nothing else.'

There was a pause. He was deeply suspicious of my good faith. Well – I could do nothing about that.

'Stella must come home,' he said.

I hesitated, recalling Stella's pale, exhausted little face.

'You wish me to rouse her and bring her home, instead of letting her sleep?'

I felt anger tingling through his silence but knew that he would not unleash it over the telephone; I waited while the battle went on. He asked, in a voice stiff with constraint: 'What is her condition?'

'Weak and shivering, but otherwise quite herself.'

'I should like to speak to Miss Fitzgerald.'

I called Pamela. She spoke gently: 'Commander Brooke, Stella asks me to tell you that there is nothing wrong – just one of her chills and a little fainting-fit; but she feels too tired to come to the telephone. She asks your permission to stay with us tonight. If she may, I will take great care of her.'

There were still difficulties; there were more assurances, and at last Pamela won his consent.

Stella sighed with relief when we told her, but asked anxiously whether her grandfather had seemed displeased. We were forced to confess that he had.

'The misfortune is,' she said, troubled, 'that he will think I have seen something, and it is embarrassing for you, also. I am afraid I have deranged you dreadfully.'

We tried to reassure her, but we were shaken and worried and not very eloquent.

Pamela asked her whether she thought she could walk upstairs. Stella hesitated.

'Please,' she whispered, 'not up there.'

'You told us there was nothing!' I exclaimed.

She looked unhappy. 'I know: it's true: I didn't see anything and I was not frightened, exactly; but something did, sort of, overpower me. I don't know what it was. But, please, don't go up there!'

'I have been up,' Pamela told her; 'there's nothing wrong.'

'She could sleep here,' I suggested.

Stella looked at Pamela pleadingly.

'What I would love, if it would not give you too much trouble, is to sleep in the little room.'

'The nursery? Your own room! Why, yes,' Pamela replied, smiling. 'It's perfectly easy to make up the bed in there.'

She went up to see to it. I was not easy about this: it was in the nursery that I had heard sighing and seen the light, but Stella's eyes were wide with joy and warm colour had come into her cheeks.

'You are both very, very good to me,' she said.

'Stella,' I told her, 'I had rather you stayed in this room.'

She was very weak still; she bent her head, saying: 'Very well, Roderick,' but tears splashed down.

I had made a mistake: Stella needed soothing, peace of mind, a long night's sleep, and I had spoilt her chance of these, because of a reasonless fear. I could not bear making her cry. The situation was becoming unendurable.

'Don't cry,' I said curtly; 'perhaps you'll sleep better in there. Do as you like.'

She smiled at me, but I could not respond. I was filled with foreboding. An hour ago all had been well; we had stood together on the edge of immeasurable happiness, but now something dark and chilling had fallen between us – a shadow out of the past. I ought never to have brought Stella to this house.

I sat in a chair beside her and said nothing.

'Please, try not to worry so much,' she pleaded again, laying a gentle hand on my arm.

Agitation and constraint made me answer harshly: 'All right; if you don't mind, I'll smoke instead.'

I was glad when Pamela came and took Stella to the nursery and I could go out in the rain and put the car in.

I returned to the sitting-room and paced up and down, all steadiness and direction lost, my mind a churning turmoil of hopes and impulses and fears.

'She's all right now,' Pamela told me quickly when she came in. 'I've lighted a fire, so she won't be in the dark.' But her voice broke, and for a moment she sat on the couch and cried; then she looked up: 'I'm going to sleep here. Like a dear, bring down my blankets.'

I fixed up a bed on the couch for Pamela and told her that I would patrol now and then during the night. We promised to call one another if the least sound was heard.

There was nothing. I kept my bedroom door open, slept only in snatches, and went downstairs several times. The lights were on in the hall and on the landing all night. The wind subsided gradually. The house was quiet; through the half-open door of the nursery came the flickering glow of the fire, and I heard, now and then, a light, easeful sigh and the murmur of drowsy words; no wonder, I thought, if Stella slept lightly and had restless dreams. My heart grew lighter: if there were some obscure menace in this house it was in abeyance now, and perhaps there was no menace at all. It was possible that the mere excitement of her evening with us, the play, and then her agitation about being home in time had caused Stella to faint. All might be well. All might be more than well. I was realising what Max had meant when he said, 'Life can be grand.'

At last the thinning of the darkness in the east and a sheen creeping over the water relieved my guard; I fell asleep and slept heavily for two or three hours.

When Lizzie called me I told her that Miss Meredith had been taken ill and stayed for the night in the nursery. Greatly perturbed lest her savoury should have been the cause, Lizzie promised to be very quiet downstairs and to go in, as soon as she heard her stirring, with a cup of tea.

I had my bath, dressed and shaved in half my usual time, and when I left my room Pamela was on her way from her bath. She said she had slept well.

'I have never seen anyone asleep so contentedly as Stella,' she said.

We stood at the banister-rail, listening. Lizzie was chattering in the nursery while Stella drank her tea. Stella's voice had a joyous lilt in it.

The telephone rang; Lizzie answered it, called me, and went on to the kitchen. When I ran down, Stella's door was shut. It was Commander Brooke. I reported all well and promised to bring Stella back within a hour.

'Quick with breakfast, Lizzie!' I called.

The sun was shining on a wet, glittering world. Stella had not appeared when Pamela came down and did not answer when we knocked at her door. We went into the garden to look for her; she was there, standing motionless beside the dead tree. She heard us and turned her head slowly. There was no need to ask whether she had slept and was well; she was brimming over with joy; tears of happiness shone in her eyes.

'Oh, why didn't you tell me?' she said tremulously. 'Didn't you know? She came to me in the night: she was with me in the nursery. I was afraid that it must be a dream, but Lizzie has seen her. It was she who was on the stairs. It is my mother. Didn't you guess?'

Chapter X

PAMELA'S EXPERIMENT

NO ONE SPOKE until we were seated at the breakfast-table. Pamela looked as desperate as I felt. None of us could eat – Stella was lost in a state of dreamy exaltation; Pamela and I, in our distress. I pushed my plate aside and questioned Stella.

'Now tell us what Lizzie told you,' I said, and Pamela broke in, 'She did wrong to say anything at all!'

'No, no!' Stella protested. 'It was simply that I told her how I had fainted, and Lizzie said she had so nearly done the same thing. She said that in another moment I would have seen her, as clear as life! Oh, why did I faint?'

'I am convinced,' I told her, 'that Lizzie only imagined that apparition.'

Stella shook her head: 'I know it is true.'

'And you want it to be true?' Pamela asked her.

'But, of course! Could anything be more wonderful?'

We were silent: this was an astounding reaction and created complications to which no end could be foreseen.

'You told me,' she said pleadingly to Pamela, 'that you believe spirits haunt the places where they were happy: why should anyone be afraid of a happy ghost?'

'Because,' I burst out, 'it's unnatural to see them! It is overpowering: it makes people ill!'

'Only if you are afraid,' she protested; 'only if you don't understand.'

'You fainted,' I said quickly, 'yet you tell me that you were not frightened.'

Stella looked ashamed.

'It was weak of me,' she said wretchedly: 'it was just that I didn't expect ... Lizzie was afraid,' she went on in a different tone, hard and angry. 'She was frightened; you'd think she had seen something evil. She talked about – about ... ' Stella choked; Lizzie had outraged and shocked her. 'About the priest,' she said.

'Lizzie is very superstitious,' Pamela said gently: 'that is why Roddy and I believe that she imagined the apparition.'

'And now,' Stella contended, 'you say that she *was* there and that she made me faint.'

Pamela sighed: 'Oh, Stella darling, we don't know what we should think. We can't *know* anything; only wonder and guess.' I sat down beside Stella and pleaded with her.

'Stella, you are a very reasonable person. Max Hilliard said a fine thing about you: he said that you have integrity of mind. That means that you have the courage to refuse to deceive yourself, no matter what you might *wish* to think. I beg you, try to have that sort of courage now: don't delude yourself about this.'

'"Integrity of mind," Stella repeated thoughtfully. 'I would like to deserve that. But I am not deceiving myself: this is true!'

'You can't *know* that it is true,' Pamela urged.

'Ah, but I do!'

'But you can't,' I argued; 'there is no proof.'

She paused, meditating. Her face was very serious; her luminous joy was gone; we had spoilt it. There was a small bowl of pansies on the table and she kept turning it between her hands. 'I am going to tell you something,' she said at last.

Shy of me, she looked at Pamela while she spoke.

'It was not there on the stairs that I felt her presence, but all night she was with me in the nursery; there is no doubt of that at all.'

'Stella,' Pamela said, 'you were asleep!'

'Not all the time; I was awake a good deal. I was happy – too happy to sleep – happier than I have ever been in my life. I just lay, warm and quiet, watching the light, and knowing that she was there.'

'What light?' I asked sharply.

'The firelight, at first, and, when I woke later and that was gone, the night-light on the table.'

I turned to Pamela and asked whether she had left a night-light in the room. No, she had not.

'Didn't you?' Stella exclaimed. 'A baby's night-light with a tiny flame? Didn't you, Pamela? Isn't that strange!'

'And isn't that a proof that you were dreaming?' I reminded her that she had told us how often she dreamed of the nursery and the light and tried to make her see how probable it was that, when she slept in the same room, the dream had returned. She smiled.

'But it was your curtains and your eiderdown! No, I was not asleep. And there was another curious thing,' she went on: 'the room was full of the scent I love best of all, mimosa, and I was wearing no scent.'

Pamela glanced at me, startled. Neither of us spoke. Stella went on:

'Once I heard a soft, whispering voice, saying pretty words, loving words; I couldn't make out what they were, but they made me feel – oh, safe, and loved, and cherished, and comforted.'

'Poor little Stella!' Pamela said.

Stella smiled at her, saying, 'You had your mother until you were sixteen, didn't you?'

It was ruthless to try to tear down this illusion, but to let Stella live in it would be worse.

'You are obstinate,' I declared.

She looked into my face searchingly, disappointed and distressed.

'I don't understand you, Roderick! Why should you try to prove that it was not my mother? Why should you mind? Because, now, you and Pamela need not be upset any longer about the haunting of your house, and for me – surely you understand that – for me it is an unimaginably happy thing?'

I did not know what to say, nor did Pamela; it was what Stella said next that fixed my wavering decision. She said, 'Another time I shall see her, perhaps.'

Now resentment rose in my throat. This situation was atrocious; it could not go on. It had been bad enough already, this cult of the sainted mother, this fixation on dead virtue, dead standards, dead taste. What ordinary mortal could hope to interest Stella while she worshipped that pattern of perfection? And now was she going to centre her affections on a *revenant* and live, obsessed, with a ghostly companion? I had seen a woman's mind wrecked by a vaguer delusion. And it was I, in my crass scepticism and stupefied absorption, who had dragged Stella into all this! Well, I would drag her out of it again before it destroyed her reason, even if, in the process, I had to half break her heart!

I said, 'You are not coming here again, Stella,' and stood up.

Stella sprang to her feet and stood by Pamela, clutching her shoulder and staring at me.

'You can't mean it!'

Pamela put a hand over hers, compassionately, but upheld me.

'I am afraid Roddy is right.' She looked very unhappy.

Stella stared at her incredulously.

'But my own mother!' she said.

'I mean it,' I told her. 'Now listen, Stella: either there is no ghost there and your imagination is running to dangerous lengths, or there is one, and you were in its presence last night on the landing, and it made you ill. You were in such a ghastly faint, Stella, that for a moment I thought you had died.'

I broke off. The memory of that instant overwhelmed me. Stella spoke gently: 'I am so sorry,' she said.

I looked at her again and, in my bitter confusion and bafflement, spoke recklessly.

'You think it was good, whatever you encountered last night. I think it was frightful, and you are never going to take such a risk again. This house is no place for you. The Commander is right, and I have been worse than a fool. But we are not beaten,' I went on, contending against the unseen enemy, not against Stella now: 'We are going to rid this place of spirits and sounds and hauntings! There is exorcism in the last resort!'

Stella screamed. It was a choked cry of horror.

'Roddy!' Pamela exclaimed, rising in angry protest. I was appalled; I had said a brutal thing.

Stella stood rigid, her fist to her mouth, wide, shocked eyes on mine.

'That's what they do to devils,' she stammered, 'to drive devils down to hell.' She was shaking.

'No, no, I didn't mean it!'

I implored her to forgive me, to be calm, but the rigidity would not leave her body or the horror go from her face.

'Stella, darling Stella,' Pamela pleaded, 'don't look like that!'

'You've got to swear to me – to swear!' Stella said, 'that you will never do that.'

It was impossible to leave her with that horror in her mind. 'I promise,' I said, 'that I will never do it without your consent.'

'If you did,' she said in a low voice, 'I think I should go out of my mind.'

'You must trust Roddy's promise,' Pamela said.

Stella broke down.

'Oh, I do, I do trust him ... Oh, Pamela ... '

I went out to get the car, leaving Stella sobbing in Pamela's arms.

Pamela did not come with us, and we were silent until The Avenue came in sight, then I slowed down.

'You have got to forgive me, Stella. I am not being selfish,' I said.

She answered in a faint voice, 'I know.'

'You think I am cruel.'

'I have been longing all my life for my mother, and she came to me, and you are separating us.'

'Stella – this is terrible.'

'But that's not the worst part of it,' she went on tensely. 'My mother isn't happy; she can't rest; there is something that she wants, and it may be something that I could do. I believe it is, and I must find out – I must! I would face anything to give her rest.'

My heart sank, listening to her: a child's wild chivalry and devotion – and for a ghost!

'Listen,' I said. 'This means as much to me as to you: you don't believe that now, and I can't make you understand, in your present state of mind. I won't say more; but I want to make Cliff End safe for you, Stella: can you understand that much? I want to be able to let you come there again. If this is the spirit of your mother that is haunting it – a spirit all goodness and gentleness and love – if there really is nothing to be afraid of, then you shall come. But we have to make sure of that. Try to be patient; give me time.'

Her face was taut.

'I don't think I can wait,' she answered. 'I don't think I can.'

We had reached Wilmcote. I drew up.

'I'll do everything possible,' I promised. 'Meanwhile, don't desert us: you'll come and bathe with Pamela, won't you?'

She shook her head.

'I'll wait until I may come to the house.'

I was hurt.

'Is your friendship for the house, Stella,' I asked, 'not for us?'

Her lips trembled.

'Don't make me cry,' she whispered, and hurried to the door. The Commander opened it; he looked keenly at Stella and said something to her in a low tone, then he waited for me to come in.

He had aged. As he stood before the fireplace in his study I saw the face of a very tired man. I told him that Stella was perfectly well again and had spent a peaceful night, and I gave him a fuller account of how we had found her unconscious at the top of the stairs. His voice was like frost:

'Where your servant believes she saw an apparition?'

'She is a superstitious old woman,' I told him, and explained why I believed that Lizzie had felt an actual psychic atmosphere but had imagined the apparition.

He listened intently; I felt he would have been glad to accept my theory but could not do so.

'What do you mean by a "psychic atmosphere"?' he demanded.

'I mean,' I replied specifically, 'some condition which reflects emotions or events out of the past and can create hallucinations and produce sensations of fear.'

His face hardened as he listened. He did not invite me to sit down.

'You will remember,' he said coldly, 'that I gave you an indication of this.'

'I appreciate that.'

'I regret that you have been disturbed.'

'We believe that if we could discover something about the cause of the disturbance we might find some way to bring it to an end – that is my sister's feeling, at least.'

His eyes flashed. 'Your sister would do well not to meddle,' he said tartly, then, recollecting himself, he begged my pardon. 'I fear,' he added, 'that you will find that you must accustom yourselves to this "atmosphere": I trust it will prove harmless to you and your friends.'

I replied hotly; his 'meddle' had infuriated me; the house was supposed to be ours, after all.

'I think you owe it to us to give us any help that you can.'

'I can give you no help.'

I protested vehemently: 'One room is uninhabitable – a friend of ours was made ill by depression there; our servant has had a shock, and I, myself, experienced the most sickening sensation on the stairs.'

I broke off; I knew what was coming, and I deserved it. His voice shook with anger.

'And yet, knowing all this, you and your sister have undermined my authority, flouted my judgment, and induced Stella to visit Cliff End!'

I had no defence.

'We supposed it was all over,' I answered weakly. 'We have told her that we feel that, until all this has been cleared away, she must not come again.'

'There will be no question of that, now or at any time,' he answered: 'my granddaughter is going abroad.'

His voice was as stony as his face, heavy and dead. I was dismissed. We exchanged formal good mornings and I left. Stella did not appear to bid me goodbye.

When I reached home I left the car in the drive and walked up the knoll; the wide view from up there, the unbroken vista of sea and sky and moorland, should have had power to quiet storming thoughts, but now it brought no relief. I loved Stella and I had done her harm that might be irreparable. I loved her with strength and simplicity that did not belong at all to our jangling, tangled civilisation, but belonged to this changeless earth and all that is unchanging in the spirit of man, and I had destroyed her peace. What was there that I could do? Yesterday I had felt a giant confidence in my power to make Stella love me; I had imagined that I was going to open to her a world of happiness of which she had scarcely dreamed; today she thought of me as an enemy, and soon she would be out of my reach.

'My granddaughter is going abroad.'

I found Pamela in the sitting-room, reading a voluminous letter written on thin paper.

'Nesta's biennial,' she told me with a wavering smile. She put it down.

I heard Lizzie sweeping the stairs, sobs and hiccoughs accompanying her broom; so Pamela had reduced her to tears! Well, Lizzie had made trouble enough.

I told Pamela that I had left Stella bitterly unhappy and determined not to see us again until our ban was removed, and told her what the Commander had said. She was dismayed.

'He'll send her back to that school,' she declared. 'They wanted her, once, to stay as a pupil-teacher … Back to that prison. She hasn't a friend in the place.'

I sat in the window-seat, submerged in the most barren of all emotions, remorse. The farther Stella went from us, the better for herself; so it seemed to me then.

'It will break her down,' Pamela said.

'Scarcely more than we have done between us,' I replied bitterly. 'He's right to send her away; he has been right all the time.'

Pamela shook her head.

'With all this behind her, and her mind obsessed with it? She wouldn't forget; she would fret desperately; it would make her ill. Roddy, we can't let her go.'

I turned on Pamela, but it was myself I was rending.

'For pity's sake,' I burst out, 'stop thinking of yourself as Stella's heaven-sent guardian! You're not! You and I have done nothing but make hay with her life for our own pleasure: now leave her alone!'

The silence lasted long enough for me to hear the ugliness of my own words. Now what would Pamela do? She seldom let real rudeness pass, and she was apt to reply with action, not speech.

'Another course is open,' she said composedly: 'we could shut up this house.'

'Where should we go? What should we live on? How would that help?'

'You would not have to worry about me. Read this – the last page.'

She handed me the letter from Nesta. Having flicked over pages concerning soil, bulbs, and fertilisers, I came on this:

When you can tear yourself away for three months, come and partner me here. You'd earn your keep and earn it hard. I've always been sorry that our old plan fell through, and I'd really love to have you at any time. So would mother. Besides, with the gift of the gab that you have and the drop of venom, you might find Dublin your spiritual home.

I handed it back.

'Well, that's always a refuge if all this becomes too much for you.'

'And you?'

'Oh, I can live in a garret and write plays.'

We were both silent. I could hear the tick of the grandfather clock in the hall. The room was full of scent from a bowl of roses and warm and sweet with the sunlight that poured in. There were two sailing-boats in the bay.

'Pamela, I'm sorry,' I said.

'It's rotten for you, Roddy,' she answered: 'worse than for me. But

I don't think,' she added slowly, 'that it will do any good to clear out now; it's too late – for Stella, I mean. Her life has been changed and can never settle back into what it used to be. I think we must stand by and see her through.'

I did not reply. I had started painting the slatted shelves in the greenhouse. I put on my overall and went on with the job now, leaving Pamela writing letters at her desk. Presently she came and stood watching while I worked.

'I have been thinking,' she said.

I was suddenly back in childhood, in Cambridge, busy with a broken bicycle, Pamela, in her gym tunic, her hair in pigtails, standing by. She would find me out on all such occasions to propound the speculations of her precocious mind. 'I have been thinking,' she would begin.

'Do you believe that Mary was with Stella in the nursery?' she asked me.

'I do not: it was wish-thinking,' I replied.

'But one could understand it so well, Roddy, and if it is true, don't you see, that may be what Mary wants – the thing that has kept her haunting and restless – longing for her child?'

'If that is so, she should rest now,' I said.

'Perhaps she will.'

'I haven't much hope of it. I don't think you are right. I don't believe Stella was near any ghost.'

'Don't you? But why?'

'She didn't feel that horrible cold.'

'Yes, that's true; she felt warm, she said, safe and warm.'

'I felt the cold; so did Lizzie.'

'I did, too, once.'

'You see!'

'No, Roddy, I don't. Because I don't think that Stella was dreaming or imagining that Mary was with her; I think it's the likeliest thing in the world that it's true, and when she told us I felt convinced … Roddy' – her voice changed – 'could there be *two* ghosts?'

I looked at Pamela; her face was alight with excitement; I stuck my brush in the turpentine pot and sat on a box to think.

'It's possible,' I replied, and added, 'Meredith was as cold as a stone.'

'As cold as a snake,' Pamela said. 'But Meredith didn't die here.'

'No.'

'Mary and Carmel, then?'

'Other people have died here, don't forget.'

'Yes – and times can mix, I suppose.'

'Time has no existence, I imagine, to them.'

'Carmel died here, and without a doctor or a priest. Father Anson must have said Masses for her, of course … '

'Didn't Father Anson promise to send you the address of that nurse?'

'Why, yes!' Pamela exclaimed. 'And she lives in Bristol. Let's try to see her on Friday!'

'I think we should.'

'I'll send Lizzie to Father Anson with a note. It will do her good. I scolded her too much.'

'Lizzie's a brick to stay.'

'Lizzie's a Trojan: her loyalty is a rock. If only she wouldn't gossip!'

'She'll do that,' I said, "while grass grows and water runs."'

'She will.'

Lizzie was cheered by her errand, which involved a ride in the local bus. She brought back a kindly note from Father Anson, expressing his deep concern, and a letter of introduction to Miss Holloway, who now ran a 'Centre of Healing through Harmony' at Clifton. He asked her to see us on Friday afternoon, telling her that we were 'anxious about certain matters concerning Cliff End,' and desired information which she alone might be able to give. 'It would be helpful,' he concluded, 'if you would treat my friends with the utmost confidence and give them particulars of the events preceding Mary Meredith's death.'

The note was stiff enough in its tone – unlike Father Anson. We observed that he did not ask her to tell us about the death of Carmel. Did he think the request would scare her off? We sent his letter, with a covering note, to Miss Holloway, feeling very doubtful whether she would reply.

The day dragged on, the longest and saddest that we had spent at Cliff End. Pamela was preoccupied; my work went vilely, and I was pleased enough, in the afternoon, to learn that we had a visitor, even though it was, as Lizzie said, 'only Dr Scott.'

Poor Scott! He was so polite and careful, so transparently curious, yet he had asked no questions whatever about hauntings and ghosts. Pamela had accepted only one of his repeated invitations to tennis and then she had forgotten to go, and now she was going to put him off again. He had brought her a present – a small black dog.

'It's a Scottie,' he explained to me wistfully, 'for her to remember me by.'

'Isn't that a magnanimous return?' Pamela said, smiling. 'Come, boy! Come, Bobby! Nice laddie! Beautiful pup!'

She picked up the quivering, loose-skinned creature and fondled it. Oh, gosh, was Pamela going to get silly about a Scottie? I had no use for these stumpy-legged terriers. A dog should be a noble, upstanding animal. Give me a wolf-dog or an Alsatian or an Afghan hound. However, Pamela had to have live things round her, and at present any distraction was better than none.

We kept Scott to dinner. Lizzie always enjoyed a visitor and rose well to last-minute demands, but she was not pleased when she discovered the dog on the scene, nor was Whisky, who accompanied her when she came in to lay the table and saw Bobby sitting in Pamela's chair. After circling with slow, tigerish movements, malign eyes riveted on the pup, he leaped on to the back of the chair and from there snarled diabolical menaces at the frightened Bobby. Before anyone could intervene, Whisky had pounced, delivered one fierce blow with claws out, and darted out of the room. Bobby was not hurt, but Lizzie's feelings were deeply wounded.

'There now! The poor little cat!' she exclaimed commiseratingly, and went to console her ill-used pet.

Scott smiled apologetically: 'I've created a situation, I'm afraid.' We assured him that it could be adjusted, since Whisky's and Bobby's spheres of influence need not overlap. To have this nonsense to laugh at was good.

Scott was good company enough when he could talk on one of his three subjects – sailing, photography, and dogs. He told us that he had a share in a small sailing-boat; unfortunately, it had a damaged keel and was being repaired at the moment, but should be ready soon. He wanted to take us to Lundy and to take snap-shots of the puffins. 'What about Sunday, tomorrow week, if it is fine?' He enjoyed making these plans. We told him nothing of our troubles or of Commander Brooke's decree and said that we would enjoy the sail.

Scott hated to leave; I suppose he was lonely and dull in his lodgings. It was after eleven when he left, and we established Bobby on a rug in the cloak-room and went upstairs. I went first and turned on the landing light. The switch was awkwardly placed, on the far side of the studio door. I resolved to have that two-way switch in the hall without more delay. The landing window was uncurtained; Lizzie would no longer go upstairs after dark. Only a faint glimmer remained in the summer sky. Pamela looked pale. It had been a miserable day. I said: 'I hope you'll be able to sleep.'

'That doesn't matter; I can always lie on in the morning,' she said absently, then gave me a quick, nervous glance and went to her room.

Pamela was rarely nervous, but there was reason enough for it. One could not move in this house after dark now without half-expecting some ghastly shock.

Was Stella lying awake, breaking her heart? My thoughts were not peaceful; it was a long time before I fell asleep.

A hideous howling woke me – it was the dog! Now Pamela, I thought, would rush down, and I did not want that. I was glad, when I went out of my room, to see that her door was shut. It was strange that it remained shut, though – she slept so lightly. Was she too scared to move? I knocked and, when she did not reply, thought she must have already gone down. The noise the dog was making was ghastly – an agonised, wavering wail; it made my blood run cold, literally – or something else did. I stood by the banisters, leaning on them, weak from the cold and overwhelmed with shame at my complete loss of nerve.

The landing was dark; no moonlight came in, but near the head of the stairs, outside the door of the studio, I began to see something

– a faint coil of blue-white light. I would have to pass close to it to go downstairs, and that I could not do. I put out my left hand, groping for the light switch inside the door of my bedroom, but withdrew it, because I saw the luminous whiteness stir. All warmth drained out of me as I stood there, watching, while the wreath of mist condensed and its incandescence intensified with a palpitating rhythm, like breath. I saw it swirl slowly and grow; it was spiralling up and, at the same time, sliding towards the head of the stairs.

The howling below rose to a crescendo of terror. I switched the light on and the nebulous thing became almost invisible; still, I knew it was there and I could not pass through it. I vaulted the banisters and tore, ahead of it, down the stairs.

The dog was in the middle of the hall, crouched, facing the stairs, crawling backwards with a vile, craven movement, his throat stretched in that frantic howl. I opened the front door and he shot out.

Where was Pamela? I called and heard her answer in a faint voice from the nursery. She was in there, lying full-length on the bed, clutching both sides of it and shaking from head to foot. She looked up at me with glass-grey eyes.

I pulled her to her feet. 'Into the kitchen,' I ordered, and we ran down the passage without looking up at the stairs.

The kitchen was warm; there was comfort and safety in it. I turned on the light. We stood, shivering, our backs against the door.

'Look at the cat,' Pamela whispered. He was standing on the table, his back arched, every hair starting, his eyes wild.

'Lizzie,' she gasped, 'I must go to her … Her heart's not strong.'

I would not allow it. I had never known Pamela to faint, but she looked as if she might do so now. I made her sit down. If I went out to the passage now, I would, perhaps, see it for myself – see what shape, whose form, what nature of thing this was. But I did not want to see it, and less still did I want it to touch me. I had made it more horrible, making it invisible, by turning on the lights. I never did anything more reluctantly than opening the kitchen door.

There was mist in the passage, that was all, as if a wreath of sea-fog had blown in; it drifted into the nursery and did not come out again.

'Are you all right, Lizzie?' I called, opening her door.

A shaking voice replied from the darkness: 'Oh, holy saints! Oh, Mr Roddy – I'm near dead with the fright! Did the dog see something? Was she on the landing again?'

'Rubbish, Lizzie! It's just that the dog was afraid in a strange place. They get hysterical; you ought to know that. Go to sleep now. Good night.'

I went back to Pamela. 'There was a sort of cloud,' I told her. 'It came down the stairs and floated into the nursery without taking shape.'

She shivered. 'I knew it was coming in there.'

'What were you doing in there, Pamela?'

'I wanted to find out.'

'You went to sleep there deliberately?'

She gave me a twisted smile. She revived the fire and put on a kettle, and we sat trying to warm ourselves at the comforting glow.

'As a matter of fact, Roddy,' she confessed, 'I panicked. The dog was too much for me. I was sure he was seeing something. In another minute, if you hadn't come in, I would have been tearing out by the window.'

Pamela's temerity had often startled me; this time I thought she had gone to extremes.

'If you're going to do things like this!' I protested.

She said, 'I wanted to know whether Stella was dreaming last night.'

'And *was* Stella dreaming?'

'No.'

'You mean – what *do* you mean?'

'It happened just as she said, Roddy. Everything was peaceful and I slept. Then I woke up and the room was – I don't know how to describe it – full of a lovely sort of tranquillity, and scented, and warm. I even saw the soft glimmer of light; I even heard whispered words.'

'What were they?'

'I couldn't make out.'

'Are you sure you weren't dreaming?'

'I tied a knot in my handkerchief: here it is.'

'Go on.'

'Then the light went out and a low moaning began. It was a piteous sound. It didn't frighten me, and I was trying to make up my mind to say something, but suddenly everything changed. I think it was before the dog started howling, and the change was in me. I felt terribly afraid. I tried to cry out. I wanted to rush out, away from it, into the garden, but I couldn't move. Then the dog began. I was able to move then, but I was in a panic. I had just sense enough left to know that if I rushed out I might lose my head and go over the cliff, so I held on to the bed.'

I said nothing. It was a bad story. When the kettle boiled I made tea, and we drank it in exhausted silence.

'You'll have to go away,' I said.

Pamela spoke obstinately, resolutely: 'No, Roddy. We are on to it at last. If we can stick it out now, we'll get at the truth.'

'And go off our heads in the process?'

'I won't sleep in that room again or let anyone else sleep in it.'

'We'll all be sleeping on the doorstep soon,' I said bitterly, and asked her, 'Do you really want to stay?'

'I do.'

'What about Lizzie?'

'I think she won't leave without me, and if she did, we could cook for ourselves.'

'You're determined to see it through, then?'

'I am, Roddy – aren't you?'

'I am, naturally.'

'I feel sure there are two spirits,' she said.

'Very well,' I agreed, 'we can work on that hypothesis; it gives us a definite problem to bite on, anyhow: who are the two spirits, and why are they restless? What do they want?'

'There is Mary,' Pamela said in a tired voice, 'Mary, who sighs and weeps, suffers a nightmare of misery in the studio, looks down in anguish over the stairs, and comforts her daughter and gives her a light. And there is the other – terrifying, unmerciful, cold.'

'I believe you could sleep now,' I said, rising.

'I'm good an' tired.'

'Come along. We can only hope that Miss Holloway will throw a light on it. She must have heard that the house is haunted and have thought about it. She can probably explain a great deal.'

'I expect she could,' Pamela said, 'but I don't, somehow, believe that she will.'

All was normal now on the stairs and landing. We went to bed.

Chapter XI

MISS HOLLOWAY

MISS HOLLOWAY wrote briefly that she would see us on Friday at six o'clock. I arranged by telephone with Milroy to come to the theatre at about three and read my play to him. His eagerness would have pleased me if I had been capable of taking pleasure in anything to do with my work, but this play, which had so disastrously blanketed my senses against the whole outside world, was itself shut out now. A few reviews and articles were all that I could contrive to write.

The nights were detestable: the house was a hollow cavern of mournful sound. To my ears, it was not sound so much as a kind of vibration, just below the range of hearing, and Lizzie, fortunately, appeared to hear nothing at all, but Pamela told me that, to her, it was a moaning human voice. She was stupefied from fatigue. On Sunday night and again on Tuesday we were both out of bed, exploring and listening. We had begun to distrust the evidence of our senses, feel our hearts lurch at shadows, and take every murmur of winds and waves for a supernatural sound.

The dog did not return. When I telephoned Scott he said that he supposed it would turn up at his place. Later he rang up to tell me that a friend had recognised Bobby in a shop, where the dog had been taken in as a miserable stray. 'He is in a bad condition,' Scott said rather crossly: 'hysterical, his nerves all to rags.' I told him he had roused us all at night with his hysterics, but I did not explain. This was unfair to the dog, but was there fairness anywhere?

On Wednesday Pamela received a letter from Stella which upset her a good deal. She read a part of it to me. Stella was more articulate about herself on paper than in speech.

> *I have told him that I will not go abroad. How could I go, when he is obviously not well? But it would be dishonest of me to pretend that this is my chief reason, and, indeed, as he says, my obduracy is making him worse. But, Pamela, I cannot go. All my life I have so longed for my mother. You would not believe how intensely I have imagined, sometimes, that she came to me at night. That was only make-believe, but in the nursery she really did come. I would have to be a poet to tell you how heavenly it was. I think she is lonely, too, and wants me as I want her. So you must let me come. Dear, dear Pamela, please try to persuade Roderick, and write to say that I may. You are my friend; you don't want my heart to break.*

Pamela put down the letter and spoke shakily.

'She is being torn in pieces.'

I was moved, but not ready to give way. I read and re-read the words of her melancholy song, which Stella had copied and enclosed … 'Fate denying … '

'All we can do for Stella,' I said, 'is get rid of the danger, wherever it comes from. Tell her we are doing our best.'

Pamela wrote, repeating the assurances that I had already given to Stella, telling her of our appointment with Miss Holloway, and promising to leave nothing undone. She said, too, that we both thought, grievously as we would miss her, that Stella would be wise to yield to her grandfather and go abroad for a time.

'It is a feeble, cowardly letter,' Pamela declared as she stamped it. 'We are letting her down.'

Pamela was haggard; Lizzie, when she came in with lunch, looked at her and then looked at me and shook her head.

'God pity you, it's like ghosts the two of you are,' she said. 'I'd be afeard, meeting you in the dark. You want to make up your minds and go from this place soon, or you'll be past having any minds to make up. The worst of it is, till I have a refrigerator, I can't make nice sweets for you, and we can't get one till you know if you can stay. The coffee-cream I'm after making won't set.'

'The situation is really becoming serious,' Pamela declared. I felt that I could forgive Lizzie a great deal; she risked her immortal soul for us, staying in this ungodly house, and she made us smile.

She was delighted to be going for the night to the Jessups', and Charlie had promised to come and carry Whisky's basket across the fields.

We would all be better for a night away from Cliff End. I hoped, too, that the visit to Bristol would give me a fresh start with the play. If Milroy liked it, he would make useful suggestions; I ought, then, to be able to get down to the revision and lend it up for final approval by Adrian Ballaster within a couple of months. If the play was put on at Bristol I could count on one or two of the London critics coming down. It was important. I must try to break through this deadly inertia – but who can live in two worlds at once? Perhaps *Salome* would help to quicken one's theatre nerve again. And perhaps Miss Holloway would give us the key to the obscure tragedy that was growing around us like a labyrinth.

Pamela became irrationally optimistic about the visit to Bristol. In spite of her fatigue, after a week of broken nights, she was in good spirits on Friday when we set out.

Claude Milroy received us in his private office at the theatre with every manifestation of delight. He squeezed Pamela's hand, beaming up at her through the rimless magnifying glasses that gave him the look of a solemn cherub. He adjusted the angle of my chair, fussed with the blinds to give me the best light, and placed a carafe of water at my right hand.

'That you should give us the first offer of your play, my dear, dear RDF!' he murmured, making me wretchedly nervous.

'Isn't it a truism,' I said, 'that critics can't write plays?'

'There was *The Green Goddess*,' said a crisp voice at the door, 'and Shaw was a critic once.'

This was alarming: Ballaster had come in. I read scepticism in every inch of his trim, disciplined figure and every line of his vigorous face. I had not wanted Ballaster to hear my rough draft.

There was nothing to be done, however; Milroy was as pleased as Punch at having secured the personal attendance of the great Adrian. I had to pretend that I felt honoured.

I read to this audience of three, stumblingly, detesting the men and my play. When I grew husky Milroy leaped to his feet and poured water for me. Neither of them spoke a word, even between the acts, and Pamela had to sit silent, too. I thought she must be bored: however, she had brought this on herself; she had chosen to hear the whole thing over again. She had one little triumph: at the passage to which she had objected – the bit about leprosy – Ballaster said: 'Tchut, tchut, tchut!' and Milroy coughed. I stopped to say that I thought of altering this, and read on.

At the end there was a pause. Milroy opened his mouth and closed it again without speaking, his gleaming glasses turned on Ballaster's face. Pamela looked pale. The pause stretched away into the future, where I saw myself, in a semi-basement in Edith Grove, trying to light a fire with damp sticks and the scripts of rejected plays. The fire had gone out again before anyone spoke.

'Contemporary; meaty; good theatre,' Ballaster said.

Milroy exploded: 'Oh, boy!' he cried, his pink face damp with excitement. 'Oh, boy, it's a play!'

They plunged at once into questions of casting. There was a contention over Wendy; Milroy did not believe she could do it; Ballaster said, 'Let her try.'

I was relieved; I would have hated to intervene, but I owed something to Wendy over this. Their views for the other parts were the same as my own. Talk about dates, sets, advertising – all matters which interested me little – took another quarter of an hour, and when these seemed settled Ballaster turned to me.

'Alter that climax, can you, and let me see it again? Give more relief in the third act and jizz up the second. Play up the girl – Jennifer. Nicolette should be good in that part. Get a touch of humour into those last scenes. It's gone sombre on you, hasn't it? Get drunk on champagne and go at it again. If it comes out the way I think it will, we'll do it in the second week of November. When can we have it? In about ten days?'

I held out for a month.

'First week of October? Good!'

Hospitality was pressed upon us, but I wanted to collect my wits before facing Miss Holloway, and made excuses to get away.

It had been exhilarating. To Pamela and me, drinking a hurried tea in the lounge of our hotel, counting broods of theatrical chickens yet unhatched, the trouble at Cliff End seemed unbelievable.

Miss Holloway lived on a height at Clifton. Her 'Centre of Healing through Harmony' was a considerable bath-stone villa on the side of the hill overlooking the wooded downs. White beds were set in open galleries; sad-looking women paced up and down the gravelled drive in sandals, with thin hair hanging loose. We waited for ten minutes in a chaste parlour decorated with reproductions of Botticelli and plaster reliefs of bambini in swaddling clothes. As six o'clock struck, the matron came in.

Miss Holloway was a tall woman, and her impressiveness was increased by the starched cap which she wore and the long, full skirt of her dark green dress. Her eyes were deep-set in a sallow, symmetrical face – dark eyes, which she used effectively, seldom blinking, and focussing on one's own. Her voice was strong, but gently and smoothly modulated.

'How is dear Father Anson?'

She sat down. Her large hands lay on the round polished table, still. I received a curious impression from their stillness: it seemed wary.

'Thank you,' I replied, 'he is well.'

She inclined her head slightly; it was the gesture of a distinguished person giving audience.

'I am quite free for forty minutes. I am glad to have been able to arrange it. You are in trouble. Can I help you in some way?'

Absorbed in the woman's planned personality, I left Pamela to tell our story. She did it well and rather fully; only concerning Stella she was reserved.

A smile came to Miss Holloway's face. I didn't like the smile.

'My poor little Stella!' she said. 'Deprived of such a mother, so young.'

'You lived with her for some years, didn't you?' Pamela asked.

'For ten years,' the musical voice replied. 'I sacrificed ten years of my career to complete the work that Mary had begun. That was my tribute to my martyred friend.'

We were silenced.

'I have not regretted it,' she said.

Pamela recovered first.

'We thought you would, perhaps, tell us whether Mary Meredith – whether she went through some great sorrow at Cliff End. We hear so much weeping,' she told her.

'Sorrow was Mary's portion,' Miss Holloway answered; 'but she did not weep.'

Pamela looked at me, disconcerted. Our hypothesis was thrown out.

'You may satisfy yourselves,' Miss Holloway said firmly, 'that if any uneasy spirit haunts Cliff End, it is not Mary's. Mary has passed to higher spheres.'

'It is a woman's voice,' Pamela said.

Miss Holloway said 'Yes?' gently.

It was curiously difficult to ask questions. Our mission was, after all, intrusive. This had been an intimate friendship, a deep personal grief.

'Perhaps,' I said diffidently, 'you would be so very kind as to tell us something about the household? I believe you knew Mary Meredith very well?'

She bowed her head in assent.

'I knew Mary as no one else ever knew her.'

What next? Nobody spoke. Miss Holloway sat still. The fingertips of one hand were poised lightly, touching those of the other; they seemed to be listening. She was not going to help us; she did not wholly believe Pamela's story and she was not sure for what purpose we had come. With extreme caution, she was deciding on her course.

Pamela said in her gentlest voice, aware that she was speaking to this woman of a dear, lost friend: 'We have no right to ask – no right at all to intrude; but we think that possibly her grief, her emotions, may have left some influence in the house. If we could understand it, it would not be quite so agitating for us: the mystery is rather tormenting, you see. And I hoped, too, that we might even do some-thing to help. You would be doing us a great kindness if you would tell us something of her life at Cliff End.'

'I understand,' Miss Holloway said. 'I will try.'

Her voice became yet more quiet as she began: 'Our first meeting took place here, in this very room. This was an ordinary nursing home at that time, and my duties were those of an ordinary nurse. Mary had been sent here to recoup after influenza. We recognised one another at once. My life's purpose – to create a centre of healing which would use means beyond the physical – found a deep response in her spirit. "Let us do this together," she said. Mary had a little money inherited from her mother, and she was eager to use it in doing good.

'Alas, there followed the journey to Spain, that disastrous marriage, and the entrance of her evil genius into Mary's beautiful life.'

'Carmel!' Pamela exclaimed.

'Carmel.'

The orderly and, I thought, not unprepared narration went on.

'They were together at Cliff End when an appeal came to my matron that I might be allowed to come to Mary as a private nurse. I was sent. Her illness was called jaundice, but to me it was apparent that it was due to grief and shock. I set to work to heal her through non-material means. I persuaded her to give me her full confidence. She never withdrew it. The illness passed, but Mary's heart was broken. "I felt it breaking," she told me, "like a bell of glass." It never gave out the sound of gladness again.'

Miss Holloway was talking and telling us nothing. This was deliberate, I felt sure of it; she was fencing: there was antagonism here, either to Father Anson or to us. If she had her way, we would leave as ignorant and helpless as we came. I was determined, at whatever cost of crude behaviour, to have facts. 'Meredith had had an affair with Carmel,' I broke in.

Miss Holloway assented with a gesture.

'But, good heavens,' I exclaimed, 'Mary knew it – you say she knew it and yet the girl stayed on!'

The matron's voice was soft and even, rebuking my outburst: 'Mary was unique: a woman of infinite magnanimity.'

Pamela had subsided into silence. I had never seen her baffled before. I carried on.

'Carmel remained in the house! She accompanied Mary to France!'

'You do not help the weak to overcome their sin by removing them from temptation,' Miss Holloway explained patiently. 'They must be encouraged to stand firm and resist. With anyone less depraved than those two, Mary's shining magnanimity, her trust, her tender, watchful guidance, would have prevailed.'

'You mean,' I said, staggered, 'that she deliberately … '

The word betrayed me: I was presuming to criticise, daring to disapprove. Miss Holloway's sallow face grew dark with anger, the hands on the table clenched, as she answered, with tightened throat:

'Mary refrained, Mr Fitzgerald, from driving a young, passionate, reckless girl out into the sinful world.'

Now the woman was trying to browbeat me; I held my ground.

'It is incomprehensible to me … '

'Mary *would*,' she broke in, her voice trembling with contempt, 'be incomprehensible to you.'

I had blundered – created resentment at the start; we should get nowhere now. Deftly, Pamela diverted the current of anger from me. She said, 'Mary even trusted Carmel with her baby, didn't she? She must have been terribly deceived.'

'Deceived,' Miss Holloway echoed. 'Yes, Mary's own charity deceived her, but not for long. She had sacrificed herself for Carmel, but she would not sacrifice her child. She sent for me.'

'To save the baby from Carmel?' Pamela suggested. 'Was Carmel doing Stella harm?'

'When I arrived in Paris I feared it was already too late. The child had been weaned; she was sickly; she did nothing but cry. She had only to cry and Carmel would rush to dandle her, rock her, put a comforter in her mouth, cover her with kisses – these peasant girls never learn.'

Miss Holloway stopped in disgust.

Pamela spoke quickly: 'Did Carmel resent your replacing her?'

A tight-lipped smile answered this.

'She was furious; she made outrageous scenes.'

I said, 'She was temperamental, I take it?'

'She was a hussy.'

The suave matron had vanished. This angry virago was much more useful to us; but I observed an effort at recovery and control. I asked, 'Where was Meredith all this time?'

Her reply was contemptuous: 'Where would you expect? Amusing himself in Paris until Mary should have made things smooth again.'

'So Carmel,' I prompted, 'was left at this milliner's and you came to England?'

'It was not a milliner's; she had a position that was much too good for her in the show-room of a famous couturier!'

Pamela looked at me. The set of her brows told me that she was reacting to Miss Holloway with as little sympathy as I, but she showed herself capable of a finesse with which I would not have credited her.

'Back in England,' she said, 'free from Carmel, I expect you had peace – you and Mary and the child?'

'Yes.'

There was a pause. The calm, lofty expression stole back to the matron's face; her hands relaxed; her voice grew reminiscent and low.

'Yes, peace; peace for two perfect years. Mary created an atmosphere of heavenly serenity; we studied together, she and I; we read child psychology and the new healing. Her father came sometimes, but only when Mr Meredith was away.'

'Did he go away a good deal?' I asked.

'He went abroad.'

'To Paris?'

'Probably.'

Pamela asked then, 'Was Mary very fond of the child?'

'She was a devoted mother.'

'Where did Stella sleep?'

'In the room beside the drawing-room on the ground-floor. We had a bay with vita-glass added. Of course the baby was out-of-doors in her play-pen every fine day.'

'And at night – did she sleep alone?'

'Naturally. You know what psychologists think of parents who keep children in an adult's room!'

I was not interested in infant psychology. I thought Pamela was taking us off the track. I wanted to know who had wept in Cliff End; who had gone through hell in the studio; who still filled the place with sweet scent and who with mortal coldness, and why.

'Then Carmel returned?' I said.

'Yes.' The voice was stern. 'In spite of the most solemn promises to remain abroad, Carmel returned.'

'How was she received?' Pamela asked. 'Was Meredith there at the time?'

'He was; it was he who opened the door to her knock. I shall never forget the look on his face. Carmel was a draggled, hollow-cheeked slut. His face became a mask of distaste. He stared at her and went up to his studio for Mary and locked himself in.'

'And Mary? Did she come down to Carmel?' Pamela asked. 'Did you see it all? Were you there?'

'I was there: I saw it. I heard Carmel's cry and ran out of my room. I saw Mary come out of the studio – she had been posing there for her husband – and lean over the banisters and look down. If she had ordered the girl straight out of the house I would have thought it justified; but Mary did not do that. She looked into Carmel's face for a long time, then she turned her head; her eyes met mine; I saw her smile slowly. She went quietly downstairs.'

'And took Carmel in?'

'Took her in, lit a fire for her in the guest-room – it was October – ran a bath for her, laid out clothes of her own. The girl coughed and sobbed and called out abuse of Mr Meredith. Fortunately, she had never troubled to learn English, and her vulgar patois passed over my head. Mary spoke to her softly, as to a child.'

'So she stayed,' Pamela said, and added, 'In which room?'

'The small front room, opposite Mary's; I gave it up to her and moved into Mary's room, but she did not stay there. Her coughing disturbed the whole house. We had a bed made up for her in the dining-room on the second night.'

'But Meredith,' I broke in, outraged by the fantastic story. 'What did he propose to do?'

'He proposed to paint her,' Miss Holloway replied.

'Good lord!'

'I heard him talking about it to Mary. "If you can put up with her," he said, "let her stay. I can use her. I've got a first-class idea."

'It seemed that he had finished Mary's portrait – at least, as well as he was capable of finishing anything – and had this idea for what he called an "old-style story-picture." He laughed to himself about it a great deal, and he said he needed Carmel for that.'

'Did she know? Did she pose for him? Good heavens – in that state!'

'No: she knew nothing about it, unless she guessed. He did not invite her into the studio; he kept that door locked. After all, he knew Carmel's face by heart. No: he would merely stare at her during meals; he would sit on and stare, after the meal was over; it made the girl cry – she was madly in love with him still; then he would run up the stairs two steps at a time. I could hear him whistling as he worked.'

'How long did this go on?'

'Nearly two weeks. If I had had my way, the end would have come sooner – and,' she said in a low, tragic tone, 'it would have been a different end. After a very few days I told Mary that Carmel must go. She was destroying the child.'

'Just "spoiling," do you mean?' Pamela asked.

'In the most pernicious sense. She broke all discipline, ignored all rules. Naturally I forbade her to go into the nursery, but it was impossible to keep her out of it; she would sneak in, even at night.'

Pamela's eyes stretched wide.

'Was it she … ? Was it against your rules to have a light in the nursery?' she asked.

'Certainly.'

'And did Mrs Meredith agree?'

'Our minds were as one.'

'I see.'

Miss Holloway looked at Pamela searchingly, as though wondering whether she had seen too much. We were being very cleverly manipulated. This woman was telling us precisely what she wished us to believe, no less and no more. Her timing, too, was perfection; I saw a glint of satisfaction in her eyes as she glanced at the clock: there would be no time for questions which she might prefer to evade. She had a brain, and a will of steel.

'Nevertheless,' I remarked, trying to force the pace a little, 'she did not send Carmel away.'

'Mr Meredith objected. "Three more days will do it," he told Mary. "Keep her here three more days and, I promise you, she'll never come back." I remember his smile as he said that. He had his way; his obstinacy was directly responsible for Mary's death.'

Miss Holloway knew how to hate.

'Please tell us,' I requested bluntly, 'about the last day.'

'I was about to do so.' Her even, repressive tone was, in itself, a reprimand. It sickened me to think of Stella's childhood, spent under this cold control.

'He was directly responsible,' she reiterated. 'It was he who drove the girl into a frenzy, and he did it deliberately. He was in one of his devilish moods. A storm had been raging all day, and the wind at Cliff End always made him insufferable. He had wanted to live in Spain. He came out of his study that evening and told Mary that Carmel could go now. He could finish without her. He was laughing. "Come and look at it," he said.

'Mary went with him to the studio, and I remained in her room reading. It was our hour for study; I had put Stella to bed. I remember the dreadful foreboding which fell over me and how I tried to attribute it to the low clouds which had darkened the sky. I put my book aside, unable to read, and strove to hold tranquil thoughts.

'In a few minutes I heard Mary calling Carmel to the studio; then there came a wild outcry and Carmel burst out of the studio and fled downstairs, crying as though she had gone out of her mind. Mary came back to me, looking pale; I was accustomed to Carmel's hysterical outbursts, but Mary had too tender a heart.'

Miss Holloway paused; tears shone in her eyes, but they did not fall. A musical peal was now sounding through the house – some sort of gong. She looked significantly at the clock: it was twenty minutes to seven; our time was up. The chiming was prolonged and repeated and at length died mellifluously away, and Miss Holloway, her voice low and unhurried, resumed.

'I supposed that Carmel had gone to the dining-room. It was Mary who realised that she was in the nursery; it was Mary,' she said tragically, 'who went down. I heard the frenzied voice and followed. Carmel was standing beside Stella's cot. She had turned on Mary like a tigress – on Mary, who had been her angel! They spoke Spanish; I could only guess what vile abuse Carmel was hurling out. Mary looked like an avenging angel, tall and shining, her eyes filled with blue fire. She never once raised her voice, but her words fell like a sword. Carmel cowered, then, screaming madly, burst open the window and ran straight for the cliff – and Mary ran after her.

'The child was clinging to me, frightened, but I loosed her hold and ran also. Carmel had been shamming, I suppose. I saw her make a clutch at the tree and check herself just at the edge. The black tree and that girl in her black dress – I can see them now, swaying together over the brink. I saw Mary fling herself towards Carmel; she cried out and reached for a bough and then … '

She broke off; her eyes rested, doubtfully, on Pamela's and then on mine, and she spoke with every sign of reluctance:

'Since Father Anson has requested it,' she said slowly, 'I will say to you what I have never said before to anyone except him: as Mary swayed there, on the edge of death, I saw a black arm swing out and strike her on the head. She went over without a cry.'

Miss Holloway closed her eyes; she remained silent, tense with emotion, for a moment, then she looked at us and rose. We stood up.

'And Carmel?' I asked.

'Carmel died, a few days later, in my arms. I had nursed her night and day, but she was almost gone when they brought her to me; the end was sudden, but I had never had any hope … Now I must go. We have music for our patients every evening: it is the heart, as it were, of our curative treatment. I have endeavoured to do as Father Anson requested; tell him so, please. I trust,' she concluded impressively, 'that I have made you both realise that if some unhallowed spirit haunts Cliff End it is not Mary's. And now I must bid you goodbye.'

We thanked her; she rang a bell and left the room. A maid appeared and showed us out.

'Curtain!' I said as I started the car. 'I have a feeling that one ought to applaud. And what do you make of all that?'

'Just what she meant us to make of it,' Pamela answered in a tired voice. 'It is Carmel who weeps.'

Chapter XII

THE TREE

'I AM so tired,' Pamela said as we wound down the hill again, 'that it would be nice to die.'

I, too, felt exhausted. Miss Holloway's handling of us, her steely grip, her histrionic performance, and the genuine, fanatical emotion which she had let loose when it suited her, had left me mentally flattened. I felt as if I had been beaten on the brain. Pamela and I talked little until we had had a Martini each and were eating a hurried meal at the hotel.

A spray of carnations and a note from Peter had greeted us. He and Wendy were 'bucked to death' at the thought of seeing us and we were to go straight round after *Salome* and have drinks at their digs after the show.

It would be fun telling those two about my play.

'Feeling better?' I asked Pamela.

'A bit ... Roddy, what does she want? Carmel, I mean. Unless,' she added drily, 'she wants Holloway hanged.'

'I'd be with her there,' I declared.

Pamela laughed. 'One of your prejudices?'

'Frightful woman.'

So was the cold beef frightful – gristle and fat; no sauce out of the variety of sticky bottles in the cruet would make it eatable.

We had let a generalised objection to 'Grands' and 'Royals' send us to an obscure hotel. Never again!

'The whole story's hideous, isn't it?'

I agreed. 'What a household! Meredith a cynic, Carmel a vixen, Holloway a wire-pulling hypocrite, and Mary a – '

'Prig?' Pamela offered.

'Well, say "a creature" much "too bright and good for human nature's daily food."'

'Yes, I'm out of love with Mary. Think of leaving the baby in those great cold hands! Poor, frightened little mite.'

'Of course it may be Holloway who's the prig,' I reflected. 'We are seeing Mary through her eyes – rather a distorting mirror, perhaps.'

'That's true,' said Pamela; 'and Stella felt such heavenly kindness and warmth ... It does go in circles, doesn't it? – I wish we needn't go to the theatre,' she sighed.

'Tired still? This meal hasn't done much to revive us! Do you want stewed plums and custard?'

'No, just coffee.'

'Would you like to stay and go to bed? I can't possibly disappoint the Careys or I would stay too.'

'An evening here wouldn't be a cure,' she replied with a grimace; 'besides, I want to see the show ... Gosh, how that woman hates Carmel! She probably strangled her.'

'She didn't have to: in pneumonia, a little neglect goes quite a long way.'

Pamela shuddered. 'We've been making ourselves polite to a murderess.'

'I'm quite ready to believe it. I wouldn't mind trying to prove it, if you could call a ghost into court.'

A greyish liquid was placed before us in coffee cups. Stirring sugar into hers slowly, Pamela said: 'If it is Carmel, I don't see that there's anything to be done.'

'Nor do I, but I don't think it is. I believe it is all an emotional echo, and there is nothing that anybody can do except wait for it to wear away.'

We both sat, depressed, smoking cigarettes at the table until we realised that it was time to go and too late to change into evening kit.

After we had driven for some minutes I remembered my script, which I had brought to show the Careys, and had to go back for it. We arrived just as the curtain went up.

Our talk had been a poor prelude to *Salome*. If the production had not been really brilliant it could not have gripped us both as it did. Peter's set was superb – civilised forms in barbaric colours; pits of darkness and splashes of garish light; it was over-stimulating: right for the play. Wendy's dress had a triumph; it sent a buzz round the house. I liked her performance.

She looked as pretty and dangerous as a tongue of flame. Her movements were sinuous, velvety, then, in a flash, wicked, like a Siamese cat's. They would do my Barbara proud, the two of them. I looked forward to supper and to giving them the good news; my mental cramp began to relax.

When the curtain fell I said to Pamela, 'I'm feeling more human, aren't you?'

'Loads better,' she answered. 'But I want coffee before we go round. I like Wendy, don't you? I'm beginning to see her as Barbara. How thrilled they'll be!'

It was in the foyer, where strong lights shone on Carey's colourful sketches and surrealist frieze, where I was crushed and pushed by laughing, light-hearted people – it was there that a desperate compulsion seized me to get back to the car and tear home.

It was Stella: danger was closing in on Stella, and she was a hundred miles away.

For a moment I was crippled by apprehension, then I elbowed my way brutally out of the crowd, gave a verbal message for Carey to a programme-seller, extricated Pamela, and hurried her to the car.

'Sorry, but I have to get home,' I told her. 'I've an overpowering feeling that something's wrong.'

I thought she would protest; such a thing as this had never happened before. She glanced at my face and simply did as I wished. I drove straight out of town.

'Have you got your script?' was all she asked.

'Yes – Heavens, I forgot the hotel!'

'There's nothing there that matters; we can phone tomorrow.'

I seldom drive recklessly, but tonight I took risks. As we came out on Exmoor a gale fought the car. The hood was up, fortunately, and my lights were good. We scarcely spoke. Pamela said once, 'It may be that horrible story,' and I replied: 'It's not.'

'Did you do anything about the nursery door?' she asked.

'I told Lizzie to lock the inside door.'

'Have you any feeling of *what* is wrong? Anything might be, mightn't it?'

'That's it: anything might be.'

Yes, there were plenty of things one could think of: burglars, fire … But it was not for the house that I was afraid.

The moon, a crazy fugitive, was flying about, seeking sanctuary among torn clouds in vain. Terror seemed to infest the night, but the wind was behind us at last and the car raced. It was not long after midnight when I was first able to hear the booming of the sea.

I shot over the Biddlecombe crossroads and turned up the lane. Pamela, infected by my panic, cried, 'Quick, quick!' I wondered why I had not turned off to Wilmcote, since it was Stella who needed help. I did not know why; I had no reason for anything that I was doing; I was obeying a blind impulse; perhaps I was going out of my mind.

There stood the house, square-set and steadfast. There was the tree, lashing itself like some demoniac flagellant. I overshot the garage and pulled up by the greenhouse; Pamela was out of the car and away round the corner of the house before the handbrake clicked. The thundering of the breakers on the rocks filled the night with noise; as I got out, the wind attacked me like a pack of hounds. Someone screamed.

I wheeled and saw the bay of the nursery lit up by a bluish gleam, then its window burst open and someone ran out – ran frantically, straight for the edge.

I could not have been in time but for the tree. She caught and clung to it and swung, like a child at play, over the brink. It was Stella. As she swung there she screamed, and I shouted, 'Hold on!'

I could not stop and would have gone over myself but that, lurching sideways, I gripped a bough. A twig whipped my face, half-blinding me, and I groped. At last I had a grip of the trunk and clung there, Stella within the clasp of my right arm.

I heard Pamela calling, 'Roddy, Roddy, where are you?' and shouted, and saw her starting to run. I yelled to her over the howl of the wind, telling her to go slow, that we could hold on. She ran down to within arm's length of the tree, where out-cropping rocks gave her a foothold, and, braced there, dragged Stella up. A leap sent me sprawling on the ground beside them and then we went stumbling up to the house.

When we were inside shut doors at last, in the lighted hall, I stood still, confused and dizzy, with blood trickling into my eyes, knowing nothing except that the danger was over; Stella was safe. I heard Pamela saying, 'Oh, your eyes, your eyes!'

I told her that my eyes were not hurt. She put her coat over Stella, who was sitting, half-dressed, trembling, and deathly pale, on the chest, then went upstairs and turned on the landing light.

'Bring her up, Roddy,' she called.

Stella could not speak; she was fighting to keep back a passion of tears. I drew her to the foot of the stairs and felt her shrinking, but she made a strong effort and came up. She did not cry until she was sitting on the couch in Pamela's room, then, her hands over her face, she let tears come, and choking sobs. Pamela tried to console her, but Stella was oblivious to everything except her own overwhelming grief. Pamela looked at me, then took lint and bandages from her cupboard and went for warm water to bathe my forehead.

I stood by the mantelpiece, gripping it, while Stella wept piteously. She took her hands from her face, stared at me with dark, dilated eyes, gasping, 'You might have been killed – oh, you might have been killed!' then she buried her face in the cushions and shook with smothered sobs.

She needed comfort, and I could only answer harshly, 'I might, and so might you!'

I was rigid with misery, in a rage of frustration. In her crazy infatuation, Stella had almost thrown herself to her death. Oblivious of me, of her own life, of all human needs and impulses, she had given her heart to this myth. And I – except as a friend, an unwilling ally in her frantic enterprise – I did not exist for her. She was no longer the Stella I understood. My wild drive through the dark, those hours of desperate apprehension, the shock she had given me on the cliff, all piled up a barrier of bitterness that kept me dumb. I could say nothing to comfort her. I would not try to compete with this mad obsession; I would batten my love for her down under hatches, until Stella was herself again.

Pamela came back and bandaged my head, then she asked me to bring in the oil-stove from my study. I did so and lit it; the room was cold. I brought up drinks. It was nearly half-past one. I sat on the window-seat and lit my pipe. Pamela made Stella drink some brandy and water. Stella was looking ghastly, her face changed and thin.

'I think you must hate me,' she said.

'No,' Pamela answered, 'because we understand.'

'Nobody could possibly understand.' Stella's voice sounded hopeless.

'I know exactly what happened,' Pamela told her, and recounted her own experience of Saturday night.

Stella listened avidly, but whispered, at the end, 'You didn't see her. I did.'

'You saw her?' I cried, startled.

Stella's face trembled; she said despairingly: 'I saw her, and I ran away.'

'No one can face it,' I exclaimed, walking about the room in my dismay. 'Of course you ran away.'

'Yes, yes, you did right,' Pamela said.

'But she is my mother! Oh, Pamela, don't you understand? She is my mother and she wanted me. I came because I knew she wanted me, and then, when I saw her, I couldn't, I couldn't … ' She was tense with bitterness now, sitting in the middle of the couch, her hands clenched.

I stood over her, telling her again that human nerves shrink from the supernatural and that running away was the only wise thing she had done.

But she did not listen; her self-contempt and misery had to find vent.

'Fifteen years,' she went on: 'think of it! Wandering about alone in the empty house; waiting and longing for someone to see her and listen to her ... '

Her thoughts appalled her; she trembled, but we could not make her stop.

'Trying to make people know you are there, and nobody seeing you or hearing you or feeling or thinking anything about you at all! And then, at last – '

She was half-killing herself with all this, but Pamela's remonstrances and mine were equally useless; a storm of remorse and compassion drove her on.

'Her own daughter, that she loved. Because' – her voice grew soft and tired – 'my mother *did* love me; I know that now. You see' – she lifted imploring eyes to Pamela as if she could hardly expect to be believed – 'I wasn't a lovable baby; Miss Holloway says I was cross and tiresome and never pretty at all, so I thought mother loved me a little bit just because she was good and did her duty, but it isn't that: it is *really* loving, as if she – as if she delighted in me and wants my love, too. It was like that last night, at first. And I meant to be brave: I thought, presently I shall see her and we'll speak to one another. Then, suddenly, everything stopped. It was as if everything was a clock and the clock stopped dead. I think I must have fallen asleep. I woke with my heart jumping, and it was cold – it was the deadliest cold I have ever known; and then' – Stella's voice faltered – 'then she began to come through the door – she came right through the locked door, like a mist. It was there, beside the bed, a tall, shining cloud, that was almost a woman. It moved. It had eyes – and I ran.'

She drooped forward, half-fainting, and Pamela caught her. 'Oh, heavens, Roddy,' Pamela gasped, 'what can we do? She'll go out of her mind.'

'I am going to take her home,' I said.

Stella lay on the couch now, limp and white, too exhausted even to cry.

'Better make hot drinks, Roddy – egg-flip or something,' Pamela begged. 'She can't go like this. I'll give her aspirin.' Thankful to escape, I went down to the kitchen. The fire was out, and I put a saucepan of milk on the primus stove. My hands were shaking; seeing eggs on the dresser, I broke one and it missed the tumbler and made a gluey mess on the floor. I assembled things anyhow on a noisy tin tray. My nerves were a peal of bells that the devil was jangling and this house was hell.

What could you do for a girl who forced her way into a haunted house, to be terrified half out of her mind by a ghost? Give her an aspirin! I heard my own half-crazy laugh. 'I bet you Miss Fitzgerald has aspirin.' Stella had said that. I could see her face now, as she said it, in the market-place, among the flowers, and hear her gay, warm voice. She had been so sweet and serious in the cafe, wondering what she ought to do, asking me for advice; and I had told her that she ought to come. I groaned and put my hand to my head. That cut was burning. I saw her again, swinging over space, clinging for her life to the swaying bough of the tree.

My misery left me. I finished making the drink. Stella was not dead – she was upstairs, here in my house, the proper and natural place for her to be. She was my darling and I loved her, and all would be well.

When I brought the tray up Pamela looked it over. 'No sugar, no spoons!'

She went downstairs. Stella lay in a corner of the couch, propped with pillows and wrapped in an eiderdown. Her anguish was spent. She glanced up at me as I stood by the fire, and I saw that she was afraid of me. Ashamed of my harshness, I asked as gently as I could: 'Are you feeling better?'

'Yes, thank you,' she said softly, and added: 'You despise me, don't you, Roddy? I despise myself.'

'On the contrary,' I answered, 'I think you were heroic. But I don't want you to be heroic: I want you to be safe.'

Her eyes looked immense in her blanched face, the long lashes wet. The defiant, tense look was gone; her lips, half-open, had a childlike softness. She sighed wistfully: 'I wish I could do something to make up.'

I said, 'You must stop giving us shocks, Stella. Pamela and I have enough to stand. We are going to try to deal with the hauntings, but I don't know what to do with you. Are you going to do this again?'

She shook her head. 'No, I promise. I won't try again unless you let me. You might have been killed.' She turned her head aside, crying again.

I said, 'Pamela's a long time finding those spoons.'

Stella looked round at me again, trying to smile. 'You saved my life,' she whispered.

'It would be a pity,' I replied, 'to throw it away.'

The smile deepened; warmth stole into her cheeks; weakness had relaxed the firm contours of her face; the schooled, reticent Stella had gone. Her eyes met mine and she flushed. Shyness overcame her and she did not speak again until Pamela returned.

Sipping her egg-flip, she smiled at Pamela and said: 'I broke into your house like a thief, and you are still my friends.'

'What about the Commander?' I exclaimed, remembering him for the first time.

She replied in a subdued voice: 'He thinks I'm at home in bed.'

'I'd better take you home at once.'

Pamela protested. 'Stella ought to have some sleep first, and an hour or two can't make much difference, now. Would you feel afraid,' she asked Stella, 'sharing my big bed?'

'Oh, no! Not when I'm not alone!'

'In a couple of hours, then,' I agreed, and went downstairs.

It was Pamela, I supposed, who had unlocked the inside door of the nursery and turned on the light. The window and half-door were wide open; one leaf of the window banged to and fro and the curtains waved wildly. I examined the wire screen outside; the padlock hung, locked, on the frame, the rusty hasp hanging from it. I had hammered it back, carelessly, into the crumbling mortar of the wall. Stella had tugged it out.

I tried to put the events of the night together. How had Stella deceived her grandfather? Was this the night on which he regularly went out? Friday: yes! And we must choose tonight to leave the house empty! How had Stella known? Had she been present when we were making our plans? Was this devilry, or chance? And what was it that had summoned me back?

Stella's coat and dress lay on a chair; there were her beret, too, and her shoes. I gathered them up. The light burden filled me with happiness: Stella was safe. She might have been below on the ledge, dead. I carried the things to my study. I sat smoking there at the window, where I could watch Pamela's door.

Stormy though the night was, it was warm. The wind was not screaming now; in those open spaces it rioted, strong and free. The veiled moon was ringed with a circle of gold. The lighthouse on the south point sent out its steadfast beam over the turmoil; I timed its rotations and made out its pattern at last; sometimes the foam of a breaker reflected the beam and a frothing silver beast leaped out of the sea. For a moment the moon shone out in brilliance and the war of wind and water was visible, a battle, shouting and exultant. Even if the powers of evil were loose in it, this was a glorious night.

Pamela's door opened. She closed it and came across the landing quickly, glancing nervously to her right. 'Roddy,' she asked, 'has the night turned cold?'

'No,' I said sharply. 'What is it?'

'That ghastly cold is seeping into my room.'

I thrust Stella's clothes into her arms. 'Get her out of the house! Don't wait to dress.'

While I stood on the landing, waiting, I watched the studio door. I did not know whether the landing light was reflected on it in some curious way or whether what I saw was a wreath of luminous mist; but it moved; it crawled and spread over the door. A chill nausea seized me and I called to Pamela. They appeared in a moment and we ran down to the hall. Stella had a coat on, but Pamela had only her dressing-gown.

'Fetch a coat from the cupboard,' I said, and she ran to do so. Suddenly Stella gasped and flung herself against me; I pulled her head

171

down, so that she should not see what I saw now. I shouted to Pamela: 'Go out the back way,' but she rushed to the front door and pulled it open and shut it behind us. We stood on the lawn, holding together against the onslaught of the gale. Even here I had to fight down panic. One minute more, and the form at the head of the stairs would have been a woman – a tall woman, with ice-cold eyes.

In the car Stella, sitting between us, trembling, said wretchedly, 'I was frightened again.'

Nobody answered; I drove fast down the lane; we were at Biddle-combe crossroads before I had recovered sufficiently to go slower. Here, in sight of houses, under the shelter of the oak trees, I drew up, and Pamela and I lit cigarettes.

'What did you see?' Stella asked shakily.

'A whitish wreath of mist,' I replied. I asked her what would happen when she went in.

'I think I can get to my room without waking grandfather,' she answered. Ashamed, but determined, she told us what she had done. 'I lied to him; I told him I had a headache and was going to bed; I asked him not to wake me when he came in. He very nearly didn't go out: he was worried about my headache and feeling rather ill himself; but Captain Pascoe always feels so depressed and lonely when there's a gale – you see, he lost his ship. So he decided to go. I was treach-erous and horrible; I don't deserve that anyone should be kind to me.'

She was silent as we drove on.

Pamela said that I had better pull up a few doors before Wilmcote. 'He may be patrolling,' she said. I pulled up and she slipped out of the car.

Stella had been crying again, very quietly.

'Roderick,' she said, 'you have truly forgiven me, haven't you? I promise solemnly that I won't be a trouble to you and Pamela any more: as soon as grandfather's better, I'll go away.'

'Don't do that, Stella! Don't go! God knows when I'd see you again!'

'But I thought you wished me to!' There was a lilt in her voice of surprise – almost, I imagined, of joy.

What had I said? The last thing I had meant to say. I tried to retract.

'No, I didn't mean that, Stella; you must get away for a time. But don't get ill; don't take risks any more; I can't stand it – promise?"

'I promise, Roderick,' she said.

Pamela returned to tell us that there was no one about.

Stella tiptoed up the garden and put her key carefully into the lock. I remembered vividly how she had opened that door to us five months ago. She looked back to smile at us before she slipped in and gently closed the door.

Chapter XIII

THE COMMANDER'S VISIT

THE HOUSE would have to go. Let it go. What did it matter? It was wrecking our lives – Stella's and Pamela's and mine. I ought to have seen that weeks ago: I had been blind.

Up on the knoll, in the grey, gusty morning, I came to my senses. The rain had blown over but the bracken was wet. I had come up with an axe and saw among the trees and brambles to cut timber for a fence. For a man who has got to make order out of emotional chaos, no advice is better than Abraham Lincoln's 'Sit down and saw wood.'

Birch and beech grew here, uncared for and crowded. I chose a tall sapling and set to work. I enjoyed the clean strokes of the axe, and felling the tree and stripping the trunk of branches, and the pliant, steady, resistant pull of the saw. It cut through my problems, too. What was a grandfather? What was a difference in age? What was a thousand pounds or a house? I had my trade. There was only one problem that remained insoluble, and that was Stella's self.

Stella's self eluded me. Where was her heart centred? What were her thoughts? I loved her; I needed her love and sweetness as I needed air, yet there was something in her – something strange, uncertain, changeable – that I could not understand.

Stella was not a child. No child could have taken the decision that she had taken when she refused either to deceive or obey her grandfather and made up her mind to come to us here; and it was no child who had undertaken that solitary enterprise last night. Stella had her own maturity, the most delicate poise of temperament, a harmony wrought out of stern discipline imposed on a nature intrinsically wild and free. There had been a dawn of wildness and freedom in Stella's eyes last night. What was that shy light that had looked out and been so quickly veiled? What did Stella see when she looked at me? A man of the world, finished with adventure, outside the country of the young? A sensible elder brother, helpful in trouble, ready with good advice? If that had happened, the fault was my own and I was going to remedy it.

My needs and purposes stood out now, as clear and clean as the stripped tree. How soon would I see Stella again?

Pamela was climbing up through the bracken. She had heard me bringing the sapling down. Yes – there was the question of Pamela and her share of the house. She wanted to fight for the house, to cling to it; so did I, but not at all costs.

She came and stood beside me, complaining, 'Must you choose a birch?'

'They were growing too close.'

'What's it for?'

'A strip of fence opposite the nursery.'

'I do hate the sight of wire.'

'So do I; we can plant gorse against it.'

'I'd like that, a hedge of gorse.'

She lit a cigarette and sat down on a stump. She had slept soundly, she told me, from about four o'clock on. So had I, out of pure exhaustion.

A hedge of gorse! Here was I, engaged in facing the fact that Cliff End was full of devilry and must be let go and at the same time cutting wood for a fence! It was extraordinary, the way in which one's daylight self refused to believe the evidence of the night.

I stood up, stretching my back, and lit my pipe.

'I have a proposition to make to you,' I said.

'You look quite fresh, Roddy! I envy you, being able to do with so little sleep.'

'Quality, not quantity: I don't dream … Look here, Pamela – now don't fly off the handle directly I mention it – just think this out: supposing that my play is a success; I mean, in London; has a run; if I were in a position to offer you your half of the price of the house, plus what you contributed to improvements, would you accept?'

'So soon, Roddy?' She was astonished and a little distressed. Then she nodded. 'If you want to live in it, yes.'

I continued to saw boughs off my tree.

'My notion might be to shut it up.'

'Just throw your capital into the ocean?'

'Exactly.'

'But – playwriting's so chancy.'

'I know.'

'It isn't as desperate as that. We won't have to give it up.'

I hesitated, then said, 'You can't stand this indefinitely, nor can I; it ruins my work.'

'For a few more weeks I can.'

'Weeks, but not months. We are not going to spend the winter in Cliff End with ghosts. Besides – ' But I decided that these were reasons enough to give for the moment. 'Would you agree?'

'I don't think so. It is generous of you, Roddy, but this was a joint enterprise. I was even keener than you. If one quits, both quit and we share the loss.'

'You'd force me to hang on longer than I want to, if you take that view.'

'I don't think so – if we fail. But we haven't really begun to work yet, properly. We can't quit without a fight.'

'I agree; but I'd like to know you would not be an obstacle if that situation came along.'

'Don't worry: I wouldn't.' She thought in silence for a minute. 'If your theory is right,' she said then, 'if most of the trouble is hallucinations, or a sort of skid in time, then we're beaten and I'll go; but I think there's a ghost. It may be a ghost re-enacting its tragedy forever; you do hear about cases like that – then, I suppose, we'd be beaten, too. But if there is a spirit who comes for a purpose and who would rest if it were achieved ... '

'Just so; that's the best we can hope for; but I am beginning to be afraid that it is a hopeless mix-up of all those.'

'I'm afraid it's beginning to look like that. I'm making a sort of chronicle of everything that has happened,' she told me, 'and I want your help. Then we can go through the whole story and try different theories. A rather awful idea came into my head just as I was falling asleep: that there were two spirits fighting – contending for Stella – last night.'

'Lord!' I exclaimed. 'I hope that isn't so! But,' I added as I thought it over, 'it's conceivable, all the same.'

'We haven't really given our minds to the question of Carmel yet.'

That was true; back in the house, I racked my brains to discover what clue it was, connected with Carmel, that I had left untouched, then I recalled the picture of which Max had spoken and the photograph which he had promised to let me see. I was about to write him a postcard when I realised that it would be extraordinarily pleasant to hear his strong, steadying voice. I put a call through to the studio in Hammersmith Mall and he answered, full of pleasure and warmth.

'I didn't forget those Academy photographs; Judith has unearthed them and she'll post them at once. You'll be interested; we were! How are things at Cliff End? You don't sound too fit.'

'A bit short of sleep,' I confessed.

'Not still? – Hell, Roderick! You don't mean to say that – '

'Hey!' I broke in. 'Don't use strong language on the telephone! You'll shock the lady at our exchange.'

Max took the hint.

'You don't tell me that damned insomnia is as bad as ever?'

'Worse,' I replied.

'How's Pamela?'

'Not too fit, either.'

There was a pause.

'I was thinking of coming down.'

'The weather has broken,' I said eagerly, 'if that's what you're waiting for.'

'Hold on a minute, will you?'

Presently he spoke again: 'Look here – Judith sends her love and warmest wishes. Her sister's going to be in town for a couple of days and she'll be occupied. Could you put me up from Thursday to Saturday?'

I hesitated; I was tempted, but not quite demoralised yet. 'That's a long journey for two nights, and the house – well, it's a bit cold and draughty just now.'

'That's settled then! Thursday evening. So long!'

Max had rung off before I could either thank him or protest. Gosh, what a lift! I shouted to Pamela. She was as relieved as I.

Lizzie arrived at noon, astonished to find us at home and foraging for ourselves in the kitchen; she had not expected us until teatime.

'But, sure, the weather wouldn't tempt you to be dilly-dawdling. 'Tis goodbye to summer, I'm thinking,' she said. 'There's a present from Mrs Jessup for you – two lovely duck eggs.'

While Lizzie cooked lunch I went outside with Charlie, who had escorted her home. I told him I wanted a short fence made inside the edge of the creek. He slapped his thigh with delight.

'That's what Cliff End wants! I told they Parkinsons many's the time. A place don't look nothing till it be fenced – savage and gardened all mixed anyhow. Wait till you see it! Just you wait!'

I enjoyed Charlie. A man who loves his job and shows it is a tonic.

Pamela wanted me to work with her at the journal, but I had to give the afternoon to my play. How crazy it seemed, to spend the best of one's energies on inventing perplexities and contriving their solutions while our own atrocious problem remained unsolved! But the thought of the picture on its way and, much more, of having Max on the quest, with his strong, ranging, subtle mind, filled me with hope. We were getting into action at last.

I set out the blue paper on which my second draft was to be written and sat down to the cutting of act one.

Revising ought to be enjoyable. Your work is no longer a mountain toppling over you: it is under your hand. Your theme has proved feasible, has shaped up; crisis and climax are in their places; your characters have life in them, you know what their reactions would and would not be. You work in confidence, no longer apprehensive that your plot will prove unmanageable or that your characters will refuse to function or that your theme will turn out to have no play in it after all. And, this time, key and atmosphere were set.

I recalled, with rueful amusement, my only other stage adventure, when *The Crucible* was produced by a small left-wing group. It had been transmuted in rehearsal from solemn tragedy to mock-heroic farce and had, no doubt, been improved by the change; but I did not think so at the time.

Well, now, my first act had to be cut.

But it was not my play which was written on the blue paper: it was a letter to Stella. It was a long letter. I wrote it and signed it and dated it and locked it away. Its time had not come.

I turned with determination to my work, marking passages to be deleted or condensed. I heard Pamela go to her room – to change, I supposed; I heard her saying something, disgustedly, about taking the car, as she simply must go out and return people's calls. Then I heard a sound out of childhood – a horse's hooves and cab-wheels outside. It stopped at the front door. Sure enough, there was the old horse-cab, driven by Wally Moss, uncle of The Golden Hind. Commander Brooke stepped out. He stood surveying the house, his face stamped with age-old pain, and his eyes, lifted to the window, met mine.

I knocked at Pamela's door and told her.

'I know; I've seen him. Roddy, we're in for it! Poor Stella!' And she added sadly: 'The poor old man!'

It was pretty bad. What had not Stella been through with her grandfather? And what would he not have to say to us? I had a keen recollection of the sword-flash of those blue eyes.

But the eyes were dull with bewilderment when we met. He was standing in the middle of the room, looking at every unfamiliar object in it as though each one caused him new distress. I was only another thing out of place, at first, then he focused on me a bitter look.

'I have called to ask you for an explanation,' he said.

I told him that I was glad to have the opportunity to offer it and asked him to sit down. He chose a dining-chair. A slow, smouldering red rose in his sunken cheeks, like a flush of shame. I waited, not knowing how much Stella had said to him. The man looked too ill to be out of his bed.

He spoke heavily: 'My granddaughter has given me her version of what happened here last night. You brought her home between two and three o'clock, encouraging her to creep in like a thief, like a – like a … ' He was controlling his agitation by an immense effort. 'I have a right to ask for your version, I think.'

I replied, 'You most certainly have.'

Pamela came in. I was a little startled. She had a look of our mother in that soft blue dress and with that grave look on her face. She said gently, 'I hope Stella is well?'

'She is very far from well,' he replied.

He had risen, with formal courtesy. When both were seated he said sternly, 'Her penitence and shame are overwhelming, as one would expect.'

'She has told you what happened?' Pamela asked.

'I believe,' he answered bitterly, 'that this time she has told me the truth.'

'I feel quite sure she has; she was so unhappy over having deceived you.'

He turned to me: 'What happened?'

I told him. I told him of our leaving the house empty and of our sudden return because of my feeling that something was wrong. I did not mention that my fear had centred around Stella. I told him about Stella's dash from the house, of her exhaustion, of the malignant cold-ness that had gathered while she was resting, and the figure which I had seen at the head of the stairs. He stared at me, appalled.

'This is worse than anything I had supposed.'

'Fortunately,' Pamela said, 'Stella thinks that the presence is a gentle and loving one. That saved her from a much worse shock.'

'I am aware that that was her notion,' he said.

'You are familiar,' I asked him, 'with the local interpretation of all this?'

'I am only too familiar with it.' His voice shook with contempt.

'Don't you think,' I went on, 'that the time has come when you would do well to help us with any information you may have?'

He broke in.

'I can give you no help whatever! I refuse, absolutely, to discuss my private memories with unscrupulous intruders – ' He paused, and said, 'I beg your pardon,' stiffly.

'You have had a distressing night,' Pamela said, exactly as mother would have said it, offering for him the apology he had failed to offer for himself. 'You see,' she went on, 'my brother and I have thought that there may be spirits – two spirits – haunting this house: Stella's mother and another. We thought– '

He turned on her, his face suffused with anger.

'Are you so superstitious as to credit these stories? So cynical as to imagine that a soul like my daughter, an unstained, saintly spirit, is doomed to a fate so horrible? That she walks the night, terrifying harmless people, including her own child? That she is not at rest? No, no, no!'

Now the blue light in his eyes shone, fanatical; his voice grew strong, his whole aspect and demeanour prophetic.

'I tell you, these phantasms are delusions, the hysterical delusions of ignorant, credulous minds, or they are the work of the Evil One! My daughter' – his voice broke; his face quivered; he bowed his head and ended weakly – 'my daughter is at rest.'

I sat silent. Pamela said quietly, 'May she rest in peace!'

She had tears in her eyes. I, too, felt sorry for the tormented man.

'I have never heard a woman praised and remembered as your daughter is,' I said.

'And *her* daughter,' he groaned, not lifting his head, 'is secretive, cunning, disobedient, a trickster – '

He raised eyes almost blank with pain and spoke without knowing to whom.

'Mary was rock-crystal, as clear as spring-water; she never lied to me in her life.'

'Stella is all honesty,' Pamela pleaded. 'She plays tricks like a child, under great temptation, and is wretched over it then.' He shook his head.

'She is her father's daughter. She remembers him; that is the trouble. She has presents that he gave her, copies of his paintings; she is proud because he made a name. She resembles him physically. The influence of that strain in her is so potent that it has been my life's aim to break it down. God knows, I've left nothing undone! When Mary died I retired from the navy and dedicated myself to that purpose – to make Mary's child the woman Mary would have wished her to be. I paid an exorbitant salary to Mary's confidential nurse; I surrounded Stella with Mary's pictures, gave her Mary's books, sent her to the same school. It was a sacrifice: I missed her. But when she returned home a year ago I was pleased. She would always be without her mother's grace, charm, beauty, but she was good. She was serious; she carried out her duties conscientiously; she continued her studies under my direction. I planned to take her abroad.'

He broke off, overcome.

'I think,' Pamela said, 'that you have every reason to be content. These little deceptions – '

'"Little deceptions"! That is how you speak of them! These are your standards! Such is your influence over Stella! The change in her was sudden: I begin to comprehend it now.'

'You can scarcely mean to be so insulting,' I said.

'My intention was to hold no discussion with either you or Miss Fitzgerald,' he replied brusquely. 'I was carried away. My purpose was to receive your explanation and to make you an offer.'

He spoke exclusively to me now.

'You are uncomfortable in this house. You doubtless regret purchasing it. You have not, as you hoped to do, found the change beneficial to your sister's health. I offer to re-purchase the house from you at the price you paid. Whatever you may have spent on it will be your only loss. I would offer compensation if I could, but I am not in a position to do so.'

Pamela threw me a warning glance. I hesitated; I was sure that there was more to come. I answered in the most non-committal manner that I could assume:

'I would think this the offer of a very fair-minded man, Commander, if you had not spoken as you did just now.'

'I may have expressed myself too strongly,' he replied unyieldingly, 'but my feelings on the subject of honour are strong.'

'So are ours,' Pamela said quietly, 'and so are Stella's. You are not allowing for the unnatural strain and pressure that she was under – even supernatural, perhaps. And, as I am sure she told you, we had nothing to do with her coming here last night.'

'Stella emphasised that fact,' he answered drily. 'She was eager to exonerate you. But influence brings responsibility, and whatever your intentions may have been, I cannot consider that you have acted in a responsible way.'

He sounded faintly apologetic; Pamela was feeling a good deal of tolerance, even sympathy, towards him and was allowing it to appear. I had never known her so patient; she was fighting very deliberately, I realised, for Stella and for me.

I, meanwhile, was revolving his offer. I was tempted. It would free me from the house without a financial loss which I might take years to retrieve. For I would never, as a dramatist, be a bestseller; I had no delusions about that; money-making did not run in our family; there were too many things we would not sell.

'If my sister agrees and if your offer is unconditional, I should like to think it over,' I told him.

Pamela said: 'I would want a few weeks in which to decide, Roddy.'

'Naturally,' I replied.

There was a pause. The Commander shook his head: 'My purpose in making this offer was to enable you to leave the neighbourhood, and at once.'

A slow fury began to consume me. I said, 'It is not unconditional, then?'

'No.'

'And what further condition had you in mind?'

'All intercourse between either of you and my granddaughter must cease.'

The silence that followed embarrassed him.

'The whole association has been calamitous for her!' he broke out. 'Nothing connected with it must remain!'

Pamela spoke quietly: 'Commander Brooke, Stella is not a child, and I am not willing to treat her as one. As I told you, we have insisted that she is not to come to the house as long as these manifestations go on. But if she wants my friendship it is hers. It is not for sale.'

We were all standing. The Commander looked utterly taken aback. After heaven knew what mental turmoil, he had steeled himself to face this scene and make this offer – to buy off the spiritual menace to Stella at the price of a thousand pounds – and his offer had failed. He had shot his bolt; there was no more that he could do.

He turned to me, almost in appeal.

'Do you endorse this – this exaggerated attitude?'

'Certainly I do.'

He looked round the room as though expecting help from it. His eyes dwelt on the fireplace, the cornices, the door, the windows, as if unable to believe that the solace he had been used to find here waited for him no more; then he moved heavily across the hall and out to the porch. He said, 'You force me to send Stella away … You force me,' he repeated, as if trying to accustom himself to the thought, 'to send her away from home.'

He climbed into the cab and was driven away without another word or glance for us, absorbed in his bitter thoughts.

My anger was dead. 'Lord,' I exclaimed, 'I'm sorry for him! He's a sick man. If he sends her away it will kill him. He'll never see her again.'

'There are too many people to be sorry for,' Pamela said brokenly. 'I'm sorry for all of them. I'm sorry for myself.'

She caught her lower lip between her teeth and hurried into the house.

Chapter XIV

CARMEL'S TREASURES

'WE HAVE BEEN on the wrong track.'

I was convinced of it, after working at Pamela's chronicle, but my thoughts led me no further; I could say nothing more definite than that.

Pamela had done a sound job – detailed, accurate, and detached. She had started her record in the form of a retrospective journal, reporting each event under its date – her own experiences, Judith's, Lizzie's, and mine. There were also the several accounts which we had heard of the Meredith story, with the differences of emphasis carefully brought out; even scraps of gossip were included, each with its narrator's name. This was important, because we were being forced to look at Meredith and Mary and Carmel through the memories of others, and no human mind is a flawless mirror. We realised that we must allow for charity and prejudice, devotion and jealousy and hate.

Pamela had worked hard, and there was a thick wad of manuscript bound in her loose-leaf book when she showed it to me on

Saturday evening. I glanced at the notebook and at Pamela and at the pile of novels which had accumulated on my table, waiting for review. I knew I ought to draft my article tonight and there was a detective story to be finished first. Things were bad enough without letting my one regular job go to pieces, but how on earth was I to give my mind to Peter Wimsey and his mysteries while our own diabolical problem was crying out to be tackled?

'For pity's sake, put it away till I have got this stuff done,' I said.

Pamela looked disappointed. It was pretty rough; she was doing everything she could think of to save my time and help me, and could not get me down to work.

'Look here,' I said, 'I'll sit up over that all night, if you like, but I've got to get this thing off. If I cast my bread upon the waters and burn my boats at this rate, we'll be on the rocks.'

I think Pamela would be able to rise to nonsense if she was on her death-bed. She answered gravely: 'In burnt boats, scrambling after our bread? I quite see! Your logic is irrefutable; go ahead!'

It was ten o'clock before I was ready. She wanted me to complete the records of my own experiences and help her with an account of Stella's. We were up until all hours, finishing these, and, at the end of it, that was all that I had to say: 'It doesn't hang together; it doesn't make sense; we have been on the wrong track.'

'We're both imbecile for want of sleep,' she answered. 'When we bring fresh minds to it tomorrow we may see clues. I wish to heaven we didn't have to go sailing!'

SUNDAY WAS WET, our wide world one blur of rain. Good! We were relieved of our promise to Scott. I was past wanting to sail or swim or do anything except quash these hauntings or quit.

It was obligatory, however, to invite Scott to lunch. The weather would not keep him away, nor would he take out the schoolmaster's car. His share in that ancient monument was confined to use for professional calls. He would push his bicycle up as far as the farm, come beating across the moors in sou'-wester and mackintosh, carefully hang these up in the greenhouse and come in, followed by a terrier which would promptly shake the rain off himself over our room. Poor Scott! It was a mistake to pity him, for his life appeared to suit him very well, but he was so consistently unlucky; this sail, now, would have given him no end of pleasure, and the day must turn out wet. He accepted my invitation with less than his usual alacrity; his voice on the telephone sounded morose. Surely he was not feeling aggrieved, still, about the dog?

The minds which we brought to the journal in the morning were fresh enough; if ghosts had walked or wept in the house, we had slept through their visitation all night. We went through the record from beginning to end, dissected every discrepancy, tried to make a pattern with all the fragments that seemed to harmonise, and failed. At last I said: 'The Commander was right and it is what I have thought all along: there is no ghost.'

Pamela looked discouraged, reluctant as ever to believe this theory, from which there was no issue, because, as she said: 'You can't either fight or pacify a ghost that isn't there.'

'Exactly,' I responded, 'and that is why they say that the way to rid a house of haunting is to burn down the house!'

She was obstinate: 'I *feel* that there are spirits in the place, Roddy. I can't put up a case against you, but it is what I believe.'

'Well, what *I* believe is that the place is saturated with passions and emotions, inexpungeable misery and despair, so that no sensitive person can be in it and not be overcome by hallucinations or depression or both.'

'If that's so, it's hopeless.'

'I'm afraid it is.'

'I don't see why you are so sure of that.'

'The subjective element in the whole thing is so strong. Each of us is reacting in a way that is obviously attuned to our own temperament, or expectation, or mood. Look here: take each of us in turn! First, Judith. Judith, naturally, is concerned for her appearance, anxious to keep her youth and looks. How does the studio affect her? She thinks her beauty is gone. I was preoccupied with my future as a writer – Max had been talking about it: what happens to me? I see myself as a failure. Then take Lizzie: her head is chock-full of stories and descriptions of Mary Meredith, and she sees a tall, fair lady with blue eyes. You hear heartbroken weeping, don't you? Well, saving your presence, that's temperamental too: you are still too much inclined to imagine that other people are having a hard time. Lizzie hears none of that weeping, and I, very little.'

'And, saving your presence,' asked Pamela, spirited even in the midst of all this discouragement, 'what made *you* feel that horror on the stairs?'

'I was brewing my play. It boiled up a few hours later. Wendy's wrecker had already planted the germ. My imagination was full already of ideas of danger and malignancy.'

'That's very ingenious,' she replied, sobered; 'go on!'

'Then, Stella,' I continued, excited and convinced by my own line of reasoning: 'Stella is obsessed by thoughts of her mother and craving for her mother's love. She had imagined her mother coming to her at night, remembered it, dreamed of it; it was the profoundest impression made on her in infancy. Up on the landing the psychic atmosphere had overwhelmed her, and then she was sleeping in the nursery, for the first time since those days. The hallucination was almost bound to come. It began, I should think, with remembering the scent. Nothing has such powerful associations as a smell. Mary had used it, I suppose, or often had mimosa in her rooms. Stella remembered it so vividly that, I suppose by some kind of telepathy, she caused us to feel it too. That scent is Mary's *motif*. Very soon she begins to see Mary – a tall, shining figure. To me, remember, it had seemed a slimy fog.'

Pamela sighed: 'Oh, Roddy, how plausible! I *cannot* be convinced: is it wish-thinking I am? My mind does nothing but run round in circles when I try to see straight myself.'

We were still lost in the labyrinth when Scott arrived, a wet, muddy Bobby at his heels. The poor pup entered the house doubtfully and padded all over the floor, his big, questing head exploring every corner before he would settle down. When Pamela asked, anxiously, how he had got over his attack of nerves, Scott replied that he was nearly all right. 'But I suppose,' he said gloomily, 'it's no use leaving him with you again.'

Pamela answered, 'Not yet, I'm afraid,' and an awkward silence followed. Scott, of course, had his own notion of what had terrified the dog but did not want to talk about it; neither did we. He looked keenly at Pamela; she had lost her summer colour and had dark shadows under her eyes, but he was not in a position to offer either sympathy or advice. He sat at lunch looking unhappy, and it took all our efforts to cheer him up. We dispelled his gloom, at last, by letting him talk about the Midlands and Devon. Scott had been born and brought up in the Black Country and had a phobia about such places, such a life. He described the terrific spurt of work with which he had fought himself into medicine and out of Staffordshire and the passion with which he had made for the sea.

'I thought I was in heaven when I got to Biddlecombe,' he said, 'and I'm not sure yet that I was wrong; anyhow, six months ago I refused a practice in Birmingham that would soon have been worth five times as much.'

He grinned over that, then looked worried again and sighed, as if he had suddenly found a reason to regret it.

'When was it that you came here first?' Pamela asked.

'Five years ago; I came as locum for old Dr Rudd; when he got past his work he had me back as assistant – that was a year and a half ago. The poor old chap died and I kept the practice on. It's interesting enough, and the hospital's first-rate.'

He sounded a little on the defensive; I knew he had a fine local reputation and wished that I could mention it, but did not know how. Pamela said, 'We rather wondered why you stayed here, but I'm glad you did.'

He looked at her gratefully and said, with emphasis, 'So am I.' Again I found myself thinking: 'Poor Scott!'

Pamela laughed. 'You know, I suppose, that you are boosted as one of the local assets? "And we have such a nice, up-to-date young doctor, my dear!" We have been having callers, you know.'

That did Scott good. When lunch was over he sat in his deep chair, smoking, his long arms and legs lying about untidily, looking a lot happier.

I liked Scott a good deal more than I had expected to. His lack of grooming, mental and physical, went naturally enough with his serious, honest, pre-occupied eyes, and his awkwardness of manner concealed a good deal of sensitiveness and tact. Scott must have heard as much as anyone in Biddlecombe about our troubles, but a worried silence when plans for Cliff End were mentioned and anxious glances at Pamela when a tired sigh escaped her were the only indication he gave us that the matter was in his thoughts; not even the Scottie's behaviour had made him encroach.

If the Commander was as ill as he looked, Scott was probably attending him. In that case, the doctor was the one link left with Stella. I was inclined to tell him something about the situation and enlist his support; his admiration for Pamela was patent; he would want to help. I hesitated, but when Pamela said, 'I'm going to tell Lizzie we are not at home to callers, I just can't do with strangers today,' and left the room, he turned to me, eager to speak out.

I watched him dismiss one sentence after another that rose to his lips. It was only decent to give him a lift.

'Give us the chance of a sail another day,' I said. 'It would do Pamela no end of good.'

His face brightened, then clouded again.

'She looks done up,' he said.

'We're having rotten nights,' I admitted. 'You've heard something about it, I bet?'

'I have.'

'What have you gathered?'

'People say this house is haunted. Some say that the ghost of Stella's mother walks. I suppose that's absolute rot?'

'We can't make out; there are all sorts of unpleasant disturbances,' I told him: 'we are not sure what is the cause.'

About Stella's feeling, I could not speak.

'What frightfully rough luck!'

'Yes; it's disappointing. And it affects Stella: the Commander forbids her to come here.'

'I say, that is rotten! She has brightened up no end since you came. I thought ... She's had such a thin time ... I hoped ... I say, what a jam!'

'It is. We would give a lot to understand what's behind the trouble here; we feel we might be able to quiet it; but the Commander won't tell us a thing.'

'That's like him.' Scott hesitated, then spoke excitedly: 'Look here, Fitzgerald: I have loathed the notion of telling you this, but I've got to – it might help – '

He shut up, because Pamela had returned. So this was why he had sounded reluctant to come and arrived in such a state of gloom!

'For goodness' sake, man, tell us anything you know! Pamela's hardened to all this.'

'I had a feeling you knew something,' she said.

'It's nothing new,' he responded: 'it's something Dr Rudd used to talk about. It happened years ago. He had a patient in this house.'

'Mary Meredith?' I asked.

'No – the girl who lived with them: Carmen, or some such name.'

'Carmel.'

'Yes. She died here, did you know?'

'Of pneumonia after exposure, yes.'

'Well – it's just that Rudd always swore that she needn't have died.'

Pamela told him we had suspected that.

'Rudd used to get fairly worked up about it,' Scott went on; 'said the woman who looked after her ought to be drummed out of the nursing profession. He said he would have demanded an inquest only that there'd been trouble enough connected with this house, and he might have been blamed himself.'

'Did he attend Carmel?' I asked.

'Yes; he was sent for by the people who found her – she was found in a ditch, wasn't she? He visited her here a couple of times. He said the household was in a rotten condition – neither Meredith nor the servants seemed to care a straw whether she lived or died, and the nurse was a stick. But he thought the girl had a simply uncanny hold on life and would pull through. He was astounded when he heard that she was dead. He never forgot it. I thought I ought to tell you, though it's not a very cheerful tale, in case it might throw a light.'

Nobody said anything for a moment. Right enough, it was a loathsome story. I saw Pamela go greenish-looking, quite frightened. After a minute she said, 'It was nice of you not to want to tell us, and to tell us … Would anybody like to play ping-pong?'

When Scott left I put on a waterproof and walked with him as far as the schoolmaster's house, where he had left his bicycle this time. He was rather silent, and when he did speak it was in a depressed tone about himself.

'A man can make awful mistakes when he's young,' he brooded, 'and in a couple of years it's too late to put them right. If I'd taken that Birmingham job I'd have been in a position to – to settle down. I'd have been in a solid position, I mean. But then, I suppose, if I'd been in Birmingham, I wouldn't be here.'

I revolved this mixture of the incoherent and the obvious on my way home and drew a simple enough conclusion. Scott was in process of losing his heart to Pamela and he knew it was no use. I was glad he had the sense to see that.

I sometimes wondered whether Pamela would ever marry. It would be a pity if she didn't, for she was a companionable person and liked the human race, but she was so darned platonic; her friendliness, her warm, candid ways were walls and fortifications: I did not see how any man was ever to get round them, and she would not yield to direct approach. Pamela would put up a considerable resistance if she felt herself attracted by any ordinary mortal, I felt sure of that. A man would have to satisfy her fastidious mind as well as her heart – heaven help him! 'You're too choosy,' Lizzie used to say to her when they went shopping together for the house. Well, Pamela had a right to be 'choosy.' But poor Scott!

AS LIZZIE WAS out on her Sunday 'Jessuping,' we made our own supper, Whisky watching us suspiciously from the hollow of the basket-chair, waving his tail with that scornful and arrogant movement, which was said to have earned him his name. Whisky had lost his confidence in us and in his home. He no longer loved the nursery, no longer paid morning calls to our bedrooms, even to scrounge the top of Pamela's egg.

It seemed ridiculous, but the reactions of Scott's dog and Whisky were, to me, more impressive and more genuinely evidential than Pamela's or my own. Animals were not influenced by auto-suggestion, one supposed.

We did not eat much supper: baked eggs, toast, and coffee, on the low table by the fire, were as much as we wanted. We finished quickly and pushed the table away.

Scott's story had made a rather sickening impression on us both – that unfortunate girl, with her vehement temperament, her mad love for Meredith, her intense clinging to life, dying of neglect – deliberately killed by neglect, here, in this house. If it was her grief and terror that persisted, the place would never be habitable again. Pamela broke in on my brooding, and her voice shook.

'Roddy, if it *is* Carmel who is haunting, I don't think I want to stay; I think I'm afraid.'

'I wouldn't blame you,' I said.

'Because,' she went on, 'if it was just revenge on that woman that she wanted, she would haunt her – haunt Miss Holloway, I mean – but I'm afraid it is just that she died in a wild state of hate and fury and wants revenge on this place where she suffered – on the whole world. I'm afraid of what she was trying to do to Stella – what she might do to us.'

'If you are feeling like that,' I answered, 'it's time to quit.'

'Let's hold on until after Max's visit,' she said.

It was a relief when Lizzie came in. She came in and sat down by the fire. This Sunday-evening chat was a ritual. We heard all about who had been at the farm, what they had eaten for supper, what they had heard on the wireless, and what Charlie's pal's girl thought of her mistress's visitors and their goings on. Pamela was less responsive than usual, and Lizzie cut her story short.

'Miss Pamela,' she said, rising, 'you get to bed with you, you are tired; go on now and get your beauty sleep for a change!'

It was a sound idea; I supported it. Pamela went, and I took up a book.

It was not long before Lizzie reappeared, hovering in the doorway.

'Could I speak to you, Mr Roderick?'

She spoke in a stage whisper and closed the door behind her with conspiratorial caution. I put my book aside, and she sat down with a sigh, then she chuckled.

'Breaking the Sabbath, as usual; well, if I'm interrupting, I may be saving you from sin; though when work's play, the way yours is, I suppose you'd need no dispensation.'

Lizzie's jocularity sounded forced; it was not for this that she had come in.

'What's the trouble, Lizzie?' I asked.

''Tis Miss Pamela,' she answered; 'for the dear's sake, get her away out of this!'

'What is it?'

'I heard her last night, Mr Roderick, crying fit to break her heart. Walking about the house she must have been, for in my room I don't hear a sound from upstairs. I got up, but by the time I had my things on she was gone. You know, sir, Miss Pamela's no cry-baby; I never knew her carry on like this, except only when your mother died, God rest her soul!'

I surprised Lizzie by responding 'Amen.' To believe that one's mother's spirit was wandering, restless – what an unendurable thought that would be! No wonder if it had driven Stella to her frantic act.

Lost in this reflection, I said absently, 'That isn't Miss Pamela.'

'Dear sakes, Mr Roderick, you're not telling me 'tis ghosts?'

Now what had I done? But there was no going back.

'Not ghosts exactly, Lizzie,' I said, 'but a sort of mournful memory that is hanging about the house. It hasn't done any harm, has it?'

These sophistications had no appeal for Lizzie. She shook her head.

'If it wasn't Miss Pamela, 'twas a ghost.'

I tried to convince her that ghosts might be harmless. 'You have heard that Mrs Meredith was a good, saintly woman: why should you be afraid of her spirit, even if it did haunt the house?'

'No good spirit spends eternity that way,' she said firmly. Father Anson's view! A reasonable one, I had to admit. 'If this house is haunted,' she insisted, ''tis haunted by devils out of hell, and what would they be wanting but the ruin of immortal souls? For God's sake, Mr Roderick, take Miss Pamela away!'

'We are not going, Lizzie,' I told her; 'not yet, anyhow. Not till after Mr Hilliard has been. Do you want to leave us?'

Poor Lizzie began to cry.

''Tis against my conscience to stay in the place, but how can I go and leave Miss Pamela in it? She'd get nobody to help her; there's not one would stay.'

I replied, 'I'm quite sure that's true.'

'I can't do it,' she moaned. 'But, Mr Roderick, for the love of heaven, won't you send for the priest? Exorcism's a fearful thing, God help us; they say any priest that does it three times will die of it; but Father Anson would do it for you if you asked him, I haven't a doubt.'

I promised to have another talk with Father Anson; still Lizzie delayed. I asked her if there was anything I could do for her; she nodded.

'I'm afeared of hearing it again. It'd put the heart across me and the palpitations have me nearly killed. Could I sleep, maybe, in the kitchen? Would you give me a hand with my bed?'

That was quickly done. We were forever hauling beds about in this house. I wished Lizzie sound sleep but felt that there was little hope of it for any of us.

Carmel … Yes, it was Carmel who filled Cliff End with horror, I reflected, brooding over the dying fire. Whether what we felt was an emanation from her past agony or the presence of her actual spirit, it was dreadful and not to be borne. Perhaps Pamela's instinct was right and her spirit was haunting, malignant, intent on revenge. Was her power growing stronger, that Lizzie could hear her lamentations now? Would she presently appear, completely materialised?

What would she look like? I imagined her dark, haggard, with hollow cheeks and cavernous eye-sockets – the death's-head that Judith had seen in her glass. But she had eyes – eyes that burned or froze you: I had felt their power. To see that ghastly form fully manifested might be too much for human reason.

Burdened with anxiety and more than ever thankful that Max was coming, I went upstairs, prepared for an uneasy night. There was nothing unusual to be seen or heard as I went to my room, and after a restless half hour or so I slept.

Pamela woke me. She had never done it before, and I was startled when I saw her standing in my doorway in her white dressing-gown, but she did not seem agitated. She said quietly, 'Please come out here.'

She made me stand by the banisters; there was nothing to be seen and no sound. Pamela did not explain, but after a moment I realised what had excited her – it was the scent: the perfume of mimosa was wafted up through the house, wave upon wave, as if on a warm, soft breeze.

'Let's see if we can trace it,' she whispered.

We went downstairs; the scent was a great deal stronger in the hall but was faint in the nursery, to my surprise. Pamela laughed softly; it was like playing hide-and-seek. I unlocked the door of the dining-room and stood, astonished. The room was as we had left it, bare except for a corner cupboard, packing cases, pictures stacked with their faces to the wall, and rolled-up rugs. There were no light-fittings in this room; in the watery moonlight it looked unnaturally still, dead, but the air was fragrant with that golden mimosa scent. It played sorcery with place and time; for a moment I was walking on the terraced hills above Portofino, treading the flower-dust under my feet.

'It makes me dizzy,' Pamela whispered. She was moving among the packing-cases. Leaning over one, she breathed deeply and beckoned me with a gesture. When I stood beside her I was sure, as she was, that the scent was strongest here. A feeling of mystery made us both talk with hushed voices and move as if in the presence of someone who must not be disturbed. Pamela lifted the loose lid of the case and laid it down quietly.

I heard her gasp and saw her leaning on the sides of the box as if she were faint.

'What on earth is it?' I whispered, standing beside her. I saw nothing but a lot of junk.

'Don't you see,' she replied, half laughing, 'it's not ours; it's the old stuff; it's theirs, stuff that was in the studio cupboards. This does mean something, Roddy. Quick!'

'In the studio cupboards!' I exclaimed. 'What do you mean?'

She controlled her excitement and answered quietly, 'They're things that Charlie ought to have cleared away. Lizzie wouldn't burn them without looking through them, and we put that off. I forgot all about them. Let's turn them out now!'

I untied a mat and laid it on the floor between the windows, where a faint beam of moonlight lay. We carried the case over, and I pulled out, one by one, all sorts of oddments which Pamela, kneeling, laid out on the floor. We were both bemused by the overpowering scent.

It was an assortment of the kind of rubbish which people hoard because it is difficult to dispose of or because it may 'come in useful' some day. There were rolls of wall-paper, scraps of furnishing material, a wall-map, lengths of stained old silk and brocade, probably used for draping the artist's models, and a tinselly Moorish lamp; there was a teddy-bear, squashed out of shape and filthy, a headless doll, and a large chocolate-box with the picture on its cover unstuck – a commonplace collection enough.

I said to Pamela, 'Are you sure we're not imagining the mimosa? Do you smell it still?'

'Indeed I do! It seems to be coming in waves, as if the air were being fanned. It is making me a little faint.'

She sat with her head drooping. I was in a daze.

'Shall we leave it?' I said. 'There's nothing else.'

'No,' she answered weakly; 'open the little box.'

I felt a curious reluctance to touch it. I would have liked to get Pamela out of the room. Mary might be all that was gracious and lovely, but I did not want her to appear to us in this moonlit room. I said, 'Leave it till tomorrow,' but Pamela shook off her faintness and, taking the chocolate-box, pulled off the lid. On the top, carefully rolled, was a piece of gaudy, striped silk – a small square shawl with a tangled fringe. She took out next a fan, made of gauze and covered with sequins, a high, tortoise-shell comb, an artificial red carnation, an empty phial, and a pair of castanets. 'Carmel's treasures,' she said under her breath.

A shiver passed through me. I struggled against the conviction that we had been forced or led to do what we had done, to come to this room and discover these things. I felt a ghostly presence too close. I scarcely heard what Pamela was saying; she repeated it.

'What's on the label? Have you a match?'

There were matches in my dressing-gown pocket; I struck one and held it to the printing on the faded label of the heart-shaped flask. '*Parfum Mimosa*' I read.

Pamela caught my arm and stood up dizzily. We left the room, and, locking the door behind me, I put the key in my pocket. Pamela sat down on the chest while I opened the front door and let the night air blow the fragrance away. When I shut it again the scent had gone but the hall was sickeningly cold.

'Did you see anything?' Pamela whispered.

'No,' I replied, 'and I don't want to. Hurry! Come up to your room!'

She hesitated, very white, but there was nothing to be seen on the stairs or landing and we ran up. We lit the oil-stove, which was still in the fireplace; Pamela was shivering; the small phial was still in her hand.

'There is no scent from it now,' she said. It was true; not the faintest trace of the perfume remained.

'Those things were Carmel's, weren't they?' she said, anxious and worried.

'I'm afraid there's no doubt of that,' I replied. 'It's the insignia of a Spanish dancer; she would pose as a dancer for Meredith. Yes, they are Carmel's.'

Suddenly Pamela said, 'Look at my hand!'

She held out her right hand in which the little flask was gripped hard. Three of the fingers were waxen.

'Take it,' she said, shuddering.

The fingers were cramped round the flask and quite numb; I had to open them forcibly to remove it. I was rubbing her hand in the warmth for a long time before the circulation came back. She kept glancing at the door.

'Now don't go attaching psychic significance to that,' I warned her. 'You were nervous and gripped the bottle too hard.'

'No, Roddy; that is not natural; my fingers never go dead,' she protested. 'I felt that cold coming, didn't you?'

'I'm not certain that it wasn't natural.' I opened the bedroom door.

'Don't go just yet.'

The landing was dim with a greyish fog, but it had no nucleus; there was no luminous centre such as I had seen before, and the cold that I felt was not very different from the raw, dank chill of a north wind. I glanced out of the landing window. There was a ragged veil of cloud over the moon, and land and sea were a blurred surface of shadow and pale light.

I went back to Pamela, shutting the door.

'There's fog and it's chilly, but it may be natural,' I told her.

She shook her head.

'This room feels as it did on Friday night, when we rushed Stella away.'

'Would you like to come down to the sitting-room?'

'No; let's wait and see what happens.'

Nothing happened. I stayed with her for nearly an hour, and by that time the temperature was normal and the fog had cleared.

Pamela put the flask away in the drawer of her dressing-table and said that she could sleep now.

'But there's a tremendous lot to think about, isn't there? There was *purpose* in it tonight. And my fingers never go dead. It's all very difficult.'

I agreed.

Chapter XV

THE ARTIST'S MODEL

'I WAS just thinking … ' Pamela began.

'So I observed!' She had been lost in frowning concentration since we sat down to lunch. As often happened, it was our first meeting of the day, and on these occasions she was usually talkative. 'Suppose,' I suggested, 'you eat for a change.'

Her Cornish pastry was eaten without attention; she looked at me with a rather awed excitement in her face.

'Do you remember saying yesterday that the mimosa scent was Mary's *motif*?'

'I do.'

'Do you think it is possible that she heard you?'

'Who? Mary? Good heavens!'

'Yes. Could she have heard you saying that or, in some way, known that you were thinking it? And then, last night, don't you see, Roddy, somehow made the scent come, to show us that she was there? I don't think it's impossible, do you?'

'I'm never going to say that anything's impossible again.'

'I feel sure that she made us find that box.'

So did I – well, not certain: there could be no certainty in this fantastic affair, but I had wakened pretty well convinced that there had been purpose behind the events of the night. My midnight credulities had so often wavered, changed into cool rationalisations during the day, that I had quite expected this conviction to flag, but it survived.

'Yes,' I answered, 'I believe she did.'

'But, Roddy, this is tremendous!' Pamela was elated; her eyes shone; not a shadow of yesterday's despondency remained.

'It opens possibilities,' I agreed.

I was resolved not to rush headlong to conclusions, but I was feeling extraordinarily hopeful: if Pamela was right, we were no longer dealing with inanimate emanations, but with an intelligence, active and intent on giving us help.

'It means everything,' Pamela went on joyously: 'it means that it is Mary, and that she wants to tell us what is wrong, and that she can reach us – we are in touch! And there was nothing frightening at all! Roddy, it's wonderful!'

'Don't forget the other,' I said.

Her eyes widened. 'Do you think the other may – try to interfere?'

'Didn't you speak of two contending for Stella? That's probable enough, I'm afraid.'

Pamela restrained a shudder.

'I have been wondering,' she said slowly, 'what Carmel meant to do in the nursery, that last evening, when she rushed down from the studio in such a frantic state.'

'Kidnap the baby,' I suggested, 'kill it, perhaps, by way of revenge.'

'What a ghastly idea, Roddy! Because – because, don't you see, if she had that in her mind – if she died wishing that she could have done it … '

'The impulse may go on?'

'Exactly.'

'I'm afraid it's possible: I'm afraid that on Friday Stella was very near death.'

There was silence for a moment; Pamela had grown pale, then the spoke hopefully:

'Never mind! If Mary is on our side, we shall win. She is trying to protect Stella – we may be sure of that. We have only to keep ourselves open to her influence and follow her clues.'

'And interpret them; that's not so easy,' I added.

'Yes. Why did Mary want us to open Carmel's box?'

'There's nothing else in it, is there? A letter or anything?'

'No; I've looked at everything again and again. I can't imagine any reason at all.'

'Imagining won't get us very far, I'm afraid.'

'There must be something we can do.'

Yes: there *was* something that we could do, and I did not want Pamela to think of it. I changed the subject, telling her, for the first time, of my talk with Lizzie last night.

'That settles it,' Pamela decreed: 'in future, Lizzie must sleep at the farm. Her heart is not strong, and everybody in this house is liable to get some frightful shock.'

I agreed. In any case, during the two evenings on which Max was to be with us Lizzie must be out of the way. If a spirit was trying to communicate with us, there was one thing that we could do: we could hold a séance.

The idea repelled me; I had a wretched boyhood memory of the effect of this sort of thing, and I realised that Pamela, with her sensitivity and galloping imagination, was the last person who ought to be exposed to the risk. Should I suggest it to her? The question churned in my mind, destroying the optimistic mood of the morning and ruining my work. Finally I decided to say nothing to Pamela until I had consulted Max.

I wasted the afternoon in my study, spoiling my play, and after dinner spent half an hour in making false starts at an article on radio drama.

Pamela talked. She rarely chattered while I was working; I knew that this meant that she, too, was obsessed. She had Carmel's box on her lap and sat, frowning and restless, fingering its contents, one by one.

'I suppose Meredith bought the perfume,' she said. 'Mimosa scent is very rare. I expect he bought it for Mary in Paris. I wonder whether Mary gave it to Carmel – or did Carmel steal it? Or had he given it to her when they were in Spain? And how did Stella come by hers? Did Meredith send her some later on? I do want to ask Stella about that.'

'That would be an odd present,' I remarked, 'for a kid of six. That was her age, wasn't it, when he died?'

'I can't think of anything else.'

'Stop thinking, then, or, at least, stop talking,' I demanded unkindly. She said 'Sorry,' and relapsed into worried silence. I wrote some acid comments on a production of a verse play, saying that it might have been interesting if the players had not been scared of verse and had been able to pronounce more than two vowels, then I struck all that out, seeing that it was born of my own nervous irritation, and began again.

I was annoyed with myself for snapping at Pamela. The whole affair was wearing her to fiddle-strings, and she ought not to be made to feel, for a moment, that she was alone with it. I put my writing-pad away and grinned at her.

'No go,' I said; 'we'll be beggared – and "I do like a little bit of butter to my bread." What's up? You were as light and airy as a canary this morning: what's gone wrong?'

'Oh, Roddy,' she replied, 'the whole thing! Our theories are skating about in figures of eight. And isn't it infuriating, if Mary is trying to make us understand something and can't? *Why* did she want us to find Carmel's box? But you've *got* to finish that article, haven't you? I'm going to bed. I have a suggestion to make – something that may really work – but it will keep until tomorrow. I believe my very thoughts are making a noise like a mill-wheel creaking round. I'll leave you in peace. Good night.'

She left me, but not in peace. I knew too well what Pamela was going to suggest: she wanted to hold a séance.

Next morning I had my first swim for nearly a week. The water was cold and boisterous, but I enjoyed it. I had slept the night through and felt my own man again, no longer the plaything of ghosts. After breakfast I went out to Charlie, who had come across from the farm with Lizzie and was starting work on the fence. From out there, I could watch for the post.

This was Tuesday. I was assuring myself that there would be a letter for Pamela from Stella. There was so much to tell us – what had happened and what was to happen now. She would not go away without writing to say goodbye.

Charlie was in one of his obstinate moods. 'I'll have to have wire mesh and I'll have to sink it,' he insisted; 'the rabbits'll devour you if I don't.' It was useless to tell him that the object of the fence was to prevent accidents, not to protect crops. A fence was a fence; a job was a job; in expecting him to do such a niggardly bit of work, I violated Charlie's pride. 'I were never asked to do the like,' he protested, aggrieved.

The postman was walking up the drive at a leisurely pace. He ought to have a bicycle, I thought, covering such a scattered round.

'Do it as I told you, with three strands of wire. Rabbits don't climb up out of the sea,' I said brusquely to Charlie, and left him.

There was no letter from Stella, only the package from Max. My heart sank; apprehensions that I had been holding at bay broke in. Stella was alone with the old man. What was he doing to her? His abhorrence of what she had done was vehement. He had spoken of her 'overwhelming repentance.' To what condition had he reduced her with his reproaches? Was he annihilating everything in her that might have flowered into love? Had he so broken her down that she would never wish to think of me again? It was intolerable to be cut off.

Pamela found me in the porch, the parcel from Max unopened in my hand. 'Didn't you sleep well? I did!' she exclaimed.

I told her that I had slept perfectly, and cut the string.

There were two volumes with a marker in each. She took one. I opened the other and sat stupefied.

This could not be Carmel! Even in early girlhood Carmel would not have been like this; she would have had a dark, hard, audacious face. The name under the picture was Llewellyn Meredith; he had painted from other models, of course. But this girl wore a fringed shawl and had a tall comb in her hair, and she held a carnation against her throat. The title was *Dawn*. She was very young, soft-eyed, and joyous, with dimpled cheeks and lips half open in a shy, wondering smile; it was a picture of the dawn of love.

Father Anson had said that Carmel was pretty, I remembered – that she had bright eyes and a sweet smile. This girl was lovely: it must be Carmel, I supposed … the carnation … the shawl … the comb … And Meredith had changed her into a malignant witch! How had he done it?

Pamela sat silent over her volume, a look of sick revulsion on her face. She passed the book to me.

'Meredith was a devil,' she said.

This was a full-page photograph. The picture was called *The Artist's Model*. His *Dawn* was reproduced in it as a framed portrait hanging on a wall. That was cleverly done, the beauty and happiness of the young face shining out. Turning away from it, with a gesture of anguish, was a woman – just the head and shoulders, filling most of the canvas. At first glance one was shocked by the contrast, simply, between youth and age, for the face of the agonised woman and the face of the girl were the same angle; then one realised that it was the same face. It was the same face and it had not aged; it was young still, but gaunt, haggard, and hungry, the pallid skin stretched tight over the bones, a hideous caricature. The stricken girl wore the same shawl as the other; her hand lay at her breast in the same position; it was an unmerciful study of decay.

Pamela spoke slowly. 'She was madly in love with him still. She came back because she couldn't bear life without him, and he did that.'

I remembered: 'Let her stay,' he had said to Mary: 'I can use her. I've got an idea.'

'He painted that when she was sick in his house.' Pamela's voice was appalled. 'He would stare at her at table and then run up to the studio and paint; Miss Holloway used to hear him whistling … He showed it to Carmel, that last day. He sent for her to the studio. He watched her face when she looked at it. He probably finished it with the help of what he saw then – finished it while she was dying.'

'And exhibited it,' I added, 'when she was dead.'

Pamela looked shrivelled with horror. I had a feeling of nausea myself.

'No wonder,' she said vehemently, 'that she rushed out to throw herself over the cliff! No wonder if she struck at his wife! No wonder if she died so full of hatred and vengeance that her spirit can't rest!'

'I can see what he meant when he said to Mary, "I promise you she won't come back."'

'He was wrong,' Pamela said ... 'What do you suppose,' she asked me, 'Judith saw in the glass? "Death's-head old age" was her phrase. She thought it was herself. Did she see Carmel, or this?'

'I don't know what she saw, but I think that she felt as Carmel felt at that moment – struck by decay. I think that feeling stays in the room.'

'Dreadful!'

Staring at the picture still, Pamela murmured, '"Looking down into hell": Lizzie said that about the woman at the head of the stairs. I would believe that Lizzie had seen Carmel, only that Carmel's hair and eyes were dark.'

I deliberated over this.

'I suspect,' I said, 'that the materialisation was not complete and Lizzie actually saw no more than I did – a misty form. Her imagination would do the rest.'

Pamela stared at the ghastly face in the picture and said slowly, 'If so, Lizzie was lucky: it would be horrible to see this.'

'And vitalised by hate – alive with hunger for revenge.'

Pamela's horrified face made me regret thinking aloud.

'I'm glad Stella didn't see it,' I said.

'Yes.'

An idea came to me; I admitted it to myself reluctantly, and it was some time before I spoke: 'Exorcism might drive Carmel out.'

'I had put exorcism entirely out of my mind, but it is possible ... ' After a moment's deep thought Pamela went on: 'If we could communicate with Mary and ask her about exorcism and if she said "Yes," I dare say Stella would agree.'

I hedged: 'If Mary gives us a sign; but we can hardly hope for that.'

'If she can communicate – '

'I am afraid she will never – '

'Roddy, we must make her! Ask her!'

'Constrain a ghost?'

'Yes, Roddy: hold a séance!'

I stood up. I was not going to be rushed into this. Without replying, I went across the grass to Charlie and worked with him for a while. While I worked I thought. This was the only active course open to us: the one thing we could do at our own will and our own time; to reject it meant waiting, perhaps endless waiting, for chance, occasional manifestations, which might or might not give us clues. I had sworn to Stella that I would try everything, and Pamela was willing to try this. If she was still willing when she knew more about the dangers, we would do it.

I called her; we walked down the drive and turned into the path among the larches, where there was shelter from the wind.

She was all ardour and urgency, but I was not going to let her plunge into this experiment without realising the risk. I asked her, 'Do you remember Mrs Lush?'

'Vaguely,' she replied, surprised: 'a woman in dripping black, who was always coming to mother in hectic joy and then bursting into tears. She had lost her children, hadn't she? I used to feel that I ought to be nice to her, but she gave me the creeps.'

'You don't remember her earlier, when she gave parties for her two kids? You wouldn't, you were too young. I do. She was a laughing, vivacious woman; I admired her no end.'

'I suppose the deaths of the children broke her down?'

'Not at first. When they were drowned she was very courageous, then someone started taking her to séances. Mother told me about it as a warning, but forbade me to tell you. Mrs Lush thought she was in touch with Tommy and Rita and was in raptures; then the medium was convicted of fraud. The unfortunate woman went to another, and it was torment: she would be in seventh heaven one minute and the next go to pieces, thinking she had been tricked again. In the end she went out of her mind.'

'Are you telling me this to scare me?'

'Yes.'

'I'm not scared. This isn't a case of communicating with someone you care for. We shan't become involved.'

'That's true, but it's a dangerous game.'

'We've got to try it. This has all become so dangerous for Stella; the danger may not be confined to this house.'

Pamela had found a conclusive argument. I said, 'Very well.'

Neither of us knew what to do next. Except for frivolous table-turning with friends in Chelsea, we had no experience of this sort of thing. We disliked the notion of employing a medium, and this kind of experiment would not be in Scott's line. In the end, of course, we resorted to Max. We decided to send Max a long telegram, asking him to try to find somebody, not a professional medium, who would help us to conduct a séance. I drove six miles to a telegraph office to send it, not wishing to start all Biddlecombe chattering about the devil-raising at Cliff End.

What would Max think of this request? I wondered. He must have realised from those photographs that Judith's vision in the studio was connected with Carmel in some strange way; he had said, 'You'll be interested.' We were. He probably detested the idea of séances as much as I did, but he would guess that it was a last desperate resort, and he would help.

I called at Scott's lodgings. I wanted to find out what was happening at Wilmcote and believed that he would know. To ask him direct questions over the telephone would be useless: he would become prickly with etiquette and shut up like a hedgehog, but if we could talk, he might become a little co-operative. His landlady told me that he was out on an urgent call; the telephone number was three seven and I was not to say she had given it to me, but she was cooking dinner and could not telephone herself. When I said I would like him to ring up Cliff End she became transformed into a lady of leisure, who would have liked nothing better than a long chat, but I made a quick escape.

Three seven was the Wilmcote number. Pamela and I assured one another that it was the Commander who had been taken ill, but we were both strained and restless, waiting for a call from Scott. He did not telephone; at about nine o'clock he came, this time in the car.

'We felt anxious about Stella,' Pamela told him frankly, 'and we hoped you wouldn't mind letting us know whether she is all right.'

'She's a long way from all right,' he replied.

I gave him a drink; he needed it, but he hesitated, turning the glass round and round, while I struggled with an impulse to question him.

'The Commander sent for me,' he said, frowning, 'and he would not like my speaking of it, but Stella begged me to. She's my patient, after all, in this case, and she's not an infant. I'm not going to let the old man stand in the way.'

Hang Scott and his etiquette and his ethics! I thought impatiently. Pamela asked quietly, 'What's wrong with Stella?'

'Insomnia.'

'That's serious,' I said. 'Is it bad?'

'This is Tuesday,' he answered: 'she has had about four hours' sleep since Friday night: a little on Saturday morning, two hours on Sunday night, and last night none at all.'

'What are you doing?'

'I got her asleep under drugs.'

'Good lord!'

'What else can I do?'

'Get her away from her grandfather!' Pamela exclaimed angrily. 'He puts an impossible strain on her; she thinks about him, worries about his approval or disapproval all the time! Heaven knows what he has been saying to her!'

'That's arranged: she's going away.'

'When?' and 'Where to?' we asked, both speaking at once.

'On Saturday; the nurse or matron or whoever she is won't come for her sooner, and of course the old man can't travel. She's going to Bristol to a rest-cure place of sorts.'

'Not Miss Holloway's?' Pamela was appalled.

'That's the name. The matron's an old governess or something of Stella's.'

There was a shocked silence. Scott looked puzzled by our dismay.

I enlightened him: 'Miss Holloway is the woman who was nursing Carmel when she died.'

He was dumbfounded.

'Do you mean to say the Commander knows that, and ... '

'And trusts her, because she was his daughter's friend.'

'Does Stella *like* the woman?'

'No.'

Pamela broke in; she was upset. 'The strain will be worse there! It may not be true that Miss Holloway neglected Carmel, but she is a dreadful person – as cold as a stone; she – she *distorts* Stella.'

'You've met her, then?'

I replied briefly, 'We have.'

'Dr Scott,' Pamela pleaded, 'can't you stop this?'

He shook his head wretchedly; he would have liked nothing better than to do battle at Pamela's request.

'Impossible! The Commander's completely satisfied with this plan, and nothing else will induce him – '

He broke off; concerning the Commander, professional secrecy was to be observed. He said only, 'I can't worry him now.'

'What's Stella's message?' I asked.

'It's an extraordinary message and there's no sense in delivering it, but she made me promise. She wants to come here for a night. She declares that if she were here she could sleep.'

'No!' To my own annoyance and Scott's astonishment, I had shouted, leaping to my feet. 'Has she not had lessons enough? Is she crazy? Has she forgotten last Friday night?'

'It is unthinkable,' Pamela said.

Scott looked from her to me, bewildered. His eyes searched Pamela's face. 'You're not sleeping properly yourself.'

'No one sleeps in this house,' I told him angrily; 'you know what's going on here! Why didn't you tell Stella to put it out of her mind at once?'

'I did,' he replied, 'and the result was a frightful upset. She astounded me; I would have bet my last penny that nothing would make Stella behave like that.'

'What do you mean?'

Quite unfairly, I felt angry with Scott.

'The change in her was incredible,' he said. 'You know her self-possessed little manner, so correct and polite? Well, when I was called in first, this morning, she was all proper and tidy, like that – and, mind you, after three nights without sleep! Most women would have been hysterical. She received me in that neat little room of hers, looking as if she had been ill for a month, but all obedience, all good manners, ready to do anything that was advised, much more anxious about her grandfather than about herself.'

'Is he ill?' I asked.

'He is in a frightful state about her,' Scott replied. 'He won't tell me why. His phrase is, "She has come under unfortunate influences," and that's all he'll say. I think, myself, they have had a big showdown and she's repentant and wants to make up. It's pathetic – the two of them there, and only some sort of a charwoman to look after them.'

'Did she tell you what was keeping her from sleeping?' Pamela asked.

'No; I couldn't get it out of her. "Everyone has their worries," she says. Ridiculous! She evaded my questions. I was helpless; you can't cure a patient who refuses you her confidence, above all in a psychological sort of trouble like this. I could only put her under drugs.'

'But,' I said impatiently, 'I thought you told us she made a scene.'

'That was this afternoon, when she woke. I went up again and waited for her to come out of the drug. She woke at about half-past four. She was in a curious state; I suppose she'd been having nightmares; she was moaning to herself; I don't think she realised that I was in the room. She kept on saying in a desperate sort of way, "He might have been killed! He might have been killed!"'

'And then?' I prompted. My voice was steadier than my heart.

'Oh, then she saw that I was there and started to cry bitterly and say that she was lonely and unhappy and couldn't bear it and I must send her away. She said, "I can't bear it here any more." It was then she came out with this notion about sleeping here. When I said the Commander wouldn't think of allowing it, and so on, she sobbed and pleaded and carried on – it simply wasn't Stella at all. In the end, to quiet her, I had to swear I'd come here and put it to you; and I had to give her a much bigger shot than I like to get her under at all.'

'That's a dreadful thing,' I exclaimed, 'cramming Stella with drugs!'

'What else can I do? If you can tell me what is on her mind, it might help. She didn't get into this condition without a reason – a girl of her age.'

Pamela looked at me. 'We had better tell Dr Scott everything, hadn't we?'

'Obviously,' I replied, 'since we are the "unfortunate influences".' Dazed by the chaos of thoughts and emotions surging through me, I left Pamela to tell him the story and stood at the window, staring out.

'He might have been killed.' In the midst of her suffering that was what Stella thought about most. 'You might have been killed': she had said that to me and promised not to force her way here again. I had not realised, then, what a sacrifice she was making. For her fright had not quelled her longing to see her mother; that persisted; for my sake she had tried to crush it down. And now she was suffering the torments of insomnia and begging for our help, and I was forced to refuse the one thing that she believed would give her sleep. She needed me, and I could neither go to her nor let her come. I was almost desperate, and yet the pain I felt was shot through with the keenest happiness that I had ever known.

Well – we were fighting: all this would pass.

Scott was listening to Pamela, enthralled.

'By Jove,' he exclaimed, 'it's no wonder she's off her sleep! How on earth does she keep all this to herself?'

She told him of her fear that Carmel's spirit was haunting Cliff End, bent on revenge, even, perhaps, set, in a sort of timeless delirium, on doing Stella harm.

He was incoherent in his concern.

'How utterly rotten for you! I'm not surprised you're not looking well. No wonder,' he added, 'the dog wouldn't stay.'

The anticlimax made Pamela chuckle.

'I'm glad,' he said crossly, 'that you can laugh.'

'We haven't despaired of coming through it,' she declared. 'Could you,' she asked him, 'take a letter for me to Stella?'

Scott looked worried.

'I can't very well do that, but I'll tell her anything you like.'

'Tell her we are really hopeful at last,' Pamela said, 'and that I'll write to her at Bristol. Tell her to trust us and be patient and to try to understand why we can't let her come. Give her our love.'

She looked unhappy; it was a heart-breaking answer to have to send.

Scott was going on to Wilmcote now. After seeing him to his car I walked across the garden and climbed the knoll. The September twilight was cool, with a moist, fragrant breeze; the cleeve of Biddlecombe was filled with a bluish mist; the golden lights of the houses twinkled out of it; here and there on the moors shone the windows of solitary farms, and minute clusters of lights marked villages along the coast. The hills on the far side of the village were dark against the afterglow. That valley was narrow; it did not seem credible that I was separated from Stella by an impassable gulf.

Was Stella lying awake? Was she thinking of me? Snatches of her naive little song came into my head:

> *May sweet angels watch thee sleeping,*
> *All through the night,*
> *Safe from harm and danger peeping,*
> *All through the night,*
> *Till no longer fate denying,*
> *Gives the meed to love undying ...*

As I went down to Cliff End a warm glow shone out from the lower windows. Stella loved this house, as I did. I could not believe that any other was destined to be our home.

Chapter XVI

A WARNING

'GET DRUNK on champagne,' Ballaster had advised, 'and go at it again.' He was right, I decided when I looked through the second act on Wednesday morning. This act, in which Barbara is filled with the exhilaration of her devilish enterprise and is still adored as a gay and generous woman, needed buoyancy, humour, wit. I knew – and found afterwards that I had been right about this – that I could rely on the players to lighten it; this morning, however, it was as heavy as clay on a spade. After an hour's sweating and straining over it I produced two amusing retorts and one pun, and my script had become a jungle of erasures, inserts, and long-tailed loops. The champagne and the jizzing up would have to wait, I decided, and turned to the last act. There was a problem here more in tune with my mood: to devise a fate for Barbara which should be grim but not horrific, unexpected and yet almost inevitable; which should derive from her character and be appropriate to her misdeeds. I was pondering over it when the telephone rang. 'Scott!' I thought, and was downstairs in two bounds.

'May I speak to Miss Fitzgerald?' The voice, strained and abrupt, startled me: it was Commander Brooke's. From the nursery window I hailed Pamela. She dropped the wire she was holding for Charlie and hurried in, signing to me to stand by.

Her face flushed as she listened; she answered quietly, 'I shall be very glad to. Yes, at once.'

She hung up the receiver and looked at me wide-eyed. 'He wants me to go to Stella.'

'Does that mean she's worse?'

'I'm afraid so; he sounded rather distracted; he was afraid I would refuse.'

'Didn't he say what's wrong?'

'He said, "she has pleaded so vehemently." He said, "naturally, unless it seemed the only thing that would calm her, I would not make this request."'

'Shall I drive you?'

'Yes, Roddy; do.'

This summons could only mean that Stella was ill or hysterical, yet my anxiety was less than my relief; we were no longer cut off.

'Make some plan to keep in touch with her,' I urged as we drove to Wilmcote. 'Tell her I'll be in Bristol; say I'll stay if it will help. In any case, I'll be there for rehearsals. Make sure of some way of seeing her; the whole thing is not to get out of touch.'

Pamela nodded. 'I'll try, but if she's "ashamed and penitent," as the Commander said, it might upset her.'

'She's over that – she was mutinying yesterday, according to Scott.'

'I think I mustn't oppose her about anything,' Pamela said. 'Whatever her mood is, I must just fit in. She has got to sleep.'

'I agree absolutely about that.'

I told her I would leave the car outside Wilmcote, walk through the grove, and wait for her near the bowling-green. 'Don't say anything to excite her,' I urged, 'and don't on any account mention the word "exorcism."'

'Good heavens, no!'

Pamela looked nervous as she waited to be let in.

I walked to the clearing on the other side of the grove. There was a sanded path here and a bowling alley with seats facing the sea. This sheltered crescent, with its fine view, background of pines, and briny, resinous air, was the sort of place which it would be exciting to come upon in its natural state, but tamed, trimmed, and populated, it was dull. Four old gentlemen were having a leisurely game, watched from one bench by uniformed nursemaids who looked as bored as their charges and, from the other, by tousled youngsters and their rosy young mother, who were enjoying some uproarious joke. This was the fashionable side of Biddlecombe; elderly couples with small dogs were to be met here; a tall girl passed, wheeling an old man in a bath-chair; two stout, hot women in black marched by grimly; they had quarrelled and kept their eyes on opposite sides of the path. It was a refreshing change to meet a young man and a girl in shorts, striding along with packs on their backs. I could have found entertainment here, but my nerves were in a contemptible state, and while I walked up and down my anxiety grew and grew. The more I recalled of our talk with the Commander, the more sure I felt that only a considerable crisis would have driven him to make this request.

At last Pamela drove up. She parked the car and joined me, and we walked into the shady depths of the wood. I could see that things had not gone well. She said, 'Stella sent for me to say goodbye.'

'How is she?'

'Quite calm, but exhausted; very fragile and pale. She has had a good deal of sleep under drugs. She begs our forgiveness for sending that hysterical message yesterday. I am to tell you' – there was irony in Pamela's voice – 'that she will always remember us both with gratitude.'

'An everlasting farewell, was it?'

'So I understand.'

Pamela had tears in her eyes.

'Good heavens, girl,' I said, 'you're not taking this seriously? She has been bullied, that's all, and she's too weak to resist. It will be a completely different story when she's well.'

'I'm not sure, Roddy: she is defeated, almost extinguished – it isn't – it isn't Stella at all.'

'But have sense, Pamela! Think of insomnia – nights and days without sleep, and then drugs. Of *course* she's not herself.'

'I know, but there is more in it than that. Her grandfather has won. He is ill; she says he is suffering terrible pain, that he ought to have an operation and won't, because of her. She wept over that. And I'm afraid he said dreadful things to her, crushing things. She kept repeating, "He forgave me and I don't know how he could."'

'Yes, yes,' I replied, 'all this is natural enough for the moment, but don't you see that it will pass?'

'I'm frightened,' she said; 'the influence goes so deep; it has been life-long, since the day Stella was born. Oh, Roddy, the deliberate pressure, twisting and moulding her! Her room –it's a memorial to Mary, that's all.'

'Now aren't you exaggerating?'

'I'm not; it's simply a shrine to her mother. Stella told me about it, in an awed sort of voice. Pale blue walls – her mother's favourite colour; marguerites on the hangings – her mother's favourite flower; Mary's pictures – Florentine madonnas; a sketch of Mary as a girl and before it, in a glass vase, one white rose; even a statuette of her mother – a white plaster thing. It's a *culte*. Oh, the piety, the austerity, the pure, virginal charm! Any sensitive girl would come under the spell – and I doubt if the man is born who could break it.'

'Sounds pretty complete.'

'And she's going to Miss Holloway now!'

'Does Stella consent?'

'She consents to everything; she consents because she shrinks from it. Stella's self-discipline is abnormal.'

'It certainly is.'

'This is surrender, abnegation,' Pamela went on despairingly. 'She said, "I have sinned and I must do penance," and as she said it she smiled. I could hear Mary saying it; I could see Mary's smile.'

'A candidate for martyrdom?'

'Yes.'

We walked deeper into the grove. The trees were tall and sombre here, the air stagnant and the closed-in odour too strong.

I loathed the story Pamela was telling me; everything in me was in revolt.

'Look, Roddy.' Pamela found a fallen trunk and we sat down. She opened her handbag. 'Look, Stella gave me these. This is for you. She said, "Tell him it's to remember me by."'

It was a small sketchbook of her father's, with pencil sketches made in Spain – details of a cathedral door, twisted olives, a beggar sitting on a step; there were drawings of Carmel – Carmel young and gay. Her farewell gift to Pamela was a heart-shaped phial about a quarter full of mimosa scent, its fragrance almost gone.

'I was right,' Pamela said; 'her father sent it to her from Seville. It was his last gift before he died.'

This was depressing; it was as if a girl going into a nunnery were giving her last earthly treasures away.

'Come out of this mortuary,' I said.

We walked back to the car. I asked Pamela whether she had had any talk with the Commander. 'Yes,' she said; 'he came into Stella's room and said that it was time for her to rest. Tears began to stream down her cheeks. She clung to me wildly just while we said goodbye, then took her arms away and lay quite still and smiled. I couldn't stand it.'

Pamela's voice shook. After a minute she went on: 'He took me to the door. He told me what had happened. Stella had made a bargain with him: she had been in a hysterical state but promised to calm herself if only he would let me come to bid her goodbye. He said, "It is goodbye, you understand, Miss Fitzgerald? Where she is going, no visits and no letters will be permitted. She will have a complete and prolonged rest, and after that she will go abroad." He really looked terribly ill. He was polite. He said, "I appreciate your coming; it was exceedingly kind." Then he opened the door. There is something indomitable about him, Roddy. I can't imagine him ever giving in; he makes me despair.'

'You have let this impress you too much,' I answered. I was not going to despair at this juncture. For the moment my enemies had prevailed. But this would not end it; even Miss Holloway's 'stony limits' could not be impregnable.

What could be done to distract Pamela from brooding over this miserable visit? 'Shall we go and see Father Anson?' I suggested. 'We ought to tell him about our talk with Holloway.' She agreed. It was nearly one o'clock; we might find him at his house now.

The red spire of the little Catholic church was a landmark, rising out of dark trees on the hill to our left. As we approached it we saw a bare, square, new-looking house, faced with cement, standing in a patch of field, the garden as yet unmade.

'That's the priest's house,' Pamela guessed.

It was, and Father Anson was in. His housekeeper received us crossly; she had just been about to serve his dinner, no doubt. The woman satisfied the regulations, being not comely and of the canonical age. Pamela told her that, if it was not convenient for Father Anson to see us, we would like to know when we might come or when he would come to tea at Cliff End. The woman's face lit up.

'Cliff End, is it? Then you'll be Miss Fitzgerald? Mrs Flynn was with me the other day and we had a great old talk. Maybe she'd come down again some time? We are both from the County Clare.'

We assured her that Lizzie would be delighted, and she took our message to the priest. He came out of the sitting-room at once, welcomed us warmly, and settled us near the window in basket-chairs. He appeared delighted to see us and talked happily about his house. His parishioners had recently built it for him; it was not as fine a house as Cliff End, but he had great enjoyment from it. They were going to start on the garden soon. He chatted about his curtains of Irish tweed, his hand-made rugs, and other comforts, looking kindly but keenly at Pamela all the time. Here was a man from whom people whose home was menaced could expect understanding. I was glad we had come. Presently he paused.

'But here I am chattering about my own concerns and I have not asked after yours. I hope you have come with good news? I have been thinking about you a great deal. Is the trouble less?'

Pamela was unhappy and tired, and his kindness sapped her control.

'It is terrible, Father,' she said.

He rose and, after carefully selecting the right key, unlocked a cupboard in his sideboard. He drew out a bottle, two glasses, and a napkin. He polished the glasses, dusted the bottle, found a corkscrew, and slowly drew the cork.

'I hope you are connoisseurs of Madeira,' he said. 'I am told this is a fine old vintage; unfortunately, it is wasted on me and has been waiting months for guests worthy of it. Now let us see whether my friend, the Abbé, was cheating me. No?'

I sipped the wine. It was delicious.

'The Abbé is an honest man, Father: long life to him!' I said.

'And to you, Father,' Pamela smiled.

'I'll give you a toast, though I can't drink it,' the priest said, seating himself comfortably in a worn leather arm-chair:

> *Health and long life to you!*
> *House and land to you!*
> *The wife of your heart to you!*

'It ends,' he added: "And death in Ireland" – but we'll leave that to God.'

His eyes were twinkling. Pamela laughed. He had achieved his object, and at once his face became grave.

'We must not despair, however terrible these visitations may be,' he said quietly. 'The Church has means of combatting them.'

I told him about Stella's abhorrence of the idea of exorcism and her nervous state. He was moved.

'Poor child! Poor, tormented child! And without consolation; without the Faith! It is difficult to know what one should do.'

He was deeply troubled, speaking as though the problem were his own.

Pamela made him smile with her somewhat ironic account of Miss Holloway.

'I have no doubts that according to her lights she is a righteous woman,' he said, 'but,' he added, the creases around his eyes deepening, 'one sometimes finds it easy to understand that the Lord loves repentant sinners best.'

He asked whether her story had helped us. Pamela told him that what we had learnt about Carmel's state of mind made us think that her spirit might be causing the sense of cold and terror that we felt in the house.

He shook his head:

'I would find that very difficult to believe.'

She recounted how we had, apparently, been guided to the discovery of Carmel's little box and asked him whether he did lot think it possible that Mary was lingering at Cliff End to protect Stella and trying now to help her through us.

I could see that this displeased him; he deliberated for a long time before he answered, then he said: 'I can conceive that Stella's mother might be permitted to protect her, but we must not make assumptions about these things; they are beyond our comprehension. You have an active imagination, Miss Fitzgerald; beware of letting it carry you too far from shore; these are deep waters.'

I mentioned the question of Masses for Carmel.

'I remember her poor soul every year at the feast of Our Lady of Mount Carmel, but I will say a special Mass for her,' he replied. Then he smiled.

'It pleases me that you should suggest this. You are only half a heretic, Mr Fitzgerald, and your sister is not a quarter one,' he said.

'We would be deceiving you if we let you think that,' Pamela answered; 'but what seems to me to matter in this case is that Carmel believed.'

The priest looked at her with deepened interest but said no more on that subject, though I felt sure that he would have liked to pursue it and was only biding his time.

'Tell me, have the disturbances been very distressing?' he asked.

As briefly as possible we described the events of Friday night – the terror which had come upon Stella, the apparition which she seemed to have seen, and her panic flight. He was profoundly shocked. He turned to Pamela, exclaiming, 'My daughter, leave that house!'

I told him that we were prepared to do so if all else failed, but pointed out that we were fore-armed against such panic, that no one would sleep alone at Cliff End, and that we were protecting the fatal creek with a fence.

'A fence!' he cried sternly. 'Do you think that a fence, or human companionship, or any precaution that you can take, of your own strength, can protect you against such forces as these? You little understand with what you are contending, my son! The danger is not danger of death.'

'Do you mean a shock to one's reason?' I asked.

'I mean possession,' he replied.

Pamela said soberly, 'I know, Father Anson; I have thought of it; I felt it one night when I tried to sleep in the nursery: the malignance would come in on you – overwhelm your mind.'

'The thing happens more frequently than people are aware of or willing to believe,' the priest said gravely. 'Lunatic asylums are full of such cases, though scientists give it other names.'

'Have you actually known cases?' I asked.

'Thank God, no. But a friend of mine had a narrow escape. She was a Galway lady. She did a very foolish, even a wicked thing: she held spiritualistic séances in her house. She entered regions where the Church forbids her children to tread. One night two strangers joined her circle; they begged her to allow them to attempt to communicate with a relative recently dead. Some exchange of messages took place which no one but those two understood. They declared themselves satisfied and went away. On the next day my friend was alone in her house. It is a tall one, four storeys high. For nearly an hour she stood at an upper window, fighting a fierce battle against an impulse to fling herself out. She learned afterwards that the dead relative of the two strangers had taken his own life in that way.'

I suppose our silence betrayed us. We could not promise him that we would not hold a séance. He looked at us with his lips compressed.

'I will let you go now,' he said impressively, 'with that warning in your minds. Stella Meredith's objection must be overcome. We must hold a service of exorcism at Cliff End. I will apply to the Bishop for permission at once. Be patient. God bless you, my dear friends.'

We drove home without talking much. Pamela's face was set in its most obstinate lines. I was almost regretting having consented to a séance.

There was a telegram from Max: 'Bringing Ingram Dublin Writers' Who's Who last train tomorrow.'

We looked him up. This must be he: Garrett Ingram; Member of the Irish Bar; a man of thirty with a curious variety of achievements to his credit already.

'He seems,' I remarked, 'to be another of these Dublin law men who do so many things brilliantly that you can never remember what their profession is.'

He had written plays for the Abbey Theatre and published verse; he was the author of a monograph on Waterford glass, which he collected, of another (with Mrs Ingram) on 'The Pigmentation of Dahlias,' and of a book called *Parapsychic Phenomena: An Analysis.*

'I hope he is not one of these debunkers,' Pamela said. 'I just couldn't do with being told "It's all your imagination" now.'

'Max wouldn't do that on us,' I said. 'The man will know how to conduct a séance, anyway; though, I confess, I'm in two minds about trying that now.'

'I'm not, Roddy.'

'So I supposed.'

'I'm glad to be warned of the dangers, all the same.'

'I wish you'd stay out of it, Pamela, and leave it to the three of us.'

She shook her head: 'None of that, Roddy, please.'

'I don't like it, Pamela; you're not the type.'

'Look here, Roddy.' She stood squarely in front of me and looked me full in the face. 'You have no responsibility for me over this. I could do all sorts of things by myself if I wanted to – sit up all night on the stairs, for instance; it might give results. But we'd make it worse for each other if either of us worked alone. I'll promise not to, as long as we can work together; but don't think you can shut me out.'

I could only grin and surrender.

'Okay, comrade!'

Pamela's intrepidity was encouraging. She was not likely to suffer from the experiment, I told myself, approaching it in that spirit. I cheered up. It was exhilarating to be preparing a frontal attack, with two men of brain and brawn to help. If our séance did nothing else, it would probably stir up whatever psychic influences were around. Watching all night, together or in pairs, we would almost certainly see something that would help, and 'the worse, the better, now,' as Pamela said.

I spent the afternoon with her, digging, and wondered how people got through times like these who did not own a bit of land and a spade. After a few hours of it Pamela felt better.

'I believe you are right about Stella,' she said after dinner. 'This morning depressed me terribly, but that is the atmosphere of Wilmcote, I think. Once she gets clear of that, Stella may be herself again. If only she were going anywhere but to Miss Holloway!'

I said vaguely, 'She may not be there long.'

My mind was playing with scenes of escape and abduction, but I kept this to myself.

Our optimism was shattered by Scott. He arrived on foot, exhausted and distraught, and slumped into a chair, saying to Pamela accusingly, 'Why the dickens couldn't you leave Stella alone?'

It was a shock.

'You've undone all my work,' Scott went on. 'She's worse than ever; the old man too. No doctor could handle them. He ignores my advice, refuses a consultation … '

'Did you want a consultation about Stella?' I broke in.

'Not yet; no: for him. I've had to send in a nurse. I've told him I won't … '

'What's wrong with Stella?' I demanded.

'I wish I knew! She's gone off the deep end again, worse than ever.'

'But she was perfectly calm when I left her,' Pamela exclaimed, 'absolutely composed and resigned!'

'You shouldn't have gone!'

'The Commander begged me to.'

'He ought to have rung me up first.'

'You wouldn't have objected.'

'I'd have warned you not to upset her.'

'I didn't upset her.'

'Well,' Scott insisted, 'all I know is that when I looked in this morning, about ten o'clock, she was in a sound sleep. Then, according to the old man, she wakes up and starts crying and fretting and pleading with him to let her see you. You come along, and I'm sent for again, and I find her like this!'

'Like what?' I asked him. 'You haven't told us. Do be explicit! Have a drink?'

'I won't, thanks. "Like what?" Like a frantic child! She was roaming about her room in her dressing-gown. She seemed to have no control of herself at all. Said she couldn't swallow her medicine, couldn't stay in the house, couldn't go to Miss Holloway's. She seemed frightened of me, of her room, of her grandfather. When he came in she turned on him; the poor man was utterly taken aback; I'm sure she had never in her life been rude to him before. She abused him and then wept – oh lord, it was tiring!'

'You've drugged her out of her senses,' I exclaimed.

He snapped back: 'Would you rather she went out of her senses without drugs?'

'Had she slept after Pamela's visit?'

'Yes, for three hours.'

'She'd gone to sleep naturally, after Pamela left?'

'So the Commander said.'

'And woke like this? It's extraordinary.'

'It's diabolical.'

I wished Scott wouldn't use words so wildly.

'And after this morning!' Pamela said incredulously. 'She was all meekness, all submission.'

Scott nodded. 'I know. I have never seen anything like it. I don't mind telling you I'm out of my depth.'

'Didn't she tell you what had upset her?' I asked.

'Everything has upset her! She's in a state of rebellion against everybody. She is simply not herself. Can you imagine Stella violent? Can you see Stella throwing a locket and chain out of a window? Snatching up an ornament and deliberately smashing it on the floor?'

This was appalling. I heard Pamela asking, 'What ornament?' as if that mattered. Then I understood.

'A white plaster statuette of her mother,' Scott said.

Pamela looked at me, aghast. I said, 'I'm afraid this is serious, Scott.'

'Haven't I been trying to make you see that it's serious,' he answered angrily, 'and can't you see what's brought it on? This visit! There's a tug-of-war going on in the girl – on one side the Commander and all her training, and on the other you two and whatever you and this house stand for in her life. And these ghastly psychic experiences on top of that. Good heavens, there's only one logical end!'

He was pacing up and down, working himself into a fever. 'What end?' I demanded. 'What are you getting at, Scott?'

'Schizophrenia,' he said.

I did not know whether I could have understood, and it was an effort to ask.

'Split personality?'

'Yes.'

I saw it clearly. This *was* the logical conclusion of the whole thing. Father Anson would have called it 'possession.'

'It hasn't happened,' I contended vehemently. 'You are making a great deal out of a fit of temper. You've lost your balance, man! She's not in that condition!'

'No, but she may be.'

Scott knew what he was talking about. I apologised. 'What's the treatment for schizophrenia?'

Scott hesitated, then said, 'I can't swear to that diagnosis. I'm not a psychiatrist. In a way, it has more features of dual than split – Or it could be *folie circulaire* – '

Maddened, I broke out violently, 'The treatment, man! What's to be done?'

His answer was evasive.

'These things aren't tackled by general practitioners.'

It told me enough.

'She'll be all right,' Pamela said shakily. 'She'll pull herself through.'

'That's the best we can hope for,' Scott replied. 'I appealed to her on her grandfather's account; I told her he was seriously ill, and it did produce an effect: she made an effort to quiet down. She cried passionately over the statuette and begged me to tell him it was an accident. I picked up the locket all right.'

'Did you tell him that?' I asked.

'Yes. Good heavens, I couldn't tell him the truth!'

'Has Stella nobody to look after her?' Pamela asked wretchedly.

'There'll be the nurse now.'

'I suppose he wouldn't let me go?'

'You!' Scott exclaimed. 'The last person on earth! Oh lord, I'm sorry,' he said. 'But I'm played out. I can't cope.'

He had not eaten. Lizzie had left for the farm; Pamela brought him cold meat on a tray. He wolfed it; he was famished. When he had eaten he accepted a drink and at last relaxed.

'I have done an awfully irregular thing, telling you so much about it,' he said, his brow contracted in a worried frown. 'Only I had to make you see that this tug-of-war can't go on. It's destroying her. One side has got to give way. I've left her quiet and docile, and that's how she'll have to stay. You two excite her; you've got to drop out, immediately and completely, that's all.'

'Yes,' I admitted, 'that seems pretty clear.'

Pamela looked at me; it was the way my mother used to look when I had ear-ache – as if to stop it was the only thing that mattered in this world. She said, 'Stella has no end of willpower. I think she'll get over this; she'll probably be herself again in the morning.'

'And who,' Scott said bitterly, 'in the afternoon? The devil of it is, the thing recurs! It's these alternations that scare me. For two days, now, she has been a stained-glass saint and a crazy little gypsy in turns.'

'A saint and a little gypsy,' Pamela repeated weakly. She leaned on the table. I thought she was going to faint. There were war-drums in my head.

'I'll phone you in the morning,' Scott said, and rose to go. He was exhausted. I drove him to his lodgings. Pamela came too. I would not leave her alone in the house. As we drove home she began to cry quietly. I could say nothing to console her. I was in the grip of deadly apprehension myself.

Chapter XVII

THE SPELLING-GLASS

I THOUGHT that it was Pamela weeping and leaped out of bed. She had reason enough to cry, but not with this abandonment and despair.

Outside her bedroom door I stood still. It was not Pamela – thank heaven for that! The sound came from farther off. I looked into the studio; the room was as empty and unwelcoming as ever. I went back to Pamela's door again, but the sound had ceased, and I knew, now, that the voice had been like one remembered, not like a living voice. Pamela called me quietly and I went in. She was all right. Her lamp was lighted; she had a bed-jacket over her shoulders and was sitting up in bed, listening.

'Did you hear it?' she asked.

'Of course – I was afraid it was you.'

'Wait for me; I'm going down.'

While I waited on the landing I heard it from downstairs. It was a distressing sound to listen to, even though I felt its remoteness from actuality – anguished weeping, with a wild protest in it, the shocked incredulity that belongs to the griefs of youth.

Pamela came out and stood beside me, listening. 'It's in the nursery,' she whispered, hesitating to go down. I thought the voice changed, presently, or something changed in the nature of the weeping; it became weak, as though exhausted with old, hopeless pain. At last nothing was left but a sigh.

We went down quietly, turning on the lights. The nursery was empty and so was the dining-room. For a moment I felt or imagined a tremor in the air. That stopped suddenly and everything stood still.

I did not like the quality of the stillness: it was as if we were in a vacuum at the centre of a vortex; heart and pulses slowed down; there was no air; it required an extreme effort to move. We broke through, running upstairs and into my room.

'The cold will come now,' Pamela said.

I gave her a cigarette. She was excited and pale, but not really afraid; she talked, keeping fear at bay.

'I'm glad you heard it so distinctly at last. It's selfish of me, but the worst thing of all is not to trust one's own senses … I think I had a hallucination tonight. I'm quite sure you would say it was that.'

A fringe of the cold was creeping into the room, yet that does not express what happened: nothing was coming in; it was rather as if the natural warmth of the air and of one's body was ebbing away.

'It was floating in the darkness,' Pamela went on, 'in the far corner of my room. It was just as I was falling asleep. It was vague, like an image in water. I was just going to speak, but it broke, as if you had thrown a stone into a pool.'

She was shivering. I could guess what was happening outside: that ribbon of luminous vapour was snaking up.

'But what was this?'

'It was the face in the picture.'

'Not Carmel's? That ghastly face?'

'Oh, no, the other one – *Dawn*.'

Pamela was crouched on the bed, my eiderdown over her. She was white now, even her lips. I found it a strain to talk.

229

I said, 'That wasn't hallucination, even; it's common enough; the retina or the brain retains an image.'

'But it wasn't exactly the same.'

'How do you mean?'

'The face looked sad. It was young and soft, but the eyes had a tragic, appealing look. I wish it had stayed.'

'You say you were just falling asleep?'

'Yes.'

'It was very natural … '

'This cold isn't natural, Roddy.'

'I know.'

I did not know how to endure it; it was this weak, bloodless feeling again, the languor that made one reluctant to move. I said, 'I'm going out to see what is happening,' and Pamela replied, 'So am I,' but neither of us stirred.

'Tomorrow will be soon enough,' Pamela whispered. She was shivering from head to foot, and my knees would not keep still. By this time, I thought, it is moving down the stairs. I wanted to see its face. We said no more until gradually the pressure lifted and the cold passed off, then I felt ashamed.

I looked out and told Pamela everything was normal.

'First the scent, then the cold; first the weeping and then the cold. I don't know what it means,' she said wearily as she went back to her room.

I lay in the warm darkness and thought of Stella. The weeping had wakened my imagination to her loneliness and grief. I thought she was lying awake, her heart almost broken, her whole being almost broken in two. But I did not lie awake; I was exhausted and fell asleep.

THERE WAS bustle in the house all the morning. It had been neglected, with Pamela pre-occupied and Lizzie with no heart, as she expressed it, for 'beautifications,' when we would likely be leaving soon. But guests were guests.

There were no pretences about it this time: the studio was not to be slept in, nor was the nursery. Fires were lighted, nevertheless, in both rooms. A bed was put in the study for Mr Ingram, and Max would have mine; I was going to sleep on the sitting-room couch.

While Lizzie 'readied' the rooms Pamela prepared patties and soup for a late supper. She was quiet and tense with anxiety about Stella. I telephoned Scott, but he was out. I drove to his lodgings, but he had not returned.

It was market-day and I had promised to bring home fruit and flowers. The splendid dahlias made my heart ache. I must not even send Stella flowers: I had to 'drop out.' Memories were bitter-sweet company – her soft, eager 'Mr Fitzgerald,' her shy, flushed face.

In the early afternoon Scott telephoned. His hurried words brought supreme relief: 'Pamela was right: Stella's pulling herself out of it; she's a brick. Don't worry if you don't hear from me till Sunday; I have a heavy case. Sorry for unloading my worries on you yesterday.'

Stella was pulling through. The horror that had weighed like a roof, cramping us into a dark cell of dread, was gone, and the wide spaces of life lay around us with clear skies overhead. The rest did not matter. Stella was herself again – which Stella? Mary's daughter, who would 'always remember us with gratitude,' or my Stella, who cried because I might have been killed? That did not matter. She was not suffering; the awful menace that hung over her yesterday had withdrawn; the rest, time, and her own patience, and our efforts, would mend.

Pamela ran about the house as if trouble did not exist. It was too stormy to swim, but we got into the car and drove southward to the high cliffs at Hartland Point; she had wanted to see the Atlantic racing and breaking here, and this was the day for it – strong wind, moving clouds, and clear spells of sun. The long ocean breakers rolled in and rushed on the rocks with a tremendous, roaring onslaught, throwing up cataracts of dazzling spray; the power and the noise were glorious; they washed through one's spirit, sweeping it clear of nightmare. Colour came into Pamela's face. She would be fresh and steady now for the evening's work.

We came back for tea, idled over it, listening to music over the air from some light orchestra, and then rested in silence by the fire.

I came out of a drowse to find the room filled with champagne-coloured light from a windy sunset. It seemed the colour of peace. Years hence, I thought, I shall wake in this chair and see the room like this and watch the light steal over the table to finger the flowers in the bowl.

But as the dusk closed down and curtains were drawn, and the time for our guests' arrival drew near, tension grew. Pamela became restless. I knew very well that Father Anson's warning and Scott's word 'schizophrenia' were making a combined assault. She said: 'I don't feel concentrated enough, somehow, to make the séance work well, do you?'

The house could not be left empty with all these fires blazing and I would not leave Pamela in it. I let her drive alone to the station. She set off at half-past nine. Lizzie had already gone to the farm.

I cleared my book-table; it was a low, round table and would probably serve for the séance. I pulled Pamela's sofa on to the landing, put garden-chairs in the hall, stoked up the fires, and filled the baskets with logs; then I sat down with the journal.

I wanted to bring it up to date and add a summary of the conclusions which we had reached and the questions which baffled us still.

Pamela had already written up her experience of the night and described the illusion in her room, but she had added: 'I thought at first that this was hallucination; now I am not so sure; this face and the weeping have the same kind of sorrow in them.' I wondered what she meant by that. I added a note: 'I have heard two kinds of weeping – one, shocked and violent; the other, hopeless and tired, as though it had gone on for a long time. The latter sounds the more actual of the two.' The first was nightmarish, I realised now, and one heard it when one was half-asleep.

A curious notion came into my mind. Were there two Carmels – two wraiths or memories, as it were, of Carmel – haunting the house? Was the whole thing due to some collision in time? I had not mastered Dunne's theory of Serialism, but I knew that he concludes that one can slip into other dimensions of time. Then there was the ancient belief in astral bodies. Is it possible, I wondered, that Carmel, in her extremities of emotion, had given off first one wraith of herself, and, later, another – one innocent, the other dynamic with hate – and that Cliff End was haunted by both?

This was too far-fetched. I did not write it down. I wrote a methodical summary instead.

I wrote: 'Note: the sensation of cold brings with it fear and either a kind of paralysis or fainting or panic. It invariably accompanies the half-materialised form which appears on the landing and sometimes moves downstairs and enters the nursery.

'Query: is this Carmel, intent on revenge? Was Lizzie mistaken? Was it not Mary but Carmel whom she saw, looking over the stairs?

'Note: light and scent produce no cold or fear; their effect on Stella suggests the presence of Mary.

'Query: is Mary's purpose to protect Stella from Carmel? Why did Mary use the scent to guide us to Carmel's box? What is the significance of the empty phial which the box contained?

'Note: the depression in the studio seems to be connected with the idea of decay.

'Query: is it a reflection of the shock which Carmel suffered in that room?

'Note: the face which Pamela saw in the dark was not the face of Carmel at the time of her death.

'Query: was this an illusion produced by looking at the picture, *Dawn*?

'Note: the weeping produces no sense of cold or fear.

'Query: are both kinds of weeping merely echoes from the past, or is one (violent) from the past and the other (exhausted) an expression of continuing grief? Who is weeping? "Mary did not weep."'

The last question was the most baffling. That and the problem of Carmel's box eluded me; but for these, I would have answered all the other questions, simply, with 'Yes.' Perhaps Ingram's brain, trained to deduction, would discover the answers, or perhaps the haunting spirits would give us one … We were about to lay ourselves open, as completely as human nerves and brains could achieve it, to the influence of those spirits, and one was malign. How would this night's work end?

At last I heard the car.

Never were men more welcome. They came in like two boys on a holiday, Max delighted with himself for having captured Ingram, and Ingram brimming with interest which he made no effort to conceal. As we sat at supper the earth settled solidly on its foundations and human beings were supreme again. Pamela's vivacity, eclipsed for weeks, had come back. Her dark red frock gave her colour. She wore, on a thin silver chain, a fish of white jade, a gift from Judith. 'It is Chinese. It wards off evil spirits,' Max explained smilingly.

The men had dined on the train, but they made a clearance of the patties and cakes.

Max knew nothing of Stella's illness and there was no need to mention it. He knew that we had been befogged in an unearthly atmosphere of tragedy and he was here to help to clear that away. His mere presence, his stalwart frame, strong voice, and contented chuckle asserted the dominance of the living over the dead.

To Ingram our trouble was merely that of people whose property is lowered in value by occult manifestations; he seemed to assume that the intellectual interest of the whole question absorbed us and envied us the ownership of a haunted house.

He was a man of my own age or younger, slight and compact, and in fine training after a month at Zermatt. His keen hazel eyes, mobile brows and mouth, crisp hair, and vigorous movements gave him an air of well-being and confidence in whose presence depression could not survive.

'A fine wild-goose chase you set me!' Max laughed while we drank strong coffee beside the fire. 'What sort of a reputation I'll go back to I can't imagine, after ringing up eleven people to ask if they knew a ghost-hunter! Most of them knew of a medium or two, but you had stipulated 'not a medium'; they all referred me to the SPR, but I rather wanted a personal link. It was by such a fluke, in the end, that I caught Mr Ingram, that I think the stars must be on our side. Lady Townside, of all people, had just read his book. She had written to tell him about some incident that she thought would interest him and had just received a polite reply sent from the Thackeray Hotel.'

'So the wild-goose was run to earth,' Ingram said, 'in the room of the British Museum.'

'How in the world,' I asked, 'did you chance to be free?'

'I wasn't,' he grinned. 'I've got to be on Helvellyn on Saturday and I had five engagements for these two days – but who could resist such an adventure as this? And my aunts can't be aggrieved, can they, when I tell them that I threw them over for a ghost?'

He began to talk, telling us a good deal about himself, which, when it is done with humour and discretion, is no bad way for a newcomer to entertain his host. As usually happens when Irish meet Irish, we discovered that we had common friends: his mother, the lady of the dahlias, with whom he lived when not in his rooms in Dublin, and our Aunt Kathleen were old friends and rival horticulturists. Ingram met Nesta sometimes at the Horse Show and Spring Show.

'She has notions,' Pamela told him, 'about growing plants without soil. I hope it works: that's what we shall have to do here.'

He was starting on an animated exposition of hydroponics, but Max seized the first chance to anchor the balloon.

'How do you find time among all this for studying occultism?' he asked. 'What started you on that track?'

'I wished to prosecute some poltergeists, and discovered that they were privileged,' Ingram answered gravely. 'I wanted to alter that.'

'Where was this?' Max asked, amused.

'In Donegal. A client of mine bought a house there. He was hasty, I admit. He found it infested: bells were jangled; there was incessant knocking; things were flung downstairs, beds dragged about. The man who had sold it to him was completely cynical; he laughed. My client came to me in a bad state, between nerves, rage, and financial panic, and I had to tell him that he had no redress in law. I spent a night in the house. It was unholy. There was no doubt whatever that he had been tricked. I carried the matter as far as I could, by way of a general protest, and the story got all the publicity one could wish.'

'Not much satisfaction,' I remarked.

'No; but, you see,' he concluded gravely, 'having committed myself to believing in poltergeists for the sake of my client, I am obliged, for my own credit, to prove that they exist.'

Pamela laughed. 'Judicial impartiality!'

'Luckily for me,' he declared, 'they do.'

'So,' I observed, 'you are going to change the law?'

'I'll get it altered in Ireland or perish in the attempt! But, of course, the research is endless; every species of haunting is involved.'

'Ireland's a happy hunting-ground, I expect,' Max said.

'Too good! But the thing is universal, and as ancient as man. Both medicine and psychology are bumping into it all the time; they just go and bury their swelled heads in the sand. It's enraging. This should be the science of our time, and, except for a few societies of amateurs, it is left to credulous cranks to expound and charlatans to exploit – a research that calls for scientific method, the strictest observance of the laws of evidence, the most hard-headed investigators!'

'Hard-boiled ones,' Max said, smiling, 'like yourself! – You should hear Mr Ingram's views on Irish politics! But not tonight.'

So that was what they had talked about on the long journey.

I told Ingram that I was sorry I had not known of his book.

'My book wouldn't have helped you,' he said. 'I hope sincerely I shall be able to.'

He said this in a more serious tone, with a glance at Pamela. 'I'm not in the least degree psychic,' he said to her. 'Are you?'

She shook her head. 'I'm thankful to say I'm not.'

'I wonder why you didn't send for a medium?'

'We don't know enough about them; I was afraid of trickery,' I explained.

'That *is* a difficulty. But I'm afraid, you know, I can only hope to be helpful as any stranger might be, by bringing an unprejudiced mind to interpreting any communications that we may get.'

Pamela asked him, 'Shall we tell you about the tragedy connected with the house and our experiences and theories, or ought that to come afterwards?'

'Afterwards, please – it will be so much easier for me to avoid suggestion. That's the very devil in these séances: what you expect is what you get. Have you thought about which method you'd like to use?'

I told him we would leave that to him.

'Then, as there are four of us, I suggest the spelling-glass. I brought a pack of alphabet cards. Excuse me; they are in my room.'

'Interesting fellow!' I remarked to Max when Ingram had gone. 'He has such a sane approach to the whole thing – analytical, sceptical, yet not too much so. You were grand to hunt him down for us.'

Max beamed. 'I thought you'd like him. He's as young as they're made. Can't you see him addressing the jury, in wig and gown? He warned me at the first possible minute not give him any hint of the story. I think that is wise.'

Ingram returned with his cards and laid them in a circle the table in order; the alphabet was broken at opposite points by cards marked 'Yes' and 'No.' He inverted a wine glass in the centre and said that our preparations were complete. No hymn-singing, no plunging the room into darkness. I was relieved.

I looked at the clock; it was past midnight. The house was quiet. From outside came the dull, rhythmic rumble of the sea and the higher and steadier note of the wind. I had closed doors and windows; the heavy curtains and the portière which we had hung over the greenhouse door shut most of it out.

We sat round the table with fingers laid lightly on the rim of the upturned base of the glass. Nothing happened. We rested, smoked for a while without talking, then tried again. First Max took his fingers off, thinking that he might be an impeding influence, then they tried without mine.

'It is seldom so slow,' Ingram said, depressed.

'Shall we try in the studio?' Pamela suggested.

'I think that's the idea,' Max agreed, and we carried the cards and the table up there.

The room held a damp but not unnatural chill. Pamela went to her room for a coat. We began without her. Again the glass remained motionless. Pamela joined us and laid her fingers on it and at once it tilted a little to one side. It was still again for time. Ingram spoke quietly: 'We are waiting,' he said.

A slow sliding movement began. The glass travelled uncertainly around the circle of letters, pausing now and then. It completed the circle, repeated the whole movement, and came to rest. It gave one the queerest sensation of watching some groping intelligence that was trying to understand our layout. It tilted again, and Ingram spoke, using the lower register of his expressive voice.

'Is there someone who wants to communicate with us?'

The glass rocked, then steadied and began to slide with a smooth, even movement, in the reverse direction from the A, where it had settled, to Y. It paused there but then glided straight across the table and pushed the card marked 'Yes.' It came to rest there. Pamela sighed.

Chapter XVIII

MARY

INGRAM'S FACE had changed: it was hard and concentrated, no longer lively, except the eyes – the face, it struck me, of a judge. He sat with his back to the door, at my left, with a notebook on the stool beside him and a pencil in his right hand. Three fingers of his left hand were on the glass, touching Pamela's fingers and mine. I had taken the chair opposite Pamela, in order to watch her. She looked strained. Max was taking the thing calmly and gave me a pleased glance when the glass moved. Ingram said gently, 'What is your name?'

The glass travelled steadily as far as M and then, after a little groping and hesitation, glided across the table and paused at A; it slid quickly to R, then to Y, and stopped.

Pamela, Max, and I exchanged excited glances. Ingram went on. 'Did you die at Cliff End?'

The glass slid away from me so quickly that my fingers slipped from it. It paused at 'Yes.'

'Did you die a natural death?'

Again the movement was rapid: 'No.'

'A violent death?'

'Yes.'

'Was it an accident?'

After a brief pause the glass crossed to 'No.'

'Do you blame someone for your death?'

I thought the glass was going to stop at the 'Yes,' but it passed and went on to C. 'Carmel' was steadily spelt out.

Pamela drew a sharp breath and Ingram took his fingers from the glass. We all rested.

'Do these names mean anything to you?' Ingram asked me. I told him that they did. He did not look as pleased as I should have expected.

'Will you take over the questioning?' he said.

I agreed, but found myself unable to think of what I wanted to ask; there was so much, and the idea that we were in the presence of Mary Meredith, conscious, intelligent, was stupefying, I nodded to Pamela: 'You go ahead.'

'Did Carmel strike you?' she asked.

'Yes.'

'Do you know that Carmel is dead?'

'Yes.'

'Do you want her punished?'

The glass travelled smoothly to 'No,' paused, began to make the circle, and stopped at F. I guessed what was coining. The word spelt out was 'Forgive.'

'Characteristic,' I said, and Ingram looked at me dubiously. 'Try not to anticipate answers,' he warned me. 'The power in your fingers responds to a thought.'

'Why, the glass *drags* my fingers; I'm certainly not pushing it!' I replied, and Pamela said: 'I feel the drag, too.'

I asked a question now: 'Have you a purpose in remaining?'

'Yes.'

'Can you tell us what it is?'

I was becoming extraordinarily tired; this was a strain. I could scarcely believe that my question would be answered, but the glass moved. It slid to the letter I. There was a little confusion then. It moved across the table and paused just between two letters – F and G – and then again between U and V; but it ran smoothly then to A and R and D. Pamela said, 'I guard.'

I was amazed – not by the answers, but by the smoothness with which the thing was working. Ingram's lips, however, were compressed; he took over the questioning and asked, 'Do you mean that you guard this house against some danger?'

'Yes.'

He continued.

'From where does the danger come?'

'Carmel.'

Pamela asked quickly, 'Is she trying to injure – '

Ingram gave her a warning glance and framed the question himself: 'Whom is she trying to injure?'

We had our first surprise now. The glass was almost wrenched from under our fingers. It rushed at the letters L and I and then at L again. There it stopped, rocking violently.

'Lil!' Ingram exclaimed. 'She threatens someone called Lil!' The tips of Pamela's two fingers resting on the glass were white and the skin of her face had a shrivelled look. I asked her whether she felt cold. She said impatiently, 'Never mind!'

Steadily the glass moved again, travelling straight across to S. It spelled 'Stella.'

'Do you mean that Carmel would harm Stella?' I asked.

At this point something went wrong. The glass rocked and then, with agitated, zig-zagging movements, careered round the table. It fell over but, as soon as it was set up again, darted straight to the 'Yes' with such force that it pushed the card over the edge. The feeling of life in the thing and this quickened conviction of danger threatening Stella, together with the freezing cold, were disabling me. Pamela clenched her teeth to keep them from chattering. Ingram was scribbling. It was Max who rearranged things and put the next question: 'Was "L I L" a mistake, then?' At once the glass moved to 'Yes.'

'Is Stella still in danger?'

Again the agitation, the rocking, and the dash to 'Yes.'

I pulled myself together. This was important. Now I was going to find out what I had wanted to know. I asked: 'What ought we to do?'

The answer was spelt out steadily:

'Send her away.'

Pamela's breath was coming unevenly now, but she asked: 'Do you mean, send Stella away from her home?'

'Send Carmel away.'

Pamela removed her numbed fingers from the glass and used her left hand. She was very white, and Ingram looked at her anxiously. His bronzed face was pale. I was trying to frame a question about exorcism, when he took his hands from the glass.

'Shall we try to warm up?' he said.

I said, 'One more question first!' and we replaced our fingers on the glass, but Pamela's dropped off at once. She said faintly, 'I'm afraid I'm too tired.' We crowded round the fire at once.

It had sunk low, the logs burnt out, and the coals were still black. I laboured with the bellows, but nothing would make it burn well; blue flames with no heat in them were all that I could produce. I gave it up.

'Better go down for a bit, hadn't we?' Max suggested, but Pamela shook her head: 'I'm all right now, and the most important question hasn't been asked.' She went back to the table and put her fingers on the glass. At once, before anyone else had touched it, the glass ran backwards and forwards between two letters: 'L I L I.'

'Lili, again Lili!' Ingram said.

Still with only Pamela's fingers on it, the glass raced round and round on the table, flinging the cards off; then it rushed over the edge itself and rolled on the floor.

Pamela was shivering violently. We all left the studio, and Max took her down to the sitting-room. 'The cold is horrible,' he said.

Ingram smiled. 'The cold is extremely interesting.'

He went to his room and came back with a neat box containing a recording thermometer. He set this on a stool in the middle of the studio, then, thankfully, we joined Max and Pamela, who were heating chocolate in a saucepan on the sitting-room fire.

Max was the quickest to recover; it was he who went to the kitchen and brought in the tray, poured out the chocolate and piled on the whipped cream. Ingram drank his absently, plunged in thought. Pamela, lying slack in her deep chair, gradually came back to normal. She was very happy. 'The results couldn't have been better, could they?' she said.

'They are infinitely better than anything I expected,' I said to Ingram gratefully.

He shook his head slowly. 'I'm not so sure.'

Max looked disappointed. 'It fits in with the story, doesn't it?' he asked.

'Yes,' Ingram replied; 'I could see that.' He turned to Pamela: 'Almost every syllable was what you expected, wasn't it?'

His tone was dry, almost sarcastic.

Pamela gazed at him in bewilderment. 'It went well, didn't it?'

'Too well.'

Our elation damped, we waited for Ingram to explain.

'Tell me,' he said, 'have you thought and talked a great deal about these women, Mary and Carmel?'

I told him that we were obsessed with them.

'And you are strongly prejudiced against Carmel?'

'Well, yes, I suppose so,' I admitted, but to my astonishment Pamela said: 'No – I was, for a time, but I'm changing my mind,' she declared.

'Since when? For what reason?' I asked severely.

She sighed: 'For no reason at all. That's the trouble. I'm crammed with feelings that I can't account for and they muddle me up.'

Ingram handed me his notes.

'Look at the answers, please. Tell me – is there one word, one syllable, or even one letter which is not precisely what you expected it to be?'

His scepticism irritated me, although I approved it in principle.

'Certainly there is,' I replied: 'this "Lili" means nothing to me.'

'Yes, that seems to be a divagation. But "Stella" means something to you, I take it?'

Did Stella mean something to me? The question took me unaware. It stung me. I almost made a fool of myself; but I collected my wits in time and replied coolly.

'Why, yes; she appears to be the centre of the trouble.'

'Just so. Was there anything else that you did not expect?'

I felt as if I was in the dock being convicted of fraud. 'There's the word "Guard." I expected "Protect."'

'But the glass paused near G and then near U – not precisely at either, I think. Given G U, what word *would* you – *did* you, in fact – expect?'

Max intervened: '"Guide" leaped to my mind.'

'"Guard"' I confessed, 'did come into mine.'

'And mine,' Pamela admitted.

With the shrug of a satisfied prosecuting counsel, Ingram said to me, 'You see!'

'Do you mean the whole thing is invalid?'

Pamela gave a quick sigh, 'Oh dear!'

'No, no!' Ingram replied, suddenly human and sympathetic. 'I only mean that we mustn't accept it, blindly, as evidence.'

'Doesn't the cold convince you?'

'It convinces me that your studio is haunted.'

'I see! But not that we were in touch with the ghost?'

'Just so. The most interesting parts of the séance, to my mind,' he went on, 'were the repetition of "Lili" and the agitated movements which flung the cards about. There, I think, a ghost may have taken a hand.'

'And all the rest was mere auto-suggestion?' I could not keep the disappointment out of my voice.

He looked distressed.

'I don't insist on that; I only ask you to consider the possibility,' he said.

I remembered that when we had tried, twice, in Pamela's absence, the glass had remained still, while with her fingers only on it, it had raced.

'You're the culprit, Pamela,' I said. 'You are charged with having a dishonest subconscious.'

'Or the sensitive,' Ingram amended.

Pamela looked serious. 'I'm afraid that may be true. I do "get inventing" as Lizzie used to say. You had better try without me, I think; but I want to look on.'

Ingram hesitated, then said diffidently, 'Telepathy is so potent … '

'I see,' she said, smiling; 'very well. I'll stay and finish the chocolate. But don't be long.'

'What a triumph of greed over curiosity,' I remarked. Ingram smiled. He had a rather pleasant smile – sympathetic and amused.

'On the contrary – true scientific disinterestedness,' he declared.

The cold in the studio had intensified, and the thermometer chart was starting a steep drop. The fire was out. We forced ourselves to sit at the table for five minutes and they seemed like twenty, but the glass did not move.

Max said, 'It seems to need Pamela,' and we gave it up.

'Yes,' Ingram agreed, looking worried; 'and I am very much afraid,' he added slowly as we went downstairs, 'that she ought not to join a séance again tonight.'

'Do you say that because you think it is her subconscious that moves it?' I asked.

'No,' he replied, 'rather because of how she may be affected if it is not.'

When we reported our failure, Pamela urgently wanted to try again. 'We haven't asked the most important question of all,' she declared.

Yes, now that we were in touch with Mary, we could ask her for her blessing on the project of exorcism. She might give us a sign. Stella might agree.

Ingram was reluctant, however, to continue the séance with Pamela. He said, 'We shall all work better after a rest.'

My own belief was that, before the night was over, there would be a manifestation on the landing. I hoped for it. I went out of the room at intervals to see whether anything was happening, and I turned on no lights out there. The cold was spreading through the house.

Ingram entered his notes of the séance on blank leaves belonging to Pamela's journal. He would not look into the book yet. 'I'll take it to my room, if I may, and study it in the morning,' he said.

Max was pondering over the word 'Lili,' saying: 'I feel that's the key.'

I pointed out that a number of people must have died in this house and asked Ingram whether he thought it possible that some entity from an earlier period might have been trying to break in. He nodded.

'That is very probable.'

Pamela had grown sleepy and closed her eyes; she opened them to murmur, 'Why do you assume that it is a name at all? Perhaps some other spirit was trying to break in with a word.'

I was just about to say that I could think of no word beginning with 'lili,' when a sighing sound made us all hold our breaths to listen. It was a long, sad, despairing sigh. It came again, as though someone were in distress. Max glanced from me to Pamela; we said nothing, watching Ingram to see how he would react. He listened keenly and then said, with a good deal of excitement: 'I don't think that was wind.'

'No,' I told him, 'that is a sound which we hear night after night.'

He sprang to his feet. I took him all round the house, looking into every room. The sighing had ceased. The cold held the studio in frozen stillness and drove us down. Returning, we crouched over the fire. When we compared what we had heard, we found no differences: to each of us the voice had seemed human and close. Ingram questioned us about its recurrence, warning us not to mention theories of its cause. He was intensely interested.

'The sound of weeping lingers sometimes where there is no other evidence of haunting,' he said. 'I heard it myself in a house in Edinburgh, but that was a nightmarish sound – not like this.'

'We have heard a nightmarish weeping, also, and it is different,' I told him.

This delighted him; he thought it would be extraordinarily interesting to hear the two kinds of sound in one place.

It was past two o'clock now. Pamela urged, 'We *must* try again.'

Ingram agreed, suggesting, 'If the studio is cold still, we might try elsewhere. I'll go up and look at my thermometer first.' As he left the room he took a small electric torch out of his pocket. 'I won't turn up lights, since we want to encourage manifestations. We're practically evoking them.'

Max was smiling. 'He has an acute sense of his responsibilities but is burnt up with excitement,' he said.

'He thinks I don't look after Pamela properly,' I declared.

'It's a pity about me,' Pamela grinned.

Ingram was down again in a minute; he said, 'The studio's as cold as the Celtic hell, and I'd rather have a hot one myself. We can't sit up there.'

Pamela stood up: 'Quick, Roddy, we'd best go upstairs.'

We hurried past the studio door, shuddering, and crowded at the landing window.

Ingram said, 'I think I'll try to go in.'

'Don't,' Pamela answered; 'that might prevent it. Wait here and watch.'

Pamela had carried her coat up with her from the sitting-room; she put it on. 'Though nothing,' she murmured, 'does any good.'

That was so: no clothing or covering seemed to be any protection against this insidious sucking away of one's animal warmth. I felt it already, while I sat on the landing windowsill. Pamela and Max were on the sofa; Ingram walked up and down, peering over the stairs. Was he case-hardened? Or was it coming fresh to the thing that made him seem half-immune? I was shrinking already under the oppressive stillness; I could hear the slow, dragging beat of my heart.

'Listen,' Ingram whispered. He was leaning over the banisters, looking down. It was a challenge, and I managed to join him. I expected to hear the moaning again, but what I heard was a murmur of soft, sibilant words. It came from the nursery, and there gleamed from the nursery doorway a faint, flickering light. On the night when Stella slept there I had seen it, and I had heard that sound and thought it was Stella talking in her sleep.

'Good heavens,' Max whispered beside me, 'who is down there?'

Pamela had not moved. She said urgently, 'Don't go down.'

Ingram had run down. After a moment the light vanished and the whispering ceased. He came, pulling himself up the stairs slowly; when he reached us his face was pale and clammy.

'It's queer,' he said, 'on the stairs.'

'I know,' I replied.

'I saw nothing,' he said in a low voice. 'We should hold a séance in there.'

'I say,' Max exclaimed under his breath, 'look at the studio door.'

I put a hand on Pamela's shoulder, but my hand shook and I took it away. My knees were trembling too. With all my heart I was hoping not to see the face of the stricken, malignant Carmel.

I could not stand it. There was no reason why I should. But there *was* a reason: some deep, secret part of me remembered and told me – it was important for Stella. I could not remember why.

It was not uncoiling from the floor this time, but emerging through the closed studio door. A phosphorescent figure, like a mummy, was growing out of the door in low relief. It drew out and grew slowly, and rounded, and at last it was free. It hovered on the landing, growing tall.

Pamela trembled convulsively. Max was stone-still, his eyes dilated, his hand on her wrist. Ingram was standing against the window-curtains, drawing hard, steady breaths. Downstairs a forlorn moaning went on. Ingram turned his head very slowly and looked at me: he had heard it too; then his eyes were fixed again on that luminous shape. I would have liked to go blind for the next ten minutes but could not take my eyes away.

It moved smoothly forward. The white, flowing shroud was a gown now, and I saw hands. They were poised over the banister-rail. I saw a long throat and a head – a head with hair hanging down. As though the mist were crystallising, the outlines were defined gradually and the features became as clear as alabaster at last, shining in their own pale light.

I saw the classic brow; the lips, fine and stern; smooth eyelids veiling the eyes. She was looking down, a marble Victory, poised to swoop. Her head was bent, listening to those piteous moans. My heart was clenching with dread. The other face would have been less terrifying than this. I could not hear anyone breathe.

She listened, then she lifted her head slowly, the eyelids lowered still, in a strange gesture of triumphing pride, and the lips parted in a smile. She opened her eyes – great, ice-blue eyes, alight with so fierce a flash of power and purpose that I closed my own.

When I opened them she was sweeping down the stairs. A cry, so low that I doubted if I had heard it, shivered up through the house, and then that dead, timeless stillness and silence fell.

Ingram did something that I could not have done: he moved; he walked forward steadily, like an automaton, and went downstairs. I wrenched myself into motion, gasping, 'Max, the window!' and, with a strong effort, reached my bedroom. I looked out, not knowing what I expected to see. The tree was a wild, black demon, lashed by the wind. I saw nothing else. Max waited with me, but nothing happened out there. When we went back to look after Pamela we met her coming from the bathroom. She said with a wavering smile, 'I feel it my duty to inform you that I have been sick.'

Ingram came upstairs. His face was greyish now, but his eyes danced.

'Nothing there now,' he said, his teeth chattering slightly; 'but that was absolutely the most perfect manifestation I have ever seen! Magnificent! By thunder, I wouldn't have missed this!'

He looked at Pamela. We were all at the doorway of my room.

'"It is well to take counsel of one's pillow,"' he quoted gravely.

She nodded. 'Yes, I'm going to bed.'

I took the men down and gave them drinks and had one myself. Then I carried one up to Pamela. She was huddled in bed, looking rather ill.

'Figures of eight again,' she murmured weakly, 'but at least Mr Ingram was entertained. Don't sit up, Roddy, will you? Sleep well!'

We all decided to turn in. The bed from the nursery had been put in my study for Max. 'I'm afraid it's a bit on the small side,' I remarked. He did not reply. He stood there, looking deeply concerned, winding his watch.

'This is ghastly for you and Pamela, Roderick,' he said. 'I don't know how you've stood it. I wish I had known.'

'I've a feeling we're near the end of it,' I told him.

I went next door to see that Ingram was all right. He had put the journal on the table beside his bed. I showed him the tree and told him that it played a part in the story that he was going to read.

He sat on the edge of the bed, still shivering slightly, but his eyes met mine, glowing with excitement and delight.

'It's the first time that I have seen a veritable, complete apparition.'

I asked him, 'What exactly did you see?'

'Why, the woman! Beautiful and terrible as an angel! Shall I read about her in this? Who is she?'

'You will. She is Mary,' I said.

Chapter XIX

DEADLOCK

THE MORNING WAS brilliant, but a rough wind was blowing and bundling puffy clouds up from the west; the sunshine would not last long. When I came down I found Ingram outside, walking on the heather by the cliff's edge, his face to the wind, avidly enjoying the air and the view. He was a new Ingram this morning, laughing and boyish, the learned counsel and the ghost-hunter gone.

'You certainly live on the top of the world!' he greeted me. 'What a coast! You might be in Kerry. Look at that water!'

Great waves were seething into the creek, flinging their crests off in its hollows, to riot there and pour out again as satiny water-falls.

'Doesn't your sister love it?'

'She does.'

'We have certainly got to lay those ghosts!'

'Do you think we have any hope?'

'Why not? – I say, this journal, this story' – he had the book in his pocket – 'it is the most enthralling thing of the sort that I have ever encountered. You know, you have a psychic-researcher's paradise here!'

'That's not quite what we wanted,' I answered drily. His undisguised pleasure in our odious situation was beginning to jar. He gave me a crooked, apologetic grin.

'Do forgive me,' he said disarmingly, 'but you can't conceive what luck this is for me. I am the nobody who benefits by your ill wind ... Did you, when you were young, think that "nobody" was a scarecrow? I did, because our scarecrow used to look so hilarious in a storm.'

'No, I thought the poor wind was sick and no use.'

He had been down early and read the whole journal through, supplied with coffee and rolls by Lizzie, who had told him she couldn't let an Irishman starve.

Ten was the time scheduled for breakfast. Max appeared punctually, looking as though he had not had much sleep. He was worrying, I could see. He looked searchingly at Pamela when she came in. She seemed thoroughly recovered and free from the depression which was weighing on me since the discovery that the haunter of the stairs was Mary had thrown my theory overboard. She had slept like a dormouse, she told us, in spite of seeing Carmel's face again.

'The vision in the dark?' Ingram asked eagerly. 'The young face?'

'Yes, and much more distinct.'

'And was there any sense of fear – any cold?'

'No; I went straight to sleep.'

'Interesting ... '

The hoverings of Lizzie, coming in with relays of waffles, held up discussion, but as soon as she had cleared the breakfast things away we set to work. Ingram, brimming with energy, took the lead.

Without once referring to the journal, he went through the Meredith story, point by point, co-ordinating the various accounts of it and getting the sequence clear. Max had not heard it and was astounded.

'What an incredible trio!' he exclaimed. 'Mary Meredith taking that girl back – it is incomprehensible.' That a painter should use his skill to do what Meredith had done to Carmel offended him profoundly. He said, 'Drowning was too good for the brute!' Ingram, studying the pictures with deep concentration, said, 'It certainly was.' He put the books away.

'And now I will cross-examine, if you agree.'

I told him to go ahead.

He looked round the table and smiled. 'I would like, please, to dispense entirely with *politesse*. You are all hostile witnesses; the truth is not in you, and I shall endeavour to discredit everything you say.'

'Good!'

He had some notes before him and ticked off or added to them while we talked.

To start with, he required from each of us a precise description of what we had seen on the landing. Max spoke first. He described the gradual shaping of the apparition and her pose and movements exactly as I had seen them, and he had felt the piercing power of the blue eyes, but he said that the features were blurred. Pamela and I declared that we had seen the features with perfect clarity and recognised the face in the portrait at Wilmcote.

'While I,' said Ingram, 'although I received a strong impression of beauty, austere, imperious, and, in some way, overpowering, could not this morning recall a single feature of the face; and to me she was as colourless as marble, even the eyes.'

'The eyes,' Pamela insisted, 'were blue.'

He looked at us with a mischievous smile. 'Here, at the very outset, we have a nice instance of the power of suggestion. Two of you had seen the portrait of Mary Meredith, and to you two the features are clear and are hers, while to Mr Hilliard and me they were vague: take warning!'

Max shook his head. 'I did not see the features distinctly, but I'll swear that the eyes were blue. They were the colour of flames when you throw copper-filings into the fire.'

'And you had not seen the picture? Or thought very much about any description of Mary which you had heard? That, then, *is* evidential,' Ingram concurred. 'Nevertheless, may we, just for the moment, call this apparition A?'

'And is Carmel B, then?' Pamela asked, smiling.

Max chuckled. 'Is B Carmel, you mean.'

'Yes, let us call the apparition in your room B,' Ingram said. 'I take it the face was not completely materialised?'

Pamela replied, 'I could see it clearly for a moment, then it became vague, as if one's eyes were out of focus. I spoke: I said, 'Carmel!' And it began to come again, but it broke up.'

'You had studied the picture. *Dawn*?'

'Oh, yes!'

'And it impressed you strongly?'

'Very strongly.'

'So you see' – Ingram smiled appealingly – 'we can't really do more, can we, than speak of apparition B? Your thoughts may have moulded that face.'

'Very well,' Pamela said with unwonted submissiveness. 'But,' she insisted, 'I think it is B who weeps.'

'Is there evidence of that?'

I said, 'We heard the weeping from the nursery while Mary was on the stairs.'

'That proves nothing except that it is not A.'

'It may be "Lili",' Max suggested.

'It may be anyone who died at Cliff End at any time.'

Ingram was enjoying this: he was judge, he was jury, and he was centre stage.

He went on: 'It may be no conscious spirit at all, but a vibration from impressions lingering in the house; or it may be a ghost repeating its last tragedy forever, or an active intelligence intent on a purpose now, or you may have all these.'

'Confusing!' Max remarked.

'Very confusing, often baffling: you realise how cautious we have to be! And now,' he said, 'let us see whether there is sufficient evidence to permit us to connect the hauntings with the Meredith story at all.'

This was scepticism with a vengeance! 'Heavens, yes,' I protested, 'there's everything!'

'The face of Mary – the face of Carmel!' Pamela exclaimed.

'Remember those portraits: a strong element of suggestion comes in.'

'The séance,' I said.

Ingram looked at Pamela diffidently. 'Will you be offended if, for the present, I discount the séance?'

'Roddy,' she said, smiling ruefully, 'you're in the dock with me! We're being debunked.'

'No, no!' Ingram protested. 'The séance may prove acceptable after all. It is only that I want to be certain we are on solid ground first.'

'Of course!' she consented quickly. 'But,' she insisted, 'there *is* evidence: there *must* be.'

'The feeling in the studio,' Max argued, 'is just what Meredith's brutality would have produced.'

Ingram nodded. 'Yes, I think we may almost accept that – Carmel's agony of mind lingering on; an impression which Judith – Mrs Hilliard – received.'

He refrained, tactfully, from referring to my painfully honest record of my night in that room.

'And there's the light,' Pamela said.

He shook his head. 'How many candles have been lighted in the nursery?'

'There's the scent!'

Ingram nodded, acquiescent at last.

'Yes, here we have a definite link: Stella possesses some of the same perfume; she connects it with memories of her mother, and there is no reason to doubt that she is right. This is really a link, a clue. If we had smelt mimosa last night, I would agree that we have seen Mary and that the scent is her *motif.*'

'It never comes with the cold,' I told him.

'That,' he declared, 'is the most curious factor of all. I believe I understand it, however.'

'And the box?' Pamela asked eagerly. 'Why did Mary guide us to Carmel's box?'

'One possibility,' he replied – 'I advance it as a possibility only, remember – is that Mary consciously wished to indicate to you that Carmel is the source of the danger.'

'We never thought of that!' Pamela exclaimed.

Ingram said deprecatingly, 'It is a little far-fetched.'

'It strikes me as excellent reasoning,' I told him. 'But what do you make of the empty scent bottle?'

'That would give Mary her link. The phenomenon of materialisation,' he explained, 'seems to have subtle and curious laws. We don't fully understand them yet. But it is probable that Mary needed some link with Carmel and with you before she could produce a guiding manifestation, and the empty phial provided that.'

'I see!' Pamela said, impressed, and Max nodded, as pleased with this ingenious logic as though he had propounded the theory himself.

'So you are satisfied to admit a connection with the Meredith story?' I asked.

Ingram replied definitely: 'Yes.'

'And you let us assume,' Pamela said, 'that it was Mary whom we saw?'

'I think we may assume it,' he agreed.

'Thank you,' said Pamela a little drily.

Ingram grinned. 'These lawyers! They go all round the globe in order to advance a mile!'

Max had been looking through the journal; he frowned.

'I want to know,' he said, 'why Mary Meredith, who was a woman of fabulous gentleness, brings that malignant cold.'

'Exactly!' Max had formulated the problem which had frustrated us at every turn and made our theories wind, as Pamela had expressed it, in figures of eight.

Ingram said quickly, 'I think I can explain.'

He leaned forward, eagerly watching to see how we would react to this.

'I think that in all your deductions you have been making a fundamental mistake. You have assumed that the sensations of cold and horror were due to a spirit's deliberate malice – arose from some mood or attribute of the woman when she died. Is not that so?'

'We have certainly done that,' I affirmed.

'But it is not necessary at all!'

He paused to make sure that he had our attention. He certainly had it.

'You ignored the question of ectoplasm,' he said. 'You know, don't you, that, in order to materialise, a spirit is thought to draw something from the human bodies within reach? That, don't you think, happened last night?'

'I certainly felt – depleted,' Max said.

'That sensation,' Ingram continued, 'produces the physical symptoms of fear, and these, in turn, produce its mental effect – something like panic terror overwhelms one – I think you will agree? But I do not believe that we should take this as evidence of any malice in the ghost.'

'I confess to the panic terror,' I said.

Pamela shook her head. 'So do I, but – I can't help it, Mr Ingram – that cold seems to me evil.'

I was astonished at her obstinacy over this; Ingram's exposition was brilliant and did away with the anomaly which had been obstructing every channel of thought.

'These feelings!' Ingram said warningly. 'They are really not to be trusted, you know.'

She did not answer. I could see that she was not ready to give in.

'I believe you've got it! That's tremendously illuminating,' I said.

Max was thinking hard.

'But look here,' he demurred; 'why is no cold felt with the other manifestations? For instance, when Mary visited Stella in the nursery that first time?'

'I am afraid Stella's reaction must be eliminated; the suggestive power of that room would be very strong.'

'You're eliminating quite a lot!' I commented lightly.

'Never mind,' Max chuckled, 'as long as he eliminates the ghost.'

Ingram sat silent. Had he taken offence? No! He looked with a rather troubled expression at Pamela and said gently, 'I do hope you understand that I can't possibly promise to do that?'

'Why, of course,' she responded warmly. 'You are helping us to understand it; that is what we hoped for; we must do the rest for ourselves.'

'That is understood, isn't it, Ingram?' Max said. 'But to come back to this problem: why was no cold felt that night in the dining-room when Mary led them to the box?'

'Don't you see,' Ingram replied eagerly, 'she was not trying to materialise? No shape became visible, did it? That is my point! As long as Mary remains invisible she causes no sensation of fear or cold, but as soon as she tries to materialise she becomes dreadful and dangerous.'

'Good man!' I was tremendously excited; this was a beautiful theory; it fitted the data. We were all talking at once.

'Well, of all the sophisticated, sceptical investigators!' Max exclaimed, delighted. 'I never heard anything so ingenious.'

'It's too ingenious,' Pamela murmured.

'There are not two spirits, then,' I conjectured. 'It is Mary all the time. Carmel is eliminated – or isn't she? You have made my brain spin.'

Ingram laughed.

'"Confusion worse confounded"! Look here – I've only just arrived at this notion about the cold myself. I haven't digested it. I would really, if you don't mind, do some thinking before I say any more.'

I endorsed this. We needed a breathing space. 'Let's leave it,' I said. 'We'll come back to it this evening. There'll be sun for another hour or so; let's go out.'

'I am sorry,' Ingram said rather wistfully as we stood up; 'I seem to have been very discouraging: the séance, and then this journal. It's such a beautiful piece of work, and the theory's consistent. It seems a shame to break it all up.'

'We are not at all in love with our theory,' Pamela was reassuring him as they went out to the garden. We spent an hour showing Max and Ingram over our wilderness and collecting fallen branches for the wood-pile, then we were ready for lunch. By tacit consent, our troubles were not discussed; we talked about the future of Ireland, in which Ingram's faith was boundless, and the war in Spain. After lunch I suggested a run in the car or a walk, but Pamela said that she thought she would idle in the garden and Ingram wanted to do some writing.

'I never know what I think,' he explained, 'until I have written it down.'

Max and I set out by ourselves for 'the Ghouls.' The sun was fighting a losing battle with three regiments of clouds, and a gusty wind hurried us along. We had a good three-mile walk before us, over the moors southward and down a steep, narrow latte and along a cart-track to the pebble beach. Max strode along clutching his wide-brimmed hat.

'Lord, this is what I've been wanting!' he said. 'What a mistake London is! It's a pity there are so many things that can't be done from anywhere else.' He told me about a series of loan exhibitions of the work of experimental painters which he was trying to organise. 'The obstacle,' he declared, 'is not "the great dumb masses" with their suspicion of everything new, but the damned articulate ignorant snobs who shout hallelujahs over the most asinine mediocrities merely because their stuff's obscure.' His wrath darkened the heavens but was suddenly forgotten. 'By the way, your young friend Carey – any news of him?' he asked with interest. None, I told him, but he or Wendy would probably phone in a day or two when they saw an article in which I had put in a word about *Salome*.

'I'd like to know,' Max said, 'whether he has heard from Christopher Pennant. I mentioned his work.'

'Lord! To Pennant?'

'Yes; he's putting on a bill of plays by Dunsany. He was tearing round in circles, looking for a man to do the *décor*, talking about all the money he was prepared to spend and the stunts he wanted to try with lights. Sounded intriguing. I thought Carey's style would be about right – that mixture of the poetic and the grotesque. Pennant lit up when I told him and said he'd go to Bristol himself.'

'Gosh, Max, Carey would be set up!'

'I hope it works out.'

I told him about my play; he was tremendously pleased and liked my theme. 'Though it can't be easy to make your Barbara convincing,' he reflected. 'It's not a recognised motive, is it?'

'I like exploring unrecognised motives,' I told him; 'and I am sure the love of power takes queer twists in women – it is so repressed. The modern, complex mind scarcely knows its own motives; there

are wheels within wheels – and look at the poisonous jungle psychologists are opening up!'

'Is it all sombre and Strindbergian?' he asked, and I explained
that I was sunk in the heavy labour of making it light. 'Things have
not been propitious,' he said sympathetically. We walked on for a
while in silence, I revolving the problem of Barbara's downfall, and
Max, I knew well, concentrating on Cliff End.

Presently he asked me about Stella and whether the whole thing
had shaken her as badly as one would expect. 'Such a ghastly idea for
the child to get into her head! She must have been frightfully wrought
up to come alone like that to the empty house. But what courage! Is
she going to be all right?'

'God knows,' I replied.

'Judith,' he told me, 'wants to know if *La Belle au Bois Dormant*
has begun to wake up. We both felt drawn to her; there's such a
bubbling spring of life and affection so carefully shut down.'

I told Max a good deal about Stella and I knew that he deduced
more. There were one or two things that I did not tell him. I could not
speak of Scott's worst fear. What I did say left Max appalled.

'What a diabolical situation!' he exclaimed. 'Surely you've got to
put a quick end to it? Can't she be persuaded to consent to exorcism?
Would Father Anson try?'

'I won't risk it,' I declared.

'Why, Roderick?'

'Because Stella might yield, but she would never feel satisfied: to
the end of her life she would never feel sure that I had not driven her
mother's soul into outer darkness.'

'It's an atrocious dilemma for you.'

'It is.'

By the time we reached 'the Ghouls' the sun was buried and
the queer-shaped rocks and islets were not showing up at their
best. Nevertheless Max prowled among them, excited. 'By Jove,' he
exclaimed, 'imagine that fellow in a low light from the east! And that
gargoyle up there! A stormy sunrise … Gods, yes, I must have a go!'

'Good! I hope we'll be here.'

Returning, we were in time to see a gleam on the knoll – the last salute of the defeated sun, blazoning the heather and gorse.

We climbed to the top and looked down at the house. It, too, was washed in the flying light, but only for a moment; shadows closed in and the house seemed to cringe and shrink.

'Supposing,' Max asked me, 'that it came to the worst – if everything else failed – if you had to choose between trying exorcism and giving up Cliff End, which would you do?'

'Give up the house.'

'I see,' Max said slowly. 'If it were Judith, I'd do the same.' We could see Ingram down on the lawn, striding from rock to rock and gesticulating loquaciously. Pamela followed him, vividly interested. She drew me along eagerly when we came down. 'Look! Mr Ingram believes we could grow gentians here – the kind you find in Galway. He says we could have a lot of alpines and a real sea-garden, with things spilling down the cliff. A friend of his mother's has done it at Howth.'

'You might have something unique,' he responded, 'but it would be pretty hard work.'

A fine time Ingram had chosen, I thought, to make Pamela more than ever in love with Cliff End.

Pamela decreed a large tea, a late supper, which we would clear away ourselves; after that the adjourned conference, and, between the two meals, sleep. There were no dissentients, but Lizzie, when told that she might leave early, looked suspicious. And what sort of goings on will you be up to, her glance plainly asked, when you have me out of the way?

Ingram had recovered from his mood of contrition. He said that he had failed to persuade Pamela to forego her conviction that she had seen Carmel and heard Carmel weep. Pamela, challenged, could still give no reason for her tenacity. 'I am afraid I've gone all feminine and intuitive,' she confessed. Ingram smiled and quoted: '"Le coeur a ses raisons que la raison ne connaît point."'

He was in high spirits. Tea was a gay meal. Max teased us. 'You and Roderick should be barred as investigators,' he told Ingram; 'you both write plays. Pamela and I are the ones with honest, undramatising minds.'

'Bless you, Max!' Pamela said.

Ingram turned to me. 'Is it awfully ignorant of me? I didn't know that you wrote plays.'

We dived into talk about the dramatist's job, and Ingram confessed frankly, about his own plays, 'They just didn't work! There was nothing wrong with the dialogue – we are all born speaking dialogue in Ireland – but the stuff wouldn't stay serious; it kept ballooning away into farce. And then when Barry Fitzgerald and Maureen Delaney got hold of it … ' He grinned. 'Before we were through with rehearsals the producer told me, "We prefer our authors dead." I said, "Unfortunately for you, even dramatists don't really die of broken hearts." But they're grand. It was great fun.'

We laughed and yawned. Pamela was beginning to look rather strung up. She rose to go to her room.

'If I don't appear by seven,' she said, 'will someone please bang hard on my door? I'll be a bit doped. Would anybody like luminal? I've got a secret hoard.'

We all refused, and Ingram said with emphasis, 'Oh, no … Please, Miss Fitzgerald,' I heard him say earnestly as I left the room, 'do be careful! I don't like drugs at all when there are psychic influences about.'

Drugs! … drugs … I went upstairs slowly, absorbed in a new and enthralling idea. Was that the proper end for Barbara? A drug addict. Yes. And her victim, Jennifer, as the innocent instrument … A hopeless addict, cut off from her dope in a hell of craving – a hell of her own making. It would be a perfect nemesis. Wendy could play it, too; I could see her – the feeble, pointless gestures, the vacant stare and incoherent speech; then the exhaustion, and the torment … I turned on the landing to speak about it to Pamela, who was running lightly upstairs with a smile on her face.

'I say, I've got an idea for Barbara's crash, instead of the end you objected to.'

'Have you, Roddy?' She spoke vaguely.

'Yes – drugs. What do you think?'

'Drugs? I've just had a fatherly sermon about drugs. Why, yes, I should think that ought to do.'

She went to her room and I to my study. Pamela was no longer interested in my play. That was not strange, I told myself; tonight's séance would be a considerable ordeal for her; yet that was not what had been preoccupying her. Why the amused, soft smile?

I went down again, feeling restless, and rang Scott's number. I was told that he had been out all day. No news was good news. I went back to work and roughed out the change in my third act.

AFTER SUPPER Lizzie left coffee and sandwiches galore on the table, chocolate in a saucepan, and cakes on a tray. Even if she suspected us of devil-raising, she was not going to let the Irishman starve. Lizzie had taken a fancy to Ingram, and Max had long ago won a place in her heart.

As soon as we had settled round the fire Ingram took up the notes that he had written and prepared to tell us the conclusions at which he had arrived. His gaiety had left him; it had gone so completely that I suddenly suspected that he had forced it in order to conceal a discouraged mood.

'I am afraid I am going to worry you a little,' he began: 'there is a point of which I find no mention in the journal but which struck me when I went through it again. It concerns Miss Meredith – Stella; excuse me if I use that name. Have you observed that the hauntings became intensified after each of her visits to this house?'

'I think we realised that,' Pamela said. It was certainly true.

'You think there is a direct connection with Stella?' Max asked him, and he replied gravely, 'I am afraid there is.'

I do not know for what I had been hoping: it had been senseless to imagine that Ingram could say or do anything to alter that dreadful fact; but my disappointment made it difficult to speak. It was Max who said, 'You have worked out a theory, I expect?'

Ingram answered, 'I have worked out two.'

'Two theories!' Pamela exclaimed.

'Yes, unfortunately. It means, of course, that I find neither of them entirely satisfying,' he replied. 'But in both of them I make the assumption which you wished to make – that it is Mary Meredith whom we saw.'

'I'm glad that you assume that,' I said.

'In both of them I reject "Lili" as a meaningless intrusion from outside or a mere chance movement of the glass.'

Pamela looked as if she was about to oppose this, but refrained. 'I think,' he went on, 'that it is important to realise how acutely Mary must have suffered and also that she had known exceptional happiness and peace. I am inclined to believe that experience of these extremes makes a woman very sensitive to others – eager for their happiness and apprehensive lest they should be enduring anything of what she herself went through. Then, Mary's faith in her father would lead her to idealise men. Very probably she had romantic illusions about Meredith. He not only destroyed those but spoiled this house for her – violated her home. In both of my theories one has to remember all this.' Ingram was speaking thoughtfully, in a low voice, looking into the fire.

'My first theory,' he said, 'rejects the séance; it supposes that there is only one ghost. I have, in fact, suggested it to you already. I imagine that Mary died as gentle as she lived. Her spirit is tender; she grieves about Stella, imagining that she is lonely and desiring to comfort her. She visited Stella in the nursery and made her feel "cherished"; she carried a ghostly light; she creates the delicious perfume of flowers; she led you to Carmel's box because she wanted you to find the scent bottle, to realise that she is here, a conscious presence, and tell Stella this. She hopes that Stella remembers the scent. She is aware of Stella's eagerness to see her and longs for contact with her child. She comes when Stella is here and returns seeking her, and when she cannot find her she weeps. But this is Mary's tragedy – '

Ingram looked up at Pamela: her face was still a little resistant. Max sat as if spellbound by the story, and I was feeling moved, convinced. Ingram went on in a tense, compassionate tone:

'Her fate is tragic, even after death: when she tries to appear, tries to make herself visible, she becomes a thing of horror and nearly frightens Stella to death. And that will always be so: Mary, materialised, visible, will always appal.'

There was silence, and then I said, 'I believe you are right.'

'Terribly convincing,' said Max.

'What is your other theory?' Pamela asked.

'May I have another cup of coffee?'

Ingram smiled; he was tired; he was putting a great deal of himself into this. I could not get the man's measure – how far was he dramatising and how far sincere? That he was sincere in wanting to help us, I felt convinced.

'My second theory,' he said after a few minutes, 'does not contradict the first one but supplements it: my belief about the effect of materialisation remains. But I accept the séance: we were in touch with Mary up there in the studio; other entities – no matter who – tried to break in, but it was Mary whose words made sense. She protects Stella and she forgives the girl who killed her. She wants to save all in Cliff End from harm. There is danger from Carmel.'

He paused; our absorption stimulated him; consciously or otherwise, he was making the most of his effects.

'Carmel,' he went on, 'as one sees from the story, was a wild, undisciplined girl. She was madly in love with Meredith. They lived together as lovers in Spain. He made her happy, then Mary came and took him away. Carmel is not a Paris *cocotte* but a Southern woman with whom love goes deep. She is cunning. She resolves to destroy that marriage. She trades on Mary's pleasure in making magnanimous gestures and secures a position as her maid. In this house she gets her way: Meredith becomes her lover again, and Mary, discovering it, falls ill. When the household breaks up she is clever – it is to Mary that she clings. She has not done with Mary yet. Stella is born, and Carmel proceeds to undermine her influence with the child. Now, at last, Mary stands firm. She leaves Carmel in Paris and brings Stella home. We know what happened. Carmel returned, perhaps out of longing for her lover, perhaps to beg or blackmail – we can't tell. But we know what Meredith did to her. It would fill any woman with hatred. Carmel's passion for revenge becomes a madness: she weeps, she rages, she desires to die. But, in dying, she will perfect her vengeance against both of them. She will destroy their child. She failed to do that – Mary stopped her – but she killed Mary. Carmel, when she was dying, was still in a frenzy of unsatisfied revenge. She is probably in an endless delirium, trying to kill Stella still.'

Pamela was lying white and faint in her chair.

'Roddy,' she gasped, 'did you phone?'

'Yes,' I replied. 'Scott's out.'

There was a pause. Max poured out drinks and handed them round. I rang Scott's number again: he was out still.

'I'm going to phone Wilmcote,' Pamela said.

'You mustn't do that,' I told her. 'Stella might answer; remember what Scott said. You know you mustn't do that.'

'Yes, I know; but I can't stand it.'

'Scott would telephone if she were worse.'

She looked as if she would cry in a moment, then she saw Ingram's face. He looked utterly miserable. 'I don't know how to ask you to forgive me,' he said.

Pamela managed to smile. 'It's our own fault,' she told him. 'We ought to have confided in you; it wasn't fair to tell you half the story. Ever since the night she was here Stella has had insomnia; but she was much better yesterday; there's really nothing to be anxious about. I suddenly panicked, that's all.'

'I can't forgive myself,' Ingram said.

Max made an effort to pull the discussion back on to general ground.

'Look here, Ingram,' he said, 'both your theories make this house seem quite uninhabitable. They leave no way out.'

'Exactly – that is what troubles me so much,' Ingram replied. 'If Carmel is haunting, it is for an evil purpose, and Mary, in her very desire to help and protect, becomes a terribly dangerous presence. It's a deadlock, I'm afraid.'

'You certainly suggest no way of doing what we had hoped to do,' I told him – 'find a means of giving the spirits rest.'

'I see no hope now,' Pamela said sadly, 'unless it comes in tonight's séance.'

Ingram said eagerly, 'There is one thing you can do: it is repellent, but I have known it work – have a service of exorcism held in the house.'

'That is ruled out,' I told him, 'unless something happens tonight to make it possible. Stella cannot support the thought of it; she worships her mother, you see.'

Ingram looked dismayed. 'But there really is a deadlock in that case – you can do nothing.'

Pamela said, 'We can give up the house.'

There was a pause. She was looking unlike herself, forlorn and dispirited.

'It is getting late,' she said. 'Let us begin.'

Chapter XX

THE SPANISH WORDS

I WAS SORRY that we had to use the nursery like this; it looked charming with the daffodil-coloured curtains and bed-cover, the green mats and lamp-shades, flounced dressing-table with yellow and white china, and the round table circled by low chairs. One could imagine the child Stella giving a tea-party here. A small fire burned brightly and the room was warm. I fancied – but would not say this before Ingram – that there was a faint, sweet breath of mimosa scent. The room made my heart ache.

The cards were set out. I told Ingram that Pamela and I were so anxious to secure a particular answer to a certain question that I thought it would be better for one of us not to take part and that if they could work without me I would take notes. He agreed. They put their fingers on the glass. There was a long wait and then, suddenly, it moved.

The circle of letters was explored, as before; the glass rested and rocked and Ingram signed to Pamela to begin.

'Who are you?' she asked.

'Mary' was spelt out at once.

'Was it you we saw last night?'

'Yes.'

'Did you wish to frighten us?'

The glass moved to N and then to O. It spelled out 'Not you.'

'Did you wish to frighten someone?'

'Yes.'

'Who was it?'

'Carmel.'

The movement was even and unhurried; there was no hesitation and no doubt at any time as to the letter to which the glass was directed. Pamela went on:

'Do you want her to leave Cliff End?'

'Yes.'

'Can we do something to make her go?'

'No.'

Pamela looked at me, her face tense, and then asked the crucial question:

'Should exorcism be tried?'

The glass sped instantly to 'No.'

We had our answer. I felt a shock of loss, a black sense of drowning, for a moment, and then relief. It was over. This meant a decision. No more of the tormenting hesitations, the refusal to accept the truth, the balancing of all that Stella meant to me against the saving of my home. It had gone on too long; this was the end of it; it was release.

I looked at Pamela and she answered my look steadily, with a little smile.

Ingram was puzzled; he said to her, 'That's not the answer you wanted, is it?'

'No,' she replied, 'but it is so much better than none.'

'Does it mean ... '

He checked the impulsive question, but Pamela answered it: 'Yes; it means that we shall shut up the house.'

'This beautiful house!' He was distressed, all his efficiency and composure gone.

'No, no!' Max protested. 'We can't give up yet! Let's ask again.'

'No good,' I told him, but he persisted. Pamela sighed; she was tired.

'We'll try without Pamela, then,' I said, to satisfy him, and put my fingers with Ingram's and his on the glass, while she lay back in her camp chair. She seemed to have lost interest in the séance; she leaned her head sideways against a cushion, and on her face came the vacant look that one sees on the faces of music-lovers when the music has them under its spell.

The glass did not move for a long time. As soon as a slight tilting began Max said, 'Mary, try to tell us what we should do.'

The answer was 'Go.'

I asked: 'Do you mean that we must leave Cliff End?'

Three times the glass moved between G and O.

'Why must we go?'

'Danger' was spelt.

'From what? From whom is there danger?'

The glass moved quickly to C A R and M, but before it had reached E it fell over and lay swivelling on its side. When we began again it ran, exactly as it had done on the previous evening, backwards and forwards between L and I and then overturned again.

Max exclaimed, 'This does mean something!' Ingram said, frowning, 'This can't be coincidence.'

Once again Max set up the glass and once again we asked a question. Max spoke:

'Would it help to send for the priest?'

Wild agitation followed. The glass slid about among the letters, flinging every one of them off the table, then it was thrown on the floor and broke.

'The priest is unpopular,' Max remarked, stooping to retrieve the fallen letters, while Ingram and I, with the help of his pocket torch, collected fragments of glass. Pamela had taken no notice of the confusion; when I stood up I saw her lying limp in her chair, asleep.

'Pamela,' I cried sharply, 'wake up!'

Ingram gripped my arm, saying urgently, 'Don't!'

Max put an arm round Pamela and raised her shoulders; her head lolled; she did not wake. He looked in alarm at Ingram. I was shaking.

'For God's sake, Ingram,' I said, 'wake her up!'

Ingram had turned pale, but he replied quietly, 'Much better not: it might shock her. This is trance. It won't do any harm.'

'Pamela!' I said again loudly. Max settled her again against her cushion, saying, 'Better take Ingram's advice.'

I could see the state that Ingram was in, though he made a great effort to look calm.

'I have often seen this,' he told us: 'it will pass.'

'You've got to wake her,' I said.

'I implore you … '

Pamela sighed; she breathed slowly and deeply, as if in uneasy sleep; her face was not paler than usual. Max sat beside her with his finger on her pulse. He nodded to me, saying, 'She'll be all right.'

Her breathing grew deeper and her lips parted; she seemed to smile. After a little she half-opened her eyes. A wind passed between my ribs and over my heart, but I stood still. Presently she spoke.

The syllables which Pamela uttered were as strange to me as the voice in which she was speaking – a light, joyous voice, soft and lilting, altogether different from her own.

'I don't know the language,' Ingram whispered. 'Do you?' He snatched my notebook and began to write. Max shook his head. 'It is not Latin or Italian.'

'It must be Spanish,' I said.

I heard tender little sounds repeated over and over again. Pamela smiled.

It is Carmel, I thought – Carmel's love-talk with Meredith; Carmel living her youth over again. This might end in possession.

I turned on Ingram: 'This is intolerable! You've got to wake her! You can't do your damned researches at Pamela's expense! Remember that Carmel was a suicide, a maniac, a murderess – '

Pamela cried out – it was a dreadful cry – then she began to moan. It was appalling – she wept with abandonment. This was the helpless sobbing that we so often heard. It chilled me to the heart to listen to it. I was cramped with fear and shuddering with cold, and I saw fear on Ingram's face.

Suddenly Max opened the door. He looked out and came in again, shutting it at once. He said, 'Take her out by the garden. Be quick.'

It took a long time to unbolt the window and half-door and to open the trellis screen. While I did so, Max and Ingram lifted Pamela between them. They carried her out and in through the greenhouse and laid her on the sitting-room couch. She had stopped moaning. She opened her eyes.

'Are you all right?' Ingram's voice shook.

She replied, 'Yes, of course!' and then exclaimed, 'Roddy, what's wrong? Why are you so white? What happened? Surely I didn't faint?'

Her voice was her own; she was herself. Almost sick with relief, I sank into a chair. Ingram said, 'Thank God!' and went out of the room. Max answered her: 'No, you went into a trance.'

She was intensely interested. He began to tell her what happened. She said at once: 'It was Carmel!'

'But Mary was coming,' I told her; 'we were only just in time.'

She took hold of my arm.

'Where's Mr Ingram? Oh, Max, please!'

Max went to the hall and came back with him. Both had lost colour and Ingram was trembling; he sat on the fender-stool, too famished with cold to speak.

Max said, 'She disappeared into the nursery: a sort of wraith, shrouded; there's a fog in there now, savagely cold.'

'It's very dangerous,' Ingram said.

Of the four of us, Pamela was the calmest. She remembered nothing that had happened after the glass had spelt 'Lili' again.

'Was it really trance?' she asked Ingram.

'Yes,' he replied: 'deep, mediumistic trance … Is your head aching?'

'It is, rather; but never mind. Tell me what I said.'

He read from his notes, trying to reproduce the syllables which she had spoken.

'It must be Spanish, and I don't know a word of it!' she exclaimed. 'I've never heard it spoken in my life. It was Carmel, of course.'

We could make nothing of the syllables, and there was no Spanish dictionary in the house.

Ingram said, 'I did not have the impression that this was intended as a communication.' I agreed and told him how I had felt that it was Carmel reliving some moment with her lover.

'The voice was very happy,' Max said. 'It doesn't seem to affect your theories one way or the other, does it, though?'

'I wonder ... ' Pamela plunged into thought, looking at Ingram's notes.

No one replied. We sat quiet, smoking and sipping our drinks, all rather appalled at what we had done and sunk in the relaxation of escape.

'I'll keep these and make you a copy, please,' Pamela said, putting the notes into her journal. Then she smiled. 'Well, here ends our investigation! I'm glad it's over. I don't suppose we shall ever know the truth, but at least we know what we have to do.'

'Come to London with me, both of you, tomorrow,' Max begged. 'Don't spend another night here.'

'It won't be London, Max,' I replied. 'Bristol for me, as soon as we've wound up here – on account of my play,' I added.

'Oh, yes – I forgot your play.'

'But definitely,' I said to Pamela, 'this is your last night at Cliff End.'

'All right, Roddy,' she replied. 'Don't worry: there is always The Golden Hind.'

She stood up, ready to go to bed. Ingram, saying, 'Please wait,' went out to explore the hall and landing. He called from upstairs: 'It is all right.'

'This is all rather horrid for Mr Ingram,' Pamela said as she left us. 'Do try to cheer him up.'

She must have found something consoling to say to him, for he looked much happier when he returned. He looked at me penitently, saying, 'You have a right to be very angry with me.'

'Not with you,' I replied, 'and I beg your pardon for bursting out so absurdly. I'm wild with myself.'

He shook his head. 'I ought to have warned Miss Fitzgerald.'

'We were warned; Pamela knew what she was risking.'

'So she told me. She says it was interesting! She is the most intrepid woman … '

He stopped, inarticulate for once.

Max intervened firmly. 'Why worry? Pamela's all right.'

But Ingram persisted. 'It all means so much more to you than I realised,' he said remorsefully. 'Your friend, Miss Meredith, involved so horribly, and this lovely place, and the frightful danger of possession – and I treated it all as an abstract problem, quite heartlessly. I can't say how I regret … '

Before I could find an answer Max broke in. 'That was my doing, Ingram! I deceived you as completely as I could. Roderick and Pamela had been stifling here among ghosts. I knew that your alpine breezes were just what would do them good. If you had guessed they were in real trouble, you couldn't have been nearly such a tonic. Isn't that so, Roderick?'

'Of course it is!' I realised just how refreshing Ingram's zest had been and how strongly I would have resented an attitude of condolence. I tried to convince him of this. 'And you have done what we wanted: helped us to make our decision,' I said.

He was looking into the fire, his elbow on the mantelpiece. He sighed. 'I wish it could have been a different one,' then he said good night and left us. He was distressed.

'I am sorry about Ingram,' I told Max.

'Don't be,' he replied. 'He's a charming fellow, but he needed this plunge into deep waters, I think. He has splashed about a bit too merrily in the shallows, I imagine. Do him good to find he has floundered out of his depth. I like him.'

'So do I.'

'Does Pamela?'

'It's hard to know.'

We sat on until Max had finished his pipe and then went to our rooms.

I SLEPT like a drunkard. When I woke, reluctantly, it was to find the study full of sunlight and Lizzie looming over me, big with reproach. She said, 'Miss Pamela's not well.'

I got my wits into gear gradually. I recollected that this was Saturday – Stella was going to Bristol and we were leaving Cliff End.

'What is it, Lizzie?'

'I'm telling you she's not well.'

'What's the matter with her?' I asked abruptly. I was scared.

'Her orders is to say it's an ordinary headache and she's afraid she'll have to rest and you're to tell the gentlemen she's sorry, and it isn't a case of the morning after the night before.'

This was authentic Pamela! I laughed with relief. Lizzie added portentously, 'That's what she said to say.'

'But Elizabeth, I take it, has other views?'

This was schoolroom strategy – to call her 'Elizabeth' when she looked formidable. It failed to break up her gloom. In a voice heavy with trouble and rebuke she demanded, 'What were you doing in the nursery last night?'

'Good heavens,' I groaned, 'did nobody tidy up?'

'Table-turning, wasn't it?' Lizzie went on. 'Heathen and wicked practices, enough to call devils out of hell! I know what the priest thinks of such conjurings and I know what he'd say to me about staying in a house where people are after doing it, too.'

'I can tell you truthfully, Lizzie, that we saw no devils,' I said.

'You saw something or heard something,' she declared, 'or why is Miss Pamela's eyes sunk like two stones in her head? No, Mr Roderick: I suspicioned it and now I know. And I won't stand for it. That's an ultimato.'

'Which means, Lizzie?'

'Which means that I … that I … ' She turned her back and gave an unneeded tug to the curtains. 'Mr Roddy,' she said in a choked voice, 'you should think shame.'

'Perhaps I do think shame.'

She turned to me, her face crumpled with sorrow and perplexity, begging, 'Won't you give Father Anson a chance?'

'No more talk about that, Lizzie.'

'But he's willing – '

'I'm not … Listen, Lizzie,' I said: 'you have nothing to worry about. There's going to be a big change in our plans. If you weren't such a chronic old gossip, I'd tell you more. You'll hear in good time.'

Dubiously she accepted this.

It was a grey, windy morning. No one else was down yet. I went out to Charlie, who was putting the finishing touches to the fence. He began to chat about the lovely hedge of macrocarpus he would plant against it. I detest macrocarpus and told him it was to be gorse; then I remembered – there would be no hedge.

'Leave that,' I said. 'Go round and give Lizzie a hand.' Surprised and affronted, he went.

There was a glint of light over the headlands northward; they floated, illumined isles, in a vaporous sea – the Isles of the Blessed – Tír-na-n'Óg. Except in the height of summer or in the murk of winter, you would never look out from here on two days running and see the same scene; the variations played by the weather and the seasons, the time of day, the tides and the winds, over sea and land and sky, were infinite. All day long the excitement of changeful beauty was quickening one's nerves. I thought I would live in a shepherd's hut on the moors rather than look out on walls.

Sea-gulls, flocking inland before the wind, swerved, screaming, to swoop on something under the cliff. Listening to the din of their raucous quarrel, I remembered Stella's picture of gulls at sunrise. 'It was magical,' she had said.

How would Stella feel, arriving in a hygienic little bedroom in Miss Holloway's Home; finding herself among those sad, drab women; living under the domination of that steely will? Would she feel a prisoner, without friends?

Surely we might remind her that she had friends! What was the name of that flower-shop in Bristol where we had bought roses for Wendy? It could not possibly do any harm – a gift of flowers sent without a name. She would guess but would not write. It might avert a flood of desolation. Or would it, I asked myself miserably, crash into a hard-won peace? I did not know what to do.

I went in and rang Scott's lodgings. He had gone out, but his exasperated landlady said that if that was Mr Fitzgerald again she was to tell him that his friend was better and was leaving this afternoon.

What had I hoped for? Stella was better. That ought to be enough, but the load of apprehension weighed on me still. In what way better? More spirited or more resigned? At least, I supposed, no longer a fury and a saint in turns – no longer menaced by that ghastly fate.

'Withers' – the name was Withers.

I found the number in Bristol and telephoned. A warm woman's voice answered me. She accepted my commission and references with interest and promised to send roses without a name or message of any sort.

Max came down and we stood in the porch. I told him what I had done. My uneasiness was so great that I poured out my fears about what Stella would go through now. He listened thoughtfully.

'She won't put up with it long, Roderick,' he declared. 'The girl's full of spirit; she'll rebel.'

'Even if she wants to, what can she do?'

'She'll write to Pamela.'

'They'll stop her letters going out.'

'It's not a prison!'

'"A rest-cure" will be the excuse.'

'She'll have to be allowed to write to her grandfather.'

'She won't complain to her grandfather: he's ill.'

'She'll do something; she'll run away.'

'Where to? We have forbidden her to come here and she won't upset him.'

'Roderick, the girl's eighteen! There are hotels. I'll send her our address.'

'She'll never receive it.'

'She must have friends somewhere.'

'I doubt if she has one. Besides, they'll take her money away.'

Max looked startled. 'Do you really suppose they'll do that?'

'The Holloway woman is capable of anything: I believe she killed Carmel,' I said.

That had been a fine burst of pessimism. I felt ashamed. Max had been unhappy enough about our giving up Cliff End; he looked wretched over this. He said, 'It's a pretty bad jam.'

Ingram's arrival was a relief. He came running downstairs, as airy as the morning, with some pleasant excitement alight in his eyes. The news that Pamela was resting disconcerted him considerably, but he enjoyed the formula by which she had assured us that she was none the worse for the séance. Over breakfast his project came out.

'If your sister thought of going to her cousin in Dublin – and it would be a splendid change, wouldn't it? – do you think she would like to travel by air? You can do it, you know, from Bristol in under two hours. I've been wanting a pretext to do it, and I could go that way perfectly well. I might have the pleasure of travelling with her, perhaps? That is, if, by any chance, she could do it about eight days from now?'

He was so delighted with his notion that I felt sorry to have to tell him that I knew Pamela had no intention of going to Ireland yet.

Max covered his silence by promising to send me a Spanish dictionary at once. He wanted a copy of the notes that Ingram had made, but Pamela had taken them with the journal to her room.

When Lizzie came to clear away she reported that Pamela was still asleep. I repeated Scott's message, telling her to give it to Pamela as soon as she woke. At eleven, when it was time to drive Ingram to his train, she was still asleep.

Ingram could not recover his spirits. He sat in the car, looking at the house with the wistful gaze of a boy being sent back to school. Max, too, was depressed.

Ingram's train for Bristol was to leave Bideford station at eleven thirty-five. Max, who was returning to London, said that he would not waste the morning in a train; he decided to walk by a roundabout route to the station, lunch at a pub, and leave by the three-fifteen. He put his bag in the back of the car. Just then the telephone rang. It was Peter Carey, in a blaze over a visit from Pennant. I told him I couldn't wait, and sent Max to the phone.

'Good luck, Roderick!' Max said. 'Judith and I may join you at The Golden Hind.' It occurred to me that he might possibly encounter Stella at the station, and I was torn between the temptation to send a message by him and the conviction that she ought to be left alone. I said nothing, either way, in the end. I left him listening to Peter with a delighted grin.

Ingram was rather silent during the drive; when he spoke, it was about the house.

'So often haunting does little or no harm – scares a child or a servant now and then; but this is so acute, and Miss Fitzgerald is so sensitive. I am sure you are doing the only possible thing.'

When we topped the Tor I pulled up for a moment, the view was so fine. The sea was leaden, blazed with silver streaks, and Lundy had a silver fringe. The sun was covered by a vast cloud, almost black, with its under-edge brilliantly white; flat shafts of light, fanning down from it, caught a headland and held it in an aerial amethyst glow.

'Gosh!' I exclaimed. 'Max is enjoying this!'

Ingram paused before he answered, then said, 'I agree with Mr Hilliard: this place must be magnificent in mid-winter.'

'I wish I could invite you to Cliff End for Christmas,' I replied. He looked at me gratefully.

'If you are in any place where I might join you for a few days, will you let me? That is, if we don't meet in Ireland,' he asked.

He showed his first sign of diffidence in asking this, and I was able to respond cordially.

For the few minutes that remained he talked in his liveliest manner about the odd places and people he had met with in the course of his researches. 'I never imagined,' he said, 'that ghosts would bring me such a great pleasure as this visit has been. Please give my warm regards and wishes to your sister. She has promised to let me know how things turn out. Give her my thanks. Tell her I would sin again to be forgiven so graciously.'

When his train had gone I found that I missed him; his vitality had been stimulating. Max would be gone, too, when I reached home, and tonight Pamela and I would sleep at the inn. Stella would be a hundred miles away.

I studied the timetable in the station. The afternoon train left at five-fifty. I must not come to the station. I must not drive through The Avenue and look at Wilmcote. I drove straight home. Passing The Golden Hind, I hesitated – ought I to book our rooms for tonight? Pamela might not feel well enough to come out; we could fix it by telephone.

Pamela was much better. She lay propped up on pillows in the half-darkened room, her headache almost gone. 'It was a splitter,' she told me. 'I was awake until five. I'm sorry about Mr Ingram ... Roddy, I want one night's reprieve!'

'Granted,' I replied, 'on condition that you stay in this room.'

'I'm too busy to move. I want to do nothing but think. We've been wildly, crazily wrong.'

'I won't have it, Pamela; you're not going to start all over again!'

'But, Roddy, I am! There's hope ... '

'Don't addle your brains with it, Pamela! Nothing will do any good, and you'll wear both of us out.'

'Very well, I won't talk till I'm sure. Tell me the news! Oh, Max came up and told me about Peter. Was there ever anybody like Max?'

I relayed Ingram's messages to the best of my ability, saying that I was afraid they had lost some of their elegance on the road. She listened with half a smile. 'What was he talking about – sin and forgiveness?' I wanted to know.

'Oh, I suppose, when he was upset last night. It really is hard luck on him, and you weren't as civil as you might have been.'

'Well, I like that! And my teeth seething with irritation and I keeping it all back!'

'You didn't! He was doing no end for us, and you treated him like ... like ... '

'Like what, in the name of goodness?'

She laughed. 'Oh, like a jack-in-the-box – bashing his head down when he popped it up.'

'I didn't! And he did pop it up rather a lot.'

'Go along, Roddy. You're making my head ache!'

'Oh, all right. Send for me when you want something to sharpen your claws on.'

Pamela regarded me with dignity.

'When I send for you it will be to announce something of the utmost importance,' she said.

Chapter XXI

RETURN

I SPENT a grim afternoon. After lunching alone, I destroyed papers, packed up my manuscript, wrote business letters, and made lists of multitudinous things to be done in connection with shutting up the house. The place could not be used for storage even; it would be too easily burgled; everything must be sent away. But where to? Where were we going to live? For a few weeks, furnished rooms in Bristol; but I could not do without books and files. And where after that?

How, among all these problems and labours, I was to finish my play up to time I could not imagine, but it would have to be done. Pamela would stand by, but Lizzie … We would not be able to afford to keep Lizzie. It was going to be hard on her.

When she brought up my tea she said, 'Miss Pamela will take only an omelette for dinner. Will a cutlet do you?'

'No, Lizzie,' I answered; 'I'll have an omelette, too, and I'll make it myself: a cheese omelette. I'll make hers as well; I wouldn't trust you to cook for her when she's in delicate health.'

I angled in vain for Lizzie's rich laugh. She stood grave as a Buddha.

'I'm not going out tonight,' she announced.

'Oh, but, Lizzie, you must! You'll be nervous here.'

'I'll be found dead in my bed, stiff with fright, in the morning, maybe, and my death will be on you.'

'Good heavens, why won't you go?'

'Because I can't trust you. I can't trust you when my back is turned.'

So that was the trouble! Lizzie was preparing to stay and protect us against devils loose out of hell.

'Lizzie,' I said, 'you have me beat. If I give you my solemn word of honour that we'll do nothing tonight that the priest wouldn't approve of, will you go?'

She heaved an immense sigh of relief.

'God bless you, Mr Roderick, I will!'

I went down to the sitting-room to sort books. It was curious, I reflected, that the rooms which we used all the time did not seem to be haunted. There had been no trouble in this lovely room. I wished Pamela would not begin playing with indecision again; it was useless and debilitating; my mind was irrevocably made up. I set to work on a review and finished it as daylight failed.

Rain was falling in a deluge, and the sound of footsteps outside surprised me. Could it be Scott? He had said Sunday. It was Father Anson, struggling along under a huge umbrella to which he clung with both hands against the wrenching wind. I hurried to open the door, and he was blown in; he was out of breath, and anxious and diffident.

'May I come in?' he asked. 'Are you well? Are you free?'

I was able to tell him in all sincerity that I was delighted to see him. The anxiety on his face was not dissipated, however. His deep-set eyes searched my face. He said gravely, 'I hope Miss Fitzgerald is well?'

I told him that she had stayed in bed with a headache but was better. He sat down, looking relieved.

'I am very happy to hear that she is not ill, and,' he smiled, 'if I am going to be told that I am impertinent, I would rather hear it from you alone.'

'You are not going to be told that.'

'Were you of the Faith, it would have been my duty as a priest to come; but as it is, my visit will really be an intrusion unless you can accept it as from a friend.'

'Thank you, Father Anson. We need friends just now, my sister and I.'

'So I fear; so I fear.'

I could not help smiling; it was so obvious that rumours of our 'wicked practices' had reached him. I cast my mind back to the morning.

'It is not as serious as you imagine,' I told him. 'I would like to explain – but first let me work it out! Lizzie told Charlie; Charlie told Mrs Jessup, who repeated it to – let me see –'

'The grocer's boy,' Father Anson contributed with a smile; 'who told my housekeeper, who spoke to me.'

Suddenly grave again, he said, 'In spite of my warning you felt driven to do this?'

'It was a last resort.'

'And has it shown you how to give the spirits rest?'

'No.'

'How could it? But now I have great hope of helping you. The Bishop's permission has come.'

The priest's tenacity was embarrassing; I had got to make it clear to him, finally, that exorcism was out. I said: 'I wish you had not troubled the Bishop, Father; you see … '

He checked me with a gesture.

'I know! I know that permission has still to be obtained from a source which' – he smiled very slightly – 'which seems to you more important. My next step will be to obtain this.'

'Stella Meredith goes to Bristol today,' I said.

'The journey to Bristol is not beyond my powers.'

'It is very good of you, Father Anson, but, believe me, it is best to let her forget; besides, no action about the haunting is necessary now: we have decided to give up the house.'

'That is a hard decision.'

'We have no alternative.'

He bent his head for a moment in thought. I hoped he was not going to revert to his theme, but he did. He looked at me very earnestly.

'Forgive me, Mr Fitzgerald, but I am going to be a little persistent about this. I am not thinking only of your beautiful home, grievous as its loss would be to you, but of this unhappy child. Is she to go through the rest of her life burdened with the thought that in this house is her mother's spirit – with that dreadful, blasphemous belief?'

He flushed in his vehemence, but was at once suave again and spoke gently.

'I knew Stella's mother; I think I may say' – he hesitated – 'I think I may say that we were friends. I have failed in my duty, in losing touch with her child. I ought to visit Stella; I intend to do so, and I am anxious to know whether, if I should succeed in reconciling her to the idea of a service of exorcism, you and Miss Fitzgerald would consent.'

I felt sorry. I felt drawn to Father Anson and would have liked to retain his friendship, but what could I say? If I told him anything, it must be the truth. Those old eyes had long ago comprehended the nature and weakness of man; he would see, under any rationalisation, any fictitious pretext, the son of Adam, the child of original sin.

I told him something of what I had told Max; I explained Stella's condition; I repeated what Scott had said. He was overcome; he bowed his head and his lips moved in prayer.

'May God forgive me,' he said brokenly. 'Have I moved too late?'

'Surely,' I protested, 'you had no responsibility in all this?' He did not reply. To distract him, I began to talk about the séance and to describe Pamela's trance, but Lizzie came in, satisfaction written all over her, to say that Pamela hoped for a sick call from Father Anson before he left. We went upstairs at once.

Pamela was sitting up, in her elegant lace jacket. Her room looked cosy, with lamps lit and the curtains drawn against the gloom outside. Sheets of manuscript lay scattered on the bed. She welcomed Father Anson warmly and said that she was quite recovered and had done a day's work.

'Do you know Spanish, Father?' she asked. Now why had I not thought of this possibility?

'I used to,' he replied.

She passed Ingram's notes to me.

'Can you remember how they sounded, Roddy? Read the words out. Father Anson,' she explained, 'these are words which I spoke last night, in trance.'

He shook his head reproachfully. His eyes lit with interest, nevertheless, and he listened intently while I reproduced the syllables as best I could – *niña mia; chica; guapa*, and the rest.

He took the paper from me.

'Those are simply words of endearment: diminutives, such as "my darling," "my baby," "my darling little girl": the words of a mother to her child.'

Pamela's eyes danced. 'So I imagined!' She looked straight in the priest's face and asked him, 'Did Carmel have a child?' He studied the paper as if he had not heard and, after a moment, replied vaguely, 'Carmel came from Spain. It was for a very few months of her life that I knew her. Many things may have happened in her own country of which she never told me.'

Pamela smiled and put the paper away.

'Well,' she said, 'you can have no objection to answering this. When you knew Carmel first, was she a gentle, warm-natured girl?'

'So indeed I believed.'

'Her tempers, her passions – were they as outrageous as people say?'

The priest smiled. 'I saw Carmel lose her temper once with my housekeeper: she was like an angry, unhappy, tearful child.'

I heard Lizzie lumbering up and went out to help with her weighty tray. This chatter of Pamela's was annoying me a good deal. None of this mattered now. What did I care if Carmel had left a baby deserted in Spain? It was not Carmel and her weeping that were driving us out.

Lizzie had brought Father Anson tea, sandwiches, and a dish of buttery potato cakes. The man must have been hungry; there was unconcealed pleasure in his face when she set the tray in front of him. 'Well, Lizzie,' he said, his eyes twinkling, 'I was just thinking out a terrible new penance for gossip, but, do you know, I believe I'll let you off.'

She chuckled. 'That Charlie! … Well, Father, I can't say in conscience I'm sorry for whatever brought you to the house! Mind the potato cakes, they're dripping with butter; look, I brought you a napkin; put that on your knee.'

While Father Anson enjoyed his meal Pamela plied him with eager questions. She was in the highest excitement and expressed herself without restraint.

'Roddy, we have been as blind as bats! Carmel was a simple, warm-hearted, loving girl, and Mary' – her voice took on an edge of detestation – 'Mary was a cold, hard, self-righteous prig!'

Father Anson glanced at her warningly. 'My daughter – *de mortuis* … '

'You agree!'

'Good heavens, Pamela, what are you getting at?' I interjected.

'Everybody's admiration for Mary is scarcely "this side idolatry"!'

The priest nodded. 'Mary Meredith inspired strong feelings,' he said.

Pamela's face hardened. 'Mary Meredith,' she said, 'was an overweening, hypocritical egoist.'

Father Anson was startled.

'What can have made you think so hardly of her?'

'What do *you* think, Father, of a woman who could leave a child in the dark, crying with terror, and refuse it a light?'

'She had her own system of discipline.'

'Just so: a system of discipline! Her code of laws for other people! She had her method of training their characters, her scheme for saving their souls! A fine system – to subject a baby to terror, and a young hot-blooded girl to temptation, in order that she might watch and guide and play the redeeming angel! Sending her husband to perdition so that she might show off her "infinite magnanimity"!'

I was astounded; but the most amazing thing was the discovery that some obscure part of me had felt this about Mary for a long time. How had Pamela worked it out?

'Talk about "venom"!' I said.

Pamela had exhausted herself; she lay back on her pillows and smiled into Father Anson's reproachful face.

'I begin to fear,' he said seriously, 'that you have not quite recovered from the trance. Oh, my child, that was so dangerous, so wrong! And now,' he smiled, 'I cannot sit here and listen to such bitter talk. Must I leave these delicious sandwiches unfinished?'

'Very well, I won't go on; but I believe you agree with me in your heart.'

Father Anson spoke deliberately: 'I agree with you to this extent – I think that Mary, like many virtuous and noble women, put an undue strain upon human nature at times.'

'That will do nicely,' Pamela said.

When the priest had finished his meal he rose, saying, 'I am afraid that I must play the beggar – eat and leave you.'

He looked so tired that I wished that I could drive him home and said so, but explained that it was too late to leave Pamela alone.

'That would be very wrong,' he agreed.

He stood by her bedside and held her hand and implored her to take part in no more séances.

'Just because you have such an ardent spirit and soaring imagination it is very perilous for you,' he said.

She replied, 'I hope we are near the end of all that,' and thanked him warmly for his visit and his concern.

Lizzie was sitting in the hall, waiting to set out. I watched them go out into the heavy rain and darkness together, Father Anson's immense umbrella protecting both; then I ran upstairs.

Pamela's door was shut. I knocked on it.

'Hi, woman, what *is* all this?'

'I'll tell you at supper,' she answered. 'I'm getting up! Run the bath for me, like a nice buffer. Start the omelette when I ring!'

My omelette lay between us on its blue dish, puffed up and shapely. I cut into it carefully and it did not subside.

'Delicious, Roddy!' Pamela said. 'Crispy as "yellow tide-foam".'

In her red dress, with rose-shaded lights giving her face colour, Pamela did not look nearly so ill, but I was still at a loss to interpret the joyous excitement that shone in her eyes. The last thing I wanted was to see her buoying herself up once more with hopes that were doomed to fail.

'I hope,' I said, 'that you have some rational excuse for looking so pleased with yourself.'

'Roddy' – she became very serious – 'I am not pleased with myself. I am extremely nervous, as a matter of fact.'

'Nervous? Why?'

'Because I don't know how to tell you about this. I so desperately want you to believe it. If you do, it will change everything.'

'Pamela, have sense! What can it change? Even if you have accounted for Carmel and her weeping – and I doubt it – I can't devote my life to combing orphanages in Spain, France, and England for a foundling abandoned years ago. And, in any case, it is not Carmel who matters: it is Mary. Nothing alters the fact that her haunting is insupportable.'

Pamela looked at me in perplexity. She was overcharged with impulsive excitement but was anxious to be tactful. She sighed. 'I wish you could think it out for yourself!'

'Think what out?'

'I wish you could see that all the prejudice against Carmel is utterly unfair.'

'Does it matter?'

'It matters enormously. Oh, Roddy, she has been so maligned! These ignorant people! Just because she was gay and foreign and they knew she had been once seduced! The Jessups would guess that. She was seduced, but she was faithful: she loved Meredith right to the end; but they put her down to a light woman, I suppose.'

'They would, of course.'

'Then Miss Holloway – Miss Holloway's jealousy of Carmel was hardly sane; and Mary had no mercy on her at all.'

'But, good lord, Carmel killed Mary – or didn't she?'

'She didn't, Roddy! That was the tree! The tree struck Mary, just as it struck you.'

'Gosh! Why didn't I think of that? And it, so to speak, hitting me in the eye.'

'Miss Holloway knew it: she knows it, and she lies. She lies to herself, to salve her crooked conscience for Carmel's death. And Mary knows it, and she lies, even now.'

'Are you telling me that ghosts tell lies?'

'"L I, L I." That was Carmel trying to tell us, trying to break through. She couldn't spell English.'

'My word, that's ingenious!'

'It's simple. Both times that came immediately after Mary said that Carmel was trying to harm Stella. No one is trying to harm Stella.'

I got up and walked about the room. Now I was interested; this was intriguing, even though it didn't help. Pamela was all wrought up. She looked at me appealingly.

'Do try to clear your mind of all these prejudices and slanders about Carmel; do try to see that she was a kind, faithful, gentle girl! Don't you feel it, Roddy?'

'The face in *Dawn* is charming,' I admitted.

'So is the face I see. I rather loved that face. And Father Anson: he knew her, and he was fond of her.'

'Yes, I imagine he was.'

'And that lonely weeping: the voice is gentle and pitiful, isn't it?'

Yes, I reflected, that was perfectly true; moreover, the voice in which Pamela, in trance, had spoken those words of endearment was the softest and tenderest voice I had ever heard. But why, I wondered, was she so insistent about this?

'And think how she suffered! Think of her in Spain, a girl who was young and joyous in love. Meredith made her happy there. Then Mary comes, all cool and English and exquisite – with some money, too, and a home. I expect he was growing tired of a vagabond life. And they marry. Was Carmel heartbroken, I wonder? Anyhow, she forgave him. Rather than lose sight of him, she became Mary's servant. I believe she meant to be good – meant to be only his model after that. But he seduces her. And then her baby, whom she adored, is taken away from her, and when she comes back – '

'Steady, Pamela!'

I stood still. The world was revolving backwards.

'What, in heaven's name, are you trying to tell me? Her baby? Stella? Is Stella Carmel's child?'

'Yes, Roddy; don't you see?'

I tried to think but could not. I could see nothing – nothing about Stella or Carmel or Mary any more. All logic was fallen into chaos. I only knew that the wind was moaning dismally and that rain was thrashing the greenhouse roof and that Stella was a hundred miles away. I put logs on the fire and sat on the fender-stool, trying to see into all this. There were a score of reasons why it could not be true.

'Miss Holloway would have found out,' I argued, 'and she would never have stayed ten years with Carmel's child.'

'She might, for the "exorbitant salary"! But I don't think she knows.'

'But in Paris!'

'The baby was weaned before she came; there was only Carmel with Mary until then.'

'Good lord! – What about Father Anson?'

'Carmel may have confessed that she had a baby but never told him that it was Meredith's. I don't know. I don't believe he has known all these years, but I think he has guessed now.'

'That would account for his sudden concern about Stella.'

'Yes.'

I sat thinking about this for a long time in silence. Pamela lighted the lamp under the coffee again, then sat curled in her chair, as cosy and limp as a cat, as though all her troubles were at an end. The rain lessened, but the moan of the wind went on. It was growing late. Pamela said, 'If things are all right on the landing, I want to try something. I want to put the oil-stove up there and see whether its heat will keep that cold away. Will you look out?'

I went up to the landing. There was no cold, no mist. A faint moaning sounded through the house: it could easily be the wind. I came down and told Pamela all was well, and for a time she left me alone in the room.

I wanted to believe this: I liked it. If Stella had in her nothing of Mary's nature, if those little tight inhibitions were all imposed, if she had warm, impetuous Southern blood … I looked again at the picture called *Dawn*. It was an enchanting face; a deep well of love and sweetness showed through those dark eyes … Just for a moment, while Stella had sat on the couch in Pamela's room, there had been a shy, soft look … And there was something in the set of the ears, the curve of the lips … By the time Pamela returned, a mood of elation had taken me. I jeered at her notion that she could down a ghost with a stove.

'It's burning, anyway,' she replied cheerfully. 'Roddy, are you convinced?'

I was not going to give in just like that. I walked up and down.

'It's sheer melodrama,' I declared. 'A woman doesn't adopt her husband's child by another woman. It's all too far-fetched.'

'Mary was far-fetched; it's exactly the sort of thing she would do.'

'I don't see a motive.'

'To keep Meredith, of course! He got bored. Spain was calling, Carmel adored him, and he was fond of the child.'

'And Mary did it to turn the scale?'

'Just!'

'But would Carmel give her baby up?'

'What future had she if they discarded her? She had probably lost her looks already. An artist's model, with a baby to keep! Meredith wouldn't stand by, and Mary wouldn't spare her. Can't you imagine the great persuasion scene? "What can you do for the child, you poor outcast? And we can give her such a beautiful life!"'

'You'd better start writing plays.'

'Its being dramatic doesn't mean that it's not true.'

'Oh, I believe you.'

'Do you, Roddy?'

'Almost.'

'Feeding-time in the lion-house. Do stop that pacing act; you distract me.'

'Oh, all right.' I sat opposite to her, across the coffee table, and said, 'I will now cross-examine, if you agree.'

She chuckled. 'Poor Mr Ingram, we are letting him down!'

'He'll bob up again! Now, point A: Mary's reputation. It's not for nothing that a woman gets the name of being almost a saint.'

'Who are the people who admired Mary? All the people who *wanted* to, Roddy. Take the Jessups and their kind. They like to be on the best terms with this house, and they would be no end impressed with a beautiful face and a gracious manner and lady-bountiful ways. She was a real lady-bountiful, I don't doubt.'

'Oh, so you grant Mary some virtues?'

'All the seven deadly virtues, Roddy! All the cold, self-conscious, egotistical ones.'

'Well, I give you the Jessups. And Miss Holloway, I suppose – '

'Miss Holloway is of Mary's type; they were birds of a feather, crammed with high-flown righteousness and with not enough natural humanity between them to comfort a frightened child.'

I grinned. 'That's what has stuck in your gullet.'

'It is! That's what made me suddenly guess. Well, look here! When Miss Holloway met Mary first, what was she? A crank-pot, with her new-fangled theories and any amount of ambition, but with not a penny to put them into effect. Mary shares her theories – and Mary has money to play with.'

'I twigged that, of course.'

'So, you see! Miss Holloway *wanted* to love and admire Mary; she wouldn't let herself see herself as a scrounger; she had to have a virtuous, beautiful excuse. Personal devotion! There you are!'

'You little cynic!'

'You blind old sceptic!'

'And how do you dispose of the Commander?'

'Poor man! Wish-thinking, again!'

'I see: he *wanted* to think his beautiful Mary perfect.'

'He had no one else; besides, she did share his standards, up to a point. She was admirable, in her own ice-cold way.'

'Are you reverting to the notion that the cold comes from the temperament of the ghost?'

'I am.'

'And are you going to tell me that Mary is "ranging for revenge"?'

'Oh, no; forgiving is what Mary enjoyed.'

'You're making her out the queerest type. Aren't you inventing rather a lot?'

'I'm not, Roddy! Think of the things we *know* about Mary: keeping Carmel in the house after she discovered … She must have *wanted* it to go on. Think of what she did when Carmel came back, desperate! Can't you see her – haven't you, actually, seen her – leaning over the banisters, staring into that ravaged face, and then smiling, realising what she could do? Not drive Carmel out: no – keep her; let Meredith paint her; let him stare and stare at that death's-head! And then – do you remember – do you realise – it was Mary who called Carmel to the studio, that last evening, to show her what he had done?'

Pamela's voice trailed off.

'You make her a fiend.'

'A wrecker; rather like your Barbara.'

'Gosh, yes, how astounding!'

'I'm not sure: it was odd, your bursting out into work so utterly unlike anything you had done.'

'You think the atmosphere of the house may account for it?'

'I wonder … It's a different motive, though.'

'No, it's not: love of power in Mary also, I suppose – power of a different kind.'

'Barbara likes the fun of the wrecking; Mary enjoys the rescuing, that's all.'

The coffee had got pretty strong, bubbling unnoticed there.

I poured myself a cup and raised it to Pamela. 'You're a better sleuth than Ingram,' I said.

'He didn't know Carmel, he hadn't seen Carmel, *been* Carmel, as I was last night.'

'I wish they were here, he and Max.'

'Roddy – we couldn't tell them.'

We were silent for a while, meditating on the implications of all this. The clock struck half-past ten. It was quieter outside now, but I heard that low, moaning sound that might be poor Carmel grieving or might be the wind.

I said, 'I hope the Commander has never suspected this.'

'Oh, Roddy,' Pamela said, 'heaven forbid!'

'It would be cruel.'

'The whole thing's cruel! Think of the cruelty to Stella, ever since she was born! You can see Carmel's nature in her, can't you? The impulsive joyousness, the affection and warmth? And all that cramped, warped, repressed!'

Pamela spoke bitterly, then, her face and voice softening, she said, 'I think, when she knows, there'll be an amazing release.'

'We can't tell Stella!' I exclaimed. Pamela stared at me, wide-eyed. 'Not tell her?'

'Of course not! After all these years of idolising Mary as her mother – it would be a frightful shock.'

'But we can't let her go on living under that lie!'

'We can never tell her.'

'Could you face Stella and keep up that sickening lie, Roddy? Besides, the distortion, the mutilation –'

I heard no more of Pamela's argument because I was listening to that moan, rising and falling, now muffled, now a long, low wail. It was not the wind.

I sprang up.

'Listen to that!' I said sharply. 'We know all this! And what use is it? Where does it get us? Listen to it! What can we do?'

Pamela stood up too, trembling slightly. 'We must tell Stella,' she said. 'Carmel wants her to know. She can't bear her own child believing all these slanders and lies, not knowing that she *is* her child! I'm quite sure that's why she stays. Ask her, Roddy! Try the glass again! Perhaps I'll be able to go into trance. Ask her and she'll answer through me!'

'No!' I said violently. 'We will not tell Stella! We will not touch the glass, and you will not go into trance! We leave this house tomorrow.'

'But there's no need! We can put an end to this now. Oh, Roddy, don't you see, Mary is haunting only because of Carmel – for fear of her telling the truth? I am sure of that, *quite* sure. If we can satisfy Carmel, and she goes, Mary will disappear too.'

This was an astounding notion. Did the key to the whole thing really lie in our hands? If it did, could we use it? I was lost in thought, trying to unravel this new tangle, when the telephone rang.

It was not Scott; it was Max.

'I've just got home this minute. How's Pamela?' he said.

'Fine,' I replied. 'I'm delighted you rang. She has just sprung an amazing theory – but, I say, you should have been home long before this; what held you up?'

A short, embarrassed laugh came over the phone. I said: 'I believe it was that cloud. Max, you missed your train!'

He answered, in an amused voice: 'I enjoyed the cloud and I did miss the train. But I meant to miss it. I had Stella a good deal on my mind.'

'Stella!'

'Yes. Roddy, I've done a rather outrageous thing. I don't know what you'll say.'

I relayed this to Pamela, who was standing by, looking anxious. She nodded. 'I can hear.'

'Well,' Max went on, 'I thought it might be a good notion to see Stella off; she didn't turn up for the three-fifteen, but I found that I could wait for the later train and get this connection at Taunton, so I did. She came in with this matron person. Stella looked pretty bad.'

'Ill?'

'More sort of scared – scared and helpless and desperate. I was glad I had come.'

'You spoke to her?'

'Yes; she flew at me. The woman rushed between us like a gorgon, but I had time to stick some money in the pocket of Stella's coat.'

'Max! Money?'

'Yes, and our address; I had it ready; I have been stuck for cash myself, and I thought it might be useful ... '

'It's the brightest idea you ever had in all your bright life!'

'I'm glad you approve! I just had time to whisper, "There's three pounds in that," when the woman came down. I was terrified that Stella was going to cry, but she didn't. She introduced us, all correct.'

'She would!'

'She told me that her grandfather was in hospital – had an operation for appendicitis early this morning. She seemed awfully anxious about him. We hadn't time for any more. The woman got a "Ladies only" ticket stuck on their compartment, so I got into a smoker. I thought I'd see Stella in the corridor later, but I didn't. Roddy, she hopped it! She got out of the train before it started!'

I laughed. I could not help it. The relief – the thought that Stella was still at Wilmcote, the spectacle of Max, playing the part of instigator, and the picture of Miss Holloway's consternation were too much for me. I heard Max ask for another three minutes and complain, 'It's funnier for you than for me.'

'What happened?' I asked, choking.

'Well, when the matron missed her she came looking for me. She made me help her to search the train. She had the guards crawling on their knees, got telegrams sent from the next stop, and I don't know what all. It was as much as I could do to elude her clutches at Taunton! I am not used to this sort of thing.'

'It's a genuine rescue, Max.'

'I thought you would have gone to the inn.'

'Pamela wanted to stay. She wants to talk to you.'

I handed the receiver to Pamela and ran upstairs. I wanted to move about. The windows were open in my bedroom and things were blowing about. I shut them. Pamela's anti-ghost stove had gone out. It was full of oil and its red door was closed; it had not been blown out by the wind. That spot at the head of the stairs where she had placed it did not seem to suit it. I pulled it a bit to one side and lit it again. I had a feeling that Mary would come tonight. Let her come! Stella was not in that prison; she was at Wilmcote: somehow, somewhere, very soon, I should see her.

I had not heard the doorbell ringing, but I heard one loud bang of the knocker. Pamela ran to the door and opened it. Stella came in.

Chapter XXII

SINGLE COMBAT

FOR AN INSTANT I was transfixed on the stairs, too astonished to move. Stella stood in the hall, breathless from the blast which had blown her in, looking at me with anxious eyes. I could say only, 'Stella, Stella, is it you?'

She spoke shakily. 'My grandfather is dying ... I thought,' she said, turning to Pamela, 'if I might talk to you, just for a little ... But I am afraid that it is later than I imagined ... My cab is there. I ... I'll go.'

'You won't go. You shan't disappear again!'

I seized her wrist. I had quite lost my head and had no thought for any danger except the danger of losing Stella once more. I heard Pamela saying, 'I can't send you away.'

Stella, still erect, but trembling, was caught in her arms and leaned her head against Pamela's shoulder.

I opened the door and found Wally Moss in the porch, the reins in his fist; the lights of his cab showed him wildly dishevelled, his eyes round with inquisitiveness. He stared at the note I gave him, saying, 'Well, baint this a wonderful night?'

'A grand, bright, starry night, Wally,' I answered, and left him thinking me mad.

Pamela, running downstairs with slippers, stockings, and brush and comb, said, 'Stella wants you to ring the hospital and give them our number, but the Commander is not to know that she is here.' She paused. 'Oh, Roddy, she ran all the way down to the village from Wilmcote!' Pamela went into the sitting-room and I rang up the hospital.

After the usual 'doing as well as can be expected,' from the porter, I managed to get the night sister to come to the telephone herself. She told me that the Commander was in a coma but might linger for a day or two, and she promised to telephone if there was any change.

'My sister or I would drive his granddaughter over at once if he asked for her,' I said, 'but if you could let him think that she is sleeping in the hospital it might spare him some anxiety.'

The sister replied, 'I quite understand, but he is unlikely to ask for anyone, I am afraid, and it might be better for Miss Meredith not to see him. He is very much changed. But I will telephone you, of course.'

She sounded a sensible woman: that was good.

Pamela, hurrying to the kitchen, said, 'I'll heat up some soup.'

I found Stella sitting in a small chair close to the fire, in the yellow frock she had worn when I read my play. She was paler, thinner; her eyes were shadowed and her hands trembled a little as she held them to the blaze; she had suffered bitterly. She gave me a quick, rather timid glance and then looked away.

I said tensely, 'I didn't know whether I should ever see you again.'

She did not turn her head.

'Thank you for telephoning. Is there any change?'

'No. They will let us know if there is and they will tell him that you are sleeping there.'

'They would have let me sleep in the hospital, but there was no room.'

'I am glad there was no room.'

She looked rigid, and her words came jerkily: 'But you didn't wish me to come here.'

'I have never wished for anything so much in my life.'

She turned her head slowly and rested astonished eyes on mine.

'Oh, Stella, Stella,' I cried, 'have you not discovered yet that wishes and wisdom have nothing to do with one another at all? I was trying to be wise for you, and it half-killed me.'

She said in a low voice, 'It nearly killed me too.'

I caught her cold little hands in mine. 'Shall we give up trying to be wise, Stella?'

She did not answer; she gave me a fleeting smile, so sweet and happy that it took my breath away, but there was a tiny gesture with it, of shyness and withdrawal, which sent me back to my chair and kept me silent until Pamela came in.

Putting the soup down beside Stella, Pamela asked lightly: 'What have you done with poor Miss Holloway? Tell us about that!'

'Miss Holloway,' Stella answered with energy, 'is a heartless woman. I hope that I shall never see her again.'

I responded fervently, 'I hope so too.'

'She had some famous doctor coming to dinner with her and she made me leave, just for that. Could you believe it? He was in a coma, but the sister would have let me wait. She said – Miss Holloway said – that she had grandfather's orders in a letter, to take me on Saturday, whether he lived or died, and she refused to wait for a later train. And you can't make a fight in a hospital. I meant to slip away from her at the station, but do you know what she did? She took my handbag, so that I had no money; I was helpless; but then the most miraculous thing – '

Her eyes opened wide; they stretched wider still when Pamela said, laughing, 'Max *is* miraculous, sometimes.'

'But that is exactly what happened!' Stella exclaimed. 'How did you know? Oh, he told you – he telephoned!'

She laughed merrily over the story of the search for her and his scared escape from Miss Holloway, but then, rather near to tears, told us how she had taken a car straight back to the hospital. They would not let her see her grandfather, saying that the coma had grown deeper and he was unlikely to become conscious again. The sister had persuaded her to go home.

'But there was nobody at Wilmcote, was there?' Pamela asked.

'No; I forgot that; if I had told her, she would perhaps have let me stay.'

'Please take your soup, Stella.'

She drank it obediently. 'I was hungry,' she confessed.

Pamela questioned her.

'Have you been sitting all alone in the empty house?'

'Yes.'

'Darling, for how long?'

'Since about seven. I ... I couldn't bear grandfather's study,' she said shakily, 'and I couldn't bear my own room, so I sat in the kitchen. I just sat there, trying ... I did try ... I did really try hard ... not to come.'

Pamela said unhappily, 'Stella dearest, if only I had known! Why didn't you telephone?'

'The telephone had been cut off, and the light, and everything. I think he had arranged' – her voice faltered – 'not to come back. Besides, I had promised not to ... But in the end I broke all my promises: I just ran out of the house.'

Still the threatening tears were held back.

'In all that rain?' I exclaimed.

'It had nearly stopped. No – it was the wind, or being in bed so long, or all the bromide – I got weak. I couldn't walk any more. But I was very fortunate; I went into Mrs Dendle's house – she does our laundry and she's a kind person. She sent her son for Wally Moss.'

'You have had a terrible day,' Pamela said.

Stella shook her head.

'Today has not been so terrible as last night. The unbearable time was when Dr Scott told me that he was likely to die. For some reason, I think I can bear that now. Life couldn't be happy for him, could it, much longer? He was tired out. And he isn't suffering today. Last night he was in such pain. His mind was wandering and he was miserable; he thought that I was my mother and that she had told him a lie.'

Pamela glanced at me, startled.

'Do you know what he thought the lie was about?' I asked.

'No: he just kept repeating, "Mary, you didn't lie to me? Tell me you didn't." And I said: "Never, papa darling – never in all my life"; then he would be peaceful again.'

I was relieved; that would have been a ghastly way for Stella to learn the truth. Perhaps Pamela was right and we ought to tell her – but not now.

'Oughtn't you to go to bed now?' I said.

'Oh, please, not yet!'

It was nearly midnight, but the house was quiet, except for the wind. I stoked the fire up; Pamela piled cushions in Stella's chair and tried to make her relax, but Stella was tense with her need to talk to us; her eyes were bright, sometimes with happiness, sometimes with tears; her voice shook now and then.

'There is something I ought to tell you,' she said, and hesitated. A look of desolation came on her face and her eyes lost all their light. 'It is about my mother,' she went on. 'You were right, Roddy, and I was childish and foolish. It was not my mother in the nursery. I imagined it all.'

This was inexplicable, and it hurt her to the heart to say it. I asked quickly, 'What makes you think that?'

She replied with difficulty: 'My grandfather told me. I tried to tell him what it was like in the nursery. It was after your visit, Pamela. He had been kind about that, and I thought it wasn't fair not to try my hardest to make him understand. I told him about the scent, and the comfortingness, and the lovely little words. I hoped that he might be glad, but he was angrier than I have ever seen him in all my life. He made me see that I had been imagining it, because, it seems' – she steeled herself to go on – 'it seems that my mother was not that sort of person: he said, "She was not sentimental about you. She was never a baby-worshipper."'

Her hands covered her face suddenly, and tears trickled through. I could have cursed the dying old man. He had robbed Stella of something that no one could ever restore to her, I thought; but then I remembered that was not so; we knew the truth.

I said quickly, 'Stella, he was wrong. He has been wrong about everything. She did lie to him, and he believed the lie.'

Stella looked at me, her face incredulous but vivid with hope, then looked into Pamela's smiling eyes.

Kneeling by Stella and drawing her hands from her face, Pamela said, 'Darling, it was not your imagination. We have found out the truth. I want to tell you, if you can be calm, but I mustn't if it will make you cry.'

Stella drew a long breath and said steadily, 'Tell me, please.'

'Your mother did love you. She adored you; she petted and caressed you and stole into your room with a light. No baby was ever more loved. She has never stopped loving you. But everyone has made an extraordinary mistake.'

Stella gazed at Pamela's face intently, then looked at me. 'Did you make a mistake too?' she said.

'Yes; everyone did.'

'I knew something was wrong,' she said slowly.

Pamela went on: 'It was your mother who was with you in the nursery and who made you happy, but, Stella, it was not Mary Meredith. That was a lie. You are not Mary Meredith's child.'

Stella stared into the fire for a moment and a few tears fell, but they were not tears of distress. She spoke in a low voice: 'I did wonder sometimes. I am so unlike her, and since I've been ill – since grandfather told me that – I haven't been able to love her properly. It was as if she had cheated me – as if everything had cheated me. I loved her and hated her at the same time.'

'And that,' I said, 'is anybody's hell.'

'I tried to get over it, for grandfather's sake, but I never did.'

She stood up and opened her hands in a bewildered gesture.

'Why am I glad? Why does it make me feel as if I could fly?'

'Because,' I answered, 'you can be yourself now, not imitation Mary any more.'

'Do you know who my mother was?'

I hesitated. I felt uneasy. If Stella should hear Carmel weeping, we would have that wretched dilemma again. We ought to have thought of that and have waited until we were out of this house. Pamela was hesitating too, but Stella read our faces.

'You do know! Can it have been Carmel?' she said.

That settled it. I found the volume of photographs and handed it to her, open at *Dawn*.

She looked at the portrait for a long time, with a tender smile.

'I have seen her face in my father's sketches and I always loved it,' she murmured. 'They say she was wicked, but of course it's not true. Her face is as loving and kind as the voice in the nursery.'

Pamela began to talk to her about Carmel, as she had talked to me, only softening Mary's and Meredith's part. Stella's face had a grave and compassionate look as she listened.

It was splendid that she had reacted like this. I felt very guilty, nevertheless. It would be disastrous if the weeping began. I went round the house, turning on lights, as though that, or anything, could avert it. I was relieved to see that the oil-stove was burning still.

When I returned Stella was saying sadly, 'Think of grandfather, cheated all these years. I'm the child of that girl he despised and that man he detested, and he has given me everything.'

I said, 'He was lucky. He has had a loving companion who was attentive and loyal to him. That's more than a daughter of Mary and Meredith would have been. And he'll never know.'

'No,' Stella said resolutely, 'he will never know. If he recovers, I'll be so good to him … But I'm afraid it's foolish to think of that … The storm is growing fierce, isn't it? It sounds as if it were angry with the trees.'

The wind had shifted and was charging over the moors like a horde of demons now; our guardian larches fought and groaned. Nobody would be able to sleep while that clamour lasted. Stella was broad awake.

Pamela, moving about the room uneasily, said, 'It seems to me that we've had mighty little to eat.'

That was true, and to keep Stella downstairs might be the wisest thing.

'Now that you mention it, I'm famished,' I declared.

'I wonder what happens to people who eat a mixed grill at midnight?'

'They bless the cook and sleep sweetly.'

'I'll lay it in the kitchen.' Pamela glanced at me and left the room.

I followed her. She was pulling rugs and coats out of the cloakroom.

'Roddy,' she said, 'I think I had better put these near the back door. If things go wrong, we could run out to the garage. We may just have to sleep in the car. I think Mary will come tonight. I think she will do her worst.'

'I feel that too,' I confessed.

'Take the garage key in your pocket. I'll cook supper now and I'll run in and out and watch. If you can help it, Roddy, don't let Stella think we are anxious – she has had too much. If things happen suddenly, you can take her out through the greenhouse. Don't worry. I'll warn you; look after her.'

'You're a good scout, Pamela,' I replied.

Stella was lying in my big chair now, tired but peaceful, the portrait on her knees.

'I have been thinking about poor Carmel,' she said. 'How she was hurt and wronged! Her lover and her baby both taken away from her, and her own child not even knowing that she was her child and giving all her love to somebody else!' She broke off. 'What is the Spanish for 'mother'?' she asked, then exclaimed: 'Oh, I remember, it's *madre* – a darling word.'

'How do you know it?' I asked.

She chuckled. 'I learned a little Spanish at school. There was a rich Castilian girl who used to get secret letters. She offered to teach three of us Spanish, but it was just an excuse to show us what wonderful love letters she got.'

I said abruptly, 'Stella, I am going to give up Cliff End. I'll be living in a mean little flat or an ugly bungalow soon.'

She gave me a quick glance and looked away for a minute before she spoke. How fine and firm the lines of her face were! It looked more mature since it had grown so thin. My heart quickened while I waited for her to speak.

Her voice was quiet: 'I am sorry for you about the house, Roderick; but it isn't *necessary* to you, is it? You'll be happy: you and your sister have each other, and it is people who matter most.'

'You loved this house so much.'

'I was childish about it, wasn't I?'

'And you have "put away childish things"?'

She smiled. 'A few of them.'

'Could you be happy in a mean little place?'

She answered in a level voice, very deliberately, without looking at me: 'Certainly I could.'

'Are you wearing mimosa scent?'

It was not what I had intended to say. I had been going to say something much more important, but the rush of perfume took me by surprise; it was so strong.

'Why, no, because I gave it to Pamela – where is it coming from?' She started to her feet, breathless with expectation. 'Does it come in this room too? What does it mean?'

It was useless to tell her anything but the truth. I said, 'Stella, try not to be upset. It never brings anything in the least frightening. I think it means that Carmel is about.'

There was not a vestige of fear in Stella's face; it was serious and still. She stood by my side, listening, a hand on my arm.

'Is that Carmel weeping?' she asked.

It was: there was no mistaking this for the wind. No human voice could have been clearer. It was Carmel, uttering deep, longing, lonely sighs.

Stella said in a low voice: 'I think, perhaps, she could hear me. I think, perhaps, she would understand.'

She moved to the door, just as if she were hurrying to console some human woe. I said, 'Wait,' and went out into the hall.

There was no cold and no snaking vapour; on the landing the red light of the stove showed clear. I switched the lights out in the hall and the nursery in order to see whether there was any trace of that evil, luminous mist; I saw none. Still, from the nursery, came the mournful sound and the flowery scent.

'She is in the nursery now,' Stella said.

She stood in the light from the sitting-room doorway and looked at me. My fear was subdued by the beauty in her face, her glowing and calm conviction of her own power to help. She said, 'Roderick, I think I will be happier all my life if I go into the nursery now, alone; but I will do whatever you wish.'

When she saw refusal in my face such a change came on hers that I felt it was inhuman to do this. 'If you will leave the door open,' I said, 'you may go.'

She slipped quietly into the dark room and I stood outside. I could hear her quick, eager breathing and Carmel's sobbing breath, as if there were two women in that room; then Stella began to speak. She began with fragments of Spanish, little words, broken phrases; then phrases of English came. But the words nor the language mattered nothing, there was such tenderness in her voice. It rose and fell, soft, persuasive, a little lyric of pity and love, as if a mother were comforting a child. '*Madre mia, madre carissima*' I heard. When she ended there was quiet in the nursery. I could hear no sound but the wind; the sighing had ceased. The scent, too, had faded away.

'Rest in peace,' I heard her say gently, and then, after a moment, she whispered my name.

'She has gone! Oh, Roddy, I believe she has gone – in peace.'

Stella was trembling. I held her in my arms. I told her it was the bravest and sweetest thing I had ever seen done, and that no one else in the world would have done just this, and that there was nobody like her in all the world. I told her that if she could not love me, I would not know how to live.

'But you know – you must have known,' she whispered. 'Oh, my darling, I would have died … '

PAMELA HAD CALLED more than once before I realised why she was calling and opened the door.

The sudden cold made me gasp. I thrust Pamela into the nursery with Stella and switched off the hall light, which she had turned on.

I wanted to see what I had to fight. Mary was coming. Well, let her do her worst!

I forced my way against an impalpable pressure to the foot of the stairs and looked up at her. She stood, taller than I had seen her before, expanding and gathering form, palely luminous. She began to float down towards me, with a slow, sweeping movement. I saw the features; the eyes were intensifying their light. I did not want Stella to see those eyes.

I stood on the second step, with my hands behind me gripping the rail. In that way I could hold myself up from falling, despite the trembling of my knees. I shook all over; my skeleton was of ice and my flesh shrank from it; I could not get my voice out of my throat; the words that I spoke were whispered and my laugh hoarse.

I laughed. I laughed because it was so incongruous – the awe and terror which had surrounded the ghost of Carmel and the harmless innocence of her spirit, the simplicity of what Stella had done. Mary, too, was laughable, with her lying at the spelling-glass and her materialising at night. Poor wraith – what did she know, what had she ever known, of the joy and glory and reckless valour of love?

She loomed there, wavering, while, step by step, I mounted up against her, pouring out my derision in blades and shafts. 'You pitiful trickster, you are finished! You are shown up! Your mummery and your poses are done with, you shallow fraud!'

The form shrank and dwindled, losing outline and light; it became a greyish column of fog with a luminous nucleus, and it bent. While I pressed upward, it doubled back. My voice was frozen in my throat, but my thoughts went on, beating it, like a flail. I saw it cowering, wreathing and writhing like smoke under a downward wind.

'There is nothing left of you, Mary,' I mocked, 'but a story to laugh over, a tale for maids to giggle at in the kitchen – go and scare crows!'

I was sick and fainting now. The cloud was cold. But its incandescent centre was dead. It thinned and grew, dissolving and lifting, and seemed to ooze away through the roof. I could not have fought any more; I had no strength left. On the landing I staggered and leaned against the studio door. It gave, and I stumbled into the room. Darkness and cold overwhelmed me and I fell.

Chapter XXIII

MORNING

IT CAN only have been for an instant that I was unconscious. The glare of flames acted like magic to bring me to myself. Stella and I were beating the door with pillows before more than the surface had caught, while Pamela, on the landing, wielded the Minimax, making a hissing steam.

The carpet was ablaze out there and the door-sill had caught. I hauled a mattress from one bed and covered it; Stella dragged the other over and we flung it to Pamela, who threw it down on the big patch of flaming oil. The blaze was smothered: there were only impudent tongues and spittings to be dealt with now. Pamela tossed wet towels and blankets across to me, and with these I fell on each flame as it spurted up. We were like lunatics, stamping and dancing on those mattresses in the thick of the choking smoke.

Presently Pamela shouted: 'Go out on the roof!'

Stella was coughing and choking; I dragged her back and made her stoop to the floor. The window stuck, but I got it open at last and we leaned out, gulping the fresh air.

I returned to the attack. The wind had blown a corner of the smouldering mattress into flames; Pamela doused them with water; they hissed venomously and died.

'It's out!' she shouted.

'Are you all right?'

'Yes – don't try to come this way; it may be burnt through. I'll get a ladder.'

I heard her running downstairs.

Stella was crying out to me wildly. We could not see one another in the smoke-filled room, but I caught her arm and scrambled out with her on to the flat roof. She gripped me and clung to me, choking and coughing and frightened, quite broken down.

The wind tore at us and smoke swirled past. I held Stella against the wall and sheltered her as best I could, but she was overcome by shock and terror now that the need for action was past.

'Oh, how could you, how could you?' she gasped. 'She was so dreadful, and you went up and up! I couldn't even scream! Oh, you were lying on the floor and I couldn't rouse you, and the flames … the flames … '

I had all that I could do to calm her. I do not know how long we were there, crouched under the wind's battering, before I heard Pamela's voice.

'It's too heavy,' she was shouting. 'I can't.'

The smoke was thinner in the room now; we went in. The damage was not much: the door was blackened and blistered halfway up; the door-sill and part of the floor-boards of the landing were burnt through and the exposed beams had been scorched, but it was easy to jump over the hole. We ran down to the kitchen and met Pamela hurrying in, as black as a sweep; she laughed when she saw us. That ended Stella's panic: she looked at me and laughed too; she was covered with smuts herself. We washed in turns at the scullery sink.

'Will somebody tell me what happened?' I demanded. 'I suppose I stumbled against the stove?'

'I don't believe it was you,' Pamela declared. 'You did mad things tonight, but not that. Oh, Roddy, I thought we'd all gone out of our minds! It was horrifying to watch you. But the incredible thing is that it worked! I know it did: she won't come back! Tomorrow we won't believe any of this! She's laughed out and burnt out. I wish we had some champagne!' She was fey with ebullience of victory and the crazy exhilaration that fire-fighting leaves behind; so was I; but Stella was lying, exhausted, in Lizzie's chair.

'Our supper is spoilt,' Pamela complained. 'I'll have to scramble some eggs.'

Whisky welcomed this small-hours' invasion gracefully, visiting each of us in turn, with excited purring and affectionate rubs; he settled in Stella's lap and began licking her hand – a supreme mark of regard. Stella contrived to stroke him and to eat her supper from a tray placed beside her at the same time.

'Lizzie will think the devil was in it this time and no mistake!' Pamela said. 'Your blankets are burnt, Roddy, and your hearth-rug, and our beautiful stair-carpet. What a holocaust!'

'Doesn't matter,' I told her; 'they were insured.'

She chuckled. 'That doesn't cover malicious damage, and this was malicious, I swear!'

'Mary's parting gesture? I'd like to see them trying to prove that.'

'As long as they don't seek Mr Ingram's advice.'

'By the same token,' I reflected, pushing my cup across the table for some more tea, 'Ingram can come for Christmas now.'

The jet of tea swerved into the saucer. Pamela set the pot down and stared at me.

'Mr Ingram? Christmas? What on earth are you talking about?'

'Didn't I tell you?'

'You did not.'

'Didn't I? How he got himself invited to come at mid-winter if we were here? It was neat!'

'This is the first I've heard of it!'

'Glory! And I don't believe I mentioned that he proposed that you should fly to Ireland with him!'

'He didn't!'

'Cross my heart!'

'I? To Ireland? With him? Well, upon my word, you old wooden-head, you might at least give a message!'

'It wasn't a message!' I tried, in self-defence, to explain that I had not thought his notion of any importance, as she would obviously not want to go.

'Oh, it's not of the slightest importance,' she admitted. 'Do you want some more toast?' She got up and scribbled a note for Lizzie: *All's well, but don't disturb anybody until somebody rings.* 'That's the only thing of real importance,' she said. She looked inordinately amused.

I turned to Stella and found that she was asleep in her chair.

The upstairs rooms were still full of smoke. We took bedclothes down, made up a bed on the sitting-room couch for Stella, and fixed a camp-chair there for Pamela, who said, 'I could sleep on a clothes-line tonight.' Stella only half-woke when we roused her to take her in.

I slept in the nursery, and I dreamed, a thing that does not often happen. I dreamed that I was bathing in a radiant sea.

THE CAT woke me: I felt his soft weight as he padded over the bedclothes on my chest. His great eyes met mine complacently; he purred and waved his golden tail. I stared at him, wondering whether the things that I was remembering could possibly have happened. But here I lay in the nursery; here was the cat in the room he had abjured, thrilling with content, and there were my clothes, smudged with soot. It was true, all of it – all of it: Carmel, and Mary, and the fire, and Stella's kiss.

I jumped out of bed to see the damage by daylight, followed by the cat. Lizzie was already at work with brushes and pail, tears falling down her face. The sight of Whisky changed her sorrow to joy.

'I couldn't believe he was in there!' she exclaimed. 'I thought he'd been scared out of the house and I'd never set eyes on him again!' She rose slowly, the cat clasped in her arms. 'And I wouldn't blame him,' she declared, 'for this house isn't fit for a Christian, let alone a cat. Where's Miss Pamela? What's after happening at all?'

'Lizzie, it's the grandest house in Christendom,' I told her, and went to my bath.

While I was dressing I heard Stella and Pamela come up. Once more incredulity took hold of me. I looked out on the sparkling, rain-washed world. The clouds, shredded to flitters by the wind, let sunlight through. I opened the window; the air was scented with heather and alive with the singing of larks. The tree which had saved Stella waved its branches – it was a friendly tree. I thought of the gay beginning of our life here and the dark shadow that had loomed up, and of new hopes, so shining that I scarcely dared to look at them yet.

After a while Pamela tapped at my door and came in.

'Are you all right, Roddy? Stella has had her bath: have you? I've put her to bed properly in my room. Ring the hospital, will you? Unless she wants to go to her grandfather, she'd better stay in bed all day. She is really terribly tired.'

'Do you know what Stella did last night?'

'I know she made one bound through the flames into the studio after you! Oh, Roddy, you scared us.'

I told her what had happened in the nursery. She stood beside me, looking out.

'So she sent her mother away,' she murmured; 'she doesn't need to love a ghost any more.'

'No, Stella doesn't need to love a ghost any more.'

'Oh, I am glad!'

'Are you glad, really?' I asked her.

'Entirely; I am happier than I have been for years. I'm going to have my bath.'

Nature can be cruel to the old, I thought as I went down to telephone. The Commander could have no share in this. This man had led an honourable, loyal, devoted life, and now – was there anyone to whom his passing would be an unmixed loss? The dark web that Mary had woven had made him its victim in the end. I pitied him; but nature and life were on my side and Stella's now.

He was failing slowly, they told me, and there had been no return of consciousness. The surgeon was with him now. They were expecting Dr Scott and would ask him to ring me up. We would have something to tell Scott.

I was as hungry as a viking. 'Lizzie,' I called, 'breakfast in Miss Pamela's room for three!'

I ran up and knocked at the door, and Stella said, 'Come in.' She looked very small, sitting up in Pamela's big bed, and pale, in Pamela's creamy lace jacket. When I told her the news from the hospital her eyes filled with tears.

'If only he could have had a little longer,' she said wistfully, 'now that I understand! But I would have had to deceive him all the time, and he would rather die than be lied to, I believe.' A few tears fell. I comforted her as best I could. I claimed a good-morning kiss. She gave me a shy kiss, like a child's. She smiled at me and sighed. 'I am happy. Is it heartless to be as happy as I am?'

When Pamela came in and I told her what the report was, she promised Stella that we would drive her to the hospital unless Scott forbade it when he came. 'Just there and back to bed again,' she said. 'I think that a rest-cure is needed: this must be your Home of Harmony, though.'

Stella laughed. 'Why is that such a funny name? It has always made me want to giggle, but Miss Holloway was so solemn about it! Oh dear, I think nobody *could* be as naughty as she used to make me feel!'

Lizzie arrived with her tray, planted it on the table and herself in the middle of the room, visiting each of us in turn with a bewildered and accusing gaze.

'I come in,' she said, 'and I find the house half-burnt down and the bedrooms all through-other and a good meal destroyed in the kitchen and Whisky nowhere to be seen. And I come up and I find Miss Meredith like a picture in a prayer-book and Miss Pamela with a smile on her face and Whisky – I ask you, will you look at him? – he that wouldn't set foot on the staircase, canoodling there for his egg! – and Mr Roderick on the top of the world: what in the name of Creation does it mean?'

'Can you keep a secret, Lizzie?' I asked.

Pamela chuckled, and Lizzie's shame-faced gurgle replied. 'I won't put my soul in jeopardy with a promise,' she said.

Stella's hand slipped into Pamela's and she smiled. 'Tell her, Roddy! I want Lizzie to know.'

'It means, Lizzie,' I said, 'that Miss Meredith has promised to marry me, and we are staying at Cliff End, and the ghosts are gone.'

Tears came to Lizzie's eyes.

'Well, if I had three wishes,' she murmured brokenly. 'Miss Pamela, darling … Miss Meredith … Oh, Mr Roddy!' Her face cleared and shone upon us, aglow with loving kindness. 'May God bless us all,' she said.